The Truth is a Theory

Karyn Bristol

THE TRUTH IS A THEORY

KARYN BRISTOL

Book design by *The Frontispiece*
Typeset in 10/15 ITC Galliard

To my parents, who have always believed in me

CHAPTER 1

She had to watch. She tried to anchor herself in the kitchen, to hot coffee and the beginnings of a list—mac & cheese, milk—but as the storm door banged shut on her marriage, she dropped the pen and rushed to the glass, to Dana's broad-shouldered march towards the car.

She opened her mouth, then snapped it shut as a jumble of longing, regrets, and wishes surged up and snagged in her throat. She reached out her hand and it stalled against the windowpane, her diamond wedding band shooting flares in the morning sun. Her fingertips pressed against the cold glass. Her hand, her body was trembling.

She willed herself numb, begged the chill of the glass to freeze her, make her immune to the pain. It was something she was good at, walling herself off from hurt, a skill she laughed off as a party trick with friends, ha-ha, just another one of her quirks. But it wasn't a trick; it was survival. Other people ask for a hug when they're feeling lonely or scared. She had taught herself not to feel.

This morning though, as she watched Dana walk away, numbness failed her. Instead, all five senses were jacked up and bombarding her, distracting her from the moment, the meaning, as if they had stepped forward and said to her heart, "Don't worry, we'll handle this. Feel this instead." Her cheek stung from Dana's weird, last minute lean-in (was it intended to be a kiss? A hug? The reality was more scrape than caress because of her surprised flinch as his face came close). Her sinuses burned with his smell—Old Spice slapped on over restless, clammy sweat—and her ears were screaming with the echo of his "okay", the only word he'd spoken this morning, choked out after he'd bent in and straightened back up. Okay what? Okay, that chore's done? Okay, I'm out of here? This is all going to be okay? She couldn't see how.

Her eyes zeroed in on Dana, his rumpled hair, his wrinkled shirt, a look that years ago boasted of a late night of exotic cocktails and a need to touch, to slide hands in back pockets, to drape blue-jeaned legs over each other, and hours later, to fight off sleep because of just one more thing to say. Now it was simply an acknowledgement of uninspired exhaustion. She wondered if he had slept in his clothes. Or slept at all. She rubbed her eyes.

She focused on his blue running shoes, knotted together and dangling off of, oh God, how many bags? Her heart skipped a beat. Clearly after all was said and done, a rapid getaway was crucial, no back-and-forth to load the car. Perhaps no "back" at all. She swallowed hard.

He was leaving.

The words had been handed to her last night over routine chicken piccata and the low murmur of the TV. His "Allie... " had jolted her, lowered her fork; not so much the gravity in his tone, but that he'd said it at all. Addressing each other by first name after so many years was like a parent starting a sentence with your first, middle, and last name.

They hadn't raised their voices; there had been no argument over the glasses of chardonnay. Dana had presented his closing summary in his smooth legalese, in the way he'd been schooled at ironing the ache out of his words, and she soaked it in, her face still, the bullet points piercing her, drawing blood but absolutely no visible tears.

He was leaving.

She couldn't hear the soft thud of each bag hitting the leather car seat, but as she stood behind the glass she could feel it, and every one punched a purple bruise on her heart. He glanced back at her as he shut the door, a quick shot of his broken expression, his weariness, and their eyes wrapped around each other.

And he was everything.

She didn't know what to do with her arms, and for a moment this frustration almost reduced her to tears. She crossed them over her chest, but didn't like that statement and thrust them down at her sides, where they hung, flaccid and useless. It was unbearable, this dilemma with her arms, and if she could have cut them off to solve it, she would have. She cast around for something to touch, to hang onto; her only option was a princess umbrella that one of the kids had dropped by the door. Without hesitation, she bent and straightened, her fingers a vise around the smooth plastic.

Dana was behind the wheel. She raised the garish pink handle to wave, and her arm—extended now like the Statue of Liberty with a Disney prop—stalled in the air. As if she was commanding *Stop!* or maybe had a question.

And the black Volvo drove away.

JOURNAL ENTRY #1
Saturday night
June 10, 2000

I'm afraid of being alone. I'm wide awake in the bowels of my first night without Dana, and although I've plugged in and clicked on every slice of artificial life I could get my hands on—lights, TV, computer, both baby monitors—it's like I've tried to light up the Amazon with a nightlight. I'm acutely aware that just beyond the yellow glow sprawls the bottomless dark, where there is no edge to my emptiness, no warm skin to delineate where I end and the dead, hollowed-out space around me begins.

Sheer desperation cracked open this journal. But the calisthenics of writing is helpful, especially during commercials when it feels like my date has just gone to the bathroom and I'm alone at the bar pretending I've got a lot on my mind. The first mark, however, was daunting. The blank page sneered, daring me to begin, but the hovering, "How did I get here?" seemed so trite. In 32 years I've walked through many doors, but it's not as if any of them loomed before me with a *Let's Make a Deal* number above it and a heart-pounding decision attached. I floated through most of my life carelessly, unceremoniously, and the unselected doors evaporated in my wake.

The journal was not my idea. About a month ago, Zoe—who I now believe is psychic—dragged me to her therapist. Sarah was younger than I expected and pretty, although she tried to mute it with a pair of thick, black-framed glasses, which probably did make me sit a little straighter. She suggested the journal. I backpedaled, stammered that when I was younger, writing in a journal was dangerous. I've always been terrified to pick up a pen and begin, lest the pen, on its own like the moving piece of a Ouija board, suddenly decided to scratch away at my smile to see what churned just below the surface.

But ulcerous desperation—which has a taste by the way, a mix of tin and white chalk—shrinks the world into black or white. Curl up into yourself, or dare.

And so, I have picked up a pen.

SEPTEMBER 1986: FRESHMAN YEAR
Erikson College

Allie Mussoni scraped her flip-flop through a small pile of sand on the sidewalk; she was going to scream if her father didn't say something soon. They had been standing among her small army of duffel bags and brown cardboard boxes for what seemed like *hours* while he wallowed in indecision about how to handle the send-off. Say something wise? That would have involved some preparation. Hug? Not in her father's repertoire. Shake hands? Oh my God. She jammed her hands into the pockets of her Levi's miniskirt and clenched her fists so tightly that her nails cut into the soft skin of her palms. The bustle of students, of the world, streamed by her; she glued her eyes to the ground, loath to offer anyone a window into her purgatory. Tiny black ants, resigned to the fact that their home had been destroyed again, marched around her feet and towards her father's—a film of dust had dimmed the sheen of his loafers. She fought the urge to tear her hair out. One, two, three.

She rose up on the tips of her pink rubber soles and gave him a peck on the cheek. "Bye Dad, thanks for the ride." She was already gliding away.

"I'll grab all this stuff after I check out my room," she said to the world in front of her. Maybe the breeze would blow it back to him.

She picked up speed and ran towards the red brick dorm, leaving him with his hands deep in his pressed khaki pockets. She turned around once, at the top of the stairs to wave, and saw him with his head bent, sagging towards the driver-side door of his sparkling silver sedan. He didn't look up, and she didn't wait.

Her flip-flops thwacked loudly as she ran down the dark green linoleum hallway; parked baggage and emotionally-charged students and parents popped up in front of her, causing her to swerve and stumble, littering crumpled sorry's and excuse me's in her wake. Number 27. She paused to catch her breath in the open door. Her new home. A square overhead light, spotted with the shadows of dead bugs, threw harshness around the room, illuminating the patched cinder-block walls, the nicked wooden furniture, the scuffed linoleum. Across the room, a redhead leaned on the windowsill, forehead against the glass.

Allie ran her hands through her long brown hair, and forced the corners of her mouth up. "So where do we pick up our leg chains and standard-issue orange garb?" She stepped into the room and dropped her purse on a gray-and-white-striped plastic mattress.

Her roommate spun around. Red, puffy eyes, but Allie could see some-one else was skilled in the decorative smile.

"It is pretty grim. But I think we can make it cute." The girl peered past Allie; Allie guessed she was expecting a set of parents to stagger in with boxes.

Allie smiled. "You're an optimist." She stuck out her hand. "I'm Allie."

Megan introduced herself and glanced at all of her latched suitcases and taped boxes stacked neatly in a corner. "I didn't want to start without you."

"Thanks. It doesn't matter which bed I get or anything." Allie surveyed the identical sets of beds, desks, and bureaus. Her green eyes darted back to one of the desks. "On the other hand, I'll take the one with 'I love Mouse' carved on it."

"You're kidding me. Mouse?"

"In flowery cursive. Frightening, huh?"

"Do you think he gave himself that name or earned it somehow?"

"I'm scared for him in either scenario," Allie said. "But the prize goes to the girl who loved him and just had to eternalize it on this sorry desk."

"Maybe he's cute."

"Mouse? Now I'm scared for you."

"I can only imagine the field day my family would have if I came home and said, 'Mom, meet Mouse.' There would be mass hysteria, and I'm not talking about panic," Megan said.

Allie dropped onto the wooden desk chair and slid her hand over the cuts on the desk. *I could come home with an orangutan and no one would raise an eyebrow.*

"Do you need help with your stuff, or... " Megan's finger scraped at the cuticle on her thumb.

"Thanks, I left it all out on the sidewalk. And there are tons of frat guys out there helping new kids move in. Super charitable." She paused for effect, "Although, I noticed they don't seem interested in helping the freshmen boys." Her eyes twinkled. "Let's go introduce ourselves and point them in this direction."

Megan paled a shade and scanned the bare walls. "You don't have a mirror, do you?"

Allie shook her head. "It's all outside. Come on, you look great."

Megan sighed, smoothed down her hair, then her shorts, and followed Allie out.

―――――

"Music or TV?" Allie asked as the last box was dumped on the floor. She wanted to dive right in; the emptiness of the room made her nervous.

"Music." Megan clicked on the stereo.

"Do you mind if I flip this on too?" Allie plugged in her TV. "It's habit; I'll mute it."

Megan pulled folded sheets and a rainbow-colored comforter out of an enormous Bed & Bath bag, and then made her bed with care, smoothing down the yellow sheets, throwing the comforter up in the air and then snapping it so that it billowed out over the bed and settled across it like a sigh.

"Don't judge," Megan said as she pulled a stuffed yellow Labrador out of a bag.

"You're safe. I definitely don't own a gavel," Allie said. She grabbed a hammer and a box of nails. "Just a hammer." She nodded towards both of their cheaply framed posters leaning against the wall. "What do you think?"

Megan stared at the lineup. "Yours."

"Really? I like Ansel Adams."

"Me too. But I bet every room on this floor will have one. Yours will give the room more flavor."

"Let's put them all up." Allie picked up her funky ad for a cosmetics company—a huge pair of cherry red lips on a metallic silver background. She climbed up on her bed. "So how was your summer?" She slammed the hammer against a nail. Cement crumbled around the hole and fell onto her bed. "Uh oh." She looked at Megan and smiled at her roommate's wide-eyed look. "It's okay, we'll just take some posters out of the frames and tape them up instead." She started pulling the frame apart. "This one can cover the hole. And then if we ever want to tunnel into the next room, we've got a head start."

Megan nodded.

Allie sat down on her bed, brushed some cement dust off her quilt, and continued to pry the frame apart. "So, your summer?"

"It was good. I lifeguarded during the day, at night I just hung out with friends."

"You're lucky on both counts. I waitressed a lot, anything to get out of the house. And I didn't see much of my friends."

Megan's quiet made Allie look up and add, "Boarding school. Everyone's all over the map."

"Wow, that's hard."

Allie nodded. "You go from being glued together twenty-four/seven to being stranded at home in a neighborhood that's moved on without you. It's all or nothing. My boyfriend lives in Massachusetts and I think I spent every cent I made this summer getting up there on the weekends. Luckily the phone bill didn't arrive before I left. My dad's gonna have a heart attack when he gets it."

"Where's he now, your boyfriend?" Megan handed Allie the next poster, a splashy vodka ad with two martini glasses bending towards each other; the tagline read Absolut Attraction. "You better take it out of the frame, I don't want to ruin it."

"Princeton," Allie said as she reached for the frame. "I know," she said when she caught Megan's impressed look. "For about a minute we considered going to the same college, but there was the small problem of the difference in our GPAs."

Megan chewed on her fingernail. "I know how that goes, my brothers are all at Ivys."

"Sounds like a lot of pressure for you," Allie said.

Megan nodded.

"Dana worked his butt off for his grades, plus his father went to Princeton, so he felt like he didn't have a lot of choice."

"How'd you guys do it? At boarding school, seeing each other all the time like that? Didn't you get sick of each other?"

"No, it was great actually. I mean, it can definitely get intense, but we had our own space too, time with friends… mostly because there's a ton of rules and a jammed schedule with classes and sports, so there's a lot of forced separation." She paused a moment. "Of course, sometimes when we were together I wanted space, and when we were apart I wanted to be together." She shook her head. "But it worked. Dana is super-driven, as in, he really wanted to get that A+, so he had to block me out sometimes." She smiled.

"And the rules blocked us too," she continued. "Early on he got caught sneaking into my dorm room; I was really sick and he was bringing me ginger ale. He even held my hair as I was bent over the toilet… "

"Now that's love," Megan said.

"That's actually how he got caught, in the bathroom, holding back my hair. They didn't suspend him because it was so clearly *not* a booty call, but we knew if he got caught again, we might both get suspended. So we didn't sneak around after that, as tempting as it was. What about you, did you leave anyone behind?"

"Not really, no. I had a huge crush on a guy I worked with, like blushing-every-time-he-looked-at-me crush. And he must have noticed because we actually got together a few nights ago at this keg party."

"Sounds good."

"Except I, mid-kiss and thinking I was so *college*, asked him straight out if this was a one-night stand. He just looked at me like I had two heads and eased himself right out of there." Megan giggled. "Clearly it was a special night for him."

Allie laughed.

"Hey, I was just getting the ground rules clear," Megan said.

"Very romantic."

"I have to admit, reality didn't quite match the fantasy."

"He sounds like a prince." Allie grinned. "But I guess you have to kiss a lot of," she paused, glanced at the wooden desk, "mice before… "

"A lot of rats. A lot of rats is more like it," Megan said.

———

Before they could see or smell the cafeteria, Megan could hear the noise.

"Ready?" Allie said as they looked through the door into the cavernous cafeteria. Allie's eyes seemed to be glittering; Megan felt dread in her stomach.

Not really was on Megan's lips, but she nodded instead and tossed her long copper hair.

Allie handed her laminated meal card to the bored gatekeeper and stepped inside for lunch. Megan followed as closely as possible and tried not to gawk. After two days of freshmen orientation, the school was ablaze with the fuel of the entire student body. The gently sloping, block-lettered signs—"Welcome Class of 1990!" and "The Choir Wants You" and "Join the Poetry Club"—that just last night had seemed friendly, and even inspiring, were now just wallpaper behind the sun-bronzed upperclassmen who were hugging, high-fiving, and screaming high-pitched, primal monosyllables as they reunited with friends they hadn't seen in months.

The freshmen, on the other hand, were trying to fade into the wood-work along with the posters; any cockiness from orientation had shriveled up and died. The class of 1990 was now fully aware of their position on the totem pole, and they were shamelessly trying to watch, listen, and soak up the unspoken laws and hierarchy of this new culture.

Megan picked up her pace to match Allie's near skip and grabbed an blue food service tray.

———

Someone at the crammed fraternity table must have seen him coming. As Gavin Keller coasted across the room with his tray, brothers slid over to make space, the Red Sea parting down the middle. Gavin eased his broad shoulders in between his buddies' football jerseys, and then without a word, two sophomores got up to make room for his girlfriend Tori and her friend.

"Good to see you, man." One of the displaced sophomores clapped Gavin on the back.

"You too. Catch ya later." Gavin bit into an institutionally flat cheese-burger. The splintered conversations around the table had stalled, only one counted now.

"How was the road trip?" a brother lobbed at Gavin.

Gavin chewed. "Awesome. The Rabbit broke down right outside of San Diego, so that's where we landed for a while." He shot a bemused look down the table to one of his traveling companions, Brian.

"You're lucky you didn't break down in, like, Ohio," someone said.

"Oh, I don't know," Gavin caught eyes with Brian again, "Ohio had its moments."

Brian chuckled.

"California must have been cool," the first brother said.

"It was." Gavin grinned. "Mikey learned to surf."

Brian full-out laughed back.

There was a seconds-long pause at the table as the audience waited for more; then the group guffawed at a joke only two shared.

Gavin could feel Tori tense beside him and almost hear her gnashing teeth underneath her bright smile. He knew his summer with the guys pissed her off, and his sporadic calls from the road had only made it worse. But he also knew she wouldn't fight with him about it. He put his hand on her thigh.

"So what do you think," she said, "should we go to the barbecue tonight?"

Gavin turned to answer her, but was momentarily stunned by a tall, dark-haired girl sauntering by the table. Her short, almost boyish haircut and subtle makeup were distinct in a sea of long hair and pink frosted lip gloss, and although she was just dressed in jeans and a white sleeveless tee, she looked like she had been put together by a stylist as no detail, from black boots to pale nail polish to understated silver jewelry, had been overlooked.

He felt as though all chatter quieted as she breezed by, and whether it did or not, he knew almost everyone in her vicinity—men and women— were assigning her a place in the world: Hook up! Sorority pledge! Competition! Zoe Chapin seemed not to notice; her piercing blue eyes stared straight ahead as if she knew exactly where she was going. Gavin was riveted, even though she was diametrically opposed to the petite, watery blondes he usually ended up with. Like Tori.

"Gavin?"

"Uh, I don't know." He ripped his eyes from Zoe and swiveled back to his girlfriend. "Why don't you go with Emily and Laura, and if we go, I'll catch you there. Otherwise, just meet me at the house later." He watched her face fall at the news that his "we" meant him and his brothers. "We're definitely having a party," he added to justify his brush off. He couldn't resist scanning the room to see where Zoe had landed with her lunch.

Tori flashed another one of her super-bright smiles, which Gavin knew glossed over a tantrum. She stood up. "I'll see you later then." She fluffed her long blond hair and eyed her friend across the table. "Ready to go, Em?"

Emily put down her forkful of salad and stood up.

Tori walked off, with one more hair toss for good measure.

"Wow, did you guys see her?" said Rich, a fraternity brother who tried his best to see everything.

"A little mad, huh?" Gavin grimaced, and again dragged his focus away from Zoe and back to the table.

"No. Well yeah, Tori was mad. But I meant that freshman striker. Tall, leggy... " Rich had created what he thought was a cool classification for girls. Striker meant really cute; bomber—really ugly. Unfortunately, it had stuck. At least with Rich.

"I saw her," Gavin said. And any thoughts of Tori being mad drifted off as his mind returned to the gorgeous girl whose name he didn't know. Yet.

————

Later that night, on the outskirts of campus, the six fraternity houses were getting ready for their first big bash of the season. Collectively, this semi-circle of plain, brick buildings was known as "The Columns," although there wasn't a porch pillar in sight. These huge red houses—no different in style from the rest of the buildings on campus—sat on a hill and towered over the spread of the campus, their throne-like perch visually reinforcing the imagined and real social clout that they held.

While the brothers were busy prepping—beer iced, toilet paper re-loaded—most of the girls across campus were feverishly primping, using the hours between dinner and showtime to select just the right "I didn't try too hard" outfit and hair. They had more than enough time to try on and discard everything in their closets, as it was common knowl-edge—even to freshmen—that no one showed up at The Columns until at least 11.

In Allie and Megan's room, the music was loud, and in the corner the glowing TV shifted in silent drama. Someone on the hall had made popcorn; the smell of salty butter drifted into the room.

Allie fished clothes from a sea of disheveled belongings on the floor, and in minutes was ready to go—long hair loose, tanned knees peeking out of Bermuda shorts, tight orange tee shirt.

"I'm guessing no one ever wears orange," she said as she tried to tug the wrinkles out of her shirt. "Plus this way you won't lose me." She lit a Marlboro Light and flopped down onto an oversized beanbag chair.

Megan continued to stare into her closet at the crisp shirts hanging in a row, the tees folded in a neat stack, the shoes lined up across the bottom in categories—sneakers, sandals, boots. She was hoping for a cute outfit to announce itself. *Allie has such great clothes*, she thought, and her own clothes, fine until a few days ago, now seemed so buttoned-up. She wished she hadn't eaten that pizza at dinner. She put her hand on her stomach and willed it flat.

"Are those your brothers?" Allie pointed to a framed picture of four redheaded boys holding Megan up in the air.

Megan nodded as she gazed at the picture, just snapped in August. It had been her oldest brother's idea to hoist her over their heads, and they'd all laughed so hard it took several tries to get the shot.

"You guys look close," Allie said.

"We are, most of the time. How about you, any siblings?"

"Paul and Kevin; I'm in the middle, the problem child. I'm pretty close with my younger brother Kevin." And then, quickly, as if she didn't want Megan to ask anything else, Allie indicated Megan's sweatpants and tee shirt with a wave of her cigarette and said, "You know, that would be fine. I'm envisioning beer-soaked floors and lots of drunks."

Megan turned her back on her closet with a sigh. "Can I bum one of these?" She lit a cigarette, inhaled, and coughed.

"Anyway, you can't miss with your hair and those big brown eyes." Allie nodded at Megan's long, copper-colored hair. "No one's going to be looking at what you're wearing."

Megan peered at Allie to see if she was being sarcastic. She never knew how to respond to a compliment; they made her uncomfortable, knocked her off balance. She was about to say, I hate my eyes, I mean, what's special about brown? and that Allie had the most amazing jade-green eyes she had ever seen, when Allie switched the subject again.

"Want to get stoned before we go?"

"You brought pot?" Megan had only been stoned once before, on a class ski trip. One of her friends had smuggled in marijuana and three of them had stayed up late in their hotel room and smoked, filling the night with heady analysis and hearty laughter. The experience had been both nebulous and intense, and incredibly bonding—they had encoded it into their yearbook comments months later—but it had been safe within the confines of a small hotel room, and Megan wasn't sure how it would feel to be high out in public. "Sure, I'll get stoned. But stay with me tonight, I don't want to make a fool of myself in front of some cute senior."

"You'll be fine, you've been stoned before," Allie said, as if there could be no other possibility.

"Only once though; I'm a relative virgin."

Allie reached over to her drawer and pulled out a plastic baggie; inside were several rolled joints. "Well, I didn't ask that! But give me a few minutes and I'll be happy to talk about anything you want." Allie lit up a joint and took a drag. "As long as it's about you." She laughed and handed it to Megan.

"Right now my problem is my wardrobe. But this should make deciding what to wear a lot easier." She inhaled, and as she held the smoke captive in her lungs she squeaked, "Weed, the true fashion accessory," and grabbed jeans and a black sleeveless shirt from her closet. She wasn't quite used to the lack of privacy, and although she tried to follow Allie's unabashed lead, she hunched over in the corner as she hurriedly stripped and pulled on her clothes.

Smoke curled around a comfortable silence as Megan, finally dressed, sat down. She was hazy, relaxed, happy; it felt good after all the activity of the day. She shifted on the hard wooden desk chair. "We need more comfortable furniture in here, especially if we're going to be doing this."

"I know. Hey, sit here." Allie started to wiggle her way out of the beanbag.

"It's okay, I'm fine."

"No really, sit here; if I don't move, I'm going to be stuck in this thing forever."

Megan reached out and pulled Allie to her feet. "I knew there was a reason I liked you."

"I have to tell you, I wasn't so sure about you when I read your roommate form. I was afraid you were going to show up with a few of your ferrets."

"What?"

"Your ferrets."

"I've clearly smoked too much. What are you talking about?"

"You wrote that you had four of them in the 'A Fun Fact About Me' section."

Megan slapped her hand over her mouth. "Oh my God, I'm going to kill my brother Brad. I don't have any ferrets. He must have erased what I wrote and scribbled that in. I wrote something totally blah about running."

Allie burst out laughing. "I kept expecting them to creep out of one of your boxes!"

"Now I'm wondering about you; some administrator thought you'd be a good match for somebody with a ferret zoo!"

They bent over in giggles, grabbing furniture for support.

"Wow, you have a lot of hair," Megan said once they had straightened back up.

Allie regarded herself in the mirror across the room. Her hair had fluffed up from the flip, and her face looked small, hidden underneath the waves of dark brown. She ran her fingers through it, tried to smooth it down. Her hairdresser had been begging to cut it for years, but Allie loved the thick curtain around her shoulders. The weight of it was comforting, as if someone had an arm around her.

"Hey you guys… " A tall girl who looked like she had been airbrushed poked her head in the door. "Can I join you? I'm Zoe. I heard you guys cracking up all the way down the hall. I was wondering what was so funny, and hoping it was artificially induced. I've got beer, if you'll share." She held out a six-pack of Amstel Light.

"Come on in and help yourself. I'm running to the bathroom." Allie handed the joint to Zoe as she passed her; then said over her shoulder, "Just watch out for the ferrets." Her eyes twinkled at Megan.

"Ignore her. Come in, I'm Megan."

Zoe stepped into the room; a light, flowery perfume wafted in with her. "Thanks. My roommate is no fun, never had a beer, is like, ready to go to bed." She shook her head. "I couldn't stand one more minute."

"I wonder what she wrote on her roommate form?" Megan said with a little chuckle, trying to hold onto the levity from a moment ago.

Zoe strode over to the beanbag chair and dropped down into it. "Well, I wrote that I didn't drink or smoke because I can control my alcohol and I didn't want a drunk for a roommate." After shifting her way into a comfortable position, she held out a beer. Megan stepped forward to take it. "But I didn't say I wanted someone without a pulse," Zoe continued. "I mean, Sandra Dee's from some hick town in Vermont."

"Sandra Dee?"

"It's not really Sandra Dee, it's Sue. But she so seems like she's from the fifties. You know—I don't drink, I don't swear, I don't rat my hair, I get ill from one cigarette." Zoe fake-coughed.

Megan suddenly felt very sorry for Zoe's roommate. "I don't think I've met her."

"Anyway, I think it's going to be a long year. That's why I was psyched to hear someone up here having fun."

Zoe's eyes swept around the half-decorated room, scanning the posters on the wall, then lingering over the photographs Megan had in frames on her bureau and taped neatly to her mirror—Megan and her brothers, Megan with arms around close friends, Megan smiling with her parents. The way Zoe was studying them made Megan want to flip them over, cover them up somehow. She crossed her arms over her chest.

Zoe turned back to Megan. "Cool posters."

"Most of them are Allie's." She felt like she was admitting she had no pulse.

"What are we watching?"

Megan glanced at the flickering TV. "I don't know, we muted it. Obviously." She rolled her eyes at herself. "Do you want me to turn it up?"

"Nah, I don't watch much TV. I live in Manhattan." She crossed her legs. "We don't watch life, we live it."

Megan's eyes widened and then escaped to her beer bottle. She twisted the cap off.

Zoe laughed, a short burst of sound that ricocheted around the room like a bullet. "Sorry, I'm into taglines, you know from ads? Sometimes I just can't help myself."

Megan signaled for the joint and inhaled deeply.

"You're from New York?" Allie popped back into the room.

Megan glowered at Allie and tried to convey telepathically, just wait until you talk to this girl. You won't believe it.

Allie hopped up on her desk. "I love New York."

Megan watched the two of them talk clubs for a few minutes and couldn't believe they were hitting it off. She had to check that her mouth wasn't hanging open. Was it her imagination that Zoe's condescending attitude was only aimed at her? She was getting the sense that Zoe was the kind of girl who had to put someone down, and she had the feeling that—tag, she was it. Although she was feeling foggy from the pot and so wasn't sure. She tried to get back into the conversation. "Wow, I'm stoned. My mom would kill me if she saw me now. I mean, I got the whole drinking and drug chat before I left. She was so earnest, I'm sure she was imagining upperclassmen plying us with toxins, never in a million years would she have thought the danger lay with my own roommate."

Zoe actually smiled, which Megan was disconcerted to note gave her a boost in confidence. She continued, "What about you guys, did you get the big Be Careful talk from your mothers?"

"My mom's not in the picture," Allie said. And then, as if she wished she could take back the conversation stopper and the tone of voice that went with it, she flashed a smile.

All eyes dropped to the floor and then bounced back up to the voiceless TV. Megan's brief confidence sagged.

After a moment, Zoe's voice tripped over the clutter of discomfort. "I know what you mean, sort of." She bit her lip. "My mom's in the picture, but when she's with her husband, my stepfather, it's like I'm not in it."

Allie and Zoe locked eyes for a beat in time that seemed to last for an entire song; then each looked away. Allie reached for a beer. "So what time do we go over to The Columns?"

Zoe checked her watch. "It's 11:30, I guess it's respectable."

———

The importance of peering one last time into the small mirror erased the awkwardness in the room, and by the time they were out in the warm, star-filled night, their thoughts were in front of them, great expectations leading the way. The growing, monotone buzz of the crowd lured them ever closer, until finally they were in the middle of a mob milling around on a huge field. Portable chairs of all kinds—plastic lawn chairs, metal folding chairs, and even wooden desk chairs—claimed territory and anchored clumps of students, giving the scene the feel of a public beach on the Fourth of July. At the far end of the field a parade of bodies marched up and back down the steep slope leading to the fraternity houses at the top of the hill.

The girls wove through the throng, up the hill, and into the nearest house, where they were immediately engulfed in a pungent smog—the sweet-sour reek of stale beer fused with thick cigarette smoke. In the dim light they tried not to trip over bodies lounging on sagging couches and tattered chairs. They followed the traffic headed back toward the main attraction—the Keg Room—a large kitchen where several dripping barrels of cheap, foamy beer were being continuously pumped and drained as lines of drunk and getting-there students waited for their cups to be refilled. The floor was indeed covered in beer, and they watched in horror as a girl in a skirt and clogs (clearly a freshman) hydroplaned across the floor—arms swinging spastically, spray kicking up behind her—and landed hard on her butt. A clump of brothers snickered on the sidelines.

Allie leaned into her friends. "I heard they give out awards for the best fall."

Megan hung onto Allie's belt as they snaked forward in line.

Once filled, their red plastic cups doubled as a handy shield as they shuffled back through the house; taking a sip gave them a chance to sneak a glance around. Without a natural place to stop and hang out, they made their way back down the hill and out onto the lawn. They gulped their beers fast, mostly for something to do, and searched for recognizable faces scattered around them in the dark.

"This marching up and down that hill could get old fast." Allie held up her empty plastic cup.

"It's called dancing for our dinner, or in this case, drink," Zoe said.

"Next time we either need to stay up there a while, or come back down two-fisted," Allie said.

"Better yet… " Zoe grabbed the arm of a skinny guy scurrying by with a full pitcher of beer. She held out her cup and clearly expecting cooperation, said, "Would you mind filling us up?"

"Very nice," Allie said after the boy walked away. "I could almost hear you purr. You didn't even have to stroke his," Allie cleared her throat, "ego." She smiled.

"Listen and learn," Zoe said.

"Got it. But he was an easy mark. You'll get extra points if they're cute."

Zoe turned towards the glare of the fraternity castles. "I think the cute ones are all up there."

Allie and Megan followed her gaze up the hill. After a moment, they pivoted back to each other with a long exhale. The party in the dark mote of the field now felt like a gathering of outcasts. Unfamiliar faces clustered in cells all around them, blackness obscured groups beyond that. In the distance, someone turned on a boom box and several bodies began to sway, the shadowed anonymity emboldening the roll of their hips. Watching, the girls shrunk into themselves.

Their little huddle of three suddenly didn't feel padded enough against the strangeness of this new social scene. Their conversation sputtered, then stalled completely. They drank their lukewarm beers and shifted their weight from foot to foot.

In seconds, the black silence enveloped Allie, and an all-too-familiar dread gripped her. The darkness took shape, became clammy stone walls inching towards her, pressing close. Her stomach churned, sour and queasy. She began to sweat.

No, not now.

Her heart revved, a trot before the full-out stampede. She shook her head, her hair swished across her shoulders and back. She tried to focus—she could harness this brewing explosion—but panic crawled up her throat and started to squeeze. She couldn't fill her lungs.

She fumbled for an idea, any idea to get them moving, talking.

"Hey guys." Her words croaked in between them. "Let's liven this up a bit. What do you say we go up there and see if there's anything other than bad beer?"

Breathe in. Breathe out.

Megan picked at her fingernail. "Should we? I didn't really see any freshmen hanging out up there."

Zoe took a step closer to Allie. "Oh come on. It's not like there's a rule about it or anything. Let's go."

Allie gulped the cool night air and put one foot in front of the other, leading the way. With each step, the motion, the plan, eased her breath back into a manageable rhythm. "And maybe we should play a game," she said, riding the relief of an averted disaster. "We each have to introduce ourselves to some guy who resembles a celebrity."

"Any celebrity?" Zoe said.

Allie nodded. "Although we have to say who we are looking for right now, before we start."

"Okay… " Megan drew out the last syllable.

Allie gave Megan a quick hug. "Come on, it'll be fun!"

"Okay, I'm in, I'm in."

Not knowing the distinct personality of each fraternity, they wandered into a second house, identical to the first in atmosphere and furnishings, and stood together in a tight little circle.

"I'm looking for James Bond," Zoe said.

"Roger Moore or Sean Connery?" Allie said.

"Doesn't matter, it's all about the attitude. And of course, the gadgets."

"Bond's too pretty for me," Allie said. "I'm going for the swashbuckling, disheveled hero-type. Let me know if you see Harrison Ford anywhere."

"I certainly wouldn't mind finding a Tom Cruise clone," Megan said, "but seeing as I don't think there's anyone here in Ray Bans and an Air Force uniform, I'm keeping my eyes peeled for Rob Lowe."

Zoe cocked her head and flipped both her palms up.

"*St. Elmo's Fire? About Last Night?* You know the type—cool on the surface, but kind of lost underneath? Stretched out sideways in the back of the class like his legs don't fit underneath the desk?"

"So Allie wants to be saved, and you want to be a savior," Zoe said.

"And you're a Bond girl," Allie said.

"Although I'm the cool spy chick who betrays him at the end and ends up breaking his heart."

"I thought James Bond never got his heart broken," Megan said.

"There's always a first," Zoe said.

"Here I go; Indiana Jones is over at the keg," Allie said.

They spun to inspect a guy who vaguely resembled Harrison Ford.

"That's quite a reach," Megan said.

"Picture the brown fedora and magic whip. Better?"

"Go," Megan said.

"Okay, if he counts as Harrison Ford, then I see Roger Moore over in the corner." Zoe tilted her head towards a blonde football player.

Allie touched Megan on the shoulder. "Are you okay, or should I wait until your charming/lost guy makes an appearance?"

"Don't worry, clearly the parameters on 'resembles' are a little loose."

Allie squeezed Megan's arm.

"Wish me luck," Zoe said as she walked away.

———

Megan, now standing alone and feeling foolish, looked around for any handsome guy with brown hair, and then dismissed the first one as too intimidating. She debated hiding in the bathroom for a few minutes instead of completing her task, but in the end, not wanting to be a wet blanket, she chugged her cup of courage and walked towards two frat brothers standing with a girl in the corner. Just as she was closing in, one guy walked away and the remaining one leaned into the girl. It was too late to turn and walk away.

"Hi, I'm Megan Riordan." Her cheeks flamed as they eyeballed her. "Sorry, it's a game, I had to introduce myself."

They sneered.

Her forefinger raked at the cuticle on her thumb. She tried to call up Zoe's sweet purr from earlier. "So, what frat is this?"

"We're just in the middle of something here," the guy said. His words swatted her like she was a fly.

She spun around and fought the electric impulse to run. She race-walked back through the house, wondering how her friends had done with their assignments, and hoping that they hadn't seen her being dismissed so quickly. In a corner she spied Allie, who after days of singing about Dana, was now enjoying a flirty rapport with her celebrity, and by the way she kept throwing her head back in fits of laughter, he was either a stand-up comedian or she was putting on a very good show of interest. In her animation, her hand kept batting his arm and actually grabbing it at times for emphasis, or perhaps balance.

Across the room, Zoe was standing comfortably in a group of four guys, none of whom was James Bond. *Okay, at least I wasn't the only one who failed.*

"What happened to James?" Megan whispered to Zoe as she slid into the little circle.

"M called."

The four brothers—their tee shirts branded with Greek letters—leaned in, Casanova-like, jockeying for position, replenishing any empty cups nonchalantly. It was refreshing after her recent snub, and Megan folded into the conversation as the loud music and sweaty bodies around her began to merge.

———

Inside the first fraternity house, Gavin was sprawled on an overstuffed chair, legs long, arms relaxed and open as if he was holding the whole party on his lap. Tori had deposited herself on his chair arm, a queen to the right of her king, as stiff a fixture as the arm itself.

Gavin had watched Zoe come in earlier with her small entourage; he told himself he hadn't necessarily been waiting for her, although he had been unusually aware of who was coming and going through the front door. So he'd also noticed her leaving the house a few minutes later with a full beer. He wasn't planning on following her; in fact, he wasn't really planning anything. But just like in the cafeteria, his eyes were fastened to her and all the nerves in his body were on fire, something that hadn't happened in a very long time. Usually girls pursued him and he coasted along on autopilot. Hey, the sex was always great—sex being sex after all—but so far he just couldn't get excited about the before and after. He wasn't sure what that said about him; he was guessing nothing good. So he tried not to think about it.

He glanced up at Tori. From her post she had to lean over to manage it, but she had her arm pasted around the back of his neck, publicly claiming him. *And she's not wrong.* They had been seeing each other for a while, and he liked her, he did. She was uncomplicated, pretty; she floated weightlessly on his arm, and left not a ripple in her absence.

Tori nuzzled his ear. "I'm going to get a beer, want one?"

He needed to move. Zoe's coming and going had made him restless. "I'll get you one."

Tori smiled. He knew she felt pampered.

He should have ended it last spring, a clean break. But there had been no reason to do it then, and he had half-hoped it would just fizzle out over the summer. He hated ending these things—hated the tears, hated the guilt, hated the indecision of whether he should stay and comfort after he'd just said goodbye. He had always been relieved in the past when his girlfriend would realize the relationship wasn't going anywhere and end it for him—an easy, get-out-of-jail-free card. But occasionally, that lightbulb never clicked on for the girl and he would get bored, or even worse she would get too intense, and he would be forced to do it himself.

He went to the keg in the corner exclusively for the brothers—better beer, no line. He filled two cups and headed back to Tori, grinning and trading one-liners with friends and fans as he walked. She was sitting in the same spot, guarding her nest, pseudo-listening to a brother whose back was to him. As Gavin approached, she craned her neck around the now unnecessary brother and beamed at him.

Oh man, how am I going to end this?

———

Allie needed air. She was drunk, underwater in a sea of people, the sepia scene around her undulating to the deep, throbbing bass of the music. An arm looped around her waist and the ruggedly handsome guy she was with—Billy, was it?—leaned in and whispered, "You okay? Want to go outside for a minute?" He peered at her; his eyes looked crossed.

"Sure."

He took her arm and maneuvered her towards the door.

"Ready to go?" Megan materialized next to her and touched Allie's free arm.

Allie took a moment to focus on Megan before pulling her arm free from Billy and stumbling towards her friend. Then as an afterthought, she tossed "bye, Billy" over her shoulder.

He scowled.

"You guys are going?" Zoe appeared as suddenly as Megan. "I might stay." She looked around. "Oh, hell, I'll go back too. We've got four years to do this, right?"

———

Back in the dorm, Zoe bid Allie and Megan goodnight and headed to her dark room. She flicked on the bright overhead light and immediately noticed her sleeping roommate. She left the light on as she checked herself in the mirror, undressed, and slipped into her navy silk pajamas. It wasn't until she had gone down the hall to brush her teeth and had come back again that she finally clicked off the light.

———

Allie staggered with Megan down the hall towards their room. Halfway there, she stopped at the hall phone and tilted her head towards it. "I'm just going to call Dana."

Megan shuffled on as Allie, feeling shaky, stepped into the phone booth and closed the glass door. She held her breath—and the tears that threatened—as the ring echoed out across the miles. No answer. She exhaled. Probably just as well. She would have sobbed with the ache of missing him, and she was afraid he wouldn't know what to say, afraid there might be silence on the other end of the phone. Or maybe he would have answered with something positive, "but it sounds like you had a great day!" which would have made her feel slightly crazy in her sadness. No, better to talk to him tomorrow when she was more composed. She hid out in the phone booth until she was sure her tears were locked down. Then she headed down the hall to her room.

Megan climbed into bed and hugged her stuffed dog. The toy Labrador was a present from her oldest brother; she knew he was probably worried about her, his baby sister out in the big world, and his way of saying it was, "I thought you might miss the dog." She did. She missed their dog, she missed her parents, she missed her brothers.

But she was also excited, a fresh start, on her own, out from under the expectations that—because she was a Riordan, because her brothers were made of gold—were everywhere she turned, like well-placed jaw-traps that snapped closed around her ankle and bit.

She turned over and closed her eyes. Tomorrow was a new day.

CHAPTER 2

JOURNAL ENTRY #2
July 15, 2000

I live on a typical Westchester County cul-de-sac—majestic oak trees drape over white porches, slate walkways bear the rush of starched, knotted dads, and blond, toned moms. Speed bumps ripple down the road, a nod to safety and to the neighborhoods of years ago when kids and pets romped freely, only culled into family units at suppertime. Now kids have guitar lessons and soccer practice after school, pets are leashed, and drivers rarely heed the speed bumps—catching air over each rise in the road shaves precious seconds off the commute.

But in the warm breathiness of a July evening, Lockwood Lane hums like it might have when I was young. The web-like heat amplifies the buzz, a full-sensory symphony of summer, complete with the mouthwatering smell of sizzling beef, the aerial ballet of hungry dragonflies, and the singsong crescendo of neighborhood freeze tag. Parents are cocktailing on patios, balls are rolling across the street, colored popsicles are dripping without prejudice down every tee shirt.

I'm soaking it all in from afar, having just poured a fat glass of wine and exhaled my way onto a porch rocker. So often I'm in the throes of family logistics at this hour—dinner, baths, exhausted silliness—and I seldom take a deep breath and reflect. But tonight, Matthew and Gillian are with Dana, leaving the house, and me, meditating and still. My own twilight.

This morning I broke a sweat just getting out of bed. I dumped ice in my coffee—which just made it lukewarm and watery—and listened to the weatherman hype a scorcher. The kids and I did not need convincing; we packed up and aimed for the swim club, with Megan close on our heels. I can still feel the sun's intensity and smell the coconut-infused suntan lotion—applied way too late—radiating off of my skin. Although I'm vigilant about protecting my kids, I still have the beauty-trumps-health mentality about myself, and so after lathering them up, I couldn't resist the narcotic lure of the sun and a chat with Megan, and I eased back on my vinyl recliner, my skin and my heart defenseless. With Megan, my soul is comfortably naked; we skinny-dip through all of life's flash floods together. I don't know what I'd do without her; she's my touchstone, my lifeline, and I know that I am the same for her.

As we melted into our lounge chairs, stress dripped off us like the condensation on our water bottles, and our conversations, idle and deep, weaved in and around the magazine articles we flipped through. Matthew and Gillian, now six-and-a-half and five, have a whole gang at the club and they splashed just within our periphery all day. Right now they both crave and fear independence, a wonderful age when they still like me with them, but I'm not their sole entertainment. I treasure these days, as I know that soon they'll choose their friends over me, blushing and perhaps even cringing when other kids spot us together.

That may kill me.

Today's only tarnish was when Dana came to the house to pick up the kids. The awkwardness was palpable, stiff-backed, a dining room chair between us. We didn't kiss or hug, and our bodies, as if unsure of the rules, twitched in the space where the embrace was supposed to be, a microscopic tilt towards each other and rapid snap back to the reality of the situation. In that moment, I think we both felt so alone, stripped of the togetherness that has cloaked us for so many years now. I wanted to reach out across the void and stroke his sandy-brown hair and his tanned and slightly grizzly face. But I held myself in check. That small gesture would have been an enormous step, as many gestures are. I'm not ready for that, not ready to begin again, or to take up where we left off. Nothing has really changed yet, not for me at least.

I'm used to feeling lonely. I've actually felt lonely with Dana for a long time. Not at the beginning; at first our togetherness filled me up, spilled over me, over us. Like two people sharing an umbrella, we huddled intimately underneath our starry-eyed devotion to each other. And then at some point in our marriage, as our pace increased and the discrepancy in our strides became more pronounced, it just made more sense to use separate umbrellas, and I found myself isolated, holding my own against inclement weather.

Deep down, I've always blamed myself for that, although on the surface, in our fights, I blamed Dana. It was just so much easier to point the finger at him than to point it at myself. But now that I'm alone, and there is no Dana at night to aim my bitterness at, I can step back and see that maybe it was both of us; maybe we were both hurting.

Yet he was the one who walked out. On some level, I've expected that since the day we got together. Expected it, and not known how to stop it. But now his leaving has forced me to try to sift out my own feelings from the tangle of knee-jerk reactions that has become our marriage, like separating a well-shuffled deck of cards into suits—my clubs, his spades, our hearts.

Maybe that was his intent when he left. His parting words to me were, "This isn't working. You need to decide what you want." Which at face value gives me the power, but really, as he's the one who made the move, I think he's holding the cards. For years I've stashed the "I can always leave" clause in my back pocket; it was my security blanket, a way to pat down my fear as I felt him—maybe pieces of him—slowly leave me over the years. As I sensed the daily "how was your day" lose any real curiosity, as it became part of dropping his briefcase and shedding his coat and recited with just that amount of heart.

To be fair, I guess my own curiosity became more and more hobbled by my hurt. And then my anger.

We've been together for a long time—15 years, since our junior year in high school. And we've been married for eight of those years. Part of what attracted us to each other, or at least me to him, was that we were different, or as different as you could be at a New England boarding school. Dana grounded my lightning, legitimized my craziness. He was Captain America—handsome, athletic, smart. He was cool in a straight-up way, sporting his seasonal numbered jerseys with more pride in the team and in the game than in the status it assured him around campus. I was more reckless, impulsive. I had my own following, and it wasn't to the library.

We met at a party. He was drinking Molson's with his buddies (in between seasons of course), and I was getting stoned with some friends. Somehow we ran right into each other (I probably wasn't looking where I was going, or maybe I just couldn't see) and although Fate might have had different plans for both of us, on that day our connection challenged those plans and forced Fate to reconsider.

Dana came from a good family—strong values, close connections. My family... well, my family hung in there as best we could, with no mother, and a father who's been haunted, bewildered since the day my mother walked out the door close to 30 years ago. I guess he did try his best to raise the three of us kids, but his best was so stymied by the hole Evelyn left that he never really pulled himself together where we were concerned.

So Dana kept me safe and in line—and possibly in school—and I loosened up his tie. And we were in love. That heady, high school love that completely swallows your heart and your life. We finished each other's sentences, completed each other's thoughts, and became each other's family. And in hindsight, that all-consuming feeling won out over any differences, or future desires, or any vague images we held of who we might become. In that cocoon of high school, where the entire outside world consists of your dorm, your classroom, and the athletic field, it was perfect.

DECEMBER 1987: SOPHOMORE YEAR
Erikson College

Allie hung up the phone and shivered, as if someone had just yanked all the blankets off of her on a dark, frosty morning. She yearned to curl back up into Dana's deep gravelly voice, to crawl back through the coiled phone wire into him. Her fingers hesitated over the numbers on the dial.

She pictured Dana cracking open a textbook, his highlighter poised and ready, their conversation already ticked off on a detailed to-do list. He would probably dive into chemistry, as he always tackled his most challenging subject first. She frowned. His down-the-hatch common sense often missed the point of right now. He always had his eye on the ball—"Hang in there honey, only seven more days… " He wasn't wrong, but sometimes it would be nice to hear that he missed her too.

"How about we only talk on Sundays?" he had pitched earlier in the semester after a particularly bad phone bill. She had wanted to slam down the phone on his oh-so-practical suggestion, and her "okay" was sharp and intended to hurt. But she had to admit (although never to him) that it had been a good idea, and not only financially. The daily heartbreak of missing Dana had been excruciating; a flicker of his earnest expression or a recent sweetness had her reaching for something solid—a bedpost, a beer bottle, a friend—so that she didn't disintegrate. Even the shadowy essence of Dana sifting through her thoughts was agony, an instant train wreck, derailing her from conversations, homework, brushing her hair; leaving her paralyzed, the words, the brush, dangling useless.

But now, with their new financially-savvy schedule, she could open up the scab and bleed heavily on Sunday, then slap on a Band-Aid, box up her heart, and stuff it into the back of her closet for the rest of the week, one precious box amidst a wasteland of dirty clothes and crumpled, red-inked exams.

She clicked on the TV and crawled under her thick down comforter, willing her mind to go blank, to start filing away the weighty ache of Dana, now pressing on her chest and threatening to suffocate her. She focused on her breathing—in, out. Easy. This wasn't an emergency, more of a standing appointment, the post-phone call hangover, the hour between the bubble-wrap of Dana and the new weightlessness of the week. She could wait it out. It was soothing to hear the low droning of the television.

Ever since she could recall, the TV had been on in her white clapboard house. Allie couldn't remember much about Evelyn, or Eva (her mother insisted Eva had more pizzazz), but she did know that television had been Eva's oxygen. During the day, Allie camped out at the base of the blue paisley couch, setting up her dolls and her stuffed animals on the rug at Eva's feet, the panty-hosed legs crossed next to her a vertical security blanket. While she changed the outfits on her dolls, the men and women of *General Hospital* and *All My Children* floated across the screen in their own ever-changing, technicolor wardrobes. Eva's rapt face and begrudging, one-word answers told Allie all she needed to know about her own precarious presence in the room. Once in a while however, with one eye still on the screen, Eva would exclaim, "Can you believe she did that?" to no one in particular, and Allie, every time like Pavlov's dog in ponytails, would leap up from her game, the honor of being included spurring her to her feet, and struggle to come up with the answer, even though the word "tree," or no word at all, would have sufficed. But incomplete attention was better than none, and Allie learned never to whine. There was no faster way to dissolve the brief commercials of motherly love.

Their routine varied once, when she was four.

Allie, waking from her nap with the bright midday sun streaming in through her window, crawled out from under the covers and gathered all of her favorite dolls into an unwieldy jumble in her arms. She bit her lip in concentration as she wobbled down the hall; she did not want to drop anyone. Habit and the chatter of the TV led her towards the den, and she stepped into the doorway with relief—She did it! No one fell!—and prepared to gently release her babies onto a chair next to the door.

Instead she froze.

The room was hot, so hot, like the oven when her mom reached in for the chicken nuggets. The windows were shut tight. The thin plastic shades were pulled all the way down and the sun outside lit them a flaming orange, like a jack-o'-lantern lit with a candle. There weren't any lights on in the room, but the glow from the television and from the fiery shades made monster shadows on the walls.

Allie's attention snapped to the couch. Her usually powdered and pressed mother was a ball of flannel—legs tucked up inside her long pink nightgown, head face down on her knees. Her dark hair hung in a stringy web around her. She was rocking back and forth, but not like Allie slowly rocked her baby dolls; her mother was rocking fast and jerky.

A small mewing sound erupted from deep inside of Allie. "Mommy."

Eva pried her head up off her knees; her cheeks were streaked with mascara, as if she had scrawled black crayon all over them. She put her head back down. The rocking stopped, but the stillness was even scarier.

Allie let go of her toys; plastic baby dolls crashed to the floor in a heap of twisted limbs and heads. She swung towards the TV for help, but the toothy smiles and red-lipstick laughter that grinned back just made the nightmare in front of her more terrifying.

Allie stumbled over to the couch and wrapped her small arms around the awkward bulk that was her mother.

"Mommy! Don't cry, Mommy."

There was no response, no change in demeanor or shape. Her little mind scrambled for a better fix. She raced by Kevin's room—door shut, still napping—and into the kitchen. A drink, something to drink. Juice. She ran over to the refrigerator and grabbed the orange juice. She was about to pull a chair over so she could climb up and get a glass when she saw a box of tea bags on the counter. Tea! She dragged a chair over, climbed up on the counter for a mug and slid back down. She filled the mug with water from the faucet and dropped a tea bag into it—string, tag and all. It floated on the top of the water and Allie paused for a moment—it didn't look quite right, but she was sure this was how her mother did it. She then put the chair and the orange juice back before she took the mug with the floating tea bag in both hands and turned towards the hall. She stopped. She was scared; scared to go, scared not to go. Her heart was thumping, which was scary too. Finally her fear of being scared all alone pushed her forward, and carrying the mug very carefully so as not to spill, she walked towards her mother.

The den was empty. The party continued on TV, but Eva was gone.

That was the last time Allie saw her.

The reasons Eva left were never discussed in the Mussoni household. But Allie—her long hair without ribbons now that her mother was gone—knew that it was her fault; she had not been good enough, she had not been quiet enough, she had not been *enough*, and she believed that her mother had left in search of better. In four-year-old Allie's mind, that was a place where kids weren't asking, kids weren't crying, kids weren't screaming. Where kids weren't.

After that, the television stayed on, and the vibrant square became the dramatic centerpiece in a house that had become an emotional vacuum. The random babysitters were more than happy to have the kids electronically entertained, and Allie's father, who arrived home from work to slump at the kitchen table, received the "Daddy, can we watch TV?" as a gift. After a while, the kids stopped asking.

"How's it going?" Megan opened the door and peeked into their sunny dorm room. These Sunday afternoon calls with Dana were part of her schedule now too and she always disappeared for a while so that Allie had a quiet place to recover.

For over a year now, the two girls had been entwined, their joy and their pain braided around each other in coded companionship. They shared an infinite, running dialogue—often laced with urgent information—even when they weren't talking. One girl's loaded smirk from across the room could tickle the other, waiting in line for the bathroom, and make her laugh out loud. Late at night in their dark dorm room, they whispered their trivia and their deeply personal stories to each other, filling and tying off balloons with their dreams for tomorrow until their heavy-lidded eyes closed and mid-sentence words became soft snores. In the drowsy sun of the morning, they picked right back up where they left off.

"I'm getting there." Allie emerged from under her covers. "Thanks."

"How's Dana?"

Allie's eyes were puffy, her nose was red. "He's taking some class that has him thinking about law school."

"Whoa."

"You're telling me. I can't even think beyond tomorrow and he's graphing out the rest of his life." She sighed. "He would be a great lawyer though, he's so damn logical, and he's an amazing public speaker. No fear."

"Remind me where he keeps his superhero cape?"

"Sickening, isn't he?"

"Sickening?" Tess Cleary stood in the doorway, her tentative smile scrunching up her freckles, which for a rare moment were scrubbed clean and on display. "You aren't by any chance discussing the chicken a-la-something the cafeteria is calling dinner tonight? Because I was wondering if you guys wanted to go get a salad… " She twisted her gold necklace, debating the importance of a salad over what she really wanted. "Or order a pizza?"

"Pizza sounds good, but let's go out and get it. I need a change of scenery," Allie said.

"Sounds good," Megan said.

"Give me five minutes, okay?" Tess turned and headed towards her room.

———

Tess had been Megan's lab partner in freshman bio, and the two of them had bonded over their mustached professor's oddities. He had a strange speech pattern, starting off each thought slowly, then talking progressively faster, so that although most students were trying their damnedest to write down what he said, their notes only captured the first half of each important point. Megan and Tess spent many a class looking at each other with a wide-eyed "Did you get that?" and then smothering giggles when it was clear that once again neither of them had.

This year, Allie, Megan, Tess, and Zoe had all arranged to live in the same dorm; it was luck of the draw that Tess had ended up only two doors down from Allie and Megan.

Tess opened up her oversized makeup bag and dumped out her social palette; dozens of cosmetics, in all shapes and sizes, clattered out onto her bureau. She separated the various tubes and compacts by function and then browsed the selection for just the right colors. After rubbing out her freckles with foundation, she swiped on blue eyeliner, black mascara, rosy blush, and pink lipstick; then she brushed her pin-straight dark blond hair until it shone. When she was finished, she dialed down the volume on her mother's imagined disapproval and scrutinized her handiwork, still amazed that she could see her whole face at once. In high school, she'd had to apply her contraband makeup in the visor mirror of a friend's Buick, which only illuminated one plain feature of her face at a time. She sighed at her reflection and clicked off the light, her mother's voice grumbling like an old muffler in the background.

———

From as far back as she could remember, Tess's mother Ann had clothed herself in the mantra that beauty shines from the inside; that looks don't matter. Trying her best to instill resilience, Ann pounded the message into her daughter at every opportunity. When Tess skipped home from school bubbling with the joy of a new friend or a scribbled note—John thinks you're cute!—her mother would glance up from the stovetop and offer solemn advice: Make sure they like you for you.

A hobby! A passion! Her mother had incessantly crowed that this was the key to happiness. Ann's was cooking; her entire day revolved around preparing dinner, the only full meal she ever consumed. Each morning over hazelnut coffee she crafted a shopping list, using special colored pens to organize the items into categories (Tess would forever associate dairy with purple ink). Sometimes she even hummed while she worked. Then, wearing whatever baggy ensemble she had thrown on in the morning, Ann wheezed and waddled her way down the supermarket aisles—"My exercise," she said—the detailed list an all-important shield against people staring, and trying not to stare, at her obesity.

From midday on, she immersed herself in her ingredients, stirring, sautéing, tasting—and tasting some more—a gourmet meal for four. All afternoon the house simmered with delicious aromas—garlic softening in butter, rosemary and basil wilting in rich sauce, thick lamb or chicken roasting. But as the aroma intensified, Ann's humming died away. Pots and pans clashed and banged like cymbals, utensils scraped and whisked as if the flavor was hiding deep underneath the metal. No one actually heard her swear, but that was because Tess, her brother, and her father stayed far away, choosing hunger over entering battle.

Her bark to dinner snapped the family to the table, tails between their legs. They placed napkins on their laps and both feet squarely on the floor, bracing at least their bodies for what was to come. A mouth-watering feast, artistically garnished with a sprig of herbs or an edible flower, lay in front of them; but no one was tempted to lift a fork. Instead, they held their breath as Ann wiggled her girth into her chair, and then, like another family's benediction or cheery "Bon appétit," Ann's mood burst. Pent-up bitterness—mean, belittling comments or loaded, glaring silence—spewed across the succulent success of her day, destroying every appetite in its path. Tess, her brother, and her father ate dinner wordlessly, tremulously, as Ann ferociously sliced and stabbed her way through every morsel—and then slapped on seconds—as though she had just had a violent argument with the Delmonico potatoes.

Tess was not keen on finding a hobby.

"You know, pizza is the white button-down shirt of foods," Zoe shouted into the bathroom as she sat on Gavin's bed and buttoned his shirt over her breasts.

There was no answer from behind the half-open door.

"Think about it, it goes with everything," Zoe continued. "It can be snazzy or plain; it can be an appetizer, a meal, or even an activity, right? I mean people order pizza just for something to do. It can even be a lifesaver for an agoraphobic." She heard the shower turn on. "Pizza; the best idea 'round." She raised her voice. "Get it? *Round?* I know you think I'm brilliant."

"Brilliant and sexy," Gavin yelled from the shower. Then he stuck his head out from behind the yellowed plastic curtain. "But right now pizza is medicinal. Pepperoni."

Zoe smiled and picked up the phone. "Okay, okay. I'm ordering now because you're naked and indisposed. But don't get used to it. When we're working down on Wall Street and you're actually dressed, I'm not going to be ordering your pizza."

She heard Gavin mumble something from behind the shower curtain as she dialed.

"What was that?" She walked towards the bathroom, trailing the phone cord behind her.

"The girl who came up with the best idea 'round is headed to Wall Street? I thought you wanted advertising."

"Can't afford it. Maybe someday, but what I want—what I need—right now is money. My own. I have the infuriating dilemma of wanting to give my stepfather the finger and not wanting to make that statement from a crappy studio apartment," Zoe said.

She could hear Gavin turn the shower off. "Yeah, I can't quite picture you brainstorming taglines from a Murphy bed," he said. "I know a wiser man would say something like, 'money isn't everything,' but I'm not so sure that's true."

Zoe knew Gavin had an older brother with Down's Syndrome, and that Gavin felt like he had to be a star, to be everything his brother couldn't. He had talked about wanting to be a teacher, to work with kids, but he thought working in finance would mean "success" to his family. Zoe happened to agree. Because Gavin in a sweater vest? She wrinkled her nose like she smelled something bad.

"It's definitely everything in my house," Zoe said. The noise of a busy pizza shop crackled in her ear; "Hello? Damn, I'm on hold."

She picked up a magazine and spread a blanket over the ripped yellow couch before dropping down on it. In anyone else's room, she would never sit on such a frightening piece of furniture, even with a thick blanket over it. Only for Gavin.

The door opened and a fraternity brother peeked into the disheveled room. "Oh, sorry," he said when he saw Zoe clad only in a white oxford and underwear.

"He's in the shower," she said without looking up. It didn't really matter who the intruder was; at one time or another over the past year everyone in the fraternity house had walked in on them, on Zoe in some state of undress. She had learned that the less she freaked about it, the smaller the aftershocks.

Gavin and Zoe had now been together, and shocking people, since the third night of her college career, when Gavin followed her into a dark corner (she would later say she had no idea he was behind her) and they kissed, a steamy first kiss that would have gone on forever if not for a brother's urgent poke and message that Tori was looking for him.

Zoe scowled as Gavin slunk back into the bright lights of the party.

The gauntlet had been thrown down.

Throughout the rest of the fall, Zoe found every opportunity—empty classrooms, quiet library aisles, dark balconies—to press herself against him. She slid her tongue over his earlobe and whispered how she wished they had more time together, and then slinked away, leaving him panting and reaching out for her.

By the Christmas dance however, Zoe was done waiting. Her date was a handsome friend of Gavin's, who—per Gavin's suggestion—politely kept his hands to himself all night. She ended up standing in a group of people who she had zero interest in, glowering into her grain alcohol punch as Tori, drunk on the same red concoction, gift-wrapped herself around Gavin and sandbagged him with her boozy gibberish. If Gavin hoped to mollify Zoe with his sheepishness, it didn't work. Every time he looked at her with his hangdog eyes, she felt as though he was lifting up his shirt and showing her the soft spot just underneath his ribs.

It gave her courage. She raised an arrow and fired a well-engineered slip-of-the-tongue, outing herself as the other woman to a loud-mouthed junior, a girl who didn't have her own social life and so scavenged off everyone else's. To complete the transaction, Zoe slapped her hand over her mouth—Oops!—after she let the tidbit fly.

The news ripped through the party like wildfire, flaming red and orange behind the eyes of revelers who had just won front-row seats to the explosion of someone's private life. A giggly Tori was grabbed and dragged into the bathroom by two girlfriends. The crowd crackled with a pre-concert fervor. Moments ticked by; conversations around the room were window-dressing, easily abandoned when the bathroom door reopened and harsh fluorescent light carved a path through the dark, smoky room. Every party guest, while pretending not to care, tracked Tori's stomp across the floor and over to Gavin; then all pretense of disinterest was shed as Tori wound up to slap him.

————

Gavin knew something was up when Tori's friends yanked her off, and so when he saw her shoot out of the bathroom and bullet towards him, he could guess what was coming. *Oh my God. Here it comes. Why didn't I end it earlier? What the hell is wrong with me? There is seriously something wrong with me.* He braced himself for the slap.

But it never came.

Instead, Tori dropped her hand down by her side. He could feel the fury steaming off her, she was trembling with it, and he could see how much effort it had taken for her to drop her hand. She leaned her face in; he could smell the punch on her breath.

"You're such a fucking cliché, Gavin." She spit the words at him. Her eyes were narrowed, focused and fierce. She eyeballed his chest and looked back up to his face. "Is there even anyone in there?"

The words, her tone, landed on him like a gob of sticky saliva. He had been ready for the sting of the slap, but this was worse. He felt exposed, ugly. He stood very still; there was no retort on his lips. The silence hung in the air between them.

"That's what I thought," she sneered. She turned and walked away.

Gavin crossed his arms over his chest and scanned the crowd to see who had gotten a load of this. Some people looked away, others weren't quick enough. He saw Zoe among the rubberneckers, hardly obscured because of her height, and he started towards her, reassuring himself as he walked that while everyone had been watching, no one could have heard what Tori said. He squared his shoulders, and with each step he put another piece of his social armor back on.

"Wow," Gavin said, and to cover up his real shame, he hung his head like a small boy in front of the principal.

"Dare I ask what she said?"

"Basically she said 'Fuck you.'"

"Creative," Zoe said. "You okay?"

He nodded, trying to regain his bearings. "Let's get a beer. I could definitely use one."

They walked next to each other, not quite touching. As usual, people shifted to let Gavin through, but brothers and guests alike were subdued as the two of them passed, a few nods and weak smiles taking the place of back-clapping. Gavin shouldered the weight of the room as he stood with his back to the crowd and filled up a pitcher of beer. Zoe stood next to him, her spine regal. She snaked a hand into his back pocket.

Gavin exhaled.

Once in the safety of his room—one of the few singles in the fraternity—they dropped onto the blanket-covered couch and Gavin filled two cups, quickly chugging and refilling his own. "I'm going to get drunk. Want to join me?"

Zoe chugged her beer in response. "Sure." She held out her cup. "I think we both deserve it."

Gavin thought Tori might feel differently about that, but he didn't say so. Instead, he reached for Zoe and pulled her into him, kissing her hard, needing to be inside of her with a voracity that still surprised him. Their sexual electricity stung him all day, every day, even—unbelievably—on the football field. A flash of Zoe's guarded blue eyes wide open in delirium often blindsided him in the middle of a play. Luckily, the blast of adrenaline in his legs compensated for the momentary mental fumble.

––––––––

Zoe undid the button on Gavin's jeans with one hand and wrenched down his zipper, desperate for him to cover her, to lose himself in her, intoxicated with the idea that she now had him all to herself. She was crazy about him in a way that sometimes frightened her; she actually looked up to him, and whenever they were together, he unleashed all the colored butterflies in her stomach.

The only thing she had in common with Tori was that she could imagine feeling the same anguish if Gavin ever dumped her. She would never advertise it of course, but she'd be devastated. She had resolved that night never to give him a reason.

Now, a year later, she was just as determined to hang onto him. She placed the order for the pizza and waited for Gavin to get out of the shower.

––––––––

A week later, Zoe paused in the front hall of her mother and stepfather's apartment and breathed in the quiet, cool indifference. It always felt good to come home, for the first 24 hours at least. The apartment's sanitized affect was the ultimate Valium, a white padded room after a semester with Ringling Brothers and Barnum & Bailey.

She was careful not to put her heavy bags down on the polished-wood floor, and she held onto all of them as her footsteps echoed through the dustless halls and into rooms filled with uncomfortable, posed furniture. All traces of life-lived had been tucked away in closets and dishwashers, leaving only expressionless reflections on the expensive tables. She noted that her mother (or her mother's decorator) had made the seasonal switch into holiday mode; the everyday white and beige linen had been glammed up with accents of gold and silver—even the sofa pillows preened in gold lamé. The red and green ornaments, the Santa candles, and the wooden painted reindeer that Zoe had loved when she was young had long ago been donated to charity. The Christmas theme at the McCallister's was now 100 percent precious metal.

She stepped into her room, an anomaly because of its bright purple walls. Zoe secretly disliked the purple as much as her mother and stepfather, but the statement it made was priceless. She dumped her stuff on the floor, flopped down on her bed, and wondered when someone would notice that she was home.

———

Christmas morning was orderly; everyone showered, dressed, and arrived in the living room promptly at nine, arranging themselves on wingback chairs around the tree for a sedate round of gift-giving. Even her stepsister Georgette, who was only five and should have been whooping it up amidst the chaos of ripped paper and ecstasy, perched with her hands in her lap and waited her turn. Zoe shared her seat with a brightly-wrapped gift, guarding it from the polite exchange. It was the only present she cared about and she wanted it to be last. Finally, when all the toys, electronics, and sweaters had been opened and properly acknowledged, she handed the box to her mother with a rush of anticipation and pride. Its obvious shape made Meredith smile, and her blue eyes sparkled at her daughter as she unwrapped.

"Oooo, black and strappy," her mother said as she held up the shoes. "Thank you."

"You're welcome." Zoe grinned. "Can I borrow them tomorrow night?"

"Haha!" Meredith crossed the room and bear hugged Zoe. "It's so great to have you home."

Zoe's squeeze back slackened as she caught her stepfather's dark eyes. His nostrils were flared, and he seemed to be peering down his nose, gloating, although he was looking straight ahead.

"Merry Christmas, everybody." Meredith balanced on the edge of Zoe's chair, her arm still wrapped around her daughter.

"Not so fast."

Meredith's arm dropped from Zoe's shoulders as everyone shifted towards William. He reached into his pocket, and with the flair of a magician, whipped out a gold envelope.

"There's one more."

Zoe was sure she saw a cruel glint in his eyes as he bestowed the envelope on Meredith, and it wasn't a reflection from the tree lights. She held her breath as Meredith slid a polished fingernail underneath the seal and pulled out two airline tickets. Her mother's face lit up with delight.

"Aruba!" She rushed towards William and threw her arms around him. The shoes clattered to the hardwood floor, the black straps askew like broken limbs.

They lay there until the next morning. After the limo raced off to the airport, Zoe gently packed them back in the box, and placed them on a shelf in her mother's closet.

Then she picked up the phone. If she was going to stay in New York over break, she was not going to stay alone.

———

The four girls were stationed in front of the enormous bathroom mirror, each zooming in on their own personal flaws, burning holes in the silvery glass as they examined every pore. Despite the acute self-absorption, they were very much aware of each other—not of the stunning mosaic they made as a group, but of the essence of other, *better* glimmering just around their edges. The beautiful company only highlighted imperfections—real or perceived—that they each saw in their own reflection. Every one of them would *kill* for something different—bigger breasts, straighter hair, a skinnier waist, a smaller nose—imagining that their lives and loves might be different if only. The mirror, mirror, on the wall and the image it cast back was the whole truth, and it brandished more power and meaning than all the personality or talent housed just underneath the eyeliner and blush. At least on a Saturday night in a bathroom with mirrors.

At eight o'clock, an announcement from the doorman in the lobby—"You have guests, Ms. Chapin"—tore the girls away from themselves, and within minutes, modish friends, friends-of-friends, and appropriate-looking strangers began to stream into the lavish apartment. After ensuring that the logistics were all set—fridge stocked, ashtrays out, music on loud—Zoe abdicated her role as hostess, becoming a very laissez-faire guest, displaying none of the typical teenage hostess' "Don't touch that!" anxiety. While much of this attitude was just Zoe's demeanor anyway, Allie suspected that a part of her was hoping someone would drop a cigarette on her stepfather's white carpet.

————

Megan wrapped her arms around Dana in a bear hug. "I haven't even said hi to you yet. It's so good to see you."

"What's one of the most beautiful girls at the party doing in here all by herself?" Dana said as they broke away from each other.

"You've obviously had a few too many drinks." She smiled.

"And you look like you were waiting for someone. Will he come over if I'm here? Am I cramping your style?"

Megan swatted Dana's arm, although he was right, she had been hoping that Ted, a guy from school she liked, would notice her alone in the kitchen and come over. "If he's scared of you, then he has no balls and I should rethink my interest, or at least change my strategy."

"You should change it anyway. The lonely damsel routine? You should go over and just grab his butt, that'll get his attention."

"You fell for it."

"What can I say, I'm a sucker." Dana raised his beer in a mock toast. "So which one is he?"

"The tall one over near the fire, talking with that guy in the green shirt. But don't let him see you looking."

Dana waited a minute before spinning around. "I actually talked to him earlier, seemed nice. I'll just go tell him you're in here."

"No!" Megan grabbed Dana's arm, pulling him back. "Why don't you go pick on somebody else?"

"Nowhere near as much fun." He grinned.

Megan leaned back against the counter. "So how are you, anyway? Have you been running?"

"Not as much as I should. You've spoiled me for company, and I couldn't get Allie to go with me. For some reason, I just can't convince her that gasping for breath and sweating like a pig are good things."

"I didn't run much either. I have to say, I don't miss getting my butt kicked."

"Don't worry. Next time I visit, I'll take it easy on you. I'm out of shape."

"I'll hold you to it, although I can't quite picture you taking it easy. Has anyone ever mentioned that you're slightly competitive?"

Dana laughed. "A few times."

"A few hundred I'm guessing," Megan said, pretending to mutter under her breath.

"I heard that."

Megan smiled. "So, how was Christmas with Allie?"

"Awesome, although when Zoe called, we were more than ready to get out from under my family." He rolled his eyes. "My sisters—well, the word dramatic doesn't quite cover it. I love them to death, but let's just say the emotional volume in my house is turned up all the way. My dad and I end up cowering in another room, staying very quiet rather than risk making it all louder, angrier, sadder, or just *more* in some way." He leaned in and mock-whispered, "And my parents... they wonder if Allie's a bad influence on me." He resumed his normal tone. "So with my mom trying to act as if nothing was wrong—extra perky if you can imagine—and the background theater of my sisters, it was interesting. How about you, how was your Christmas?"

"Great, nice to be home; sleeping, seeing old friends, being tortured by my brothers, not necessarily in that order. But I'm ready to go back."

"Me too, I guess. I may have to kidnap Allie though, I can't imagine saying goodbye to her again."

"Kidnapping is a felony. And I'd miss her too much."

Dana's brown eyes grew somber. "I know. I'm glad you're there for her."

"We're there for each other. Speaking of which, where is she?"

"I don't know. I was trying to give her a little space and not be the nightmare who's stapled to her side all night because he doesn't know anyone." Dana smiled, his eyes twinkling. "See, so actually, I was the damsel in distress, and you fell for my scheme."

Megan glanced out into the living room to see if she could spot Allie, and paled a shade when she did. Allie was hunched in a far corner, a dark-haired guy leaning into her, his hand on the wall above her as if for balance. The silver bracelet Dana had given Allie for Christmas sparkled as her fingers raked through her hair.

Dana followed Megan's gaze across the party, then turned back with some serious question marks in his eyes.

"Some guy from school, I forget his name." Megan licked her suddenly parched lips. "Do you want a beer?" she asked, and without waiting for an answer, she opened the fridge to steal herself a moment. Then she handed him a bottle and started talking, this time with a mission. She had to keep him in the kitchen until whatever was going on with Allie and Kyle ended. As much as she liked Dana, it was Allie who she was going to protect at all costs. And at times, Megan knew, Allie needed protection from herself.

Out in the living room, Allie was panicked. She hadn't known Kyle would be at this party and was completely unprepared to have both him and Dana in the same place at the same time. From the moment Kyle had slinked through the door with his smoldering Italian good looks, Allie had steered clear of him. Now however, she was trapped. Kyle had literally backed her into a corner and he was both drunk and pissed off, a dangerous combination. Allie, drunk herself, spied Dana out of the corner of her eye and wished that she and Kyle were in a more private place to have this out.

Their relationship, as it was, had started out innocently enough. Kyle was not subtle about his interest in Allie—enthusiasm skipped in his eyes whenever he saw her—and over time his obvious desire ratcheted up the night's verve. It was an extraordinary booster shot to walk into a fraternity and know that someone was watching for her, hoping for her, and she soon found herself searching the dark rooms for him too.

She loved Dana, that was concrete. She knew he loved her too; but she often felt like an afterthought. In the frat party, in the dark, in the adrenaline of Kyle looking at her like she was the only person that he wanted, she was not an afterthought. She knew it was wrong. And she was magnetized.

She told herself it was harmless, and she had staved off guilt by penciling rules around their drunken hookups—no real dates, no sex. She had not paused to consider that someone, any of the three of them, might get hurt. Tonight was sobering however; someone was going to get hurt. Although the jury was still out on who.

And it suddenly seemed monstrous, and frightening, that she could box up her feelings for Dana so easily and be with someone else.

"Does he know about me?" Kyle's eyes bore into hers, his rage oozed through his growl.

"No, he doesn't. And he can't." Allie held his eyes and tried to keep her face from registering alarm. The pleading in her voice however, betrayed her.

"Well, this sucks. I haven't seen you in weeks, and you want me to sit here and watch you with him?" His face was red; she smelled tequila.

Oh my God, oh my God. She had assumed that Kyle understood the situation because it was so clear to her. Obviously not. There was no way she could explain it now; his eyes were wild, his muscles clenched. She tried to think. If she could just placate him, get him to back off tonight, she could deal with the whole thing back at school.

"Kyle, you know how I feel about you." She willed her voice to mellow, her eyes to soften. She put her hand on his arm; his bicep relaxed slightly. "But I've been with Dana a long time; it's just not that easy." She stole a glance at Megan and Dana. Tess had joined them, and the two girls were keeping his back to the living room. "I don't want to hurt him."

Kyle leaned in to kiss her.

She tried not to recoil, but there was no way she was going to let him kiss her here. In one fluid movement, she grabbed his hand and pulled him down the hall.

"I'm sorry," she said, the small words an envelope for the whole predicament. "I never meant this to be such a mess. Don't be mad, and don't do anything that will make it worse than it is. Let me deal with it my own way. Please?" She gazed up at him, her green eyes welling up with tears.

He stared at her for a long moment, and then exhaled. "Okay." He leaned in to kiss her again, and although her stomach shriveled, she let him. Her only goal right now was to untangle herself from him as quickly as possible.

After he walked away, she sagged against the wall, fighting waves of nausea. *What am I doing?* Shame and relief flooded through her.

This was all so unreal, a soap opera; although the heroine (or villain as it were) never heaved into a toilet after the dramatic scene. She stumbled further down the hall in search of a safe place to pull herself together. She opened a bedroom door and jumped back. She had interrupted Gavin and Zoe. Gavin and Zoe, always together, the perfect couple. They were lying on the bed, fully clothed, but Allie didn't stay to find out whether they were involved in an intimate conversation or foreplay.

She slipped into a bathroom. Closing the cover on the toilet, she sank down, trying to lower her blood pressure and call up her earlier lightness with a cigarette. She smoked it down to the butt. When she stood, she caught herself in the mirror; the fluorescent light accentuated the circles under her eyes. *Ghoulish. Serves you right.* She half-heartedly shook out her hair, applied fresh lipstick, and as she emerged from her tiled sanctuary, hoped that the light was more forgiving in the kitchen.

She joined Dana, Megan, Tess, and Ted, who had finally made his way over.

Megan raised her eyebrows slightly. *Is everything okay?* she asked with her eyes.

Allie opened her eyes wide. *Oh my God.*

From across the circle, Tess handed her a cold beer and she gulped it gratefully. Dana's brown eyes were dark, perplexed, but he was involved in a conversation with Ted and so luckily couldn't ask her any questions. She nuzzled up to him, and he cast his arm around her, hopefully stifling any uneasy feelings he may have had.

Allie tried to join in the easy banter of the circle, but she felt disoriented, the trauma of the past half hour still writhing in her mind. She was hyper-conscious of Kyle lurking somewhere behind her, and the hair on the back of her neck prickled with the thought that he might be watching her. Not wanting to incite additional fireworks, she fought the impulse to turn around and see where he was. All she wanted was to be alone with Dana, to curl up into his broad chest and feel his strong arms encircling her. If they could just be alone and shut out the world, she was convinced her shame could be shut out as well.

She tensed as someone came up behind her and grabbed her butt. Terrified, she whipped around to see Zoe's grinning face.

Zoe leaned over and whispered, "You okay?"

Allie smiled wanly as adrenaline coursed through her.

"He just left," Zoe added.

Allie's whole body sighed.

Zoe then sang out to the group, "Just getting some beers," and she grabbed a six-pack out of the refrigerator and started back towards the bedroom.

"Are you guys ever going to make an appearance at the party, or are you going to stay holed up in the bedroom all night?" Dana teased.

"You guys seem like you have it all under control," Zoe said over her shoulder as she breezed away. "So I'm going to go with the latter."

Allie knew that if Zoe had her way, she and Gavin would never come out.

CHAPTER 3

JOURNAL ENTRY #3
August 11, 2000

I'm never sure how to start these entries. The whole Dear Diary thing seems so prepubescent, as if I'm writing in a pink vinyl journal dressed with a tiny faux-gold lock. But without a greeting, I'm an overbearing stranger breaking into a private conversation. No good morning, just here's what I think. It doesn't seem very Emily Post.

The kids and I just got back from a week on Nantucket. I wasn't sure how it would feel to be there without Dana; the island is stuffed with memories of the two of us walking the beaches and cobblestone streets, first holding hands and enjoying five-star restaurants (when the food and the hand-holding was just a prelude to electric sex), then strolling pregnant (when the hand-holding was more of a seat belt and eating anything was a highlight), and more recently, toting kids' sand toys and sippy cups (when handholding was impossible because we were juggling, juggling, and if we had 10 minutes to inhale a burger we were lucky). In all those times there was shared happiness; we melted together on that sandy oasis in a way that carpools and to-do lists on the mainland prohibited. Any ghosts from the past or demons of the present were swept away in the damp, textured breeze off the Atlantic.

Of course this year, our family has been radically sheared, and Dana's absence was a dark, brooding shadow hovering just to the side of every ice cream, every bike ride. It was Sarah's suggestion, sort of, to go on vacation;

she said that the kids and I should do the things we'd normally do, not just hole up in the house, within myself, which is how I've handled this separation so far. We agreed it would be good for us to get away, but also, I think she wanted me to really experience how it felt to be on my own. Without Dana, going about life-as-usual.

What we didn't discuss however, was that my usual has always been Dana.

I had cheated on Dana before we got married, but never after. No, instead of acting out my loneliness in the arms of someone else, I acted it out in the arms of our relationship. It was on my face, in my attitude, part of my posture. And underneath that, I was screaming at him—silently—to see me.

Help! Can't you see my flailing arms?

Of course he didn't hear, couldn't possibly hear. But he noticed. And he must have interpreted my expressive S.O.S. as distance, as coldness, as dissatisfaction. He became defended, poured himself into work, and the stones between us piled up. The answer seems so simple: talk to each other. But in imaginary conversations, I heard myself whining, pleading, for what, attention? If he loved me, shouldn't that come naturally? To beg for it made me needy, clawing, the original ball and chain. Not something you strive for.

As a result, I did become distant and cold.

Dana is a good man. He loves me, loves the kids, he takes good care of us. And he loves being a lawyer. He thrives on the challenge of each case, the camaraderie of his colleagues, the accolades he has won. He suits up early in the morning, earlier than necessary, to shoot the shit with his co-workers and begin his day with an un-frazzled mind. He then stays late to ensure each exquisite detail has been honed to perfection. He is a star.

And I was invisible. A ghost who did laundry.

I blamed Dana for that.

"Get a job! Volunteer! Do something about it!" I can hear Zoe stomp her polished black boot. But I couldn't abandon the kids when they were young, and once Gillian was in kindergarten I felt like I had missed the boat. I went on one interview, for an entry-level position, and passed a girl who had clearly just traded in her red-and-white pom-poms for a jaunty navy suit. My wedding ring, the kids that I had just put on the bus, my stretched-out stomach all made me feel like a dazed tourist in a foreign country. My friends, who had been working for years, were at least halfway up the rungs of success, if not farther. Starting as a receptionist or gopher at 30 or 31...

See, I am whining. What a cliché, the hard-working man and the bitter housewife.

My mother's life.

This was not what I believed love and marriage were all about. And I had the best role models—Walt Disney, must-see TV, *Pretty Woman*. So where was my life's soundtrack of catchy top-40 tunes?

When I was young, the TV was my mother, my babysitter, my constant companion. Instead of soothing warm milk and a cuddle before bed, I was served True Love and Happily-Ever-After with technicolor frosting and a witty-banter candy rose. And I devoured it. I would curl up on the rug, my face aglow with the fluorescent reflection and the company of men embracing women in adoring looks, all-forgiving hugs, heart-soaring reunions.

In those days, TV dramas didn't progress week to week; each episode stood alone, its own unit. The best episodes (during Sweeps Week) had the hero falling hard for someone, head over heels. But alas, this soulmate always met an unfortunate end (as the hero had to be single and fantasy-ready again for the next week). The final minutes of the hour would be a real tearjerker as the devastated tough guy would lean over his love's deathbed and spill his heart out, the few tears he shed hard evidence of his heartbreak.

Nothing warmed me or made me want to pirouette around my bedroom like these snippets of true love, and in the dark I would imagine hearing those words, feeling that power, seeing see my hero bowed to his knees by emotion. By me.

As I got older and graduated to the big screen, love could take another hour to bloom and there were often obstacles to overcome, but it was always electric and absolute, and it was understood by all in that dark theater that when the lovers finally got there, that was it. Happily ever after. Without dirty dishes and misunderstandings.

I guess it's no surprise that the fairy tale became branded into my expectations, a blueprint for my own love life.

I don't have to go farther than my living room to witness the silver screen's power on the psyche. Moments after watching any kind of fight scene on TV, Matthew is karate-chopping Gillian or sword-fighting with the dog, his cardboard paper towel tube slicing through the air with rabid machismo. And to this day, I cannot swim in the ocean without visualizing my legs dangling, baiting the vacant pair of eyes and razor sharp teeth that I am coldly certain lurk just underneath me.

I can live without riding the ocean waves, but it's hard to avoid romantic movies and love songs. Hell, even during some commercials I get a disbelieving "Are you *crying* Mom?" It's everywhere, the idea of being swept off your feet, perhaps against all odds, and falling into a passionate love...

Big sigh. And fade to black.

Obviously, the trick is not to let it fade to black, to instead define your own happily ever after. But the definition is hard to create in the bright light of day, when you've misplaced the magic under piles of bills and dirty diapers. It flickers in the beat of each other's hearts during a stolen embrace amongst the chaos of dinnertime, in a moment of real affinity while the water on the stove next to you bubbles and boils. But inevitably the demands of the uncooked pasta, the whines of the hungry dog, the shouts of *more milk!*, and the burdens of homework and lifework nose its way back in between you and force you to let go. And the curtain closes again.

And so, against the backdrop of dramatic, cinematic romance, I hold up my life. Is this it?

APRIL 1989: JUNIOR YEAR
New York City

It was a cloudless April Saturday and New Yorkers—finally stripped of their heavy coats and winter blues—were nodding, smiling even, as they jostled past each other. The whole city was out strolling on the street, running in the park, or spilling into sidewalk cafes, something only city-dwellers find indulgent. Crammed into a space the size of someone's dining room, your chicken salad an arm's length from toxic exhaust and giant, swinging shopping bags, intentionally dressed New Yorkers slip on their sunglasses and snub the lines at TKTS for a more entertaining matinee: people watching.

Ready for the show, Zoe had planned to meet Gavin at their favorite Saturday afternoon rendezvous, Carmichaels. Gavin arrived first, and after a brilliant smile and a deep-bass hello that wrapped around the hostess' shoulders, he was ushered to a coveted corner table outside. He ordered a Heineken and sat down to wait for Zoe. The sun warmed his back, interesting people wandered by, a cold beer was on the way. And so was Zoe. His foot jiggled under the table.

The whole restaurant sat up straight when she arrived, late as usual, and he watched her from afar, mesmerized as always by her long stride and by the way her clothes—dark jeans and a snow white sweater—hugged her in all the right places, as if they were tailor-made, which Gavin knew might not be far from the truth. She sailed right by the hostess, who opened her mouth to utter a canned greeting and quickly found herself staring at Zoe's cashmere back. Gavin leaned back in his chair, his foot momentarily lulled into stillness, and enjoyed Zoe's approach with the first sip of his beer.

She navigated the tables as if she was on roller skates, gliding fluidly through the busy restaurant and out onto the cordoned-off cement; her creamy neck provided a full ruler of separation between her head and shoulders, her high-heeled black boots added a sexy sway to her hips. The hostess, hot on her heels, had to trot to keep up.

"Can I help you?" the hostess said to Zoe's back.

Zoe spun around, her eyes flicking from the hostess' shoes to her hair. "A glass of chardonnay." The hostess was left teetering in her wake.

Zoe marched right up to Gavin and kissed him hard on the lips. "Hey handsome." She flashed a full, red-lipstick smile and dropped her overnight bag at her feet.

"Hey yourself. You look great."

Zoe slid into a chair.

The hostess put Zoe's glass of wine down and then put her hand lightly on Gavin's shoulder. "Another beer?"

"That'd be great, thanks."

Zoe said, "I had to walk from Penn Station, couldn't get a cab." She shook her head; her diamond studs sparkled in the sun. "It's such a beautiful day, you'd think there would be plenty of cabs, that people would want to walk."

Gavin was about to tease that clearly *she* hadn't wanted to walk, but he stopped himself. He shouldn't get pulled into their banter, their rhythm. He had a different agenda.

"Zoe."

She lowered her chin. Something in his voice had scared off her smile and the muscles in her face tightened.

Gavin's shoulders rolled in and his fingers opened and closed around his beer bottle. He bumbled through several false starts, and then launched into a breathless monologue, his words tripping over each other in a race to get through it.

He tried to keep his eyes on Zoe's face as he talked, but as her eyes grew wide and her mouth fell open, he feigned fascination with his green bottle. When he looked up again, her eyes were narrowed, her mouth was clamped into a tight thin line.

He stopped talking and exhaled. *There.* They sat in an eggshell of silence among the clatter of the tables and the bustling street beyond. His fingers picked at his beer label while he waited for her to say something.

"Tess?" Zoe said. "You're in love with Tess?"

Gavin reached across the table and took her hand. For the first time in his life, he wanted to handle this honestly, to do the right thing, for himself and for Tess, but also for Zoe. He wanted to make sure she was okay, although he had convinced himself that once she understood the situation, she would be okay with it, possibly even happy for him. And happy for Tess of course. "Zo, I'm so sorry. I never meant this to happen."

She jerked her hand away. "How did it then?"

Gavin sighed. "I don't know. We kind of ran into each other about a month ago, over spring break. When you were in St. Bart's. I didn't even recognize her at first. I mean, I didn't know her very well at school."

Zoe sat motionless, her long legs crossed and her manicured hand around her wine glass. Her eyes were fixed on his face.

"She was in New York on an interview for a summer job. We literally bumped into each other in a bar afterwards. She was with some friends, no one I knew, and I was with some people from work. Like I said, I didn't really recognize her. She recognized me though... "

Based on Zoe's shudder, that was the wrong thing to say. Now he had made it sound as if Tess had come onto him; as if it was Tess's fault.

"But as soon as she introduced herself, I realized she was your friend, and I felt like an ass for not recognizing one of your friends. So I invited her over to our table for a drink." Too much detail, he tried to wrap it up. "And, I don't know. It just kind of happened from there." Another mistake. "Not that night, I mean." God, he was an idiot. No wonder he usually just kept his mouth shut during breakups. A thin line of sweat trickled down his spine.

Zoe was not going to let him sum it up so fast. "So... what? You guys made plans? You asked her out on a date?"

"It wasn't a date. Just dinner. She was going to be in town for a few days..." What could he tell her? That he had fallen in love with her that night? Love at first... conversation? He had seen Tess around Erikson before of course; she was one of Zoe's friends. But besides Allie, he didn't really know her friends—they'd always hung out at his frat. Zoe had never complained, and he got the sense that she didn't really care anyway. He couldn't picture her sitting around in flannel pajamas pouring her heart out to a bunch of girls over milk and cookies. Zoe kept herself so closed off. That restraint fired him up—every single time—but he didn't know her very well with her clothes on.

Tess was different. The funny thing was that he would never have looked twice at her; he *had* never looked twice at her. It wasn't that she was unattractive, she just blended in.

He had invited her to the table in the Hawaiian-shirt way he invited everyone everywhere; his sweeping invitation wasn't meant to be poignant, not at all. He assumed after a drink she would fade away into the crowded bar. But then Tess had fixed her big, brown eyes on him and hooked him somehow, made him ignore her aggressive blue eyeliner and look at her once, twice.

The wide-eyed way she gawked at him wasn't new. Most girls, most guys for that matter, looked at him that way. He had practically been crowned prom king in kindergarten, hoisted on the shoulders of his peers (and some teachers) as he rode through the halls of adolescence. But this applause, this insta-power made him feel phony. Not all the time—and he certainly wasn't knocking it—but the idea that he was a con man often nibbled at his edges, just out of bounds, making him peek around the cafeteria to see if anyone noticed that he wasn't as shiny as they all believed.

But that night there was something besides adoration in Tess's eyes, a raw vulnerability mixed into the awe, and her open, agenda-less gaze grounded him, made him feel real, solid.

Tess had stammered, said a little too loudly, "So, Gavin Keller, I've always wondered, what's the worst part about being you?" She blushed a deep red, but held his gaze.

He remembered that, he remembered being taken aback by the question, and interested in it. He knew the answer—and there wasn't just one— but he had never said any of them out loud before. He wasn't about to give voice to them then, but he was intrigued. He looked at her a third time and pulled a chair over.

Zoe snapped him back to their conversation in Carmichaels. "Come on Gavin, say it. You asked one of my closest friends on a date."

Gavin wanted to dispute the "closest friend" comment, but he bit his tongue. "It sounds terrible, it is terrible. Zoe, you know I care for you. I'm so sorry."

"Care for me?" Zoe was no longer sitting still. Her legs were uncrossed now, and both feet were planted on the floor underneath the table, as if at any minute she was going to leap up and knock it over. He braced himself for the crash. "You care for me? You've *cared* for me for two and a half years? Oh, you're cold, Gavin."

Now Gavin was incredulous. Was she in love with him? It wasn't possible. She had never shown signs of it, and he knew the signs.

She leaned across the table; her thoughts had snagged on something. Her light blue eyes drilled into his, and she spoke slowly, enunciating each word. "Wait a minute. You said a month ago. You said that this all started a month ago." She bit her lip, then her words fell over each other and her hands gripped the table, her dark red nail polish bloodlike against the white-knuckled grip of her fingers. "What's been going on since then? You've been dating her behind my back? You've been cheating on me?"

"No, I haven't been cheating on you. We haven't been together at all. Not at all." He wanted that part clear; they had only kissed. It was killing him, but that's how Tess had insisted it be until he had talked to Zoe. "She went back to school. We've talked a few times on the phone." A few hundred. "Neither of us wanted to do that to you. I mean, you're important to both of us, and I didn't want to say anything over the phone, I wanted to talk to you in person. This was the first time you could get to New York."

Her features folded in on themselves as she struggled to absorb the "we," the "us" that no longer included her.

Gavin wanted to hug her, to comfort her in a way he had never had occasion to before. He was about to get up and try when suddenly, as if she had flicked a switch, Zoe was serenely composed again. The anger and upset were gone; her affect was again unreadable. Gavin knew that he had witnessed something rare: Zoe's inner feelings. Her anger, briefly on the table like a paper napkin crumpled in a fit of rage, was now in check, smoothed out again in the shame of exhibition. She sat back in her chair; her voice was butterscotch, her face placid.

"You expect me to believe that you fell in love with her after one or two nights? That you guys haven't fooled around?" She sneered. "Gavin, I know your track record. You forget, I was the one you cheated with not too long ago." She lifted her glass. "Tess? Come on Gavin, you'll be bored in five minutes."

She slugged down half of her wine and stood up, reaching for her leather overnight bag. "You just threw away the best sex you'll ever have." She put her sunglasses on. "Enjoy Cindy Lou Who. I'm betting you'll be back."

She spun on her heel and maneuvered through the tables of insignificant New Yorkers with the liquid grace of a swan—spine straight, head high, gaze focused down the street.

She didn't lift her hand to wipe her tears until she had rounded the corner and was out of sight.

———

Back at school, Tess, who had been worrying about the scene in New York all day, was holding court with Allie and Megan, finally spilling her halcyon, Gavin-loves-me secret as if a levee had broken. With her cheeks blushing pink, Tess detailed the whole story, starting with how she had wanted to crawl through the floor when he had no clue who she was. She had to introduce herself—"I'm Tess… Zoe's friend?"—and with a blustering apology, Gavin had ushered her over to his table for a beer. She followed his broad back through the bar, berating herself for not having the courage to just say no to what was obviously a pity drink, knowing that she would be ignored once they exchanged a few "So how's life?" pleasantries.

Gavin, already peripherally involved in three different conversations, summoned the waitress with a wave. Over the roar of the crowded bar, someone across the table shouted for his attention. As he turned away, Tess—dreading irrelevance—ransacked her mind for something, anything memorable. Out spurted an inane question; she wanted to smack herself the minute it hung in the air. But he looked at her with a little tilt of his head, and then noisily slid a wooden chair over.

They were talking! Or rather, he was talking and she was focused on what she was going to say next. She threw out a comment and he chuckled; Tess wasn't sure whether it was because of the content or the manic delivery, but it didn't matter because he focused both green eyes on her, and suddenly she was ablaze, sizzling with her own out-of-nowhere vivaciousness and his obvious amusement. She launched into a story about her blundered interview that morning, about how she had tripped through the office door and into the arms of a young account executive—her interviewer—and as he was trying to extricate himself from her tangle of elbows and apologies, and she was trying to hold onto her papers and find her footing, her hand had grazed his penis. She had been "mortified—all caps," and scrambling around on her knees picking up the contents of her purse—ten thousand pens, lipsticks, and tampons—hadn't made the situation better. Tess smiled at Gavin and shook her head, and said that maybe the guy would give her the job to avoid a sexual harassment scandal. Gavin laughed and said that maybe he'd give it to her in hopes of igniting one.

One drink turned into many.

He was gorgeous. She was staring at the sun; she knew she should look away, but couldn't. He was focused on her, and at a table filled with his buddies, his gaze carved a quiet circle around the two of them and made her feel uniquely golden. A giggle lodged in her throat, threatening to erupt and never stop.

She knew that when the clock struck 12 she would revert back into Zoe's shadow and Gavin would fade away. End of story. But as he walked her to Grand Central and asked her to dinner the next night, that script seemed a little less solid. Her stomach flipped when he kissed her on the cheek goodbye.

She skipped to her train.

She spent hours getting ready for dinner; is-this-a-date-or-not outfits littered her bedroom, different-colored lipsticks stained tissues in the garbage. Her mother's raised eyebrows and heavy sigh as she left did nothing to assuage her uncertainty.

But at the restaurant, Gavin stood when she walked in, he pulled out her chair for her to sit. A glass of white wine was waiting at her seat, shimmering like liquid gold in the candlelight. "You look nice." He held her eyes and she felt her knees go weak.

They talked about work—Gavin was a trader, he had slid into it for the money, but he wanted to be doing something else; school—Tess was taking a public speaking course, "not my forte, I'm panicking the entire time I'm talking"; and family. Tess was worried about her younger brother; he'd always been quiet, too quiet, and with her not home... she shook her head.

"It's hard to be away from family when stuff's going on," Gavin said. He massaged his chin. "My brother Henry has Down's Syndrome. He's awesome, but it can be a lot for my parents." He paused. "Luckily I'm easy. They can ignore me."

She thought she saw a flash of sadness in his eyes, and she felt sad for a moment too, but then he smiled and his twinkle returned, and if the feeling had been there at all, it had been erased. She smiled. "I wish my mother would ignore me a little more," she said.

When Gavin asked her out for her third and final night in town, she threw her arms around him and kissed him in the middle of Grand Central.

She rushed through her morning interview, eager to hit Bloomingdale's—black heels, red sweater—and get a manicure. At home, as the unwanted perfume of her mother's spaghetti and meatballs infiltrated the bathroom, she showered, shaved, ripped the tags off her new clothes, and presented herself to the mirror for the final polish. Her brown eyes and freckles stared back at her as she began her routine, foundation, mascara, blush... she felt Gavin's breath, which just last night had stroked her cheek. She could feel his finger caress her eyelid, gently touching her eye makeup, his voice whispering in her ear, "You don't need all this."

A shiver rushed up her spine. She put the eyeshadow wand back in its case and snapped it shut.

Her mother's eyes followed her out of the house, but no eyebrows were raised, no dramatic sighing or grumbling floated after her.

————

Gavin was waiting in front of the restaurant, a boulder in the middle of a whitewater of people, his blond hair ruffling in the human tailwind. For a few moments he didn't see her, and then a gap opened up within the mash of New Yorkers between them and they locked eyes. Gavin grinned and put his hand over his heart.

She knew she was walking because her heels made a clacking sound on the cement, but she was unaware of commanding her body forward. Then she was in front of him with a shy smile and Gavin kissed her, a behind-closed-doors kiss, one that she could feel all through her body, in her groin, down to her toes.

Tess didn't want to think about tomorrow, didn't want to think about the fact that she would have to endure watching Gavin and Zoe together forever more.

————

"So this is tricky," Gavin said after dinner as they were walking hand-in-hand down Third Avenue.

She forced herself to focus on his green eyes. "It's okay, I understand. I won't say anything to anyone."

Gavin nodded. "You shouldn't. I should be the one to tell Zoe."

A flock of startled, winged questions flapped loudly through her head. One all-white dove circled. And circled. "Tell Zoe?"

"Well, we can't keep sneaking around."

The street was a blur of color; traffic buzzed in her ears.

"Tess? Right?" Gavin said.

"Um, what exactly are you going to tell Zoe?"

"That it's over. With Zoe. That I think I'm falling for you."

She stepped backward, wobbling in her new heels.

Gavin reached out to grab her. "Whoa. Are you okay?"

"Oh, yeah." She smiled up at him. "I'm okay."

––––––––––

The following few weeks back at school had been awful and wonderful, the secret both fuel and poison. Every time the phone rang, her heart thumped and her second thought, after thinking happily *Gavin!*, was that he was calling to say this was all a big mistake, some kind of elaborate gag. But that never happened. Instead, each night she curled up onto the hard plastic chair under the hall phone and twirled the black phone cord around her fingers while they talked. When other girls banged on the glass door, she put her palms together and mouthed, *please?*

They let her be.

––––––––––

Megan listened to Tess tell her story and didn't know whether to cheer for her or cry for Zoe.

"So he's telling her today?" Allie said.

Megan glanced at Allie. *Iceberg, straight ahead.*

"Yeah, I mean, that's the plan." Tess looked at her friends. Her bright smile faded. "I'm sorry, you guys."

"No, hey, it's complicated. Relationships are complicated," Allie said.

"And you and Gavin are trying to do the right thing." Megan shot another glance at Allie. She mouthed, *sorry.*

Allie shrugged.

Megan tried to ignore the queasy tension in her stomach, a hangover from a rare fight she and Allie had just last night about "the right thing," about Allie's cheating on Dana.

Megan had stayed in to study for a physics test as the rest of campus was out partying with an I'm-failing-anyway attitude. She had slipped on comfortable pajama pants, tucked her typo-free English essay—1,500 words exactly—into her notebook so she wouldn't forget it in the morning, and opened her fat physics book. The phone rang down the hall. Being the only one around, she ran to get it.

"Hey little sis."

"Brad!" She grinned.

"How's it going? Mom told me you have a huge physics test tomorrow."

Of course. Her life was always fodder for the grapevine.

"Don't worry about it," Brad said, "the math gene runs in the family. My strategy was always to take tests hungover, let instinct sit for the exam. Too much thinking gets in the way."

Right, for you and Charlie. And Ben and George. She picked at her cuticle. "Thanks for the advice. Actually, I'm just on my way out."

"Really? Good for you. Mom was worried you were committing hari-kari or something."

She fought the urge to slam down the phone and instead, injected sugar into her voice. "No, all fine here. But I've got to run. Talk to you soon." Then she marched back to her room and threw her book at the wall. Damn it! It was so unfair! It all came so easily to them, and she always had to work so hard for everything.

Her anger shifted quickly to embarrassment as she stood in the middle of the room, alone. She un-clenched her fists and scurried over to pick up her book, worried that the binding might have ripped. She tried to settle back into equations.

The phone rang again. She hurried down the hall.

"Hi Meg, it's Dana."

"Hey. Allie's out."

He was quiet for a moment. "You okay?"

"It's just the whole world is out and I'm chained to my desk. It sucks."

"If it's any consolation, I'm studying too."

"It's not." She sighed. "Sorry. I'll tell her you called."

As she walked back to her room, her anger at Brad turned on Allie. *What the hell? Why does she need someone else when she's with Dana? He's such a good guy, isn't that enough? And how is it that she can just look at someone and five minutes later be lip-locked with them?* She flopped on her bed and screamed into her pillow. "Ugh! What's the matter with me? Why is it all so damn easy for everyone else!"

She rolled onto her back as her angry adrenaline deflated into guilt. She knew that for Allie, the casual hookups weren't about sex, they were more about not succumbing to some black emptiness that lurked just below her sunny surface. The drug of being wanted in real time, in real arms somehow kept her from drowning. And Allie never got naked with other guys—it was really just making out.

But Megan believed in black and white, in right and wrong; the muck of gray didn't make sense to her. And she cared about Dana, which made it worse. She had been urging Allie to talk to him about her feelings for months. "I think he'd understand. Maybe he even feels the same way; you guys could agree to see other people while you're at school." But it was too hard, too scary, too *something* for Allie, and it hadn't happened.

Megan forced herself back to her physics book, but when Allie finally tap-danced into the room, giggling and drunk at three in the morning, her anger fired up again.

"Dana called. Twice." Megan kept her eyes on the equations in front of her, her voice a solid steel door.

Allie checked her watch and announced she'd call him in the morning.

"That's great, that's just great. He's waiting for your call, you know."

"Okay... "

Megan slammed her book closed, and the empty coffee cups on her desk rattled and then fell onto the floor. "God Allie, I feel like I'm lying to him. I know I'm not actually lying, but covering for you, or whatever it is, feels awful. You know I love you and I'd do anything for you, but I feel guilty. And if I feel guilty, how the hell don't you?"

"I do. But... " Allie ran her hand through her hair.

"Look, if you can't talk to him about how you feel, maybe your relationship isn't as strong as you think."

"You know what Meg? I don't need this right now." Allie stomped out the door. Then she poked her head back in. "And P.S., I never asked you to lie." Her clomp-clomp echoed down the hall.

———

In the watery light of morning, Allie opened her eyes to see Megan asleep at her desk. Allie, head throbbing, shook her gently.

"Meg, your exam."

The room pulsed to life as Megan sprang from her chair and wrenched her hair into a ponytail.

Allie gathered up textbooks and papers and handed them to Megan. "I'm so sorry."

"Me too," Megan said.

They hugged tightly.

"I've gotta go." Megan broke out of the hug.

"Meg, I'm going to talk to him."

Megan held Allie's eyes. "Let's figure it out later." And she was off, a blur in a sweatshirt and plaid pajama pants.

———

Megan grew up in a big yellow farmhouse littered with balls, bats, lacrosse sticks, and sneakers of every size; for the Riordan family, game-playing was second nature. Fun was the goal both on the field and off, but as in any game, rules were important too. So while at home the golden rule was say what you mean, when you mean it, her brothers usually lobbed in their truth with sarcasm or a joke. When the kids were young that meant running for your life after pitching a zinger at a sibling; when they were older it meant rounds of verbal chasing around the dinner table.

Meals at the big wooden table were memorable more for the personality than the food; the lasagna was just a vehicle for the riot of one-liners and hilarious daily moments piling on top of one another like a rugby scrum. Early on, Megan's mom tried to enforce showers before dinner, but with the jigsaw puzzle of practice schedules, their dinner window was small enough as it was. So she surrendered, and the family gathered religiously for dinner, often in dirty practice uniforms, and often, because Brad was a practical joker and Charlie was a reptile fanatic, with a lizard or toad underfoot.

Megan was the family mascot. She followed the boys everywhere, often uninvited, but usually acknowledged with a squeeze or a playful tousle of her hair. It was common knowledge with the neighborhood boys that if the Riordan brothers were playing kickball—and it wouldn't be a competitive game if they weren't—Megan played too. No one minded much, as she hammered the ball with her small Converse high tops and ran as if a nightmare was chasing her. She always slid into whatever sweatshirt or Frisbee was base, proud of the holes in her jeans and the dirt on her knees. But it was her brothers' loud whooping and clapping that made her feel like she could fly.

As neighborhood scrimmages evolved into school sports, Megan became a fixture on the sidelines of her brothers' games. While other siblings played tag and turned cartwheels far from the field, Megan was the team megaphone, jumping up and down and cheering loudly as the action heated up, a huge mesh jersey flapping around her knobby knees. She knew all of their teammates by name and number, and as a party trick she could recite everyone's stats. The best part of the season however, was the awards banquet; on the car ride home her brothers let her hold their gleaming gold trophies.

In sixth grade, like all the other girls her age, Megan put on a leotard and joined gymnastics. Coach Russo was handsome, with curly dark hair and endless shoulders, and tough—his occasional praise a single butterscotch dropping from an unforgiving piñata. Megan loved the team. She was early to practice and often the last one on the mat, pushing and praying her body into backbends and handstands that other girls smiled right into. Each time after she mastered a new move and re-centered herself, her eyes scanned the gym, only to rest on Coach Russo's back as he worked with someone else.

Then one afternoon, in the middle of an otherwise ordinary practice, he was beside her, inviting her to try a back-handspring. His brown eyes were encouraging, his flatline expression had softened. He placed his huge hand on her back to spot her. Thrill and fear battled it out in her veins, and with his firm support, she flew through the trick over and over again. Then he stepped back with a solemn nod. Megan's toes gripped the red foam mat, her arms stiffened at her sides, her back contracted. Girls in colored leotards gathered around, urging her to go for it. Coach Russo towered in the background, arms crossed over his chest. This was the moment. *DO IT!* Megan silently screamed. She could almost touch the smooth pride beckoning from the other side of the leap, could almost feel the heat from Coach Russo's clipped "good." But her body refused her command.

Practice ticked away, teammates drifted back to their own routines. Coach Russo's neutral expression hardened.

An hour later, Megan unclenched her toes in the empty gym and slumped towards the locker room. Out of the corner of her eye, she saw Coach Russo near the door, talking to his assistant. She aimed her eyes at the wood floor but pricked her ears in case he said something. It wasn't until she had turned the corner that she heard him mutter, "You'd never know she was a Riordan."

———

As a freshman in high school, Megan tried out for field hockey. Right away, the coach pegged her for a Riordan by her copper-red ponytail, and although Megan missed the ball just as much as she hit it, the coach shouted "Good job today Riordan!" as Megan limped into the locker room.

Days later, when cuts were posted, she rushed to the list with all the other hopefuls. From the back of the jockeying, elbowing fracas, she glimpsed her name on the varsity list. *As a freshman!* She wanted to jump up and down. She soared out of the throng, only to crash down to earth as someone elbowed her hard in the back.

The next day, before her first varsity practice, her stomach was double-knotted. She shut the door on her organized metal locker as the room began to fill up with clumps of chatting players, and smiled timidly at a group of older girls who had dropped their bulging backpacks near her. Her cleats made an empowering clatter as she headed out.

"Of course she made it, what'd you expect? Have you checked out the Best Athlete plaque lately—all Riordan."

Megan's cleats suddenly felt like clown shoes.

She finished out the day, finished out the season, giving her all during every practice, warming the bench during games.

Sophomore year she started running; not for a coach, not for a team, not for a race. As she wound her way through the backcountry roads of her town, she discovered she had found something all her own.

———

Thanksgiving of Megan's junior year in high school: the two oversized fireplaces were alive and crackling, a huge turkey was sizzling in the oven, the rich smell intensifying with each loving baste, and the Riordan house was reaching its typical crescendo as her brothers barreled home from college and nascent careers bearing dirty laundry and new friends. The boys reclaimed their rooms quickly, their crumpled jeans, jockstraps, and unique smell of Rite Guard and dirty socks restoring rooms that hadn't changed in years to former glory. Piles of *Sports Illustrated*s still teetered on bedside tables, dusty trophies preened on bookshelves, uninhabited lizard cages lay dark in the corners.

Down the hall, the flowery scent and yellow paint of Megan's room caused double-takes on the way to the bathroom. Gone were the Joe Montana and Chrissy Everett posters and in their place were cut-up magazine collages with words like "flirt" and "boys," "Maybelline" and "party" glued to poster board. Colored scarves dangled from the corners of a huge mirror, symmetrical perfume bottles and an earring tree adorned her bureau, a red velvet diary and a neat stack of *Seventeen, Mademoiselle,* and *Glamour* magazines graced her desk.

At the dinner table, the brothers' guests, who for months had listened with half an ear to stories about a gawky baby sister, were enthralled by the curvy redhead with the tentative smile. The four Riordan brothers hung on the sidelines of the conversation, shooting raised eyebrows and amused smirks to each other across the mashed potatoes as Megan bloomed in the spotlight. Her own amazement grew throughout the meal as the guests fell over each other trying to impress her, and as she nibbled on her apple pie, it dawned on her that maybe she had found a playing field her brothers couldn't best her on.

She went back to school with a new tilt of her chin, but within hours was shoved back in her place by queen bees who were not about to move over and make space in the varsity dating game. Megan assumed she wasn't pretty enough, and re-consulted beauty magazines, tried new makeup and diets, believing, as the headlines advised, that "The Ten Steps to a Sizzling Romance" was something she could control. If she just worked hard enough.

––––––––

Now a junior in college, Megan had been involved in several relationships, and in all of them, the initial rocket of feeling had crashed and burned into a debris field of broken promises, returned sweatshirts, and a fervent belief that it must be her, and that if she was just thinner or prettier she would be able to change her luck.

But maybe, Megan thought as Tess continued to talk about Gavin, *this time would be different*.

She and Baker had already hooked up a few times and had been out on two official dates—pizza and beer—during which they had experienced several eye-opening "Wow, you know what I'm talking about" moments across the red plastic tablecloth. Baker was edgy, everyone knew it; he slid late into the back of class, lurked in the shadows of frat parties, was rumored to be involved in a secret Black Eye society that was the baddest of the bad. And he was cute, in that unshaven, black-leather way that often hides a wound. His attention made her both excited and nervous.

So far she had backed away from his obvious impatience to have sex, but she had debated the color of her underwear tonight—white cotton or black lace—deciding after a few changes on the black lace. Just in case. She had only made love once before, with her freshman-year boyfriend. Their breakup had been messy, and she knew their intimacy had made it more so. Which until recently had confirmed that there should be yellow caution tape around going all the way.

But lately the rules around getting naked were becoming blurry. Megan was surrounded by people who vaulted into bed without blinking—certainly many of her friends, but also people whose faces graced the glossies, whose attitudes jumped off the screen, and whose lyrics and sultry voices crooned the benefits of "Sexual Healing." It didn't matter that these strangers were polished for publicity or acting in a scene, they created a cultural pool, and even if she didn't dive in, she was getting splashed just sitting on the side.

What's the big deal, why am I holding out? Maybe I'm nervous because I'm inexperienced. And there's an obvious remedy for that._

Part of the hesitation stemmed from the fact that Baker had a reputation for being a ladies' man—*all right, a sleaze*—but she wasn't so sure that rumor was fair. And as Tess waxed on about how Gavin was not the cad that he seemed, Megan was inadvertently giving Baker the benefit of the doubt as well.

Even if he had mistreated girls in the past, she could be the one to change him. Eventually someone would, and so far he had been sweet. There were certainly times when she questioned his sincerity, times when he purred something sweet in her ear with perhaps more than just a thank you in mind. But maybe he was being sincere, both in the niceties and in the feelings underlying them. And as Megan turned her attention back to Tess, she was now starting to think that Baker could be The One.

————

As anyone could have told her, Baker was most definitely not. Down at the Columns after Tess told her story, Baker sidled up to Megan and held her hand through a night of drinking, dancing, and shouting simple comments to each other over the noise of the mobbed fraternity. The clincher for Megan was when Baker called her "my girl" to a couple of his friends.

They later staggered back to Megan's room for tepid, drunken sex. The intention had certainly been passionate, but the alcohol dulled their urgency and it had been more grope-and-grind than rapture. It had been satisfying enough however, and as Baker rolled off her, Megan didn't have any regrets.

The quiet awkwardness that followed was broken by a buck-naked Baker getting out of bed to fish a cigarette out of the ripped back-pocket of his

Levi's. He lit it, offered it to Megan, and then lit one for himself, dragging deeply before pulling on his jeans. *No underwear,* she observed. She smiled; she hadn't noticed that earlier. They'd been in too much of a hurry.

She was still quite buzzed, but she felt good—warm, sexy, and risqué, something she had never felt before. She lay in her narrow twin bed with the sheets pulled up over her breasts and smoked her cigarette, relishing the feeling that she and Baker had a secret, just the two of them. She liked the familiarity of him sitting on her bed without his shirt. She inhaled and exhaled slowly, gazing at the smoke slow-dancing in the air, gazing at Baker just beyond it. She liked the way his brown hair, disheveled at the moment, was long in the front and hung over his right eye.

He caught her look and his mouth stretched into a smile.

God, he's cute.

He leaned over and kissed her in between drags, then grabbed his tee shirt next to her.

Megan wasn't sure what to think as he reached for his sneakers and slid them on. She hadn't considered his spending the night, but in the face of a hasty exit, the lights seemed to brighten, harshly illuminating the tangled sheets. Her muscles tensed. She snuffed out her cigarette and while she watched him, reached out with both her hands and smoothed down the sheets around her like she was ironing wrinkles out of a long dress. She realized they hadn't said a word to each other since he'd pulled out of her.

"Thanks Megan. Fun night." He smiled his molasses smile, slow-spreading and sugary, and leaned over to crush out his cigarette in the ashtray next to her bed. His hair swung over both eyes, a shade being drawn.

She blinked.

"And we'll get together." He rubbed the ash on his fingers onto his jeans as he stood up.

Although the sheet covered her, she was suddenly acutely aware of her nakedness. "Okay," she said with feigned enthusiasm.

"I've gotta go. See ya later, Megan." And he was out the door as her "Bye" floated after him.

Megan had an immediate, desperate need for clothes, and she sprang out of bed and yanked on her plaid flannel pajamas. She reached a shaky hand into her drawer for another cigarette. *Don't panic.* The warm feeling of a few minutes ago evaporated in a rush of sobering adrenaline. *Maybe the whole post-coital thing isn't his strong suit. Or maybe he felt strange being in my room.* The more she thought about it however, the faster the seed of discomfort in her stomach was growing into a very large pit. *That was weird.* She peered out the window in hopes of seeing Allie walking home. *Very weird.*

The next few days went from bad to worse. Baker didn't call, wouldn't even make eye contact when they were near each other in the cafeteria. Had she done something wrong? She continued to create excuses for him—maybe he thought she didn't like him, maybe he was embarrassed because there hadn't been fireworks. At first, she smiled tentatively at him whenever she walked by to show him she hadn't been disappointed. Then, she pretended she didn't see him, in hopes he would somehow reach out to her. She wondered if she should call him.

The humiliation sank in slowly. As it became clear that he was not only avoiding her but taking great pains to do so, she felt sick whenever she thought she might see him. She would never miss a class, but she refused to go anywhere she didn't have to, including the cafeteria. Part of her figured no one knew, and she tried to hold into that as she walked around campus, but at times she just couldn't—like when she passed a huddle of fraternity brothers—and she felt exposed, like her naïve miscalculation was a big, black tattoo on her body.

Then, just as she had almost convinced herself that people didn't know or didn't care, she overheard two girls in the bathroom, talking loudly between stalls as if the gray metal half-wall between them was soundproof.

"I hear she was all over him at Beta, and then pretty much dragged him back to her room."

"Really? I hardly think he needs to be dragged."

"He's so hot." The faceless voice giggled. "But that's what I heard. And that he was in and out."

Megan put her toothbrush, paste still on it, down on the counter and held her breath. She knew what in and out meant; in and out of her room, in and out of her.

"Who told you?"

"Joe. I guess Baker told the whole fraternity during their Wednesday night pong game."

Megan paled. She tiptoed out of the bathroom, leaving her toothbrush on the counter and praying her bare feet wouldn't make any noise on the tile floor. Then she sprinted to her room.

"Allie." Megan slammed the door and burst into tears. "Oh my God, Baker told the whole fraternity about Saturday night. And he made it sound like I was begging for it."

"What?" Allie clicked off the TV and beckoned Megan to the couch. "Sit down, tell me."

"In the bathroom, two girls were talking about how Baker... about how I... how I dragged him up here and that he was in and out." Megan slumped down next to Allie.

"Who were the girls?"

"I'm not sure, maybe Patty Bennett. It doesn't matter, they said he told his whole frat."

"He's such an ass. The whole school knows he's such an ass."

Megan's face crumpled.

"Oh, Meg, I'm sorry." Allie put her hand on Megan's shoulder.

"No you're right, I heard all that stuff about him too. I thought things might be different. God, I'm such an idiot."

"No you're not. He totally poured it on. Of course you believed him, that was his goal. And you did because, why in the world would you ever think someone would be that slimy? He's dirt, Megan."

Tears streamed down Megan's face as she berated herself for the millionth time.

"Don't beat yourself up again." Allie hugged her. "He did a complete number on you, it's like he put a target on your back."

"Why would someone do that? Does it give him a sick thrill to treat girls like that?"

"Maybe. Or maybe he only knows how to close the deal and then get out, before whoever he's with sees the real dirtball inside. You know, leave them wanting more, instead of leaving with his tail between his legs."

The door opened and Zoe waltzed in. Her smile withered as she took in the scene before her. "What's up?" She glanced back and forth between Allie and Megan.

Megan looked up at Zoe with bloodshot eyes. "Baker's not only completely ignoring me, but he told all of Beta that he was in and out."

"Oh." Zoe dropped onto Allie's bed with a deep sigh. Then she shook her head. "It's all just a game of cops and robbers; someone always bleeds."

Megan held Zoe's eyes. "You don't actually believe that, do you?"

Zoe exhaled again. "No."

Someone yelled "Pizza!" from the other end of the dorm; the word bounced up and down the long hallway.

"Hey," Zoe said. "This whole thing just looks bad for him. He thinks he's adding another notch to his bedpost, but with all the sane people on campus, he's lost a notch."

The surprise at a sympathetic Zoe stunned Megan out of her distress for a moment. The room was quiet.

Then Megan wailed, "How can I go out there?" She waved her hand to include the whole campus. "I can't leave the room knowing everyone is staring at me and thinking Baker just fucked me and tossed me aside like a used condom."

Zoe did a tiny double-take. "Fiery," she said. "Use that." She shook three cigarettes out of a pack on the desk, lit one and passed it to Megan. "Look, hiding is just what Baker's hoping for. He doesn't want to be confronted with his own bullshit. If you're not around, it's easier for him."

Megan took a drag on her fresh cigarette and focused on Zoe.

"This is all a way of making himself feel powerful." Zoe passed a cigarette to Allie. "If you stay inside, he wins."

Megan nodded solemnly.

"You need to use that fire and parade around like nothing's happened. Twirl your baton, do a few flips; you know, stick it in his face. He can't touch you, Megan. His words are garbage; *he* is garbage." Zoe paused and lit her own cigarette.

"Zoe's right," Allie said. "He's expecting you to cower. You're stronger than that, Meg."

"I'm not sure I am." Megan sniffed. "But I know you're right. I don't know why I'm so afraid of him, why every time I see him I feel like I'm going to throw up."

"Because he's a disease," Allie said.

Zoe looked Megan in the eyes. "It's not as hard as you think, look at me." She inhaled and then exhaled slowly, watching the smoke twist exotically and then dissipate into nothing. "This whole thing with Gavin and Tess? Do you know how destroyed I was, how destroyed I am?" Her eyes flitted to Allie, who had sat with Zoe through several tons of Kleenex. She looked back at Megan. "No, everyone thinks I'm fine, right? No big deal. Even Gavin, who you'd think would know better. Even he thinks I'm fine."

Megan and Allie nodded with this truth.

Zoe sighed. "Actually sometimes I wish they understood how much they hurt me, because then maybe they'd feel guilty or something. The fact that they think I'm fine makes them feel better, like what happened is all perfectly kosher."

"I don't know how you do it," Megan said. "Listen Zoe, I'm so sorry about you and Gavin. I haven't said anything to you, for just the reasons you said; it seemed like you didn't care, like you were okay with it." Megan put her burning cigarette in the ashtray and leaned towards Zoe, stopping short of touching her. "But I should have said something. I knew how much you loved Gavin." Megan's tears started again.

Zoe smiled halfheartedly at Megan and patted her shoulder. "It's better for me to be mad than sad. Sad feels too helpless, anger feels better." She stood up abruptly, as if eager to move on. "So even though Tess thinks everything's peachy, I'm mad as hell. But you know what? I'll never let her know because it gives too much away. Of me. And she doesn't deserve to own a piece of me."

Zoe studied herself in the mirror above Allie's bureau and set her shoulders. "And anyway, if Gavin thinks he's in love with Tess, he's a bigger fool than Baker. If that's even possible. When he's bored, Gavin will be back." She walked over to Megan and leaned in to her. "The key is, don't ever let them see you bleed."

Zoe started to walk out, but stopped in the door and turned around. "You guys want to go and get a drink or something?"

Allie glanced at Megan, who nodded. "Sure," Allie said.

"I'll just grab my wallet," Zoe said over her shoulder.

Megan tried to smile at Allie. "Who was that masked woman?"

Allie threw her arm around her friend and squeezed her in.

CHAPTER 4

The kids started school this week, summer is over, and the school of life begins again. I love September, it always feels fresh; much more of a new year than New Year's. But summer, well, summer is velvety chocolate frosting swiped with a finger from a bowl. Real life, or the September through May cake of life, has more ingredients in it—bland flour, dramatic baking soda, life-giving eggs, heart-attack salt—and you never stick your finger in for a preview. Of course, real life can still be sweet, but the summer—basically sugar and butter—makes it all worthwhile.

Anyway, with routine starting up and bare feet behind us, we are all grumpy—me, Matthew, Gillian, even Dana. I wonder if any of us thought this separation would drag on past the heat and humidity. I'm not sure I had any expectations, be it length of time or anything else (this wasn't *my* idea, I want to scream when Dana scowls at my door. Our door.) I think that especially for the kids, it was easier during the summer to deny that all this was happening. The way the unstructured energy of the day leached into dreamy twilight somehow made it easier to believe that Daddy was just traveling or working late. Anything besides just *not here*. But now that we're back into the cake of life, where every hour has an obligation scribbled in ink next to it, Dana's absence in our lives is glaring. There's a hole in the evening when Daddy is supposed to walk in the door with his brown leather briefcase and his weary-eyed, but smiling greeting.

So I get the grumpiness, especially from the kids. They don't really know what's going on, they just know they feel bad. Sometimes I think they blame me for Dana's moving out. Certainly in my meaner moments I hope they blame Dana. But deep in my heart, in a dark place that hurts, I know they don't blame us.

They blame themselves.

Although their slitted eyes and full-lipped pouts may be an effort to shoot blame at one or both of us, at their age, things are simple. They are the center of the universe; things happen to them, for them, and most importantly, because of them. Underneath their cozy comforters at night, snuggled in with all of their favorite stuffed animals, they agonize about whether it was their last tantrum, their picky eating, or their missed soccer goal that caused this fissure in their life.

I know.

"I promise I'll be good. I'll be nice to Kevin. I won't scream in the supermarket." The supermarket promise was my boilerplate. For some reason, when I was little I always melted down in the store—sobbing, howling, a full-blown tantrum—and Eva's response was to park the cart (with me trapped in it) and move on to another aisle. I would scream harder, my feet kicking against the silver bars of the cart, my small fists pounding the red plastic grip.

She must have returned to collect me at some point.

"I'll be good in the supermarket" was my go-to currency, offered up from underneath my blanket of guilt and shame. The promises floated away. The guilt and shame buried in deep.

So I can understand Matthew and Gillian being cranky and mean-spirited. And as much as I get down on my knees and assure them that our separation isn't their fault, they don't buy it.

This wretched futility must be why parents try to hold it together for the kids. It's a pretty powerful deterrent to understand that a divorce will drive over your children and flatten them like asphalt, no matter how hard you try to turn the wheel.

But here I am, here we are. I have not only mindfully crushed my children, but I am now alone in trying to pick up the pieces. Of course Dana is bending over and gathering pieces as well, but we're not collaborating, we're not sharing—in tiny increments in front of the toaster or while carrying brown paper bags in from the car—the raising of our children. We're each working alone, in the corners of their world, hoping to mend what may be broken now right down the middle.

As if parenthood didn't feel overwhelming before.

I've never been more aware that the buck stops here, because now it really does. Our partnership, even when it was crumbling, was always a fender for each other's blind spots. Now there is no buffer, no luxury of a united front. I alone am responsible for shaping these unblemished kids, for laying all the bricks in the right place. My every move, my every mood is modeling something for my children.

It really hits me when I see Matt or Gillian doing something exactly as I do it, or saying something in my exact tone of voice. It's awesome when what they're doing is special or brave, and I know that somehow I've contributed to that. At those moments I feel as if I could rocket skyward on the wings of pride. That's my child! I helped him develop that self-esteem, those skills!

But it's horrifying when I see them doing something nasty or mean or yelling at each other while mimicking my own venom. The times when they imitate the frustration or anger that is spit when I totally lose it with them; those countless times when I'm threadbare and my bag of tricks is empty, and still my buttons are being pushed and punched and so finally, exasperated and at my wits end, I explode. Literally explode—words flying like shrapnel. And in those minutes when the anger is frothing up and out of me, I'm out of control. I'm not able to count to 10 or take a deep breath or in any way exorcise the lunatic I've become.

In the aftermath of these explosions, my guilt alone is toxic; but when I think about the underlying repercussions of my eruption, self-loathing devours me. I have just taught my children something. I have just demonstrated rage. I have just screamed "STOP SCREAMING!" That's when I truly just want to lie down and give up. Or disappear.

I'm only human, I tell myself. I'm going to have bad days, ugly moments, angry words. In my head, I know this. In my heart, I cannot forgive myself.

Maybe this is universal, this belief that no matter how hard I try with my kids, my own humanity trips me up. Maybe it's the underbelly of motherhood, this nagging feeling that I'm not quite doing it right, don't have quite enough patience, am not quite giving it my best. That no matter what I do, at times I am wounding my children; that someday, they'll blame a repugnant personality trait on me, on our relationship.

"You can't be perfect," Sarah says. "And that's a great lesson to teach your kids." Yes, yes, I nod. But inside I'm not so sure.

A mother's impact on her children is all-powerful. Even absence does not diminish it. The wound Eva left me with will forever bleed into my thoughts and impact my actions.

I try so hard to be flawless because I know only too well what damaged feels like.

MARCH 1990: SENIOR YEAR
The Florida Keys

One by one, every passenger who steps off a plane in Florida and onto the top of the metal jetway performs a sequence of gestures that just might be the secret handshake to vacationland. Puff out chest, deeply inhale the welcome heat, and rapidly salute, using your hand as a vital visor from the sudden, blinding glare. The throngs of college students who descend for spring break are the exception however, as when they disembark, they're already wearing sunglasses (and brightly colored flip-flops). For these furloughed adolescents, vacation starts on the way to the airport.

Having already lived through the traditional, wild spring break twice, Allie and Dana—who had whooped when they'd discovered they had the same week off—decided to pass on the wet tee-shirt contests and try to find a more sedate vacation. Allie did the research and discovered a small condo complex on the beach in the Keys, which was inexpensive (not surprising when you split the cost 10 ways), with beds for eight and plenty of floor space. Dana and nine of his friends rented a condo there too, and the scene was set for a small getaway from the senior grind. Unfortunately, their well-kept secret was not so well-kept, and before they knew it, a crowd had jumped aboard their plan and turned their intimate escape into a much more raucous affair; although still tamer than the frenetic chug-til-you-throw-up scenes of spring breaks past.

The seven days flew by, and what had started out as an ocean of time in front of them had evaporated down to a puddle; one more night. Although a clump of guys had been boozing since breakfast, it was now late afternoon—a more appropriate cocktail hour—and the aluminum crack-and-sigh of cold beers being opened was a subliminal invitation for all those still sipping soda. Out by the pool, lounge chairs were being pulled and scraped into a new alignment as the afternoon shadows stretched longer and slowly encroached on the last precious minutes of sun. This was crunch time; all SPF lotions littered the deck and baby oil was being passed from chair to chair like a glowing joint.

Allie—awash in oil, sand, and salt—raced inside to use the bathroom; even five minutes out of the sun was panic-worthy. With full intent to dash back to her chair, she changed course mid-stride as she noticed Dana sitting out on the tiny balcony.

He held up two beers as she came out to join him. "Your condo was closer." He extended an open beer towards her.

"Thanks." The balcony was only big enough for one chair, so Allie hopped up onto a sunny spot on the balcony railing, her back to the oval pool, the ocean glittering beyond that. The bottom of her black bikini peeked out from under a big white tee with the sleeves rolled up, and her long dark hair, even wavier than usual because of the wind and water, was loosely pulled back into a ponytail. She lifted her face to the sun and closed her eyes. "Can we just stay here?" She sighed. "I can't believe we have to leave tomorrow."

A full minute of silence passed. Allie opened her eyes and took a closer look at Dana.

―――――――

Dana propped his bare feet on the deck railing under her and stared out at the ocean. He was drunk, having worked his way through a cooler of beer with his buddies on the beach, just a few yards and several towels away from Allie and her friends, who were flipping through magazines and sipping Diet Cokes.

Senior Spring Break, the source of much planning, much anticipation; now almost relegated to a dusty photo album. Dana wondered if in a few years he would remember the leashed agitation that lay underneath his brown, smiling face in the pictures.

He kicked himself for not paying more attention to his gut as he and Allie planned this trip. Instead, he had convinced himself that their vacation with friends would be a grand finale to college life, and he held onto that conviction as the small group grew, and grew. When the final tally reached 80, he geared up for a different kind of vacation, and judging from the tower of empty kegs in the parking lot, it had been a success. Everyone would go home sunburned, exhausted, and saying with a smile, "Now I really need a vacation".

Dana's burn, however, came from something other than the sun. The simmering stew of personalities had scorched him with the reality of the whole "dating other people at school" deal he and Allie had agreed to last year. The original—and he had to admit, theoretical—idea of Allie having dinner with someone else now seemed much more threatening than a simple breaking of bread. He had never been in a fight before, but he had clenched his fists and set his jaw many times this week, wanting to pummel the Erikson boys who had been leering moths to Allie's effervescence. It didn't help that everyone was pretty much naked the entire week. Each time he came upon her in her tiny bikini or gauzy sundress chatting with some of her guy friends, his mind went into overdrive, and he pictured Allie with her eyes closed and some other guy on top of her...

Allie shimmied off the railing and sat down on Dana's lap. "I don't know if I can go back to missing you again." She nuzzled his neck.

He didn't move a muscle; he held onto his beer in one hand, and kept the other planted on the arm of his chair. "I'm sure you have ways to compensate."

Allie picked her head up and peered at Dana. She reached out towards his dark Ray Bans and started to slide them off his face; then she hesitated and her hand dropped down to her lap. "What?"

"You heard me. I'm sure you don't miss me too much."

"You're kidding, right? You know how much I wish we were together."

"If you missed me that much, you wouldn't be so interested in other diversions." Even through the shaded lenses, he couldn't meet her eyes, and he continued to look beyond her out to the water. He knew he sounded like a petulant child, but he couldn't stop himself. He took a long drink from his beer.

"You're drunk," she said, getting off his lap.

"Yep."

Allie sighed. "Do you really want to have this conversation now?"

"I wish we didn't have to have this conversation at all," Dana said, still not looking at her. They sat in silence, which contrasted sharply with the music and laughter floating up from below them on the pool deck. Dana finally looked at her.

"Isn't this enough, Allie? I mean *us*, aren't we enough?"

Allie took a deep breath and fiddled with her ponytail holder, pulling it loose. Her hair fell across her shoulders like a dark curtain. "Dana, I love you more than anything I've ever loved in my whole life."

But... Dana waited. He had an urge to flee. He itched to get out of here, away from the tension and from the churning feeling in his stomach. But he couldn't run, he had started this. The bile in his stomach erupted into words. "Yet you're screwing other people."

"I'm not *screwing* other people. And hey, you agreed to this. You practically jumped up and down when I suggested it."

"I was being supportive."

"Supportive?" Her green eyes were on fire, her fists were clenched. "I wasn't looking for support, I was looking for a conversation. And the way you grabbed pom-poms and did a little cheer pretty much told me where I stand with you, how you feel about me."

Dana was quiet. His head was spinning. He loved her and didn't want to be fighting with her. And yet, he'd started it. He was afraid to open his mouth, he didn't want to make it worse. He wished he could rewind the last 10 minutes.

"And... ?" Allie drew out the word, waited a moment, and then punctuated it with, "Quiet." She mumbled, "Typical."

"Anyone for nachos?" Tess sailed out onto the deck with the gourmet concoction of tortilla chips smothered in hot Velveeta.

Dana stood up. "You're right. I don't want to have this conversation now." He turned and walked through the sliding glass doors and down the stairs.

───────

A moment later the two girls watched him march across the pool deck below.

Tess covered her mouth with her hand. "Oh my God, I'm sorry, I totally interrupted you guys."

"Don't worry, he would've walked out whether you came along or not. He's good at that."

"Are you okay?"

Allie's eyes were glued to Dana. She swallowed the bitter taste in her mouth. "It's been brewing all week." She sank down onto the chair and twisted a chunk of her hair around her finger. "Oh Tess, I don't know what to do. Sometimes I just feel so stuck." She leaned over and put her head in her hands. "Why is this so hard? I thought love was supposed to be easy."

───────

A little while later, down on the beach and away from the crowd, Megan was stretched out on a bright yellow towel, relishing the last of the sun's searing rays. Lying on his back next to her, with his arms crossed behind his head, was Mark Skillen, a junior from Erikson. Mark and Megan had only known each other by sight back at school, uttering courteous but empty greetings as they passed on campus. But well after midnight on the first night of vacation, with the silky, tropical darkness cut only by the greenish glow of the pool light, they found themselves draped on deck chairs discussing the essence of politics and music and sibling relationships. Finally, at four in the morning, as their yawns swallowed more and more of the starry sky, they bid each other goodnight and retired to their respective condos. The goodnight kiss that Megan had been half-anticipating and half-dreading hadn't happened, and she went to bed surprised and intrigued.

"So you were out late last night," Allie said the next morning as Megan straggled into the kitchenette wearing a tee shirt that was as crumpled as her hair.

Megan yawned and reached for the coffee pot. "Unexpectedly."

"Mark Skillen?"

Megan poured her coffee. "Wasn't he in a class of yours?"

"I was trying to remember, I think it was Western Civ. He was pretty quiet, cute. I think he plays guitar in some band."

"He does. With Delusion, we saw them last year at Springfest. They're pretty good." She picked up a Sweet-n-Low and shook it. "I guess I can see quiet. He was very... earnest last night. We talked forever, about everything. At one point we even talked about grandmothers." She ripped open the pink packet and dumped sweetener into her coffee. "He is cute, isn't he?"

"Wow. I haven't heard you say that in a long time."

"Weird, huh?" Since the Baker incident last year, she hadn't so much sworn off men as she just hadn't found anyone worth the risk. "And you know what's strange? There was chemistry there, but we didn't even kiss. It was like he knew a kiss would have changed the night somehow, made it less-than. Does that sound crazy?"

"No." Allie paused. "Wow, grandmothers and chivalry. Maybe you've stumbled into a gentleman."

Megan stirred her coffee.

———

When they finally did kiss, two nights and many long conversations later, Megan made sure that it was more than just a gentlemanly impulse that was holding Mark in check.

"I need this to happen slowly," she said as she pulled back from his embrace. Excuses and history jumped up and down on her tongue; she swallowed them back.

He leaned in, his face close, his eyes on hers. "I get that." He kissed her again and Megan melted into his lips.

"How come we get the best sunset on our last day? It's like a cosmic, haha, you're going back to snow," Megan said as she gestured to the rich collage of orange and pink above them.

"Do you think we can call up this moment when we're knee-deep in finals?" Mark said.

"I don't even want to think about exams."

They had been basking for hours, purposely separated from the spirited mob, listening to the wind-whipped music from the distant party and the sound of the crashing waves. After chugging his beer, Mark rolled towards Megan and began to kiss her. She responded enthusiastically, and the two of them wiggled closer to each other and continued to kiss, gently at first, and then harder, their tongues hungrily exploring.

Mark's hand started tentatively down her body, and goosebumps popped up all over Megan's skin from the combination of the disappearing sun, the ocean breeze, and Mark's touch. She pulled back abruptly, as if she knew that if she didn't do it fast, she wouldn't have the willpower to do it at all. She was very turned on, but she was also aware that they were completely exposed, with only a bathing suit between the thrill of exploration and the roped-off, unbounded danger zone.

"Not now, Mark," she said with a small giggle that sounded more ragged than amused. She sat up and fiddled with her top, making minor adjustments for maximum coverage.

He propped himself up on his elbow and looked at her with a quizzical half-smile.

"Someone could walk by," she said.

"You're right, I'm sorry. I just couldn't stop myself."

"It's okay." She turned away from him and grabbed her half-full beer, which was planted in the hot sand next to her. She took a sip and then gagged. "It's hot. I'm going to get a new one."

"I'll come, I could use a new one too." Mark got up and reached for his towel.

"Do you think anyone motivated and got stuff for the barbeque tonight?" Megan said as they started walking.

"I think Allie said she'd go, or maybe it was Steph."

"It definitely wasn't Allie, she hates the supermarket."

Mark looked at her.

"She says it's a giant petri dish of kids behaving badly."

Mark chuckled. "I've never really thought about it. I only notice the mind-numbing muzak."

"Well, I hope someone went, because I'm starving." She hadn't eaten much all day and the beer was undulating in her empty stomach.

They ambled up the beach toward the bright colors and dark tans of a mash of kids, fused together by the high of carelessness and top-40 tunes. Mark took her hand; it felt comfortable in his now. She snuck a glance at him. Every night he had backed off with an easy smile whenever she slammed on the brakes, although his foot was always heavy lead on the accelerator until the last minute. She wondered if he was getting annoyed. She sighed. As much as she liked him, if going all the way became a deal-breaker for him, then so be it. There was no way she was going to have sex with him so soon in their relationship.

The smell of grilled burgers and charred hot dogs made Megan's stomach roll with hunger as they approached the party, which was already in full swing around the pool. A sweating keg sat in a tub of ice in one corner and blenders were whipping up colorful fruit and alcohol concoctions at every outdoor power outlet. Even though some people had showered and changed out of their wet bathing suits, skin remained the fashion must-have of the evening.

"I'm going to get us some beers and grab a shirt. I'll meet you back here in a few minutes?" Mark leaned over and gave Megan a quick kiss.

She smiled warmly. *Wouldn't it be amazing if this worked out?*

She headed towards her condo. What she really wanted was a shower, but she'd settle for just changing out of her bikini; she knew that eating was the priority. She wove her way through the crowd, cheerfully greeting everyone she passed.

"Hi!" she called out to Dana without missing a step. "Where's Allie?"

"Don't know," he answered gruffly.

Megan stopped walking; Dana was never unfriendly. "Are you okay?"

"Sorry. I'm fine. Allie and I... we needed a little space." He shrugged his shoulders, and the movement unbalanced him for a moment. He grabbed the back of a chair.

"Is there anything I can do?"

Dana shook his head. "Nah, I'm fine, we're fine, everything's fine. We're on vacation, right?" He raised his beer bottle in the air.

"Right. Okay. See you later." She made a mental note to check on him.

Inside the condo, Megan peeled off her suit and pulled on clean underwear and a midnight-blue sundress that was cut to highlight her curves. Without a shower she needed all the help she could get, and everyone had always complimented her on the dress. She appraised herself in the mirror. The threads of gold in her brown eyes flickered warmly against her tan face. She shook out her long copper hair—sand rained down on her bare feet—and smoothed it out with a brush. *Not bad. Some sun can enhance anything.*

She followed the animated voices coming from the kitchen, and found Allie and Tess sitting at the breakfast bar, eating tortilla chips and drinking red frozen drinks.

"Here you are." Megan leaned over and grabbed a fistful of chips. "Sorry," she said with her mouth full, "I'm starving."

"Want a daiquiri?" Allie stood up to get a glass.

"Absolutely." Megan pulled up a stool. "They look great."

"Where were you?" Tess said.

"Down on the beach with Mark." Megan blushed through her tan.

"Enjoying your last day in paradise?" Allie said.

Megan giggled. "Mark's great; he seems great at least."

"He *is* great... if his friends are any indication, which they usually are, don't you think?" Tess said.

"We'll see. I mean about me and Mark; we'll see when we get back to school if he's still into it."

"He will be," Allie said.

"You guys don't know how lucky you have it. This dating thing sucks." Megan crunched on a chip and turned to Tess. "Did you finally get hold of Gavin?"

Tess's face lit up, her spine sprung to attention. "Finally is right! It's so weird that we haven't talked in a few days. He said he's been working a ton." She fiddled with her necklace. "He sounded really tired."

———

Tess had been dating Gavin for a year now, and she still couldn't believe her luck, especially when she remembered that he'd fallen for her while he was with Zoe. *Zoe.* For the life of her she had no idea how that had happened. All her life she had run with the homecoming queens, never for a moment considering herself crown-worthy. She was always the brainy sidekick to the cheerleader, the plain bridesmaid to the luminous bride. She had never wowed anyone before, especially not with her looks. Yet here she was, in a serious relationship with Gavin Keller. He introduced her as his girlfriend, he told her she was beautiful. It was electrifying, mostly because while his warm words washed over her, she actually felt beautiful.

After the warm shower passed however, and Gavin's attention was momentarily elsewhere, she was alone again with the cold, damp chill of her own insecurity. Her gushing delight and wide-eyed adoration would suddenly seem foolish, childlike.

Get a grip.

But she didn't want to. There was nothing better than being in love with Gavin. It was like the joy of learning to ride a bike—the exhilaration of flying, the rush of the wind in her face, the ballooning pride as she catapulted along the concrete. But along with her euphoria, she was always aware that a cutting crash was imminent. And Tess knew when that happened, she wouldn't just suffer a skinned knee; the repercussions of a crash with Gavin could be life-threatening.

"I can't wait to see him next weekend. It's only been three weeks, but it feels like it's been forever. I wish he could've come on this trip; our weekends are always so short." She beamed at Allie. "I've been jealous of you and Dana all week; I would kill for seven days together in tropical paradise."

"I still can't believe you and Dana ended up with the same break," Megan said. "Speaking of which, what's up with you guys? I just saw him outside and he seemed pretty raw."

"See what paradise does to you?" Allie said to Tess. She put down her daiquiri. "I need to go find him. He was upset about the dating-other-people thing, and we kind of got into it—or should I say, he threw a grenade and walked away." She shook her head. "We've been having such an awesome vacation, or so I thought. I'm not sure what triggered it. Maybe the fact that he's swimming in beers."

Megan looked down at her drink.

Allie touched Megan's arm. "Not your fault."

Tess looked back and forth between Allie and Megan.

Allie said to Tess, "Megan now feels responsible whenever Dana and I bump heads." She turned back to Megan and squeezed her arm. "You didn't push me into that conversation with him last year. Well, actually you did, but you were right, as always. It felt good to tell him how screwed up I am." She smiled weakly. "I was finally honest, but I'm not so sure he was. Although if that's the case then he deserves an Oscar for his portrayal of a man set free."

"We all put on a costume from time to time," Tess said, sipping her drink.

They were quiet for a moment. Then Megan said, "But then he can't be mad at you."

"Tell that to Dana." Allie sighed. "Maybe tonight it will be Dana's turn to be honest."

"I hope not," Megan said, stuffing another chip into her mouth, "He was pretty wasted."

"Fabulous," Allie said, shaking her head. "I should go get him." She looked more closely at Megan. "You look great by the way; even with chips all over your face."

"Oh, I haven't showered or anything." Megan stood up and brushed the chips off her dress. "And I can't stop eating, I'm starving. I didn't eat lunch." She stole one more fistful. "I'll walk out with you. Coming, Tess?"

———

When Allie spied Dana outside, she broke away from Megan and Tess. "Wish me luck," she said in a low voice. She sidled up to him and put her arms around him from behind. After a moment, the girls saw him turn into her and give her a long hug, and soon after that they watched Allie and Dana slip down towards the beach with their arms around each other.

"Phew," Megan said to Tess.

Tess wished for the umpteenth time that Gavin was here.

———

Much later that night, after the kegs had been pumped dry, the bottles of vodka and rum had been emptied, and the last of the food had been ravaged, Megan and Mark headed down towards the beach as well. As Allie and Dana had hours earlier, they walked in the wet sand with their arms around each other, the warm surf licking their bare toes. But unlike Allie and Dana, they staggered and weaved in the dark, the waves tripping them at times, their footprints making a dizzying zigzag. Megan, who had only eaten tortilla chips for dinner, leaned against Mark as he steered her down the beach, as if there was something he wanted to show her out where the glow from the dying party didn't extend. After a few minutes they trudged out of the wet sand and collapsed up on the dry beach, which was still emanating heat from the burning rays of the day.

"So can you believe—" Megan stopped when Mark leaned over and brushed some sand off of her face. They locked eyes.

"You're beautiful," he said.

"It's dark out here."

He leaned in for a kiss and she met him halfway. "I hope that when we get back to school you're not going to forget my name," he whispered into her ear.

"Never, Brian."

He pushed her on her back and rolled on top of her. "I knew it!"

She smiled up at him, and as he lay on top of her and they started to kiss, she was relaxed and happy.

———

Mark was happy too. What an awesome break; the fling with Megan had been an unexpected bonus. This was turning into an unprecedented spring. He had just found an amazing drummer, a freshman that took his band and their fans to a new high with his chops. And with a girl like Megan in the front row while he rocked his guitar, he couldn't lose. He had a real thing for redheads, especially curvy ones, and she had brains to boot. He didn't just bide his time through their conversations, he actually enjoyed talking with her, even learned a few things. And her innocent coquettishness, the whole start-and-stop game she played really turned him on. The week had been one long, quivering foreplay. The explosion was going to be mind-blowing.

He had devoured all the rumors about this girl; well, maybe not about her, more about her entourage, but those four girls were like glue, and one for all and all for one, right? Two of them had gone out with Gavin Keller for Chrissake, and he had seen her friend Allie wrapped around one or another brother in a dark corner on more than one occasion.

Mark moved his hand up Megan's smooth calf and lifted her dress as he slid his hand up her thigh.

———

Megan groaned a little with pleasure and anticipation and moved her hips into Mark slightly. She was confident that they were not going to go all the way—she had made that point very clear all week—so she felt safe relaxing into the moment. She continued to kiss him hard as she played with his hair on the back of his head. She was feeling wonderfully warm and woozy—the rum worked its magic from the inside, the thick blanket of sand cradled her underneath, and Mark's warm body was on top of her. His hand was gently caressing her thigh, which was sending delicious chills up and down her spine. She moved her hand from behind his head and slid it slowly down his smooth back. His hard penis strained against his dry bathing suit and she reached underneath the fabric to caress it. She gasped as his hand touched her cotton underwear; he reached inside and stroked her.

She suddenly wished she had put on more than a sundress and cotton panties; she wanted zippers or buttons or some kind of additional boundary between her and...

"Mark." Her voice was ragged as caution and thrill caught in her throat at the same time. This felt so good, her body yearned to keep going, but she shouldn't. She didn't want to. She'd regret it if she made love with him now; that was not the person she wanted to be. She knew he'd understand. They'd gone far enough.

"Mark," she said again in one sharp syllable. She grabbed his hand and moved it away from her. She wiggled her body in an attempt to slide out from under him.

He began to move off her. She was just about to utter a blanket "I'm sorry" that was more about acknowledging collective remorse than accepting blame, but before the words could find air, he was in motion. In one swift movement he rolled to the side and yanked her underwear down. Just as quickly, he ripped his own bathing suit down past his knees and plunged back down on top of her, his knees forcing her legs apart.

Megan's mind reeled. "Wait!" Her earlier excitement vanished in her rising alarm.

"It's okay, baby." His tongue was in her ear.

"No, wait!" She tried to push him off, but her muscles were weighted with rum. Her earlier blissful wooziness was now a detriment; everything worked in slow motion. Could he hear her? He must not be hearing her; maybe she was so drunk she was speaking gibberish.

His gentleness had now become agitated action; he was kicking his suit off and at the same time rubbing her all over with his hand, on her breasts through her sundress, on her now unclothed vagina. His weight on top of her made it impossible to get any leverage to move. She tried to clamp her legs together, but he was lodged in between them. She could feel his penis between her thighs; his legs were trying to pry her open.

Megan's shock exploded into panic. Every bone in her body was desperate to get him off her, to make him stop. At the same time, it was inconceivable that he wasn't going to pull back, to hear her, to understand her adamancy and quit. She tried to sit up, to again push him off. He was so heavy and she was pinned underneath him, lying deep in a sand compression of her own body.

She couldn't move.

"NO!"

"It's okay, Megan." Mark jammed his penis into her.

"NO! Mark, don't!"

"It's great, baby." He pumped manically. He was on another planet.

"MARK!" Her forearms were the only things she could move. She clawed at his back. His eyes opened wide as he came inside of her and at the same time seemed to realize that something was wrong.

He was panting as he rolled off of her. "Megan?" He looked confused.

Megan rolled on her side away from him and hugged her knees to her chest. Her dress was hiked up over her hips. In a distant part of her mind she wished for her underwear, but once she was cocooned, she couldn't let go of herself. She was numb. She didn't speak, she couldn't cry.

"Megan?" He peered at her over her shoulder.

She stared out at the blackness, at the rhythmic sound of the waves.

"Are you okay?" He gently tried to roll her over. When she didn't respond, he sat back on his knees. The ocean thundered. "Was that not good?" He paused in the darkness. "Let me make you feel good." He couldn't move her, so he started to caress her back.

"Don't. Please don't." She tried to curl further into herself. She prayed for him to go away.

He sat there for a minute or two in silence. "Just go, Mark," Megan whispered. She cleared the anguish from her throat. "Please go."

"Megan." He started to lean in.

"Don't touch me."

Mark leaned back, waited another moment, and then got up and walked slowly off. A minute or two later, she heard a splash as he dove into the dark, rolling water, and then a series of smaller splashes as he waded back out onto the beach.

Megan stayed in the fetal position for a long time, not moving a muscle except for her mind. *I shouldn't have done that. I shouldn't have done that. I shouldn't have done that.*

And as the inky black sky relaxed ever so gently into blue, the seagulls screamed their elation for the coming day.

———

At first, Megan didn't tell anyone what happened. The only person she wanted to talk to was Allie, but in the scramble to pack and make the flight there was no time. Megan was quiet, bordering on mute, and although Allie noticed, there were too many chattering friends around to ask her outright, so all she could do was shoot Megan some questioning looks. She answered back with a somber stare that verged on tears. And one word. "Later."

Allie gave her a squeeze and stayed close to her for the rest of the long travel day.

———

All of the girls were ambivalent about getting back to school. They were now in the final stretch of their college careers, with graduation and all that it symbolized lurking just on the other side of exams. Most hadn't thought twice about choosing an escape in the sun over a week of more mundane job hunting and future planning. And so most of them thought it was strange when Zoe of all people—who'd probably never had to work a day in her life—had decided to forgo the spring fling and pound the pavement in New York City. Now on the heels of their vacation, some of the girls on the plane back to school quietly wondered whether Zoe, or any of the other students who had decided to be proactive about their careers, had had any luck. They would feel better about their own sunny choice if they hadn't.

But Zoe had indeed had luck. Not with any career advice or new job, but with the real reason she had been city-bound: attending to an essential item on her to-do list. For once in her life she had tackled her homework with gusto, and it had paid off on the third consecutive night of dragging her high school friends to a specific Upper East Side bar. This time, surprise, surprise. There was Gavin.

Zoe's heart skipped a beat when she spied him at a corner table—she had only seen him from afar since their breakup a year ago—but she willed her heart to slow and forced herself to bide her time at the long mahogany bar. She half-listened to her friends' conversation, tossing in a one-word response when indicated, but her attention was focused on the back of the bar and on Gavin. Out of the corner of her eye she watched his every move, his every gesture. *He looks so good.* It was all she could do not to go over and melt into him, into what they used to be. She shifted in her seat and dragged herself back into the conversation around her. Her friend Jane was debating the merits of living in LA.

"I'm only looking in New York; I'm not interested in being anywhere else," Zoe said.

Jane continued to talk, flabby words that floated beyond Zoe's reach. In her mind, Gavin's green eyes gazed into hers. And then, because she couldn't guarantee that he would ever look at her that way again, the familiar fury at Tess raged up inside of her along with her desire for Gavin. She reached into her purse for her red lipstick. She swiped it expertly across her lips and was tucking it away again when she realized the girls had gone quiet around her. They were clearly waiting for a response.

She looked up. "I'm just going to the ladies room." She finished her half-full vodka collins, checked herself out in the mirror above the bar, and walked slowly through the masses, ignoring as always, the attention she garnered as she brushed by people. She didn't look directly at Gavin, but she was never more aware of the angle of his head, the direction he flashed his smile. Finally, as the people at his table began to notice her approach, Gavin's head turned. Electricity connected them.

Zoe couldn't breathe.

"Zoe." Gavin was so startled that he knocked his beer over, but true to his athleticism, he righted it before it fell.

"Gavin, oh my God."

Gavin pushed back his chair with a loud scraping noise and came over to her to give her a hug. It was an acquaintance hug, and Zoe was disappointed with its brevity.

"How are you?" His smile was genuine.

Zoe didn't have to fake her happiness to see him—she felt like she was going to float away.

He took a good look at her. "Wow. You look great."

She knew she did. Her outfit had been picked out carefully (the third fabulous outfit of the week): a dark red sweater that contrasted with her light blue eyes, tight black pants and black leather boots that made her look even taller and more lean than she was already.

"Thanks, so do you. I'm not used to seeing you in a suit."

"What can I say? The corporate uniform."

The waves of curiosity tumbling from Gavin's friends at the table almost knocked the two of them over. They both started talking at the same time, and then laughed.

"Let's have a drink," he leaned over the table and grabbed his beer. "Over here," he indicated another table with a tilt of his bottle. He suddenly hesitated. "Or are you here with someone?"

"No. I mean, yeah, I'm here with friends. But I'd love to have a drink with you." Internally she was applauding herself; she couldn't have orchestrated it better.

A few drinks, a few appetizers, and lots of voltage later, all of their friends had gone and Gavin and Zoe remained tucked away in their own little corner of the world. Zoe had done her best to restrain herself and start the evening with subtle flirting, allowing herself with each new drink to ratchet it up a notch and increase the frequency with which she accidentally touched his hand or bumped him under the table. She knew she had her work cut out for her once they left the bar, and she was trying to think of a way to get herself up to Gavin's apartment. If she could do that, she was home free. It was out on the street, when they were physically and symbolically between the innocent public flirting and the much more inappropriate being alone together in his apartment, where she knew she could lose him.

Gavin seemed reluctant to leave, which Zoe reasoned might be a good thing. Maybe he knew that he had a decision to face once they were out of the safety of the crowded pub. Finally though, they were out on the street.

"I still can't believe we ran into each other. It was great to see you, Gavin." Zoe took a deep breath, preparing for the plunge. "So great, in fact, that I hate to end it." She held his eyes, willing him to dive in after her.

Gavin looked like he was searching for a neon sign telling him what to do.

"You know what?" She lightly touched his hand, drawing his focus back to her. "I'm still hungry. Do you feel like picking up a pizza and going back to your apartment? I'd love to see it."

Gavin smiled. "Sounds good."

Zoe nearly clapped.

"You realize my apartment is nowhere near your standards. No decorating theme, no curtains, and definitely no cleaning lady," Gavin said.

"Please don't tell me that there are weeks-old pizza boxes all over the furniture."

"Nope. The pizza boxes *are* the furniture." He laughed. "No, let's just say that I'm organizationally challenged. And speaking of furniture, you may recognize some of it from school."

She made a face. "The couch?"

"The couch."

She swatted his arm. "Maybe your apartment needs my attention."

"Just your money."

They laughed. Only Gavin could joke with her that way. *God, I miss him.* She locked her arm in his and they set off for his apartment.

Once there, the hot pizza was extraneous. Gavin grabbed beers from the fridge and Zoe pulled off her boots and made herself comfortable on the tattered mustard-yellow couch, a piece of furniture that had always made her cringe, but that now represented a shared history. After he sat down, Zoe slid in close and swiveled so that she was turned sideways, pretzeling her long legs so that her knees touched his thigh. He didn't flinch, which she took for a good sign.

She started talking as if there was nothing odd about the fact that she was sitting so close to him. Although everything about her demeanor suggested nonchalance, she was so desperate to physically connect with him that she had to concentrate on keeping her hands to herself, and she picked at her beer label to keep them occupied. A remote part of her was disgusted at her longing for him; she had never wanted something or someone so much, had never been in the vulnerable position of risking herself for something. And although she tried not to think about it, this same tiny part of her recognized that if Gavin knew how much she loved him, he would shut her down in an instant. He wouldn't want to risk Tess with something that was emotionally poignant. Physical betrayal was easier to justify. He was only here now because she was making it all so casual.

She kept up the lighthearted banter while she plotted how to move in for the kill. He was obviously fine with what was happening, but he was never going to make the first move. It had to come from her. Finally, when she thought she was going to jump out of her skin, she looked at Gavin with a sly smile. "No one will know that I was up here."

"That's probably a good thing."

"And I was wondering," she leaned in a little closer, "what it would feel like to kiss you again." She gazed into his eyes. "We used to have some pretty intense moments."

Gavin swallowed.

She wasn't sure who moved in first, but a minute later they were kissing and touching each other as if something between them had combusted. Any thoughts of Tess flew out of both of their minds as they became totally immersed in igniting each other.

Her plan was working.

For the next few days, Zoe made it her mission to keep Tess in deep background. Whenever she thought those puppyish brown eyes might be haunting Gavin's thoughts, Zoe scared them away with a wickedly sexy smile or a wildly sarcastic comment. She had nothing else planned for her

New York visit—Gavin *was* her agenda—and so when he wasn't in the office, Zoe was by his side, prohibiting reflection or second thoughts by remaining composed and in charge. Everything about these few days, everything about Zoe, was spontaneous yet measured—she was a ballerina executing a gorgeous leap, appearing to soar effortlessly, while her every muscle strained imperceptibly with the exertion of precise position.

Tess's name never slipped into conversation; they never spoke of her or of their respective relationships with her. Zoe didn't dare mention her for fear of bursting the fragile and iridescent bubble she had carefully blown around the two of them. She wasn't sure why Gavin didn't mention her and she didn't care.

The only time Tess permeated their space was when the phone rang in the apartment. The first time it happened, they were happily squashed into Gavin's small kitchenette, chopping tomatoes with spreading knives, trying to make spaghetti sauce with a bachelor's paucity of utensils. The cheap chianti was flowing, Bruce Springsteen provided a raw, fervid soundtrack; whether or not the meal was a success, there was no doubt what the post-dinner entertainment would be.

The first ring of the phone exploded between them like a parent interrupting two teenagers on the couch. They looked at each other; the tomatoes on their hands amplified the feeling that they had been caught red-handed. Gavin dashed over to the intrusive machine and turned it off before any voice belched out into the room. After that, the answering machine remained off and the only discernible clue that something wasn't quite kosher was when the phone would ring. And ring. And then the red blinking number of unheard messages would increase yet again.

———

Gavin rehearsed his excuses in the bathroom mirror one morning as he knotted his tie.

"Tess, I love you." *Good, an honest start.*

"Hell, I think I want to marry you." *So actually that's why it's good that I'm with Zoe now, it could be the last time I'm with someone else.*

Nope, can't say that._

"It just kind of happened. It has nothing to do with you." He rubbed his hand over his chin. *If I can't come up with anything better, I deserve to get caught.*

"It wasn't like I was out searching for something new. I was just closing a chapter."

Oh God. Maybe he should just stick with "Sorry." But as he regarded himself in the mirror, now tied and ready to go, he knew that it didn't really matter what he planned to say. If he got caught, there would be no second chances.

But he was confident that he wouldn't need one. No one would know; no one would get hurt. He and Zoe were in this with their eyes wide open. She was going back to school in a few days, and she had nothing to gain by telling Tess. Or anyone else for that matter, as her friends were all close with Tess. *Maybe that's the key; keep your affairs close to home.*

When it came time to say goodbye at the end of the week, they stood in the doorway of Gavin's apartment (he hadn't offered to escort her to the train). The mood between them seemed shrouded in casual banter and good humor, almost as if they were sharing an inside joke, which in a way, they were. Sharing something, anyway.

"What can I say?" Gavin grinned. "It was great to see you."

Zoe returned the grin. "That was some drink."

Gavin laughed, leaned in, and kissed her for a full minute. "One for the road."

Zoe was hating this moment, and there was nothing about this goodbye that felt casual or good to her, although her face displayed nothing but a smile; if her affect could wink, it would have. She didn't want to leave, and although she was confident that this wasn't the end of her and Gavin, she wanted him to say something she could hold onto as she walked away. When it was clear that wasn't going to happen, fury at Tess flamed inside of her again. She needed to go before she said something to tarnish these picture-perfect days she had planned to leave him with. She turned and started down the stairs.

But she couldn't resist one little jab into the fat of his self-satisfaction. "And don't worry, your secret is safe with me." She looked back over her shoulder at him and grinned like a Cheshire cat. "Unless she finds that red bra I lost in your apartment." She sashayed down the stairs and out the lobby door.

———

Gavin chortled once, a lame guffaw that was lacking in mirth, and took a step back into his apartment and closed the door. A wave of uneasiness swept over him. "She was joking, wasn't she?" he said to the John Wayne poster on the wall.

He peered discerningly around the apartment.

———

When Allie and Megan finally put their duffle bags down in their dorm room, Allie shut the door behind them. "What's going on?"

"Oh, Allie." Pent-up tears leaked down Megan's face. "Last night. I had sex with Mark last night."

Allie searched Megan's face. "Okay... "

"I was really drunk. Oh God, I hadn't planned on it. I think I drank too many daiquiris. And I didn't really eat much." She took a breath. "We were walking down the beach, and I was happy, thinking what a great break it had been."

Allie nodded.

"And the next thing I knew we were lying in the sand. I didn't want to. I mean, not lying in the sand, that was fine. That was, I mean, we were having fun at first, but I don't know, it happened really fast."

"It's okay Meg." Allie hugged her, and was taken aback by the trembling in her friend's body. "Here, honey, sit down."

"I didn't mean to have sex with him. It was very clear in my mind. But one minute we were fooling around, and the next," she shuddered, "he was inside of me." She sat down and stared at the floor. "I shouldn't have done that."

"It's okay. You guys were drunk, on vacation. Mark isn't Baker, he'll call you."

"He *was* drunk." Then, in a softer voice, almost to herself she said, "I don't think he could hear me."

"Hear you?"

"I was trying to tell him to get off me, to stop. Oh Allie, I couldn't get him off of me."

Allie inched closer. "What do you mean, you couldn't get him off of you?"

An edge of hysteria sliced into Megan's voice. "I tried, but he was too heavy."

"You tried to get him off of you and he wouldn't get off."

Megan nodded.

"He wouldn't stop when you asked him to."

Megan looked down and ripped at a cuticle.

"Megan. It sounds like you were raped."

Megan looked up at Allie with brown eyes rimmed in red.

"Were you raped?" Allie said softly.

"No. I don't know, it happened so fast. One minute it was fine, I wasn't stopping anything because we were having fun. I wanted to be there with him, I wanted to be fooling around with him. And then the next minute, it was horrible. There was no time to scream because up until the very last second I believed I could stop it, that he would hear me saying no and just stop. I mean, you assume someone is going to stop when you say stop, right? Until he was inside me." Megan shuddered again. "But rape? Mark? He's not the type. I thought he was so nice. I liked him."

"There is no type. It sounds like rape to me."

"And afterward? He certainly didn't think it was rape. He didn't even know anything was wrong. I mean, he knew something was wrong I guess, but it wasn't like he was psyched because he just got laid. He was confused."

"That doesn't mean he didn't rape you."

Megan wasn't so sure. She couldn't help feeling like she had played a part in the awful scene. *If only I hadn't gone down to the beach. If only I hadn't been so drunk. If only I had protested more loudly, hit him.* The only thing she was sure about was that she did not want to see Mark again.

He called a few times over the next week, but Megan made Allie tell him to stop calling. Twice he started towards her in the cafeteria, but she fled before he got anywhere near. After that, she'd see him look questioningly at her from across the room, but he never tried to call or approach her again.

His few attempts at contacting her confused her more; this wasn't a rapist. How could he be if *he* didn't even know it? The whole thing was just an evening that had gotten out of hand.

And she had let it.

CHAPTER 5

One of the hardest things about this separation, now in its fifth month, is when I randomly run into Dana. It shocks me every time—I literally gasp, then jerk my hand to my mouth and clear my throat or fake a cough. Of course I never see him from a distance or when his back is to me. No, he jumps into my line of vision from around a corner, or maybe he leaps down from the top of the canned goods, and my heart races and I want to throw my arms around him and hold him and there is nowhere to hide and I... cough.

I'm much more composed if we've arranged to meet. I have makeup on, I've contemplated my outfit, and we have an agenda—a meeting at school, a dance recital, or when one of us tags the other for time with Matt and Gillian—and we have time to emotionally prepare and suit up with the appropriate armor.

No, it's being blindsided that knocks me down and hurts the most. The most familiar images are jolting in their intimacy when I come upon him. The way his brown hair waves slightly around his ears; the way his favorite blue jeans fit, bagging just-so underneath the back pockets; the way his crooked front tooth gives his smile a twist of mischievousness. Then in an instant, those very same things become strange as we face each other in our new disconnectedness. It's as if he morphs into something foreign right before my eyes.

And then, as if just running into each other isn't enough, we have to chat. The weather, what movie we're renting; whatever it is, it all has to be vanilla, because anything more complex unleashes a thousand vultures. Even a simple "What're you up to?" opens up a hunger: What are *we* up to? Are you thinking about me? And most importantly, do you still love me?

So two people who have been naked and stripped of pretense with each other, and who've shared seasons of Olympic agony and ecstasy, face each other in a crowded store and discuss traffic. It's the most disavowing experience, and walking back to my car I feel hopeless. Without anchor.

I've been adrift like this before. Growing up, my family never had a true anchor. After my mother left, we bobbed among the deep bottle-green waves in three different rubber lifeboats, for years at the mercy of life's wind and tides. Kevin and I, terrified and clutching each other in one boat, prayed to be rescued. Paul, in another, was tethered to us by a long rope, but for some reason, he couldn't or wouldn't pull himself over and climb in with us. Our father was in the third boat, not tethered to anything. His back was to us, and he was craning his neck out to sea as if looking for the Coast Guard, or an island, or just something to grab onto.

Funny he never looked to us as a rescue party.

And he certainly never rescued us. Not once. I have years of scar tissue on my heart—that pink, healed over new skin that looks so shiny and strong but is unforgiving and easily torn when tested. Once when I was about seven, maybe eight, I had thrown myself face down on my bed, sobbing because of something mean a friend had said or done. I can't remember what; but I do remember sensing my father behind me. The air had shifted slightly, maybe I smelled the sharp spice of his aftershave. He had just come home from work, and he stood in the doorway of my room and paused, as if he was taking stock of the girl, the heaving shoulders, the poofy pink comforter, the dolls for the first time. I wished him over, prayed for him to sit down and put his hand on my back, to tell me it was all going to be okay. My sobbing became more dramatic, with tiny pauses in between the wails so that I could hear him, gauge where he was, be ready for him. He was a statue in the doorway for a long time. Too long.

Then he slunk away.

I was shocked into silence. I forgot what I was even crying about. I spun around. He was shuffling down the hall to his office; his bulging briefcase weighed down his right arm.

He had stopped the tears, that's for sure.

Maybe he thought the dolls would handle it.

MAY 1991

New York City

The sun bounced off the shiny Midtown skyscrapers and down onto the sea of sunglasses like a rubber Superball ricocheting around a crowded room. It was one o'clock on a Friday in May, and busy professionals had left their jackets on the back of their chairs and were stealing a few extra minutes over lunch to enjoy the spring sparkle. Allie and her friend Eliza were sitting at a bustling café eating salad and drinking cold iced tea with Sweet-N-Low, the standard pre-Memorial Day lunch for a 20-something woman working in the Big Apple. Allie, as a doctor's receptionist, had an entire hour to kill, while Eliza, a trainee at a nearby bank, had about half that. But Allie had arrived early enough to get a table near the open French Doors.

The two girls were part of a growing crowd of recent college graduates who lived on the Upper East Side and spent their money in the same neighborhood bars night after night. The dimly lit dives with graffiti-scribbled, one-stall bathrooms served beer and shots conveyer-belt style, and bartenders often had to slide drinks around patrons dancing on the bar, who may have been so moved because the booming music made conversation challenging (and because, why not?). The clientele was an easy-going, eclectic group with energy and humor, and through their frequent juxtaposition and strange "small world" coincidences ("you grew up with my roommate" or "my brother works with your girlfriend") a core group had gelled. They no longer just happened to run into each other—the 30 or so young adults planned events, or at least what bar they would start off in, through furtive phone calls on the company dime. A real-life game of telephone.

Allie and Eliza dug into their salads and amused each other with their versions of last night's antics at The Dugout. Their crowd worked hard and played harder, often stumbling home at three or four in the morning for a few hours of sleep before trudging back in for another long day at work. The next day, the rehashing of the stories was always entertaining—it varied whether it was a comedy or horror show—and usually just a preview of the evening's coming attractions.

As Allie listened to a story about Eliza's roommate, a sixth sense made her turn from the tale in time to see a couple strolling by, holding hands, their leisurely pace and casual blue jeans unique among the scurrying neckties on the sidewalk. It was Dana. And a very cute blonde.

Eliza, mid-sentence, stopped talking. "Are you okay?"

Allie didn't answer. She was riveted to the couple crossing the street and gliding into the corner bookstore.

She finally looked back at Eliza. "Actually, no. I need some air." Allie wobbled as she tried to stand. She grabbed the back of the chair as a wave of nausea punched her in the stomach.

"You look green. Maybe my story about Amanda's hangover reincarnated yours." Eliza half-smiled. "I'll get this," she indicated the tab, "and meet you outside."

Allie raced through the noisy café and out into the bright sunshine. She paused to get her bearings, to try to clear the affective smoke threatening to choke her. Then, unable to stop herself, she crossed the street and followed Dana inside the store, completely forgetting about Eliza and her half-eaten lunch.

The Book Stop was small and cramped, with books stacked everywhere, and almost as an afterthought, narrow passageways cutting through them. The aisles converged in the children's section at the back of the store, a welcome open space with stuffed animals and huge Babar posters. In the corner, a group of preschoolers were absorbed in story time.

Allie's eyes swept down the aisles and zoomed in on Dana and his cute sidekick in the back browsing through picture books and talking in library voices. They hadn't noticed her, but she was an ill-fated deer in the headlights anyway. She had no plan. She couldn't just stand there. If she ran out, they might look up and catch her fleeing the scene. Or worse, all the children in the corner might rat her out by yelling and pointing at the crazy lady with the brown cape of hair. And she really didn't want to leave; she didn't want to be left holding the happy picture she had just framed. She needed details. She scoffed at the shrill alarm in her head, shoved her shaking hands in her pockets, and marched over to Dana and the Blonde.

"Dana!" Allie grinned as if this was the best interruption to her day.

He glanced up. Surprise, then rapidly guilt, flashed across his face, finally settling into a resolute stiff lip. "Allie."

"What a surprise! How are you?"

"Good. Fine." There was a pall of silence. "We just finished exams."

"So school's out. That's great."

Dana's restraint in the face of her Shirley Temple cheer made Allie's skin crawl. Her grin felt frozen and ridiculous, and despite her struggle to hold it, it slipped from her face. She bit her tongue so that she didn't quip, "Can you believe this weather?" and glanced down at the book Dana was clutching. *Goodnight Moon*. She had a momentary snapshot of being curled up on a kindly neighbor's lap.

Dana noticed her eyeing the book. "We're picking out books for Robin's birthday."

"Your cousin? She's going to be two, right?"

Dana nodded.

The petite girl by Dana's side—who kept shifting her weight from hip to hip as if she was waving herself—was as conspicuous as Babar himself would be if he had stepped down from the poster on the wall. Allie was dying to ask, "Who the hell is this?" with the emphasis on *hell*. She didn't know whether she should continue to ignore her, as Dana seemed to be doing, or introduce herself. She decided on something in between and eyeballed her.

"Oh," Dana said. "This is Nina, a friend of mine from Boston."

Nina stopped moving. Her perfectly tweezed eyebrows squeezed together at the term "friend," but she smiled and stuck out five light-pink polished fingers. "Hi."

Allie stuck out her hand too, which was now surprisingly steady despite the fact that she had so many emotions flooding through her she felt like she might have a stroke right there during story hour. She didn't know what she was feeling; jealousy certainly, but a resounding sadness too. Mostly she just wanted to smack the smile off of Nina's face and scream, "I'm Allie. ALLIE. You must know who I am." Instead she just checked to make sure that her smile was plastered in place and said, "I'm Allie." She watched Nina's reaction closely.

Something flickered across Nina's eyes—recognition?—but her smile remained neutral. "I've heard a lot about you."

Really? Interesting. She glanced at Dana for a clue. He was giving her nothing, and in fact was suddenly studying the three bears in chairs as if it was his law textbook.

Now that she was an official entity, Nina put her hands on her steady hips and looked expectantly from Dana to Allie. *Was she enjoying this?* Tears of frustration welled up as Allie's need to connect with Dana somehow—through a look or a hug or a tone of voice—was thwarted by Dana's refusal to look up from his book.

"I should get going," Allie said. "Got to get back to work and all that. It's good to see you."

Dana slowly raised his eyes from the green and red illustrations. "Allie... "

She turned around; held her breath.

He looked at her intently. Allie's wish for connection was granted through his long look, but it was a tortured and painful connection, and she didn't feel better for it. Then he sucked any escaped emotion back in and locked the door. "Good to see you too."

Every molecule in her body spurred her to sprint, but she forced her feet to walk. Walk and pretend to glance at a title or two. Oh, interesting! She made herself touch one of the books on the shelf. The clogged aisles stretched out longer and longer in front of her, a carnival trick.

She stumbled back to work, blind and disoriented in the sunshine. The rest of the afternoon, through the scheduling of appointments and the greeting of patients, thoughts of Dana tormented her, the emotional aftermath of their encounter hung on her like a cumbersome overcoat she couldn't shake off.

Dana. She loved him; that hadn't changed with their breakup 10 months ago. They had kept in touch over the phone, straining to be chatty while tamping down the deep ache of missing each other. "Hi, how are you" was always saturated with hope—that this call might be different, that this time they might compromise and get back together—and tinged with trepidation, because nothing had really changed, their feelings for each other were just as strong as their impasse. They both knew that 60 seconds in they would hang up feeling frustrated and unfulfilled, and a few quips later this certainty would pan out, as their words hollowed and led to a goodbye full of unspoken feelings and reawakened hurt. They had talked less and less throughout the year, but were unwilling to completely let go. The last conversation had been five weeks ago.

Allie loved living in New York with Megan. Their apartment was tiny, a cubicle, known in real estate jargon as a "one-and-a-half bedroom" because the original bedroom had been partitioned off into two. But it was home. Their group of friends was a riot and their escapades spontaneous; you never knew what the night would bring, who you might meet, what fling or adventure might be around the corner. Just the other night they'd divided up into three teams, and armed with a Polaroid camera and a list of destinations, they had raced around the city on a whacky, pictorial scavenger hunt. Allie's team of 10 had asked strangers to photograph them piled in the back of a taxi, in front of a pyramid of fruit at the corner deli, and standing on the bar at their favorite pub.

Her job was fine, it was a job; a stress-free, nine-to-five chore that paid the bills. Professionally, it was a dead-end; answering phones and scheduling appointments wasn't challenging, and there were no promotions for a receptionist in a doctor's office. She had no interest in medicine, but nothing else captured her imagination either. So she stayed at her desk, smiling at the parade of patients, filing her nails in between filing intake forms, and flipping through *People* while she answered the phone.

Some of her friends were also receptionists, group-assistants, and gophers, but their jobs were stepping stones to coveted careers. Megan had landed a sought-after group assistant job at J. Walter Thompson, one of New York's premier advertising agencies. She was paid next to nothing, worked killer hours, and had used her brain maybe once in the past month, but she was in heaven.

And of course Dana was on a different path, at Boston College Law School, now with one year under his belt. *And perky little Nina under his belt too.* Allie looked at her watch. *Three more hours.* She rubbed her temples;

her whole body ached as if she had just been picked up and slammed into the Brooklyn Bridge. She opened up her desk drawer and shook out two Advil.

The minute the clock struck five (other people had lightbulbs in their heads, she had a five-o'clock chime) she was out the door and race-walking the 30 blocks home, with a pit stop for a cheap bottle of chablis on the way. She dumped the accoutrements of her day in a heap by the front door—heels, blazer, enormous black leather bag (a vessel that held makeup, tampons, her Filofax, a bottle of water, numerous magazines, and hundreds of matchbooks that were not only functional, but also served as miniature cardboard mementos)—and gathered up everything she would need to wait for Megan—cigarettes, a glass of wine, the clicker, and the latest copy of *Vanity Fair*. The nondescript glass ashtray, pocketed from a nondescript bar, had several butts in it when Megan's key finally scraped into the lock.

The walls of the apartment seemed to sigh with relief as Megan stepped through the door.

"You'll never believe who I saw today," Allie said.

Megan raised one eyebrow and studied Allie's face. "You're right, I don't think I will. Who?" She stepped out of her heels.

"Dana."

"In New York?" She walked a few steps into their kitchenette—as far as conversation was concerned, it was the same room—and poured herself a glass of wine. "Something tells me I'm going to need this."

"You will." Allie lit up another cigarette. "He walked right by me with a cute blonde on his arm."

Megan's eyes widened as she sat down.

"I almost died. I stalked them like a crazy person and then basically threw myself at them."

"Oh no. Did either of them catch you?"

"I fell flat on my face. And Nina, *Nina*, was quite the attentive observer. She soaked it all up."

"Did she get an earful?"

"Not really. Oh Meg, it was terrible. I've never seen him with anyone else. I thought I was going to throw up all over her brown leather sandals and perfect pedicure."

"I thought law students were supposed to be dowdy and pasty from studying all the time."

"Apparently not." Allie made a face.

Megan slid a cigarette out of the pack on the table. "How was he? How'd he handle it?"

"He seemed a little shaken up; not as much as me though. I was a wreck. I've been shaking all day." Allie held out her hand as evidence. "I probably scheduled surgery for people who wanted a check-up."

"I bet he was a wreck too. Cute blonde or not, he loves you, Allie."

"You're going to think I'm crazy, but I've been thinking about it all day. I'm jealous, okay? But it's more than that." She looked straight at Megan. "I want him back."

"Okay... " Megan exhaled the word and the smoke from her cigarette at the same time. "Hold that thought." She jumped up and grabbed the wine bottle out of the refrigerator. "We're going to need some help." She filled up Allie's glass. "Devil's advocate?" She put the bottle down on an old wooden trunk that was their coffee table. It was stained with an intricate pattern of perfect circles, evidence of the many bottles and glasses that had sweat there over time.

"Please." Allie relaxed and sat back.

Megan picked up her burning cigarette from the ashtray. "Fact: I know you love Dana, and I know Dana loves you. And I definitely know that you've missed him."

Allie thought about all the nights she had sobbed in Megan's arms.

Megan continued, "But you've also had fun dating. And this is what you wanted, you chose being single over being with Dana last summer."

"But only because he forced the issue."

"So what's changed?"

"Being separated from him feels all wrong. I can't stand that we don't know what's going on with each other, that we're not part of each other's lives. I swear, I was in the twilight zone in that bookstore making small talk. How do you do that with someone you know so well?"

"It must've been awful."

Allie leaned forward and dropped her head into her hands. "I just miss him."

"I know." Megan squeezed Allie's shoulder. "But are you sure that means getting back with him?" They were quiet for a moment. "I can say all this because you know how much I love you, right?"

"This is great; I need to have this conversation."

"Then, can I remind you of last summer when you guys broke up? He wanted to live together and you didn't?"

"I wasn't ready. I was scared."

"I know. But how do you know you won't feel that again?" Megan dragged from her cigarette. "You know if you decide to get back together—if Dana wants to, which I would put money on—it's going to be forever. He's going to want a commitment from you."

"I know." Allie had been thinking about last July's breakup all day, about the intense feelings that had been put on the table and had at the end of the day, caused them to go their separate ways.

———

The heat and humidity hung like a wet washcloth that Fourth of July, and after a long day of jumping in and out of the Sexton's country club pool, Allie and Dana sat wilting on Dana's back porch, their arms and legs splayed out across their wooden chairs. Dana's mother Sharon was adamantly opposed to air conditioning, and on that day, even though a ceiling fan spun frenetically in every room of their large house, the thick air refused to relent.

The air was just as oppressive out on the porch. And away from the whirring of the fans, it was eerily quiet, as if the birds were too weighted down to sing. Despite the hush however, both Allie and Dana were jumpy, teetering on the edge of a serious discussion about the next step in their lives. The cord between them had been taut with anticipation for over a week; each of them had rehearsed their lines over and over, and each had already thrown a syllable or two into the ring before quickly retreating when the moment, the mood, the quiet had shifted. Life with the Sexton family had a definite rhythm to it, even in the summer: breakfast at nine, tennis at ten, lunch at the Grille. There wasn't much time when either Dana's mom or his three sisters weren't jumping into the conversation, or just plain stealing it. Late afternoon on the porch wasn't perfect either, as Dana's father was due home any time, signaling the beginning of cocktail hour and the first of his several stirred martinis ("Obviously not a Bond fan," Allie had once whispered to Dana). But Allie couldn't dance around the tension any longer.

"So Megan just lined up a job at J. Walter Thompson; she starts in five weeks." Allie twirled a chunk of her hair. "She's looking for an apartment, and I think I'm going to look with her."

"Just steer clear of Zoe's realtor."

"Ha! We definitely couldn't afford anything in her league."

"We?"

She looked at Dana and took a deep breath. "I didn't mean just help Megan look. I meant look with her, for me too. Roommates."

"In New York?"

Allie nodded and looked down at her bare feet.

Dana shifted forward in his seat. "Actually I was thinking, hoping that you could get a job in Boston." He put his hand underneath her chin and gently lifted it up. "I need a roommate too, you know."

Allie's heart leapt. It felt so good to have Dana look into her eyes and be so heartfelt, so tender. His eyes were warm, soft, loving, so different from the casual, composed way he usually looked at her. She wanted to melt into him.

And then the fear rushed up and grabbed her by the throat. *People leave you. He will leave you. If you open your heart fully, he's going to crush it.*

Dana filled in the silence. "We could get a cheap one-bedroom. It'd be so great! I'll be pretty busy with school, but you can get a job in Boston as easily as you can in New York. How awesome would it be to live together? We wouldn't have to worry about traveling to see each other, phone bills, anything. We'd come home from work to our own place. Of course, you'd have dinner waiting." His smile slipped away when he saw her face. "Okay, so we'd get takeout."

"I don't know."

"What don't you know about?"

"I've already told Meg I'd live with her."

"She'd understand."

Allie swallowed hard. "Dana." She slid her chair closer to him so that their knees were touching and she leaned in close, despite the fact that they were both sweating in the heat. "I love you. God, I love you so much." Her voice was violent with conviction. "You know that I hope…"

She paused for a full minute. His knees felt warm and slick with sweat against hers. She desperately wanted to feel more of him, more of this body that was an extension of her own, but she fought the urge to crawl into his lap. She knew her next words would not be greeted with open arms. "But I'm just not ready to live together."

Dana took her hands in his. "I love you too. I want to marry you. Hell, I would ask you to marry me today if I thought you'd say yes. But I know the whole marriage thing scares you, so I'm willing to wait. For that." He hesitated. "But I need some kind of commitment from you."

There was a dead-end in his voice. Allie felt sick with fear.

"I don't want to do this separation thing anymore," Dana continued. "I can't do this separation thing anymore. And I definitely can't do the seeing-other-people thing. I can't stand thinking of you with someone else, and I certainly don't want to be with anyone else. It just doesn't make sense to me."

"Okay, so let's not date other people. I don't want to do that either."

"It's not enough, honey. I don't want to visit you anymore. I want to live with you."

His last words echoed through her head as if they had been shouted in an empty, cavernous room.

"I'm scared," Allie whispered.

"I know you're scared." Dana squeezed her hands. "I know you see the marriage that your mom and dad had, or didn't have, and it feels like a precedent has been set for you. But Allie, there are plenty of marriages that work."

"My mom married young." Allie gazed out over the yard, her voice carrying only slightly more emotion than if she was reading off of a tele-prompter. "I'm guessing she was happy when she said yes. And then she had a house and three kids, the American dream. Except for her, I guess it was a nightmare, because she bolted. From me." She swallowed. "*I* must have been a nightmare." That was something she had never said out loud before.

Dana glanced out over the yard, following Allie's gaze, but there was nothing but shady trees and green grass. He looked back at her.

"Hey," Dana said softly, "we're not talking about marriage. Just being together. Living in sin."

Allie looked at him, her green eyes despondent. "I can't lose you." Fat tears inched down her face.

Dana reached over and wiped them off.

"But I'm not ready yet. I can't, Dana." She was filled with dread. "Please." *Please.*

Dana sagged back in his chair.

Allie sensed that his reclining away wasn't a good sign, and so she continued—urgently—to explain herself. "I don't know, it's like this wall around my heart." She paused, shook her head. "No, it's like this vise around my chest that squeezes me, tries to suffocate me, hisses that this would be a mistake. That *I* am a mistake. That one day when I least expect it, you're going to see something in me that will send you running in the opposite direction." She knew she wasn't making sense, knew there was no way she could make him understand her sense of foreboding.

"So I'm trying to understand." He massaged the back of his neck. "You love me. You want to be with me. But you can't bring yourself to do it and you're not sure when you'll be able to."

Allie sat back too. Her words sounded crazy, even to her.

"I'm a mistake," Dana said.

"Not you, me. *Me.* I'm a mistake." She was desperate for him to understand. "I'm damaged, Dana. People walk away from me when they really see me." She swallowed hard and said in a small voice, "I don't want to be your nightmare."

"Seems to me like you're the one walking away now." Dana's voice was flat. "I can't live in different cities anymore. It's too exhausting for me. I love you Allie, I want to be with you. Now that we can be together, it doesn't make sense to choose to be apart." He exhaled loudly. "I just don't understand."

Tears streamed down Allie's face.

A lawnmower hummed in the distance.

Dana waited a moment and then stood up and walked inside the house. The screen door slammed shut behind him with a loud thwack.

"I know," Allie said aloud to no one.

―――――

Many times at her desk today, and for that matter, many times throughout the past year, Allie had thought back on that Fourth of July, and when she did, the hopelessness she felt when Dana had pushed himself out of his chair and walked away flooded her all over again.

Megan was right; nothing had changed. Except time. But today it was obvious that if she didn't face her fears and give this her best shot, Dana would slip away. He was already slipping away. In shielding herself from the worst, she was actually making it happen. And the bottom line was that she could not live her life without him. She had always assumed they'd be together in the future, she just had never thought through how it would come to be.

Megan spoke into the silence. "I can't imagine the two of you with anyone else in the long run. But I think you get one 'back together' chip to play, and that'll be it. You need to be sure you want to use it now."

"I think I do." Allie locked eyes with Megan. "I do."

"Okay then."

Allie grinned. "I'm going to call him."

"Now? You don't want to sleep on it?"

"No time like the present, right? And I'm feeling brave. Besides," she smiled, "I know he won't be home, so I can leave him a message." She jumped up, spilling a little wine, and gave Megan a kiss as she passed her. "Thanks, Meg."

"Anytime," Megan said, and she walked into her bedroom to peel off her skirt and put on jeans.

―――――

Just jeans. Not jeans over tights with a camisole and a tee shirt and a sweater draped to her knees. Just one layer. Normal. Megan smiled.

A year ago, in the weeks and months after... well, Megan still wasn't sure how to label that dark night on the beach. And really, back then it didn't matter because she didn't want to think about it. She had banished it from her mind.

Yet it was all she could think about.

The bright balloons of graduation, moving to New York, finding a job, were all punctured by the dark dagger of that night. And the harder she tried to ignore it, the harder she tried to erase it from her consciousness, the more it assaulted her in sneaky, insidious ways.

She had "daymares," flashbacks so real that she could actually feel Mark's weight on her, his heavy body grinding into her, crushing her into the sand. He attacked her at random times throughout the day—while shopping for groceries his ragged breath would graze her ear, during a business meeting his hips would hammer into her, lying awake in bed at night his voice would claw at her.

She couldn't sleep anymore; she kept a vigilant eye on every shadow and she startled with every hiss of the heater, every whoosh of the elevator out in the hall. Some nights, Allie—somehow sensing Megan's wild eyes in the next room—would come in and wordlessly lie down next to her, a dozing safety blanket, while Megan stayed board-straight and clutched her quilt under her chin (she could feel his damp skin sliding over her...). Her only reprieve was when a siren would scream down the street, a brief lullaby for her restlessness, promising that help was nearby if she needed it.

Daylight ushered in different hurdles; just getting out the door now took forever. Allie often brought her a steaming cup of coffee and pulled back her curtains, a not-so-subtle nudge that it was time to start her day.

"Did you sleep?"

Megan would shake her head, her disheveled hair swaying in one big tangle. Her body was so tired, she felt like she was wading through water (she could hear the crashing waves of the dark ocean...). But her mind was alert, wired, battle-ready. It felt like hadn't closed her eyes in weeks.

If it were physically possible, Megan would pull on every piece of clothing in her closet. As it was she wouldn't leave the apartment without layering on underwear, tights, a long skirt; a bra, undershirt, two more shirts, and a blazer or a coat. It was never enough.

One morning, Allie touched Megan softly on the shoulder. "Meg, it's going to be 60 today."

"I know." (She could feel her underwear being ripped down her legs...) She needed all these clothes. Her body felt loose-limbed and fluid, Gumby-like, as if there was no physical delineation to her, as if pieces of her were oozing out onto the concrete sidewalk and into the spaces around her as she made her way down the street. The layers were an attempt to physically contain herself from spilling out. She looked into her mirror. "It hides the bruises."

Allie stood behind Megan and looked at her friend's reflection in the mirror—dark circles underneath exhausted, frantic eyes. She said softly, "You don't have any bruises."

Megan just held Allie's eyes for a minute. Allie finally looked down.

———

After the initial weeks of trying to fight back against the army of ruthless images and sensations, Megan changed tactics. Maybe it would be better if she intentionally thought about it, talked about it.

"It takes two to tango." Megan said one night to the girls as they were eating ice cream and drinking wine. She tried to keep her voice steady, but it quavered and threatened to break.

"What?" Zoe looked ready to slap her.

"He didn't have a gun. And I was drunk, that was my fault."

Zoe was red-faced. "Being drunk isn't an invitation to be raped."

Megan cringed.

"Sorry." Then Zoe said more softly, "You said no."

"But I didn't punch him."

Tess looked back and forth between Megan and Zoe and twisted a napkin in her hands. "Why do you want to make this your fault?"

"He was inside me!" The wineglass in Megan's hand trembled. She put it down.

"Because he's bigger than you, not because you invited him," Zoe said gently.

"I was attracted to him."

"That's why it's called—"

"Okay hold on, I get it, I understand," Allie said, leaning in. "Meg, you know what I think; but I get where you're coming from." She put her hand on Megan's leg and said softly, "You're an expert at beating yourself up."

Megan chewed on her fingernail. Lately she thought that if she had wrestled with him, scratched him, kicked him, it might be easier to define it as everyone else did, as rape. But she hadn't hit him, she hadn't stopped him; he had penetrated her. How could she explain that twisting that night into a drunken mistake—*my mistake, and therefore my decision*—helped her feel a little less powerless? At least for a minute or two.

With her fingernail still in her mouth she said, "Maybe there was a reason I didn't fight him off."

Allie looked straight at Megan. "Couldn't fight him off you mean." She squeezed Megan's leg. "Just because I understand doesn't mean I'm going to be quiet."

———

It was August; they had been living in New York for three months. "Come to the Dugout tonight, a group of us are going," Allie said one morning as they were walking out the door to work.

Megan didn't answer. For a few weeks now, she had been worried that her friends' concerned and sympathetic padding was wearing through at the knees. Zoe's original protective rage—Allie had to talk Zoe down lest she lash out at Mark—had dissipated and Megan believed, had been replaced by a cool impatience. She could almost hear Zoe shout "Enough already! Get over it!" Tess would never shout, but Megan knew the idea that she had been overpowered chafed at Tess's insecurity about her own social strength.

Thank God Allie remained strong and true, although Megan believed that even Allie wanted her to move on, not because she was tired of listening or because she doubted her in any way, but because she simply wanted to see her friend happy. Even these good intentions carried a certain amount of pressure, however.

"Please? You can't stay in the apartment for the rest of your life. Come on, put your toe in. Just one drink." Allie put her hand on Megan's arm. "I won't leave you alone."

Megan relented, and then cursed herself as she stood at the bar that night with Zoe. Allie was in the ladies room; Tess hadn't arrived yet.

"How are you doing?" Zoe said. "It's pretty crowded, is that good or bad?"

"It's okay I guess."

"Aren't you hot? Take off your jacket and stay awhile."

Megan half-smiled and pulled her coat tightly around her. "Not there yet."

Someone grabbed Zoe's arm and started to drag her away. "Wait, stop!" Zoe shouted as the person continued to pull. She looked back over her shoulder. "Megan, you okay?"

But Zoe was eaten by the crowd before Megan could answer. Megan's eyes darted around the room—*where was Allie?*—then she turned into the bar and grabbed on.

"I'm pretty sure the bar is nailed to the floor." A hulking guy in a Giants jersey and a mouthful of white teeth leaned in.

Megan nodded, but kept her eyes on the dark wood of the bar. She knew how ridiculous she looked, and so she reached for her beer, but held fast to the bar with her other hand.

"Do you want a drink?"

"Got one, thanks."

His mouth closed over his teeth and he drifted away.

"I actually think he was one of the good guys," the bartender said with a smile. He had long dark hair, hair that was long enough for a ponytail, but was loose and tucked behind his ears. In another lifetime, Megan would have thought he was cute.

The music howled; the air was humid and thick with the smell of sweat and perfume and beer breath; people pressed in and around her in a life-or-death push for a refill. Megan started to sweat under her jacket, her knees felt weak. She shifted her weight from foot to foot. "I can't tell anymore."

The bartender peered at Megan, then turned to the person on the barstool next to her. "Hey man, can you give this lady a seat?"

"Sure." He smiled as he stood up. "She can have anything she wants."

Megan shuddered. Was he joking or serious? She couldn't focus. "Go to hell."

The guy recoiled as if he'd been slapped.

"The seat's enough, thanks." The bartender said with a warning in his voice. The man sidled off. The bartender pointed to the stool and looked at Megan. "Sit. This one's on me."

He put a beer down in front of her, and started pouring a drink for someone.

"Can I ask you something?" Megan put her hand around her bottle; it was icy. She put her other hand around it too, clasping it like it was a marble pillar. She fought the urge to rub the cold glass over her forehead. "Did I just say something to that guy? Because lately, I think I've said something, and then I'm not sure."

"Oh you said something."

"And he heard me?"

He looked up from the bottle he was holding. "Ah, yeah."

"How do you know?"

The bartender peered at her. "Are you here with anyone?"

Megan nodded. "Ladies room."

As soon as Allie came back, Megan stood up. "Okay, I put my toe in. Now get me out of here."

———

Work was the one place where Megan felt safe and whole, and she threw herself into even the most menial projects. Each morning it was the piles of paper and the deadlines that towed her out of bed and out of the apartment. The nightmares tried to creep in, but there wasn't much space when she was buried in a project. And the buttoned-up atmosphere and predictable office hierarchy made her feel safe.

It was work that helped her heal, work that carried her through the fall and winter and into the warmth of spring, work where she discovered she could think about that night without ripping open scabs and bleeding all over herself.

And then, in the spring, she discovered there were weeks when she didn't think about it at all, and that while there were scars, the scabs were gone.

CHAPTER 6

The other day, Gillian was curled up on the couch in her routine I've-just-woken-up-so-don't-talk-to-me funk, drinking in an early morning video like a strong cup of coffee, when she spit her thumb out of her mouth and exclaimed "Look Mommy, Anita's a ghost!" I looked up from my own morning ritual, *The New York Times,* and glanced at the video de jour, 101 *Dalmatians.* Anita was dressed in white, gliding down the aisle towards her waiting groom. The dress and veil looked dreamy, princess-like, but I could see that without instruction as to what was going on—yes, maybe an overly accessorized ghost. I smiled at Gillian and explained that no, she's not a ghost; she's a bride.

A bride. Is there any other word, one word, that has the power to evoke the full gamut of emotion (often all at the same time)? Love, hate, envy, regret, sorrow, panic, awe, hope… Girls spend years, sometimes decades, planning to be one; guys spend, well… *time,* trying to catch one (perhaps after years of trying to run from one). People who won't pull over for a screaming ambulance brake to gawk at a white billowy dress in the park, guests who spend hours applying makeup weep it all away as the bride floats down the aisle. This fleeting title is one of the most esteemed and coveted, arguably more so than Birthday Girl, Olympian, Head of School,

Congresswoman, CEO. *Brides* magazine has a larger readership than *Business Week*, *Forbes*, *Fortune*, or *The Wall Street Journal*.

I tried to describe to my daughter the personal significance of my own wedding, now carefully wrapped in mental tissue paper and gilded with a golden glaze of genuine happiness. The details are easy, they're engraved in my mind like the invitation that is framed on the shelf behind me. Gillian's eyes danced as I talked, and as they did, it all came alive for me again too; I could hear the swish and rustle of the snow-white silk, smell the sweet perfume of the white peony bouquet, feel the rush of seeing Dana—handsome and smiling—in his elegant black tux.

My voice tripped over the lump in my throat as I tried to describe the emotion of the day, of the ceremony in particular. Not surprising, as even now a few notes of Beethoven's "Ode to Joy" on the radio renders me weightless, a thousand tiny quivers ferrying me out of my Suburban and back to my trembling march down the aisle, to the feeling that this is it, this is The Moment.

Was it sad, Mommy? Gillian's voice crackled with confusion and the red flag of worry that shoots up when a parent is upset. No, it was a wonderful, happy day, I told her as I remembered the tears inching down my face at the altar, the catch in Dana's voice as he echoed back his vows, my friends sobbing in the pews. No, it wasn't sad, I assured her as my voice wobbled.

Why do people cry at weddings? Why aren't we smiling, giggling, or even applauding as the bride waltzes down the aisle? Yet tears are a given. Some people well up at every ceremony, they expect it and pack tissues, like you pack an umbrella for impending rain. I've heard friends forecast, like meteorologists—I'm going to be a mess at this one—well in advance of the event.

So what's with the tears?

Tears of joy? Tears of loss? Maybe the specific emotion isn't important. Maybe it's the intensity of what we're feeling that evokes the tears, along with the permission to publicly feel it.

For most of our lives, our deepest emotions are kept well hidden, only daring to peek out in private. In casual cotton or professional wool, uninhibited ecstasy or unmanageable grief makes other people uncomfortable, squeamish even, and causes them to back away, to run. But once in a while, at a wedding for instance (or a funeral), off-the-Richter-scale emotion is publicly sanctioned. Up on the altar, two partners stand up and profess their profound vulnerability. And it's contagious. Down in the pews, our own throat-clogging mash of feeling, emotion that is usually filed down and polished for public consumption, is uncorked under the auspices and the camouflage of the moment, the mood, the magic. And suddenly, we aren't just witnessing something rare; we're experiencing it, feeling it ourselves. And no one's backing away, no one is running. We're sitting in a room full of people and a husband is squeezing his wife's hand, a mother puts her arm around her daughter, a friend takes out two tissues and hands one to her left. And for one dazzling moment, the private, powerful feelings we guard in our hearts, in our souls, feelings we've tempered so that we don't appear histrionic, are not anomalous. They are universal.

And they well up and out of us.

For a just moment. Until we wipe our eyes, put our hands in our pockets, slide our sunglasses on, and stride out into the bright sunshine.

Weddings and funerals.

As I think about it now, I never told Dana how lonely I was as things got quieter and more distant between us; I never told him how much I missed him. I showed him irritable, I showed him mad, but I never showed him lonely. I learned as a kid to never show that, to never show vulnerability. Because really, no one cared. So instead I slapped Dana in the face with my frustration, like a kid packing a knapsack and irascibly shouting "I'm running away" while deep down pleading, "See how upset I am? Please hold me. Don't let me go."

Weddings and funerals. And maybe goodbyes.

JUNE 1992
Sudbury, MA

Allie felt the warm sun spill into the room before she opened her eyes. She had tossed and turned all night, scrolling repeatedly through details, lists, and possible crises like a secretary after six cups of coffee. Her sheets were tangled and her pillow had been punched and plumped so many times it was amazing it had any poof left. When she finally did doze off, her body remained stiff, anxious, half-listening for the alarm. The minute the morning sun caressed her face, her eyes snapped open and she was wide awake.

She took a minute to inhale the quaint room she had lived in for two days. Storybook New England, with its dark hardwood floors; white lace curtains waving in the breeze; and crisp blue and white checkered quilts that usually dressed the two twin beds, but were now heaped on an overstuffed, blue toile chair in the corner. Rooms like these always ignited yearning deep within her; she was a girl at a sleepover, wishing her room was this color, her den had this couch, her house was this attended to, this loved.

She kicked the covers off her and jumped out of bed. Out the window the sky was light blue—promising turquoise with the still-climbing sun— and there were a few cotton-ball clouds meandering by, window shopping on the world below. A beautiful day, an ode to great things ahead for her and Dana. She wondered if the whole "it's good luck if it rains on your wedding day" had been thought up by a frantic bridesmaid during a storm.

Her green eyes snapped to her wedding dress. Still there. It was hanging on the outside of the closet door, pristine under the clear plastic, waiting for the moment when she would step into it and become a bride. It seemed to wink and whisper to her, a friend with a secret she was about to share. Allie itched to pull it on.

Birds chirped in stereo outside the window and although she didn't feel rested, she knew she must have fallen asleep at some point, otherwise she would've heard these loud and rather annoying songs earlier. She glanced at Megan, asleep in the next bed. The jubilee clearly hadn't disturbed her, unless it was background music for her dream. *Cinderella* maybe, or *The Birds*. Allie smiled. She had an urge to poke her or shake her awake, but instead she rummaged for a shirt and shorts with a little more clatter and clomp than necessary. When Megan still didn't stir, Allie gave up and went to find a cup of coffee downstairs in the inn's sunny kitchen.

The dining room was empty, all the tables waiting patiently with little napkin teepees and fresh daisies. "Good morning miss," she heard several times as her sandals clicked across the polished floor, and she felt as if "bride" were beaming on a marquee over her head. Steaming coffee was presented to her with panache, and once armed, she wandered outside onto the porch and dropped into an oversized rocker.

The birds had followed her, although out here, overlooking the oval pool and colorful gardens, they weren't annoying. They were the backup band to the singing in her heart. All her screaming fears about marriage had been silenced over the past few months. She couldn't put her finger on exactly what had changed, but whatever adjustment had occurred in her mind, it had been bolstered immeasurably by Dana's conviction, his unwavering belief that their marriage was the most important ingredient in their lives. "I feel it in my bones," he liked to say. And when he dressed up as a skeleton on Halloween, she had thrown up her hands and laughed.

"I believe," she said. And she really did.

She twirled the small diamond ring on her right hand and watched the sun dance in its fire, still astonished at this most unexpected gift from her father. Earlier in the week, he had driven up to Dana's house unannounced, appearing at the Sexton's door just as Dana's father, Chris, was stirring his martini.

Joseph Mussoni stood tall at the door, offered his hand and a warm hello to Sharon and Chris, and then caught eyes with Allie standing behind them. He stammered through the rest of his greeting.

"I thought we could, um, have a quiet dinner together."

They hugged—two stiff bodies meeting but not softening, a double pat on the back like a rap on a tight drum, and then a rapid step back.

Allie could hear her heart hammering in her ears, and that pissed her off. How dare her heart go from zero to 60 for this man. *Why hadn't he called?* He must have known that she would whip up some excuse, some prior engagement to shut him out. Or maybe he had wanted to leave himself an out in the event that his feet became cold en route; with no plans in place nobody would've been the wiser.

Whatever his reasoning, by just materializing from out of nowhere Allie had no choice but to accept—graciously of course, as they were surrounded—his invitation to dinner. Underneath her royal composure however, she was flailing. He had intentionally cornered her, and perhaps even more criminal, he had thrust their alien relationship onto center stage, so that the entire Sexton family—all of whom had magically appeared from every corner of the house—could witness their uncomfortable reunion.

Joseph was ushered into the house with a flourish by Sharon and Chris, and folded into a suddenly interesting cocktail hour. Allie excused herself from the brie and first-date conversation and escaped upstairs to "her" guest room, ostensibly to change, but in reality to take a deep breath, gather her thoughts, and moor her pounding heart. She sank onto the bed. *Why is he here?* Curiosity seesawed with fear. Any good news he had to share with her could have been discussed over the phone, or at the wedding in a few days. *Did he lose his job? Does he have cancer? Was something wrong with Paul or Kevin? No, if it was bad news, he wouldn't be chatting and sipping away downstairs, would he?* She slammed her fist down on the quilt. *Damn!* The mailed, formal invitation had been specific in its time, date, and attire.

She heard feet taking the stairs two at a time and seconds later Dana burst in. "Are you okay?"

"I just needed a moment. What's happening down there?"

"My mom is in her element; they're all chatting away, lifelong buddies." They shared a smile over Sharon's hostess skills; she could make a serial killer cocktail-party appropriate.

He sat down on the bed next to her. "Do you want me to come with you to dinner?"

Part of her wanted—needed—him with her. She sighed. "No, I should do this on my own. He is my father after all," she rolled her eyes, "and for whatever reason, he suddenly felt the need to talk to me. In person, no less. I guess I should hear why."

Dana opened his mouth to say something, and then shut it. "Okay."

She stood up and smoothed down her white linen pants. "We should get back to the festivities. Give me a minute so that I look like I was primping up here and not just freaking out."

She took her time in front of the mirror, resisting the pull from downstairs with the concrete task of brushing her hair and applying makeup. Then, freshly perfumed and lipsticked, Allie rejoined cocktail hour, slipping into a corner chair next to Dana and wishing she could disappear inside the chatter that whirled around her. Someone asked a question, and while her father answered, she studied this stranger sitting casually in an armchair in the middle of her life.

The breeze of his perfect manners and appropriate modesty felt familiar, and she felt woozy from the déjà vu of the many times she had sat across the room from him, gawking at his social smoothness like it was a strange outfit he put on before a special occasion. He was involved in a genial back-and-forth with Dana's parents about golf (*oh Jesus, did he even play golf?*). The light repartee however, did not gloss over the fact that there was something somber about him. He had perfect timing and all the right lines, but behind the casual smile, he seemed deep inside himself, somewhere else entirely. Allie wondered if today he was unconsciously feeling her lack of respect. Unlike at his big corner office, here in this living room he had no uppercase, gold-plated title; here in front of his estranged daughter, he was just dad. Lowercase d.

She wondered what the Sextons thought of him; they were all skiing gracefully through the moguls of this unexpected encounter, but she knew they would only let their real, uncensored feelings fly afterwards, over the scrape and clatter of the dirty dishes. Knowing she wouldn't be around for the dishing, she tried to assess Joseph through their eyes. Tall and slim, words that could have been a prelude to "handsome," but in this case were a kind whitewash for gaunt. Sharon always said that the eyes said it all, and his brown eyes were not an asset; like thick, burnt coffee, they swallowed rather than reflected the light, and did not shade and soften along with the emotional gradation in the room. The Sextons would appreciate that he had taken care with his appearance however; he had cropped his gray hair rather than comb it over a bald spot, and he had added a tie and a flawlessly-cut navy blazer to his off-hours uniform of khakis and a starched button-down. Despite the expensive clothes however, the man was muted, camouflaged within the waspy cocktail conversation. Perhaps that was his intent.

On the way to the restaurant, Allie was silent. She sat in the far right corner of the passenger seat; if she could have hung out of the window to put more distance between them, she would have. She was a young girl again, being driven to a friend's house, suffering the 10 minutes or so in confined, bitter silence; hating him for not speaking, snapping a sarcastic reply when he dared try. Then and now, the radio did its best to fill the morose void.

Unfortunately, inside the restaurant there was no such audible filler. For a short time the menus consumed their undivided attention, but when that paper barrier was pried away by the waiter, it was either conversation or silence.

"Dana seems like a good guy."

"He is."

Joseph fingered his empty wine glass. "And you're happy?"

Not at the moment. Her brows furrowed together. "Are you?"

The waiter arrived with their drinks. Allie took her wine right from his hand. "Thanks," she said to him. "Oh, and you can bring the salad with the steak, we don't need a first course."

Joseph took a big sip from his cabernet. He cleared his throat. "How's your job?"

"I just quit." She saw him wince, and she took a deep breath, filed down her sharp edge. "I had to. Dana and I are going to live in Boston, at least until he finishes law school."

"I think you'll like Boston."

How the hell would you know? "How's Paul?"

They batted information about other people—family, friends of the family, then old neighbors—back and forth until their meals arrived. Then they turned their attention to their food.

"So are you ready for your big day?" Joseph asked after several quiet minutes and half their meal had disappeared.

Allie reminded herself that her knife was for cutting her meal only. She looked him in the eye. "I'm taking his name, you know. I'll be Allie Sexton."

He put his knife and fork down and reached across the table to take her hand. She instinctively recoiled, and his hand froze halfway across the white tablecloth and hung there, limp and without purpose.

"Allie… "

Their eyes locked together; for the first time in as long as she could remember, neither of them looked away. He cleared his throat. "I know I've been a terrible father to you. I haven't been there for you when you've needed me, and well, I haven't been there when you haven't needed me either." The corners of his mouth trembled into a sorrowful smile. "I've failed you, and Kevin and Paul, and for that, I'll be forever ashamed."

Oh God. Please don't. She had the urge to put her hands over her ears. Instead, she let her breath out slowly.

He must have taken her exhalation as a prelude to a response; he held up his hand. "Wait, let me finish, because this isn't about me, and I'm not looking for forgiveness from you. I'll take it," his smile flickered again, "but that's not why I'm here. I want to give you something, and to tell you something."

He took a deep breath. "I can't imagine what my failure as a husband and as a father, and what your mother's… absence has done to you, and to your feelings about family, about marriage. We made irreparable mistakes…" His voice drifted off for a moment and he gazed out across the crowded restaurant.

Allie was scared to move as he lifted his wine to his lips and sipped, as if for fuel. His eyes found hers again. "But you must not let our failure impact your future. Some marriages are solid—your grandparents' for instance. They loved each other, they had a good partnership. I'm sure they made mistakes too, but they worked them out together. You never knew them—they died when you were so young—but they were good people and good parents." He pulled a small velvet box out of his coat pocket and looked at it in his hand for a moment. Then he reached across the table and put it in front of Allie. "Anyway, I thought you should have this."

Allie, floating above herself, watched her hands take the box and slowly open it. Inside was a small, emerald-cut diamond ring set in a simple platinum band. She gaped at her father.

"It was your grandmother's engagement ring. I want you to have it. Maybe it will remind you that marriage can be healthy and enduring. That it's something you cultivate and create, just you and Dana. I want you to have it so you'll know that although I've never been able to find the words or the time or the… well, you've turned into an extraordinary woman. And Dana is a lucky man." He stopped abruptly, as if his cue cards had fallen to the floor.

"Thank you." Allie said the words so softly that she wondered if the noise from the restaurant had swallowed them up. She held the ring for a moment, felt its weight, watched the light flicker inside the stone. Then she slipped the ring onto her right ring finger.

She felt dizzy as the familiar, silent awkwardness flooded back in between them, and she wished for Dana, if only so that someone could confirm for her later that this hadn't been a very strange dream. The musical conversations continued around them, but their brief, heartfelt bridge had vanished. Allie didn't know what to say, and Joseph was all talked out; he had finished his well-rehearsed speech, and there was nothing left in his repertoire. A few minutes later, the waiter bustled by and cleared away their half-eaten dinners.

It wasn't until she was back in her little room at the Sexton's and her dad was well on his way back to New Jersey that she realized he had never said, "I love you."

————

Allie finished her coffee as slowly as she could, and then brought two fresh mugs of it back up to the room. Megan was still asleep, but this time, Allie put the coffee on the bedside table and gently shook her.

"Okay, okay," Megan mumbled. "I'm up."

"Sorry, I just can't wait anymore. I've been up forever."

"I know, I heard you getting dressed a while ago. You're very graceful." Megan sat up and reached for the mug of coffee. "Thanks for this." She wrapped both hands around the smooth ceramic. "What time is everyone getting together for breakfast?"

"Sharon said nine."

Megan smirked at Allie.

Allie smiled. "Nine's fine."

"What's she going to do with herself after today is over?"

"Dana wouldn't let her touch the honeymoon, so my guess is, start planning for the grandkids."

Megan rolled her eyes. "Poor kids."

Allie chuckled, then caught herself. "Or lucky, depending on how you look at it. I couldn't have done all this without her."

Allie knew that Sharon and Chris had cultivated weeds and weeds of doubts about her over the years. The party line had always been that they were "fond" of Allie, but it was clear that underneath her perfunctory hug, Sharon was busy scanning the room for a more suitable girlfriend for her son. But both of Dana's parents had smothered their doubts and embraced Allie wholeheartedly when they announced their engagement. And moments after the announcement, Sharon leapt into a second career: wedding planner extraordinaire. "We'll need to reserve the country club, the florist, find a band... Oh, I'm sorry! I just assumed, will you have the wedding here?"

Allie and Dana had already talked about it; she wanted to walk down the aisle in Dana's hometown. Although her father would finance the wedding, she didn't want him even peripherally involved in the planning. Not that he would want to. But this way, Allie couldn't be disappointed by her father's indifference. All he had to do was show up and walk her down the aisle. And until he had shown up with her grandmother's ring, she had been afraid to even count on that.

Allie put her coffee cup down on Megan's bedside table. "Let's go for a swim."

Megan cocked her head.

"Come on, it'll wake us up and wash away any of last night's cobwebs. We can take our coffee down to the pool." She giggled at Megan's reaction. "Come on, it's a beautiful morning."

"I'm not sure you need any additional waking up, or any more caffeine for that matter." Megan eyeballed Allie's coffee cup. "But it's your day, I'm at your mercy. Just tell me you're not planning on skinny dipping."

"I wasn't, but it's a good idea."

They changed into their suits and brought their coffee down to the deserted pool. Megan gratefully stretched out on a lounge chair while Allie walked up to the edge of the pool and dove in.

"Whoa!" Allie sputtered when she came up. "It's freezing!" She swam over to the side where Megan was lying and hung onto the edge of the pool. "A wee bit hungover this morning?"

"A little." Megan shielded her eyes from the sun as she squinted at Allie. "Aren't you?"

"Actually, I think the adrenaline has outbid it for my attention. Thank God, it would be awful to be hungover on my wedding day. I didn't mean to drink that much."

"Me neither. All that wine snuck up on me."

"It was all the toasts." Allie grinned at the memory of last night's re-hearsal dinner. So many good friends and family members all clicking glasses together; it was a night that even her father, who had remained on the sidelines of the alternately touching toasts and ribbing roasts, couldn't cast a pall over. The whole thing had been exquisite, and she assumed it was just a prelude to tonight's even bigger celebration.

"Speaking of drinking a lot, what'd you think of Zoe's date?" Megan eased off of her lounge chair. She sat at the edge of the pool and dangled her legs in. "Oh my God, you're insane! This water is icy."

Allie laughed. "I think I'm numb. Bob? Gorgeous, of course. I don't know beyond that, I didn't talk to him much. Seemed nice enough."

"They work together. I guess he does really well at Goldman, Sachs; makes a ton of money." Megan swished her feet under the water.

"I could've guessed that. What'd you think of him?"

"He was a little... slick. I'm imagining a gold chain and muscle tee un-derneath his Brooks Brothers shirt."

"Now that doesn't sound like Zoe. The only chain she would go for would be attached to the key to a Porsche."

"The necklace was there somewhere, if only in his history." Megan giggled. "For a random guest, he made himself quite at home. He held court with that Jägermeister bottle like he was mayor."

"He did have a pied piper-like quality at the bar. I'm glad I stayed away from the shots. I wonder how Dana feels this morning."

"Fabulous, of course," Megan said in the most robust voice she'd had all morning. "It's his wedding day."

Allie was warm all over, despite the frigid water. Last night was pure magic; they had been flying as if doused by pixie dust, the stolen and pub-licly applauded kisses a physical connection to the spiritual fusion that Allie already felt in her heart. She was sure that what they shared was stronger, more authentic than any other love before them, and the soul-shifting looks that Dana shot her from across the room were confirmation that he felt the same way. The vows they planned to repeat in the church today were just redundant. *Til death do us part?* No problem. It was inconceivable that anything else could dim this radiance.

"Your brother Kevin was adorable," Megan said. "He was watching out for me last night. The whole time I was talking to Neal, he kept walking by and giving me this 'you okay?' look, like if I needed an out to just let him know."

"Did you? Need an out, I mean."

"Actually not at all. Neal was really sweet; cute in a Richie Cunningham way. I've never spent much time with him one-on-one. We had a good time together."

"He's a great guy. Of all Dana's Princeton friends, I like Neal the best," Allie said, wondering how Megan would take what she was going to say next. "Dana says that he's had a crush on you for a while."

"Really?" Megan smiled. "Interesting."

Allie, bolstered by Megan's smile and lukewarm reaction, continued, "I think that Kevin may have a crush on you too. He's taken the best-man/maid-of-honor thing to heart, like you guys are mandated to be a couple now." Allie lightly splashed Megan. "You're the belle of the ball."

"I hardly think so." She took a deep breath. "All right, it's now or never." She let herself fall into the cold pool.

———

A few hours later, Allie, Megan, Tess, Zoe, and Dana's three younger sisters were secreted away in a suite that Sharon had reserved for the bride's preparations. Crystal, Sharon's hairstylist, was waiting with suitcases of colorful pots and cases when they all trooped in at two o'clock, three hours before the ceremony. At three, Sharon bustled in with chilled champagne and a platter of cheese and crackers, which she instructed all the girls to eat. "I don't want anyone to faint in the church." The girls snubbed the food, not wanting cheese on their breath or congealing in their stomach (and maybe making it bigger), but everyone grabbed a glass. The champagne was like cold flutes of giggles.

"So where are we?" Sharon said as she surveyed the seven young ladies fluttering around the room in various stages of dress. She walked over to Allie; Crystal was piling her long brown hair up into a romantic twist.

"You look beautiful," Sharon said as she tucked a stray piece of Allie's hair up into the coil.

The girls all grabbed their cameras; six clicks captured the moment. Seconds later they were back to chatting and zipping each other up in their long navy dresses.

"The navy really looks good," Sharon announced to the room.

"I still wish it had sleeves," Dana's sister Julia said. "My arms look fat."

Sharon glowered at her.

"But I love the length," Julia said as she skulked away from her mother.

Allie peeked at Sharon in her long, form-fitting black dress, and concluded once again that it was her confidence that made her so striking. Her shoulder-length blond hair was swept back off her face; she didn't hide behind bangs or wisps of distraction. Her face was chiseled, her chin never dipped down in despair. Her brown eyes—Dana's eyes—softened her; they were warm with gold flecks of kindness. Allie hoped she looked that good when she was Sharon's age.

Sharon turned to Allie. "Ready for the dress?"

Allie smiled and stood up.

Megan carried the dress over and held it open while Allie stepped into it. Then Megan and Sharon pulled it up in a rush of rustling tulle and silk. Allie shivered, and for a moment couldn't catch her breath. Cameras clicked, the room almost broke out into applause. Megan zipped her up, and then began the task of buttoning all the tiny buttons over the zipper.

"Dana's going to have fun with these." Megan smirked, and then glanced at Sharon.

"Oh Megan, I'm not *that* old," Sharon said.

Six girls bustled around Allie, fluffing and spreading out her snow white skirt, while Crystal wove the last of the flowers into Allie's hair and touched up her minimal makeup. Allie stood in the middle of it all, radiating happiness out of every pore, casting a golden glow over the room.

When the last of the primping was done, Sharon stepped towards her with a Tiffany box. "I'd be honored if you would wear this." She lifted a pearl choker out of the white silk lining. "I wore it on my wedding day," she smiled over her shoulder at Megan, "not so long ago."

Allie couldn't speak; she was afraid her heart would soar out of her body and fly away. The only noise in the room was the click of cameras as they hugged and

Sharon clasped the pearls around Allie's neck. The stones felt cold and smooth against her skin, and their weight grounded her, held her in the moment.

"I think I'm ready." Her voice wobbled.

She studied herself in the full-length mirror. Her sleeveless dress was simple and elegant—a fitted bodice, a big cloud of skirt. Other than a band of tiny white silk roses around the skirt waist, the nubby silk of the fabric was the dress' only adornment. Her green eyes sparkled out from her clear, tan face.

A wave of melancholy swept through Allie, and in a room full of people, she suddenly felt alone. Even her reflection had momentarily abandoned her. *Does my mom know I'm getting married today? Wherever she is, does she have a solemn feeling, a feeling that today is important?*

Megan appeared behind her and handed her a tissue. "Don't. It'll ruin your makeup."

"I wish she could see me." She still nursed a flicker of hope that some-how, Eva might show up.

Megan gave her a squeeze. "You'd take her breath away."

Allie dabbed at her eyes and willed herself back to the effervescence of the room. All of the girls were now dressed and milling around like sheep corralled in a pen, refusing to sit for fear of wrinkling. As the clocked ticked closer to five, the mirror—even more than the bride—became the primary focus of the room, and restless chatter propelled the girls back and forth in front of it.

Finally, Sharon announced that it was time to go and herded them through the door. Allie, Megan, Tess, and Zoe maneuvered their way into a shiny black limousine, finally forced to sit. Sharon and her three daughters piled into a second black chariot. And away they flew.

———

Dana stood in the bathroom with his best friend Neal, fumbling with the strip of black fabric that was supposed to twist somehow and become a bow tie. His hair was wet, his face was smooth, his cummerbund was buckled, but *damn this bow tie!* Exasperated, he gave up and leaned on the bathroom sink with both hands.

Since the moment he'd opened his eyes this morning, his space—personal and otherwise—had been invaded by doting family and friends, all hovering around him underneath a large tent of prattling anticipation. He glided through the late morning brunch and touch football game on autopilot, but he hadn't had a minute to breathe, to think. Maybe that was the point.

"What's going on?" Neal said.

Dana stared at himself in the mirror. "I'm about to get married."

Neal started to smile, then paused. "That's a good thing, right?"

Dana closed his eyes.

Allie. He had loved her from minute one, as if he had an epiphany when they met, when she had quite literally fallen into his blueprinted life, and by instinct he had caught her. As he helped her regain her balance, her green eyes had looked up at him and underneath her long lashes and giggling "Sorry" he had glimpsed a haunted, anguished shadow that didn't coincide with the smirking, warm girl he held in his arms. He had the desire to reach down and wipe her tears away, although there were no tears on her face.

With that passing soulful gaze, Allie had opened up a space in his heart that he hadn't even known was there. And as she sashayed away from him with her long hair streaming down her back and a peek back over her shoulder, he felt tied to her; and not just because of the sexual chemistry, although there was most definitely that. For the rest of the night, he caught himself searching for her, visually checking to see who she was talking to and whether she was still smiling, laughing. She found his eyes each time, and as they connected over the clamor of the party, it was as if they had found a spot that was still, that was omniscient in its certitude. In the silence, without a word, they were bound.

Dana opened his eyes. "Do you remember Christine?" His words were heavy; they fell through the air like stones.

Neal closed the toilet seat and sat down. He spoke slowly. "The blonde, senior year at Princeton?"

Dana was staring into the sink. "She was smart. Not so fun though."

Neal watched Dana, waited.

"And Lindsay?" Dana said.

"The girl you dated a year or so ago. The girl with the big..." Neal cleared his throat. "Yeah."

"Pretty sexy. But out of bed… well, she was good in bed."

"Dana." Neal snuck a glance at his watch.

"I've dated all these girls, and none, not one of them compares to Allie. Both in who she is and in how she makes me feel." Dana turned around and looked at his friend. "She's always been it for me. She's home."

He leaned back against the counter. "When she called me last year? Everyone warned me, don't do it, don't get back with her, she broke your heart. And I didn't, not at first. But I knew I would."

Neal waited.

Dana ran his hand through his hair. "What am I doing? I'm only 24."

Neal leaned towards Dana. "I've known you a long time, and I've never seen you waver. About anything. You know what you want and you put in the sweat. Hey, when the coach implied—merely hinted, mind you—that we needed more finesse out on the field, you suggested ballet. Everyone laughed it off as a good joke, but God love you, I think you were actually ready to humiliate yourself to get better." Neal smiled. "It's freakish really, you're like the poster boy for Hard Work Pays Off." He paused, and held Dana's eyes. "And always, always, you've been in love with Allie. I don't think that's going to change."

"But I pushed her, I was full steam ahead. And I'm not so sure she was really ready."

"Yeah, you can be a freight train."

"Sometimes I get this feeling that she wants something from me, and Oh God, I have no idea what it is. I'm not even sure she knows. But it hovers between us, this unspoken way that I'm not quite getting it right, that I'm failing her." He looked at his friend. "She's had so much chaos in her life, I just try to be solid, you know? I try to keep the noise to a minimum and to keep us moving forward." He smiled weakly. "Okay, so maybe like a freight train."

The room was quiet.

"Did I just propose to her so that I could hold onto her?"

"No. You proposed to her because you love her. And she said yes because she loves you back." Neal stood up. "She's said no to you before pal, she's not afraid to say it."

Dana nodded.

"She's going to walk down that aisle—smart, sexy, and fun—and you're going to be standing there waiting for her in this monkey suit. And you, and Allie, and the whole damn church is going to know, going to feel, that this is right."

Dana looked at Neal gratefully.

"It's called cold feet, buddy." Neal smacked him on the back. Then he reached for Dana's bow tie and slapped it into Dana's hand. "Now get this on. You've got a date."

———

The lavish reception, like all wedding receptions, was the stage for many mini-dramas set against the confetti of the newly minted couple. As Mr. and Mrs. Dana Sexton dutifully made their rounds, the bridesmaids—having taken the requisite snapshots of the bride and groom—put down their cameras and their formal duties and skipped out into the celebration to pose for their own memories.

"Do you want to dance?"

Megan smiled as she put her hand in Neal's and let him pull her out of her seat and onto the dance floor. Then she full out laughed when Neal started waving his arms and his body around in exaggerated, spastic movements.

"I can't dance," he said. "So I just want to lower all expectations right now."

"Okay, okay. They're lowered." Megan reached over and put her hands on his arms to bring them back down his side.

Neal grinned. "And don't think I'm intimidated by tall women."

"I'm actually not that tall." Megan's eyes twinkled.

"Shhh. It helps my little man complex to think you're super tall."

"I could take off my heels."

"No way. You look beautiful."

Megan blushed. And then realized she didn't feel an icy rush of panic, a need to punch and run. Amazing. Her shoulders settled onto her back and she shimmied with ease on the polished floor.

"So you're a copywriter," Neal said.

"Junior copywriter." Megan beamed. She loved her job.

"And Dana tells me you're a runner."

"It's how I stay sane." Running had been her religion—and her vengeance—over the past two years, and she ran every day, no exceptions. She either woke up at dawn to get on the treadmill or left her office at five to sprint through the park for an hour before returning to work, sweaty and glowing, to finish her day. She was invincible and powerful as she pounded past the pedestrians on the busy streets or along the FDR, and she pushed herself to go faster and farther, not satisfied until she was floating above the pavement in a godlike high, her whole world distilled down to the rhythm of her music, her feet, her breath. "Do you run? I know you used to play lacrosse."

"Not regularly, I'm more of a weekend warrior." He paused. "It sounds like our friends have been whispering our bios to each other."

Megan nodded. Allie had raved about Neal, telling her, "What you see is what you get." And so far, Megan liked what she saw. More importantly, she felt safe with this friend of Dana's. She looked around the room, at her friends who were giving her the thumbs up with their eyes. And this time, she wasn't agitated by their shaking pom-poms on the sidelines—"Go team go! Get your man!"

I may not get my man; I may not want this man. But at least I feel like it's up to me.

Over at the bar, one of the cheerleaders leaned against Gavin as visions of her own wedding danced through her head. While Gavin ordered a beer and a glass of chardonnay, Tess played, stopped, and rewound her well-worn video, editing the scenes as she guessed at Gavin's preferences. They had never discussed their own wedding; their future togetherness just seemed a fait accompli, referenced off-handedly like an indeterminate, but anticipated inheritance. As yet however, the wedding itself, and its inherent commitment, was free-floating in Tess's imagination. A big red balloon that was bumping along the ceiling, just out of reach.

Throughout Allie's ceremony, Tess—up on the altar with the other brides-maids—could not keep her eyes or her mind from wandering down into the pews, down to Gavin, who was sitting serenely in his navy suit, his legs spread apart a little, his hands clasped loosely between them. He looked comfortable, both in his suit and on the hard bench, but then, Gavin would be comfortable wearing boxers in a blizzard. His blond hair was freshly cut, and it lay so straight the scissor marks were still sharply etched in the boyish style. Her eyes swept over the deep cleft in his chin—an exclamation point on his sexiness—and she longed to run her finger over the baby-smooth dip and on up to his mouth. Even in church, where he was restrained from breaking into his wildly enthusi-astic grin, his mouth was prepped for it, turned up at the corners in an amused smirk, chomping at the bit for the tiniest of life's tickles to swing it into full gear.

She beamed at Gavin as he handed her a glass of wine. "After three days on the beach, it's weird to be back in the thick of it, isn't it?"

"I'm all for making a run for it. We could be back on the beach in a couple of hours." He raised his eyebrows.

She swatted him.

"I'm joking," he said. "I promise to have fun."

Tess had surprised Gavin, and herself, by planning a three-day getaway on Cape Cod before the wedding. The lazy days at the ocean and the sensuous nights in their canopy bed had been nirvana, and she had con-sidered, just for a second, skipping Allie's wedding so that they could hole up a little longer.

For three days, Gavin had been sweet, loving, and best of all, attentive. When they were back in the city, there were so many distractions; a quarter of Gavin's energy was focused on her, while the rest of him was buzzing over her head, puzzling something left back at his desk, plotting tomorrow's big move, or scanning the bar for friends, co-workers, new connections. In New York he was permanently plugged into the supercharged atmosphere, and until he was out from under its fluorescence, he couldn't turn himself off. It wasn't a big deal, that was Gavin. But once in a while, it was nice to have all that wattage shining on her.

"Gavin?" A woman in a short red dress grabbed his arm.

"Beth, wow." Gavin leaned over with flourish and kissed her on the cheek. "Tess, have you met Beth? We worked together when I first moved to New York."

"Hi." Tess had never met this brunette, she would have remembered. She laced her fingers through Gavin's.

"You look great," Gavin said to Beth. "How do you know Allie?" His gaze was on Beth's face; Tess was hyper-aware of the red silk body underneath.

"I don't. I went to Princeton with Dana."

"I forgot you went to Princeton." He grinned. "So we're on different sides of the aisle."

Tess heard the unspoken *now* loud and clear.

"You're friends with the bride?" Beth asked Gavin.

Is my bridesmaid dress invisible? Tess ran her free hand through her just-lightened blond hair. "We went to college with Allie," she answered for Gavin. "But Gavin didn't really know her until we started going out, what, three years ago?" She looked at Gavin. "And then you know how that goes, he's got a whole pack of insta-friends."

Gavin dropped Tess's hand, looped his arm around her shoulders and squeezed her in. "I love your friends. Well okay, most of them."

Beth's dark eyebrows shot up, and she looked more closely at Tess. Tess was used to this astonishment, had expected it actually. She knew that people viewed her differently when they discovered she was Gavin's girlfriend; like a paintbrush, this piece of information instantly touched her up—made her brighter, more colorful—and increased her general currency.

Tess leaned into Gavin's squeeze. "Yeah, that's why our plans always revolve around yours." That was true; the sarcasm was for show. Tess was content to leave the planning of their social world to Gavin. *That way, if the experience de jour isn't high on the scale of Exceptional Times, at least I don't feel responsible.* And her breezy "whatever" in the face of the options was for the most part how she felt. Just being with Gavin was enough. She never knew what stories they would have to tell the next morning. And there always were stories; Gavin incited outlandish merriment by the sheer power of his fireworks-smile, his "I'm game for anything" restlessness.

Beth regained her composure; she put her hand on her hip. "Tell me you're not still hanging out at Wolfe's."

"Guilty. But sadly, it hasn't been the same since you left."

Beth laughed. "I'm sure. Have you been there, Tess?"

Tess mustered up a smile. "Not in a while." Evidently though, she needed to get down there more often. Long ago she'd decided to give Gavin a lot of space in their relationship; she had a sixth sense that if she remained glued to his side, demanding his all, she could be left with nothing.

"You're smart. It's such a hole in the wall," Beth said.

"Hey, the best of the best come to pray at that wooden altar," Gavin said.

"To spit and drool maybe," Beth said. Her red lips spoke to Tess, "I guess you don't work downtown."

"Midtown. I work in PR."

"She's an account exec," Gavin said.

"Really. What account?"

"Mostly Hanes," Tess said.

Gavin grinned. "Boxers-versus-briefs has a whole new meaning in our house."

Tess smiled and rolled her eyes; this was one of his favorite lines.

"Hey, I'm not complaining! Either way, I'm set for life." Gavin said.

Comments like these gave Tess the fresh thrill of being chosen, every time. And Gavin was not stingy with them; they often peppered his conversations. As Beth drifted away into the crowd (Tess hoped their implied commitment had sent her running), she caressed several of his comments from their weekend together, stuffed in her pocket like polished charms.

She could clearly envision the cloudless sky, the sparkling ocean, and a gaggle of kids tumbling by with their sandy buckets. Gavin, eyes closed to the searing sun, had said, "How many kids do you think we'll have?"

"Maybe three? What do you think?"

"Three. Or four maybe." He slid his foot over to tickle hers. "Four could be great—two boys, two girls. Or three boys and one girl."

"Okay four. If you promise to be pregnant with at least one of them." She felt as if she could just reach out and touch this colorful future, that if she just blinked her eyes, those kids on the beach might be theirs.

In her mind, Tess fast-forwarded to window-shopping a few hours later. Gavin's arm was draped around her shoulders as they passed a small art gallery, and one piece in the window drew their eye and consideration. It was a photograph of a yellow kayak bobbing in the steel gray ocean; a storm on the horizon had canvassed the sky above it in various shades of blue-gray.

"Let's buy it; our first piece of non-poster art. We can hang it in our first house, and then re-hang it after we make millions and move into a mansion." He squeezed her hand.

The promise was warm and definite, and Tess had returned the squeeze as happiness ballooned inside her.

The next night, over a leisurely Italian dinner and bottle of wine, Gavin had said with a sigh, "This has been so great, promise me we'll always spend our summer vacations here."

"I promise," she said as if her hand was resting on a bible.

Moments like these were caught on film in her mind, and she clung to them whenever the subject of weddings cropped up and Gavin recited his mantra (which he was saying right now at Allie's reception, perhaps as an addendum to his earlier we're-set-for-life comment), "We're too young to get married."

"I agree." Tess nodded her head for emphasis.

"I mean, what's the hurry?" Gavin said with a low voice, out of respect for the just-married couple. "What are Dana and Allie thinking? They're only two years out of college, why not enjoy being single a little longer?"

"But they weren't single." *And neither are we.*

"You know what I mean though, right?"

"I guess. But they weren't single." Tess let that hang for a moment; when he didn't answer, she scanned the room. "Allie looks beautiful, doesn't she?"

Gavin considered Allie. "She does." He focused back on Tess. "So do you." He kissed her cheek. Out of the corner of his eye, he spied Zoe.

———

A few minutes later, Megan wandered over, giving Gavin an opportunity to sneak a better look at Zoe, who was across the bar flirting with her date for the wedding, Bob Falco. Gavin frowned. He knew Bob from work and had introduced him to Zoe. Big mistake. Gavin was not a fan; Bob made a lot of money and threw it around loudly. Everyone within shouting distance knew how much he spent whenever he opened up his fat wallet.

Gavin had to admit, he couldn't stand to see anyone with Zoe. But then again, he usually didn't have to. These days, whenever they were in the same place, it was either alone in her apartment or out at a bar where the crowded drinks-after-work were just an understood prelude to their later fusion. Ever since their relationship had rekindled two years ago, both of them had continued to toss paper on it. They now fired each other up a few times a month.

They both worked down on Wall Street, which was a world unto itself; a very separate fishbowl from midtown Manhattan in both its location and its singularly focused energy. It would be unusual to wander downtown without a specific purpose, especially as "wandering" would entail a long taxi or subway ride. Typically the only people at the local happy hours were people who worked nearby, making it just a matter of time before he and Zoe ran into each other. From there, the ice that they had already broken continued to melt.

In the beginning, Gavin worried that Tess would somehow discover his extracurricular activity. He soon realized however, that he could engineer the risk to almost zero. Tess never popped downtown, and he and Zoe always wound up in Zoe's apartment, locking away any clues Tess could stumble across. Of course there was always the possibility someone could catch him slinking out of Zoe's late at night, but the odds were slim, so slim that he no longer let himself worry about it.

He had synced it so well that although they were all in the same group of friends, Gavin could count on one hand the times that he, Tess, and Zoe had been in the same room together since the girls' graduation, and at each of those events, a quick whisper to Tess about his desire for the two of them to be alone, and any seeds of panic blew away in the wake of their rapid exit.

Today however, at this crowded reception, Gavin was claustrophobic. There was no logical excuse he could cook up to escort Tess out, and for the first time in two years, a needle of terror lodged into his supreme invincibility. He had no reason to believe that Zoe wanted to upset the delicate balance they'd created; however, it was dangerous to have her loose in the same enclosure with him and Tess. He had to ensure that Zoe didn't smell blood, because like a shark cruising a swimming area, even if she didn't outright attack, a calculated brush of her razor sharp wit could be bloody.

He took a swig of his beer to quench his now desert-dry throat and angled himself so that he was facing Tess, but had Zoe dead-on in his sight over her head. He tried to focus on what Tess was saying to Megan, but Zoe was too compelling. She was the most beautiful girl in the room. He wondered if Bob was feeling the same desire to yank off that bridesmaid dress.

Zoe slowly turned from Bob and shot Gavin a smile; how her smiles always seemed wickedly sexy was beyond him, but they did. He swallowed hard and lifted his glass to his lips again.

"Gavin?"

He moved his eyes slightly and tried to refocus on Tess's freckled, ivory-soap face.

"Do you want anything to eat? Cheese and crackers?" she asked for the second time.

Megan shot Gavin a curious look.

"No thanks." *Pull yourself together.* He smiled at Megan.

As Megan and Tess drifted off in search of hors d'oeuvres, he ambled back to the bar to refill his now-empty beer. *What the hell am I doing?* He shook his head. He did not want to lose Tess. *But Zoe knows I love Tess. And no one's getting hurt.*

He visibly relaxed, accepting a beer from the bartender and leaning back against the bar to survey the reception.

Zoe, never one to miss an opportunity, sidled up next to him. "Hey handsome."

He grinned at her. Her perfume wafted up to him and provided him with a quick Polaroid of the two of them entwined together. She was wearing a delicate gold necklace that hung down into her... Gavin forced himself to look back up. He longed to touch her, but even after checking to ensure that Tess was still across the room, he put his hands in his pockets.

Zoe locked her blue eyes on his. "It's always so good to see you." Her eyes sparkled; her lipstick glistened. "You know I always wish I could see more of you," she said in a voice for the other people at the bar, while she slid her gaze from his shoulders down.

"My sentiments exactly." He gave her a look that undressed her with his eyes. "It's important to stay on top of each other," he cleared his throat, "of all that's going on with each other."

Zoe laughed. "Yes it is. We shouldn't let so much time go by, we might miss something interesting."

"Oh, I don't think so. We're both pretty good at laying it all bare."

Zoe wrapped both hands around her glass.

Gavin leaned in so that their shoulders touched. "I have missed you, Zo. It's just hard to find the time… "

He felt her body stiffen.

Zoe took a step sideways, out of brush-by range. "So Allie and Dana finally did it."

Gavin heard the change in her tone, from melodic to snipped. He took his hands out of his pockets and picked up his beer.

"Can you imagine the boredom?" Zoe said. "I mean, I love Dana, but one person forever and ever? I don't know, I'm not sure that's me."

"Really?" He smiled disarmingly. "Come on. You'll find yourself settled down one of these days. Well, maybe not settled down; I can't quite see you barefoot with an apron." Gavin glanced at Tess laughing with her friends across the room. "And I guess I will too," he said thoughtfully.

He knew he had said the wrong thing, as honest as it was. He fired up his grin. "Not right now, mind you. We're all way too young. In fact, Ms. Chapin, it's too bad you have a date."

"Your loss." She moved her hand behind him and pinched his butt hard—too hard—and then strode back to Bob.

The rest of the night Gavin watched Zoe's fireworks; they were hard to miss. She was the life of the party—flamboyant, flirty—matching Bob drink for drink, line for line, loud laugh for laugh. And it seemed she was always in Gavin's line of vision.

Jealousy surged through his veins, and its toxic fever thrust him into overdrive with Tess. He recycled all of his pent up frustration about Zoe into passion for Tess, and was attentive to her with an amorous wildfire that he could tell from her face was catapulting her over the moon. Part of him loved seeing her so happy; part of him thought, *oh man, I'm such a jerk.*

He couldn't resist one more glance at Zoe.

————

And Allie and Dana, dancing and laughing and soaring on an incredible romantic high through well-wishers and great expectations, were oblivious to the powerful undertow of jumbled emotion surging through the country club dining room. Any cold feet from earlier in the day had been warmed and transformed by the intensity of their feelings for each other and by the dazzle of their new commitment.

Their grins were so wide that they almost connected in the small space between them as clung to each other and swayed to the music.

"I love you so much," Allie whispered into Dana's ear.

He looked into her green eyes; his heart was bursting. "I love you too."

CHAPTER 7

JOURNAL ENTRY #7
December 12, 2000

History evaporated with my mom's desertion. She swept all of the Mussoni annals and anecdotes into a clean, white sheet, tied it into a bundle and attached it to her hobo stick on her way out the door. Afterwards, there were no tender moments on my dad's lap, listening to his love for me swirl through his hushed tales of when I was born, when I took my first step, when I uttered my first word. Come to think of it, I don't even know what my first word was. Probably Mama.

So it's not surprising that I don't remember much about my childhood. And of the memories I do have, it's hard to know which are truly my own, and which are implanted from scraps of dog-eared stories and pored-over photographs. Mental archives are like folded notes in pockets—we touch them accidentally, handle them deliberately, and sometimes even send them through the laundry. Each thumb-through modifies them somehow, so that eventually, the facts become irrelevant. Even at base, memories, like conversations, aren't exclusively factual. They're infused with emotion, colored with nonverbal nuance, and filtered through our unique perspective, and it is that subjective core that lingers once the who-said-what-to-whom fades away.

Mostly what I remember from when I was young are boxed-up feelings and blurry scenes rather than sharp, zoom-lens details. Except of course for the day, the hour, that my mom left. I remember terror once I discovered she wasn't in the house, and remember being alone with Kevin, which was scary too. He was two-and-a-half; I was four. We waited, holding hands, cuddled together on the couch with our little legs sticking straight out in front of us because the bend in our knees was nowhere near the edge of the cushion. I remember thinking we were in trouble because Mommy had left, thinking she must have left because we were too noisy; which was kind of funny because we were never too loud. Our house was blanketed in a tiptoe hush, as if there was a billboard on our mantel with a black and white cartoon lady holding a finger to her bright red lips. Before my mother left this signage was insinuated; after she left it was just redundant.

I remember that Paul was playing next door at his friend Jim Dayton's, and when it was dinnertime, Mrs. Dayton had walked Paul home. They arrived to find Kevin and I still huddled together on that blue paisley couch. Mrs. Dayton, who I imagine was appalled, gathered us up and shepherded us over to her house for dinner. That was the beginning of many afternoons over at the Daytons', which then became many afternoons of different Mrs. Dayton-like women who briefly passed through our lives only to continue on with their own.

But what I remember most from that day were the mascara-stained tears snaking down my mother's cheeks, as if her sorrow had been slow-dripping forever and had finally reached overflow.

That moment in time, that haunting still life of black tears and anguish burrowed deep into my psyche, and it crouched there, smoldering—crouches there still—flaring up and scorching me whenever the world around me rests. I've studied that image until it's become tattered and pulpy with my desperation, certain that it would give me a clue as to why she left, where she'd gone. But I never found answers in her sorrow; I only found the unbearable sorrow itself.

In the end, the only answer that made any sense at all came not from her face, but from the corner of that moment, from the center of our lives, from the most important prop in any snapshot of our family. The answer teased and twinkled from the TV in poreless sensuality: *there's something else out there.*

And she wanted it. Our life, our family, this family that she created, could not compete with the idea that there was *more*, a promise that curled its finger and beckoned us every day from the magnetic box in our living room. We weren't living in black and white mind you; we had a good life—tossing bread to the ducks on weekdays, building stick forts in the yard on weekends.

But *better* was captivating.

My conclusion was never disputed, never challenged by my father. After initially telling us that Eva was visiting friends and that she'd be back, he never spoke about her again. Maybe he thought that it would stir us up, make us too sad; maybe he thought that if he didn't bring it up it would just go away. As an adult I find this inconceivable, irresponsible, and even cruel. But to be fair, maybe that's what he believed, or at least what he hoped. At some point though, it became clear that she wasn't coming back. I don't know whether this was weeks, months, or even a year later, but whenever it was, it had been long enough that it wasn't a lightbulb clicking on with a news flash. That awful knowledge had been infecting us for some time, flatlining our smiles, weighting our feet at the playground, keeping our thumbs in our mouths long past appropriate. After a while it just became normal, and verbally at least, it was as if she'd never been there.

Did she leave a note? Did she write in the months or even years after? Did she ever call to find out if we were healthy, happy? I've never been able to summon the courage to ask these questions of my dad, to further traumatize him. That's the impression he gave, as if any mention of her would open old wounds and cause him to bleed out.

It's remarkable how a tragedy can alter not only someone's state of mind, but also their general appearance. In pictures of my father before Eva left, what's most notable is his comfort, his easy smile; he's ripe, puffed up. In the pictures of him after, he's puckered, shriveled, a peach left on the counter too long. His strong Italian nose and thick eyebrows jut out from his hollowed face, and his shoulders are hunched—I think of him shuffling along, although I don't know if he really shuffled. He just radiated defeat, like George Bailey when The Building and Loan collapsed.

I own one black-and-white picture of my mother. She was captured as she was turning towards the camera, as if someone had just called her name and pressed the shutter, afraid of missing the shot, of missing her. The pivot, or perhaps the breeze, has swirled her long, dark hair around her pretty face, her full lips. But it is her eyes that are the picture. They are bottomless. You can see all the way into her soul, all the way down into naked sorrow. It is painful to look at, yet I can't look away. It feels like walking in on someone crying in a corner and you don't know whether to tiptoe out or move closer.

But maybe I'm the one who's injecting the sorrow into the black and white. Maybe the way I see my parents is the way I want to see them, the way I need to see them. It's my version of the truth, and I use my pictures and memories as evidence of that truth. Photographs are two-dimensional; they can't describe the complexity of the person or situation behind the image, and so they beg imaginative context. Photographs—and life—are a Rorschach test; everyone sees different meanings hidden among its simple lines.

We are the photographers of our own history. In the moment, as we experience something, we are manipulating the shot and the characters with angle, exposure, and shutter speed. The person next to us is doing the same, with their own lens.

So is there ever just one truth? Or is it just the truth according to me, according to you, according to that person over there? Do we each just hold our own piece of the whole picture, our own piece of the truth?

MARCH 1993
Boston, MA

The kitchenette was a disaster. Dirty pots and bowls were teetering on the counters like a city of Jenga towers; topless jars from cupboards and a big mixer with chocolate batter dripping from its silver blade fought over any remaining counter space. Allie was singing and dancing her way through a cake recipe while the radio tried to keep her in tune and on tempo. Dana had called earlier to say he had news. She wondered if it was a job offer, and she hoped, and tried not to hope, for New York.

She slid the cake in the oven, and closed the heavy oven door with her hip, in time with the song's last drumbeat. She didn't hear Dana come into the apartment—the music was too loud—but the air shifted around her, and it wasn't into low grade where it often slipped when Dana dragged in from his day, it sprang right into fifth gear. She wiped her hands on her favorite jeans and pranced out to meet him. "Hi honey!" She greeted him with the same ebullience every night, dropping whatever she was doing to wrap her arms around him.

He always kissed her, a good kiss. His lips wore the weather from the streets of Boston; tonight they were cool, wet with rain. The pressure of his kiss usually expressed gratitude; it made her feel that her smiling energy at the door each day was important. Tonight though, there was playfulness on his lips, the quiver of a surprise.

"How was your day?" he said. He was holding something behind his back.

Usually her first words would unroll slowly and reach out for him as he trudged down the hall and into the closet-sized room they had made into his office. She would wait in the hall and listen to his heavy books thump down onto his desk while her words, the answer to his question about her day, hovered briefly in the space between them and then quietly wafted to the floor like bits of ash. Once in a while, he reappeared and they would open a bottle of wine, but most often he would be lost to her for the night, absorbed in text, his face a frown of concentration, his finger tucked under a page. She would swallow down the rest of her words and slip silently into the kitchen for yogurt, a box of Grape Nuts, and the clicker.

Tonight however, he stood and waited for the whole answer.

She smiled and tucked a stray strand of hair back into her ponytail. "I was busy."

He wiped some flour off of her face and glanced into the war zone behind her. "I can see that. What's cooking?"

"Chicken with lemons and olives, but screw the meal. The news, what's the news?" Allie danced around him and tried to peek at what he was holding.

"Not so fast." His smile stretched past his ears; his excitement was static electricity all around him. "This is a big moment. And it definitely calls for..." He pulled a green bottle from behind his back.

"Champagne!" She clapped her hands.

Dana started towards the kitchen. "I'm going in for a dishtowel. If I don't reappear in five minutes, call 911."

Allie laughed; Dana's mood made her want to swing from the light fixtures. "I can find it." She smiled at the exaggerated doubt on his face and pulled a towel out of a drawer. "See, there's a method to my madness."

"Ah, so that's it." Dana draped the towel over the bottle and popped the cork. He poured the glittering liquid into two juice glasses. "Well, there's no method to mine, and I'm too lazy to find champagne glasses." He handed her a short glass.

"You could pour it straight into my mouth for all I care." Allie trailed him into the living room. "So, tell me."

Dana sat down on the couch with a sigh. "I'm sorry to have to tell you this, after all the painting and curtaining you've done to this apartment. But we're going to have to move." He paused for effect. "To New York."

Allie squealed and jumped into Dana's lap. "Crabtree Taylor Drake?"

Dana confirmed with a proud nod.

"Congratulations." She hugged him.

"Thanks." He raised his glass to her and then paused before taking a sip. "And really, thanks for this year. You've put your life on hold for me for nine months. I know it hasn't been easy."

She slid off his lap and clicked her glass against his. "Anytime."

She had been duly warned; before they were married Dana had tried to prepare her for his grueling last year in law school. "I've been lucky, I've been able to hide a major character flaw from you all these years," he had said to her a year ago over dinner.

She tilted her head.

"It actually hasn't been a flaw yet, but I've never been married before, and I don't think Neal really cared." He smiled. "I get lost in my work. I mean, truly lost. You know how some people can breeze through homework by doing the bare minimum? I'm not one of those people. You know me, I can't do something half-assed, I'm compulsive that way. It's all or nothing. Which is a good thing; if I do well this year, it'll be great for us." He leaned forward. "And I promise to try to skim a chapter or scribble an essay, but I have a feeling I'll sneak back in the middle of the night to redo it."

She had shrugged his worry away. "I've always wondered why you and Megan didn't fall for each other."

"That's the other thing I wanted to talk to you about."

She threw her napkin at him.

She had never complained; she was proud of that. She didn't want to be a burden, and he wouldn't know what to do about it anyway. She'd been lonely before, she could handle it. She didn't complain to her friends either, who were all having the time of their lives in Manhattan. The young marriage, the move to a new city, this was the life she chose; bemoaning it felt like admitting to a fatal error in judgment. Allie was afraid she'd hear a nasal "I told you so" if she started to tell it like it was. So she rarely did.

Instead she had tried her best to keep busy, silencing her loneliness and wriggling doubts with a steely, *I am not my mother*, and throwing herself into a project, any project. The apartment was her first, and with the music and daytime TV for company, she repainted and re-outfitted their small living space in outrageous colors that made Dana raise his eyebrows. When there wasn't a corner left to enhance, she traded in her *House Beautiful* magazines for *Gourmet* and cooked her way through roast duck and home-made sourdough bread and five-layered flourless cakes. Then she joined a gym (to work off all the food); strolled her way around all the side streets of Boston; thought about training for the Boston Marathon; researched getting a puppy (but settled on Harold the fish); and although Dana's trust fund made it so that she didn't have to work, found a job at a funky clothing boutique—Anastasia's—where she befriended the owner and namesake of the shop, and spent her earnings on clothes.

"So now it's your turn." Dana settled back into the couch cushions with his champagne and propped his feet up on the coffee table. "What do you want to talk about, think about? Your job? Where to live? When to call the girls?" He smiled.

"A job. That's a buzz kill." She held up her hand. "Not for you I know." She sighed. "I don't know. I just can't seem to settle on anything. Almost everything sounds interesting, exciting even, like, I can do that! And then when I need to commit, I get twitchy." She half-smiled. "So instead I throw a party."

They had hosted a few wild parties over the year for Dana's law school friends. Allie always insisted on theme——a black tie New Year's Eve, a Valentine's red cocktail competition. Her favorite had been the Halloween party. They'd turned the apartment into a haunted house, and guests had gone all out with masks, makeup, and colorful costumes. Allie had dressed as a flapper in a dazzling silver dress; Dana was a lifeguard.

In terms of a career however, Allie felt like the last person at the party, standing alone among the drooping crepe paper and half-empty plastic cups.

Dana peered into her eyes. "You'd be good at anything you put your mind to."

"But there isn't something that's pulling at me, that's wrapping its arms around me and saying *this*." Allie reached for her champagne glass. "Let's talk about where we're going to live."

"Okay. East side? West side?"

"Or the suburbs."

Dana's glass stopped moving halfway up to his lips, and he cocked his head. "The quiet suburbs doesn't sound like you."

"I know. I love the city," Allie said, "but I figure we'll be in there a ton anyway. I was thinking maybe a cute little house with a lot of potential, so that we can fix it up, make it ours."

Dana raised his glass the rest of the way up to his lips and sipped thoughtfully.

Allie bounced once on the couch with her growing excitement. "Wouldn't it be great to have a place all our own, something permanent?"

He smiled at her. "It would be great."

"Really? But it has to need work. Moving into a primped and perfect house wouldn't feel like us. Everything would be just an inch out of place, just a color shade off. Maybe not enough to change it, but enough so that it just wouldn't feel right. We'd be intruding on someone else's dream." Allie paused. "Or nightmare." She coiled the thick rope of her ponytail around her fist. "I wonder if whoever moved into my old house feels the emptiness seeping out of the walls?"

Dana put his glass down and wrapped his arm around her. "Maybe houses are like seashells. Maybe once a family moves out, they take their memories with them, leaving only the shell, rinsed out and waiting for someone new."

"Maybe. But I still want to wipe ours clean, tear down a few walls, put up new ones, paint."

"Okay, Martha Stewart. Just promise no orange this time."

Allie's eyes twinkled. "And what size should our shell be? I mean, how many of us sea creatures are going to be living in this shell?"

"Unless I don't know something," Dana moved back a bit to take a better look at Allie, "I guess two to start."

"Don't worry, one headline for today is enough. I was just thinking, wouldn't it be nice? Starting our family, having a baby?" Even as the words were coming out of her mouth, a part of her was thinking, *What?* This was not something she'd been consciously considering. But just now, in the arms of Dana's tenderness, the discussion, the idea, felt safe. And the minute the words floated between them, she sat up straight. *Yes. This is what I want.* And something that had always felt like quicksand was suddenly solid. A family, a baby.

Dana pulled her in close and whispered in her ear. "It would be nice."

She cuddled into him and he kissed her. *I can be a good mother; I want to be a good mother.*

"So, how many babies are we talking here?" Dana said.

"Most people start with one."

Dana laughed. "But then, more than one, right? But less than five. What do you think?"

"I'm actually more interested in *when* right now." She reached over and pulled at his belt.

He mock-eyeballed his watch while a smile teased at the edges of his lips. "Definitely not right now. I've got one last paper to write." He started to get up off the couch.

"Not so fast." Allie grinned, grabbing the back of his belt and pulling him down. "You'll just have to tell your professor you got waylaid."

"Waylaid, huh?" Dana started to kiss her neck, her lips as he eased her back on the couch. "That's a lot better than the dog ate my homework."

The tiny white house was so similar to the one in her daydreams that her mouth hung open as they drove up the potholed driveway. Allie tried to tune out the chatty realtor as she breathed in the details. Hunter-green shutters, a wide front porch, even a white picket fence. Granted much of the paint had peeled off, and the gate looked broken, but it was a white picket fence nonetheless, and it encircled a decent-size yard. Grass seed, weed killer... a list was already forming in her mind. She couldn't wait to get inside.

Dana smiled, then mouthed *stop smiling*. He tilted his head in the direction of the realtor.

But it was hard to lid her enthusiasm. Walking through the quaint two-bedroom cape only confirmed that this was it, a fact that seemed to be sending the realtor into overdrive. The upstairs was small, with one pink-tiled bathroom sandwiched in between the two flowery wallpapered bedrooms; Allie was already retiling and picking paint colors. But the four downstairs rooms and half-bath were all spacious, certainly big enough for the two of them and the small amount of Ikea furniture they owned. The tile was chipped in the old bathroom, and the kitchen was sagging and neglected. *Perfect.* The dream shimmered at her fingertips, something all her own, their own. Not just a house, but a home.

41 Juniper Lane. It was musical. She silently thanked the Sextons once again for the down payment; a most extravagant wedding present. She and Dana had squirreled it away until he finished law school and his job dictated where they would settle.

They called the realtor that night with a bid.

At the end of the summer, after all the paperwork had been signed, sealed, and delivered, the house was theirs—had been theirs for three days—and they were living among the ruins of partially unpacked boxes, arbitrary piles of their life, and mountains of balled-up packing paper. It didn't matter to Allie. Nothing could rock her euphoria, not even the sweltering August heat, the sweat dripping off her, or her sore and grimy knees. She wiped her forehead with the bottom of her shirt and surveyed her kitchen. It winked back at her. She had spent the better part of the day on all fours scrubbing the layers of dirt and grease from the floor and cabinets, and she was proud of the transformation. The worn linoleum now had a new luster; the cabinets, a brighter face.

The round wall clock, which right now was propped up on the counter, clicked loudly as its shiny black plastic hand moved to the top of the hour, prompting Allie up the stairs and into the shower. Dana would be home from his golf game soon, and she wanted to surprise him with a nice dinner. A thrill surged through her as she thought about tonight. She wanted it to be perfect.

After drying off with a thick, monogrammed towel—one of the many wedding presents that were now scattered around the house, finally in use—she stepped into a pair of linen shorts that hugged her perfectly and pulled on a white camisole and a white lace tee. She had thought long and hard about what to wear tonight, and had almost called Anastasia to send some ethereal white sundress from the store, but reconsidered when she pictured Anastasia's amusement at her desire to make this a Kodak moment. In the end, she decided to dig through her closet.

She wiped the foggy mirror with her hand—remembering too late that this huge smudge across the mirror was a pet peeve of Dana's—and left her hair to air dry. She brushed on a little mascara and blush and appraised herself, analyzing first her front, and then turning sideways to check out the view from the back. *It won't be too long before I have to say goodbye to these shorts.* She placed her hand on her flat stomach.

She came down the stairs slowly, her damp bare feet silent on the worn hardwood steps. Following the sounds from the kitchen—backdoor slamming, footsteps clomping, a box being pushed out of the way—she tiptoed up to her husband.

"Hey." He kissed her, did a double take. "You smell nice."

It was so refreshing to see his smile without the usual tension etched across his forehead, and she thought again that this summer reprieve in between school and the start of his first job had been healthy for both of them, and for their marriage. Dana had been so present, so unhurried. She felt safe, loved; even though she knew it was just the calm before the next storm of life.

"Unfortunately, I can't return the compliment. You're soaked with sweat!"

He grinned and grabbed for her again. "I was just thinking about you in the car. It got me all hot and bothered."

Allie stepped back out of his reach. "What can I say? I have that effect on people who've been playing golf for hours in the sun. It's either hot and bothered or sunstroke." She opened the fridge. "Go shower and I'll bring you a beer."

"Such service. Are we going somewhere? You look so nice. I was expecting to come home and find you dressed as a dusty cardboard box."

"Well, I too, was hot and bothered." She handed him a Heineken. "I just thought we'd clear a path through all this stuff and have a nice dinner together. You know, relish suburbia, celebrate our new kitchen table and chairs."

"Just give me a few minutes," he said over his shoulder as he charged up to the shower.

"How was your game?" Allie called up the stairs after him.

"*My* game sucked. But *the* game was fun. It was good to see those guys." He poked his head back over the railing. "They say hi, by the way."

When Dana came back down a few minutes later, Allie was arranging brie and crackers on a colorful ceramic cheese plate with a matching knife. "Maybe we should fix John up with Megan."

"I think," Dana said grabbing a cracker, "that you should stop worrying about Megan so much."

"It's my job." She did worry about Megan, although she had never told Dana the real reason why. She had wanted to, many times, because it felt strange to keep something like Megan's rape from him. But she didn't think that Dana needed to know all of her friends' secrets. And she had promised Megan she wouldn't tell.

Dana looked up. "Hey, it wasn't an accusation. I just think that Megan will find someone in her own time. Let fate take its course."

Allie raised her eyebrows at his use of "fate."

Dana laughed. "I believe when it helps my case."

"You can't be a fair-weather believer."

"I'm a lawyer."

She giggled. "I almost forgot. Okay, so what's your take on our getting together? Fate or accident?"

"Neither. I tripped you." Dana grabbed another cracker. "It was just good common sense."

"Maybe all this talk about fate is just a cover for the fact that you don't want to go on a double date."

"See? When it helps my case. And anyway, I thought that was in my contract at the wedding—no more dating, double or not."

"You misread the fine print. It is now our job to fix up all of our friends, so that they too can enjoy marital bliss, or at the very least, coupledom."

"Ah. I did miss that fine print. We'd better get to work then, we've got a lot of friends to fix up." Dana pushed a box out of the way and fell back onto the couch. The corners of his lips flirted with a smile. "Let's start with Sean. Which one of your friends gets the privilege?"

Allie threw her hands up in exaggerated exasperation; she couldn't stand Sean. "You win. No matchmaking."

She sank down on the couch next to him and draped one leg over his. They chatted away about nothing and everything, and when they finished the cheese and crackers, Dana lit the grill and they enjoyed a simple dinner of grilled steak, potato salad, and fresh corn on the cob. Allie had set the table with as many wedding presents as she could—embroidered napkins, fine china, white tapered candles in crystal candlesticks—answering Dana's "Who's coming to dinner?" with, "We may as well use them, all the boxes were out." Afterwards, they lingered in the flickering candlelight, comfortably full, comfortably quiet.

Finally, Dana pushed back his chair. "Should we clean all this up and watch TV?"

Allie cleared her throat. She had been waiting all night for the perfect moment, the perfect opening in their conversation to tell Dana her news. But there had been no ideal segue, no one-liner to give her a jumping off point. She was just going to have to dive in without it. "Dana."

He leaned forward, covering the gap between his pushed back chair and the table with his torso, and looked at her expectantly.

Allie smiled. "I'm pregnant." She paused. "We're going to have a baby." She held her breath.

His eyes widened in the soft, shadowy light, and the happiness illuminated there said it all.

———

The next day in Manhattan, Zoe, who had not shopped for an ethereal white dress in which to pee on a stick, was digesting her own news.

"Holy shit," she said out loud to her reflection in the bathroom mirror. Her sharp blue eyes glared back; what the mirror didn't show was the panic underneath the anger. A thin white stick with two distinct pink lines quivered on the counter next to her. She leaned over the sink as the room somersaulted around her.

It was Bob's baby, she knew from the timing. But as she had waited for her period, with her mood lurching from denial to stomach-churning angst—one week, two weeks of agonizing before she had finally bought the home pregnancy test—she had given birth to a plan that she thought might just work, and might just give this pregnancy a silver lining. *If that was even possible.*

She and Bob had now been dating for over a year. He was entertaining, although sometimes too loud and obnoxious, but she liked him well enough, and especially liked his social and drug connections. She didn't have to love him; she had Gavin to provide the passion in her life. She still believed that one day Gavin would tire of bouncing back and forth between her and Tess and come to his senses about where he belonged. She and Gavin had been together for seven years for Chrissake; although yes, in Tess-limbo for four. But he clearly couldn't live without her, and when they were together, she never saw him sweat an ounce of remorse about Tess.

When Zoe was alone, it was easy to believe that Gavin loved her, that Tess was the interloper. She never let herself dwell on the few times that she had made up her mind to confront him, had marched in to meet him full of bravado, fists balled tight, prepared to give him an ultimatum—fish or cut bait Goddamnit!—and Gavin would flash a smile that lit him up, literally, like she had flipped a switch by just walking in. It always loosened her fists, and melted her heart, her resolve, and the demand that she had been about the pound on the bar.

No, she didn't want to think about those times. Right now she preferred to think that maybe he just needed a little nudge, an excuse to dump Tess and marry her. A baby could be the shove she'd been looking for.

She wasn't exactly excited at the idea, even a baby with Gavin was a baby she wasn't thrilled about having, and they might decide—together—not to have it. But even that decision would cement them to each other, create a lifelong bond. She threw the little white stick with the big news in the garbage, and went into her tiny kitchen to fix herself another vodka tonic and plot the conversation with Gavin.

————

He was waiting at the bar, everything she wanted in a dark gray double-breasted suit and red tie. His smile embraced her as she approached. Her heart soared and she couldn't help but grin, as hard as she tried to clamp it down. She realized how much she'd missed him; even though they'd talked on the phone once or twice, it had been three weeks since they'd been together.

He was tanned from his Labor Day weekend—probably some Hamptons getaway with Tess. The sharp teeth of jealousy bit her so fiercely that she moaned, and her hand instinctively rushed to her mouth, a physical barrier against any further sound effects. But muzzle or not, her confidence was punctured, and the gush of potential disaster turned her legs to jelly. She slowed and willed herself to forget the plan for right now; she couldn't have the conversation here anyway and didn't want her nerves to ruin their reunion. She concentrated on being jaunty and slid onto the barstool next to him.

"Hi." She grinned again. As always, she had to straightjacket herself from hugging, kissing, touching him somehow along with the verbal salutation. They were in public, and she knew that when they met in a crowd, PDA was strictly off limits.

He leaned over and kissed her on the lips and then laughed at her surprise. "I scoped the place out. It's clean."

"If that's the case, get naked."

He got off the barstool and reached for his belt buckle.

She giggled. "Okay, we all know you've got balls. We don't need to see them."

He got back on his stool. "Oh all right. Maybe later."

"Only if you're good." Zoe smiled.

The bartender appeared with an Absolut and tonic; Gavin must have ordered it for her as he saw her come in.

She picked up her drink and tipped it in a silent toast. "Just what the doctor ordered." She took a long, deliberate drink. *Although the doctor's probably not an OB-GYN.*

"So how are you? You look amazing as usual," Gavin said.

"I'm good and thank you." She was wearing a short black skirt and a light blue silk shirt, the exact color of her eyes. Her long tan legs were bare and punctuated by a pair of high black heels. "How about you? You look like you've been away." She regretted that; she didn't really want to hear about his weekend.

"I took an extra day last week and made it a four-day weekend. Went out to Amagansett and hung at the beach. How about you, did you get away?"

He never mentioned Tess directly, in fact he even omitted the "we" in his sentences. Zoe had always believed it was because Tess was immaterial, but right now, on this barstool, she wasn't so sure.

She, on the other hand, had no qualms mentioning Bob, and in fact relished dropping his name to remind Gavin that she wasn't sitting around pining for him. "Bob had tickets to the Open on Saturday—center court—and so we spent the day there. Then on Sunday we headed out to my stepfather's at the beach for the rest of the weekend."

Gavin sighed. "I love that house." He rattled the ice in his glass, then took a big sip. "Was Bob impressed?"

"Bob's never impressed."

Gavin snorted. "How's work?"

"Great, busy." She twirled the diamond in her ear. "You remember Charlie, right?"

"The one with the triplets?"

Zoe nodded. "He just announced he's quitting, apparently moving to be closer to his wife's family. Everyone at work is abuzz about who's going to step up the ladder."

"Are you a contender?"

Zoe shrugged.

"Where's he going?"

"Ohio." Zoe crinkled her nose. "Can you imagine? Leaving Manhattan and moving to Ohio?" She shook her head. "I don't get it. He was so adamant that the babies weren't going to change his life at all. Now he's mumbling about his hours and balance... " She took a slug of her drink. "Just hire some help!"

"Man, triplets. My sister has one and he's a little homewrecker." Gavin smiled. "Cute though."

"Charlie's wife must have him on a tight leash." Zoe's nostrils flared, she pressed her lips together.

Gavin chuckled. "It's called compromise, Zo."

"Never heard of it." She grinned. "And I'm taking a shot in the dark here, that neither have you."

Gavin laughed. "Not my strong suit." He paused. "Although I am slowly getting a tutorial."

What the hell was that supposed to mean? "Really?" She raised her eyebrows. "Tess is getting a backbone?"

Gavin cocked his head and opened his mouth, then closed it. He shrugged. "You could say that." He finished his drink in one smooth gulp. "Another?" He aimed his smile at her.

Zoe nodded, hoping that the noise in the bar had drowned out the bitter tinge she'd tasted in her voice. *Get a grip.* Her heart was galloping crazily, The Conversation in the saddle, kicking her with spurs and stomping out her earlier supreme confidence. She gulped her drink, praying the burn of the vodka would help her relax. She had a fleeting thought that she shouldn't drink this much, but the baby wasn't real to her yet, not until she and Gavin had decided its fate together. And besides, she needed the vodka right now.

"Absolutely." She put her empty glass on the bar. "So, how's work for you?"

The edges of their conversation grew warm and fuzzy as the bartender refilled them several times; the tingling, not-so-accidental brushes of skin became bolder—shoulders leaned into each other for exclamation, hands grabbed thighs to emphasize a talking point. Just under the ecstasy of flirtation however, the pregnancy remained an irritating alarm, screeching whenever Zoe swam in Gavin's eyes, so that by the time they stumbled into the back of a dirty yellow taxi, the siren in Zoe's head was so loud she couldn't focus on Gavin's crushing kisses. She clung and clawed in response to his vehemence, but it was panic and fear that drove her lips, her hands, the press of her body.

They stumbled into Zoe's apartment and onto the couch, shirts launched overhead, buttons fumbled breathlessly. Even though they were shuddering with anticipation, they stripped everything off, right down to Gavin's dark socks. Wholly naked; this was the heart of their relationship, a place where they knew each other intimately—their smell, the smooth contours of their muscles, the tender spots that elicited primal groans. A place where they could allow themselves to be vulnerable where they couldn't, or wouldn't, emotionally. It was here that they truly savored each other; and despite the fact that they'd been entwined a thousand times, there was nothing rote in their actions. Every feather-light stroke, every almost-painful bite, every thrust of their tongue was, even after all these years, an exploration.

Afterward, they lay lax-limbed on the overstuffed cushions of the couch; Zoe's cheek nestled into Gavin's blond-haired chest, his arm hung around her. These few hushed, satiated moments when their breathing slowed and the thump-thump of Gavin's heart flowed into her veins were religious for her. Usually. Today however, the warm, skin-on-skin felt blasphemous. She knew the words on her tongue were serrated, no matter how smooth the delivery, how shiny the wish. She had a flash of the wet blood she was about to draw, as if she had turned her head and taken a jagged bite out of his chest.

Horror clogged her throat. She levitated off his chest.

"Gavin," she choked out, forcing herself to concentrate on the plan. The Plan. She sat up and shoved her arms into his oxford shirt. Gavin's body expanded into the place she had occupied, his muscular legs stretched out over her thighs. She felt trapped, and wasn't sure whether that was good or bad.

"Gavin."

"Mmmm?" His eyes were closed; he was unconcerned. *Just wait,* she thought apologetically.

"Gavin, I love you." *WHAT?* Zoe's eyes widened and she yanked the shirt tightly across her chest. *Where the hell did that come from? Oh my God, I didn't mean to say THAT.*

"What?" Gavin opened his eyes. He tried to sit up.

"I'm pregnant," she blurted out to cover-up her last statement.

Gavin's arms and legs were suddenly spastic; he struggled to get into a sitting position. "What?" He cast wildly around for his boxers. "What?"

Gaining confidence by the fact that she had no choice but to keep going, she said in a steadier voice, "I'm pregnant."

He slipped into his broadcloth boxers in one movement and sat back down on the couch facing her. She felt strangely adrift without the weight of his legs over her.

"Oh my God Zoe. Are you okay?" Concern wrinkled into his forehead, his green eyes searched hers.

"I'm okay," she said slowly. She liked the fact that he was worried about her. But it looked like he wasn't going to grasp the whole situation by himself.

Then it came over him, an understanding pulled over his head like a sweater. "Zoe." She could actually see the color drain from his face, as if someone had sucked it out of him with a straw. The momentary concern for her was gone.

He ran his hand through his hair. "I'm sorry, but... whose... I mean..." He massaged his forehead. "Is it mine?"

Zoe was paralyzed by the pallor of his face, the dread in his eyes. *He's scared for the two of us,* she tried to convince herself. But she knew he was afraid for himself, for his own situation. For Tess. The bottom of the room dropped away, and Zoe was suddenly falling, falling into a deep dark hole, like a cartoon character that falls spread-eagle into a black abyss. The only thing that held her to this spot was that Gavin held her heart in his hands. And it was stretching, stretching like a rubber band.

"No," she whispered. "No, it's Bob's." A loud sob escaped her lips as her heart snapped out of her body and Gavin let go of it at the same time.

The following few days Zoe burrowed into her dark abyss, curled up in bed, shades wearily shut. Her heart, her whole body, had a migraine; the thought of daylight, of motion was excruciating. Her boss called her on the first day, and she croaked so horribly into the phone that he backpedaled from irritable and told her not to come in until she was feeling better.

She couldn't remember when or how Gavin had left the apartment, what he had or hadn't said, what she may have replied. At one point, she lifted the phone to call Allie, but as she held the cold receiver in her hand, she remembered that Allie was flying on the news of her own growing womb. Zoe carefully, noiselessly, put the receiver back into the cradle and lay back on her pillow.

The knock on her door on the third day woke her from a restless nightmare. She yanked a pillow over her head and silently commanded the knocker to go away. A key scraped into the lock and the next thing she knew, Gavin towered over her war-torn bed. Dressed in jeans and armed with plastic bags and two cardboard cups of coffee, he prodded her out of bed and into the shower. She did as she was told, and when she emerged from the steamy bathroom in sweatpants and an old tee shirt, her hair soggy and unbrushed, a small feast had been laid out for her on the tiny kitchen table: fat deli sandwiches, crisp potato chips, a pint of Ben & Jerry's, and a cup of hot coffee.

"Pick your poison." Gavin leaned against the counter on the other side of the table.

He might as well have been wearing a Halloween costume. Gavin bearing get-well supplies? It didn't compute. "And who are you?" Her voice was hoarse, she hadn't used it in days.

"Just a friend," he reached for his cup of coffee, "who heard through the incestuous downtown grapevine that a certain beautiful girl hasn't been at work."

Zoe stepped towards the table and picked up a cardboard cup. She took her time pouring sugar into her coffee. "Maybe I quit," she finally said. "What business is it of yours?"

"Let's figure this out together," he said quietly.

"How do you know I'm not going to figure this out with Bob?" She lowered herself gingerly onto a chair, as if she was in pain.

Gavin took one step towards the table and stopped. "The other night you said you hadn't told him yet. I may be wrong, but it seemed like you weren't too excited about telling him." Gavin held her eyes. "You told me. I want to help."

"I don't need your help. Or anyone else's."

"No, you don't. Of all the people I know, you just might be the most capable, or maybe the most stubborn." He took another step and eased himself into a chair across from her. "But I'd like to help, to at least be a friend." He paused. "Can I help you, Zoe?"

This was so disorienting. Zoe dropped her head into her hands. This wasn't the Gavin she was used to. She had fantasized about just such concern and tenderness from him once she had told him that the baby was his. But somehow the worry and compassion he was offering now felt very different from what she yearned for, and she understood that now, mixed into his sincerity was the implicit knowledge that it was very much over between them. The banter was gone, the electricity was out. They were on uncommon terrain.

"Gavin, what are you doing here?" She looked at him for the first time with no guardrail, no defense, no strategy in mind. Her mascara-less eyes were bruised with exhaustion.

He took a sip of coffee. "The other night, I hurt you. I saw that, I felt that. I'm not sure what kind of reaction you wanted from me, but whatever it was, I didn't give it to you. After I got home, at first all I could think was 'Thank God it's not mine.' I thought about how it would've been to tell Tess that you and I were pregnant, and I couldn't even imagine the conversation, let alone the aftermath." He cleared his throat. "Honestly, it scared the shit out of me. I could have easily been the father here."

Zoe raised her coffee cup to her lips. *You have no idea.*

Gavin continued, "And then, after a while of thinking about myself and how my life might have changed, I finally," he sighed, "got around to thinking about you and how you can't say 'Thank God' right now. And that even if I'm not the father, I have a responsibility here. We've been together a long time. I want to help you, I want to do the right thing." He reached across the table and laid his hand over hers.

Tears welled up in Zoe's eyes. It was partly from his sweet earnestness, his sincerity, but mostly, she just wanted to cry. The whole thing was so overwhelming and her head hurt and she just wanted someone to make it all go away. And the tears that were erupting from the bottom of her heart were also because it was all so clear: he didn't love her, he loved Tess.

And because what wasn't being discussed, what wasn't even being mentioned, was that she had finally told Gavin she loved him. Did he even remember it? Or had her confession been lost in all the confusion that followed? She might never know. But what she did know was that she meant it then, and she meant it now. She loved him. Her heart ached for him, and although she knew now that she had to, she wasn't sure she would ever get over him.

She looked up at his face, at the caring that was emanating from his green eyes. She dropped her eyes to the table where his big hand covered hers. Her instinct was to pull it away. She wasn't sure she wanted help from him; she didn't think she could handle being pals with him.

Her head throbbed. She left her hand where it was, and took a ragged breath. "Oh, Gavin. I don't know what to do."

And he was on his knees next to her chair, hugging her before she even finished her sentence.

———

A week later, after a leisurely Saturday morning latte, Megan and Tess were browsing their favorite SoHo shop, a tiny store filled with eclectic jewelry and vintage clothes. Although it was only September, the people out the window had their lightweight jackets zipped against the biting wind, and they scurried by, their eyes on the concrete in front of them. Inside the vanilla-infused store it was warm, and as the two friends chatted, they floated down the aisles, eyes on the merchandise, hands sliding over fabric, their attention partially on the dialogue, partially on the fabulousness of the garment in hand.

"So how's Gavin?" Megan peeked at the price tag on an ivory lace blouse.

"A little intense lately, if intense is the right word." She shook her head as she ran her hand over a lavender cashmere sweater. "I don't know, something's different. At first I thought something had happened, like he'd been fired, but now I think… it's like he's had some kind of epiphany."

"What do you mean?"

"He had this big presentation last week, and he was a little nervous about it, although the only way I knew that was from the hours he spent glued to his computer." She guffawed over a ruffle of irritation. "I assumed that the night after the presentation we'd celebrate, but he called from a bar and said he was with the work crew and would see me later. Which was fine," Tess said quickly, "I didn't care. But when he did come over later that night, he was really, I don't know, distracted." She rolled her eyes. "More than usual I should say."

Megan put down the dangly silver earrings she was holding and faced Tess.

Tess continued, "He said the presentation had gone well, but something was weird that night. And now he's completely attentive, which as you know is a little out of character. Don't get me wrong, I like it. But it's weird."

"Maybe the pressure's off at work and he can concentrate more on you."

"Maybe. I actually gave him a litmus test, asked if he wanted to go out to Fairfield and have dinner with my family. He said fine. That's when I knew something was up. I mean, *I* don't even like to go to my parents' for dinner." She paused, and said to the rack of clothes in front of her, "If I didn't know better, I'd think he cheated on me the other night." She glanced at Megan out of the corner of her eye.

Megan didn't think it was such a far-flung theory, Gavin being Gavin, and well, men being men. "No." She tried to sound more definite than she felt. "Gavin wouldn't cheat on you."

"I know. Though I swear if he shows up with roses tonight, it's all over."

Megan thought, without malice, that if Gavin showed up with roses, Tess would be ecstatic. "What are you guys up to tonight?"

"Going to dinner; I'm not sure where yet. You know Gavin, he's got a whole agenda. What about you?"

"I'm meeting Jared at Carmine's." Megan blushed and examined an ugly brown turtleneck like it was the most beautiful piece of clothing in the world.

"Oh?" Tess smirked.

Megan focused on the turtleneck to hide her own smirk. She was half-ashamed and half-amused. Ashamed because in the world of office etiquette, a woman falling for a younger assistant was a major faux pas; amused because she didn't care. Which was surprising because she was passionate about her job. She wondered what her indifference said about her feelings for Jared and she put another check on the "pro" side of her mental list.

Jared was not the type of guy she was usually attracted to, but she knew that might be the best thing about him. He was smart and decisive; at 22 and only one year out of college, he was curiously composed, with none of the gimmick-wrapped, pink-faced insecurity that defined the other assistants. In the looks department he was Everyman: medium height, medium build, brown hair, brown eyes. He would be a defense attorney's dream—he so resembled any guy next to him that his inclusion in a criminal lineup would confuse a witness trying to make an ID. The only feature that gave him any distinction were the wire-rimmed glasses he wore over his observant and kind eyes.

In a very public job—the four group assistants for the team had desks, but shared space in a big, common area—Jared was most notable for what he wasn't. He didn't chatter incessantly about his social life like Sue; he didn't have Jim's rapid-fire, often inappropriate sense of humor; he didn't have Nick's GI Joe good looks. While Sue, Jim, and Nick yucked it up over the tops of their computers during the day, Jared smiled and laughed, but kept his focus on the grunt work in front of him.

It was understood by the rest of the group that if something needed to be done right, it went to Jared.

He and Megan, as part of a team, had slaved for hours on the advertising for their client's new suntan lotion, a breakthrough product that would antiquate a beach bag full of different SPFs. This smart product sensed information about the skin, analyzed the sun's rays, and then protected each specific body area appropriately. So by smoothing on one lotion, a person could have SPF 45 on their face, 15 on their shoulders, and 4 on their legs. The lotion was named SunSense, and Megan had been the one to suggest the tagline that stuck: "Don't get mad, get even". (She had later joked with Zoe, "That blast of genius came from spending so much time with you.")

Megan was thrilled to be in on the campaign. It meant long days and even longer nights at her desk, but per her usual style, she dove right in, these days not so much as a healing mechanism, but simply because she loved it. If anyone from the team was chugging caffeine and grinding away late into the evening, Megan's cubicle lamp was on too, glowing yellow over her disheveled piles of paper and open bag of dinner—extra salty pretzels.

Jared provided the team's between-meal sustenance: gum. He chewed constantly; his desk drawer was stuffed with packs of every imaginable flavor from Bubble Yum to Teaberry, and he was more than happy to share his habit with anyone who passed by. The best part about his stash was that he had an open-drawer policy; when someone needed a fix, they didn't have to create a conversation to approach him. Many an exec reached into his drawer for a stick of Juicy Fruit or a chunk of Bazooka after dropping a project on his desk, as if the gum was a reward for finishing a draft. Others with less hefty titles, Megan included, helped themselves more frequently, especially when they were in a creative funk. It became a standing joke that the gum was why the team was so prolific, and why Jared's inbox was always so jammed. The three other GA's blithely accepted the gum as the reason their inboxes were not as popular.

When Jared first joined the department, besides the gum drive-bys, he and Megan didn't socialize. After work, although the whole team would often unwind at the same bar, Megan and Jared's hierarchical allegiances assigned them to separate areas of the room. Anyone who had their own office, or cubicle even, gravitated to a big round table in the back, where relaxation was served in a glass; the group assistants gathered around the oblong bar for bottles and rapid-fire refills. Jared, by age and position, was delegated to the bar, where he would shed his suit coat, loosen his tie, and ease into a more denim version of his professional self. While Sue shrieked loudly at Jim's manic commentary of Nick's pickup lines, Jared drank his beers, chewed his gum, and enjoyed the show, the tortoise to their hares.

In the gray time between the office and the cocktails however, it wasn't long before Megan and Jared discovered each other coming and going from the building in their after-hours Adidas attire, and brief conversations about running soon served as a courteous segue from "hi" to "here's something I need done right away."

One bleary-eyed morning, as Megan ordered her light coffee and everything bagel from her favorite deli, she heard "I'll have the same" from behind her. She whipped around.

"So we've got another thing in common," Jared said.

Megan inwardly groaned. She didn't want to get caught up in a conversation; she hadn't had her caffeine yet.

"Are you running today?" He nodded to the cumbersome gym bag slung over her shoulder.

"If I can sneak out for a while." She gathered her covered cup and plain brown bag and began to maneuver through the throng of people; not an easy feat with her huge duffel bag.

"Do you knock down little old ladies with that thing?" he called after her.

She smiled. "Sometimes."

"Maybe we could run together sometime."

"Sure." She escaped out onto the crowded sidewalk and picked up her pace.

At six o'clock that evening, as she emerged from the elevator into the lobby in her black Lycra tights and big baggy sweatshirt, there was Jared, stretching by the center fountain. *Unbelievable.* She glanced around for a way to sneak by. Of course, at that moment the plaza was empty. She walked towards him.

"This is weird." She smiled neutrally at him.

He nodded. "Twice in one day. Which way are you going?"

She sighed. "If we go together, we could head over to the park."

Running on the busy streets of Manhattan was an exercise in agility, and they started out in single file, weaving their way through briefcases, Bloomies bags, and the honking gridlock of the evening commute. Once they entered the park however, their pace synced up and heavy breathing and short gasps of office gossip filled the space between them. Megan exhaled a few tales of a monster exec, and Jared panted through interesting tidbits he had picked up from the other GAs. It wasn't until the office building was back in sight that they tread on anything remotely personal.

"Thanks for the pace, you really pushed me," Megan said as they slowed to a trot. "Have you been running for a while?"

"About a year. It's part of a whole 'get healthy' kick I'm on."

"Trying to impress the ladies with a makeover?"

"What I'm really trying to makeover is my lungs. I used to be a pack-a-day guy."

"Really? I can't imagine you with a cigarette." They were walking now, their breath slowly settling.

"A year ago, you wouldn't have been able to imagine me without one. *I* couldn't imagine me without one. It was kind of a family hobby; my dad owned a garage and all the guys who worked there smoked." Jared smiled. "I spent all my time there tinkering with engines, and of course, smoking. I was hooked before I picked up my first cigarette."

"So how come you're not on the Subaru account?"

"I go where I'm told."

"But you know a lot about cars?"

"Yes ma'am, I'm a grease monkey."

"So why advertising?"

Jared rubbed the fingers of his right hand together, signaling money. "Cleaner fingernails." He smiled. "Actually, the best part of the garage for me wasn't working on the cars, it was hanging out with my dad and my 'uncles,'" Jared made air quotes, "listening to them talk. They talked about carburetors and old Corvettes, but also about life, telling old stories, throwing out bits of wisdom, sharing regrets and mistakes. And the way they told their stories, so passionately. They were like brothers—cutting each other off, finishing each other's sentences, laughing before the punchline. For me, the cars weren't the point, the comfort was. It was like our version of family dinner. Except our meal was a pack of Marlboros."

Megan wiped sweat off her face with the bottom of her sweatshirt. "So why'd you quit?"

He looked straight at her. "My father died of lung cancer."

Megan stopped walking. "Oh Jared. I'm so sorry."

"Me too." He shrugged. After a moment they began to walk again, this time in silence; there was no pressure to fill it.

"Funny thing is," Jared said after a minute, "it didn't even occur to me to quit when he was diagnosed; I was a chimney all through that year. But after he died, at the reception, Oh my God I was so sad, so empty." His voice wobbled; he cleared his throat. "So I grabbed my pack and my lighter and headed out onto the porch, desperate for a smoke, and for a connection, because that's what smoking is, right? At least that's what it was for me, a breaking of bread of sorts. And there were all my heroes from the garage—all of them, in their ill-fitting, scratchy suits—scattered around the porch, with their shoulders at odd angles to each other like they were trying to block each other out." Jared shook his head. "They were all smoking—aggressively, desperately, like some people might chug a Jack Daniels and slam it down on the bar for a refill. As if, on a porch with all the people they loved, that cigarette was the only sustenance in the world." They stopped walking and faced each other. Megan watched his eyes; Jared was focused on something above her head. His tone shifted, floated with disbelief. "It was so quiet. I stepped out there, and they all just turned their heads and looked right through me. No one said a word. All I heard was the tap-tap of flicking ash." He looked at Megan. "Later that night when I was home, I lit up, and when I tapped my ash, I couldn't stand it. It's barely even a sound, but it made my skin crawl." He took a deep breath. "I started running the next day."

Megan didn't know what to say. She reached out and put her hand on his arm.

"You're blushing." Tess put her hand on Megan's arm and drew her mind back into the store, back into their conversation.

"I know, I've been like this all week. I don't know what's going on."

"You want me to fill you in?" Tess smirked again. "We've all known for months now."

"It's not like that. We're just really good friends. Hell, he tells me all about his dates."

"Meg, it's clear he likes you."

Megan's brow furrowed. "You know, once in a while I think that." She shook her head. "But I'm kind of his boss." She flipped over a price tag. "Plus we've been friends for too long now, I know too much about him. It would be weird."

"What do you mean, you've been like this all week?"

Megan picked at her cuticle, her eyes locked on Tess. "Last weekend at dinner, I told him about Mark." In between the salad course and the spaghetti she had poured out the story of her rape, as if the narrative had been waiting in her throat, lingering in the recesses of her mind for the right person, and then the right situation in which to spill out. And though she hadn't spoken of that night in a long time, and had only ever done so with the girls, she didn't edit herself. It was the first time that she had ever definitively said it was rape. She had never had the courage before to admit that she had been finally, truly violated.

Jared had listened carefully as the blurred melody of forks clattering and voices chattering continued all around them. His eyes never left her face, his wire-rimmed attention forced the rest of the world to the side. He never once interrupted her and when she was finished, he didn't ask for more details. He just reached out and held her hand across the red-and-white checked tablecloth.

"And okay," Megan said to Tess. "After I got home on Saturday, I realized I had feelings for him. He was so tender, so sweet. It made me feel safe. I haven't felt that way in... well, ever."

Tess squeezed her arm.

"But so what, right? That doesn't mean we should get together. I can't imagine kissing him." But she had fantasized about it all week. She blushed again.

"Best friends falling in love, that's the ultimate," Tess said.

"In the movies. What if we kiss and it's terrible?" Megan groaned. "Or only good for one of us?"

"Or what if it's amazing?" Tess said.

"What if it ruins our friendship?"

"Or what if it's amazing?"

Megan smiled. "Or what if it's amazing. Oh my God, I'm Allie—zero to a hundred in a matter of seconds."

"It's not seconds. It's been almost a year."

"How am I going to act normal with him tonight?"

"Why act normal?"

"Now I'm nervous." Megan checked her watch. "I need a drink."

"Why'd you pick Carmine's for dinner? You're going to reek of garlic."

"Maybe it'll be a good litmus test."

———

That night, Megan tried to relax as she and Jared settled into their usual debriefing and sipped their way through their second glass of wine. *Nothing unusual, a typical evening; although someone tell that to the popcorn kernels just heating up in my stomach.*

"I went out with Suzanne last night," Jared said.

Megan's heart dipped, but she smiled. "A third date. How was it?"

"Actually, great. She's hilarious. I hadn't really gotten that before. We went to this sushi place and ate tons of raw fish and drank a lot of sake. She cracked me up all night." He paused. "Although I guess she did get funnier as the night went on, so maybe it was just the sake I enjoyed." His brown eyes twinkled.

Megan laughed. "How much did you drink?"

Jared made a face. "Too much."

"Are you going to ask her out again?"

"Probably." He shrugged.

The waiter bustled over and scribbled down their order of Caesar salad and shrimp fra diavolo.

"Mind if I get serious for a moment?" Jared leaned in after the waitress hurried away. "Is anything wrong? You've seemed really distracted this week."

Megan blushed. "No, nothing."

He waited a moment; watched her take a sip. "Are you sure you're okay with what you told me last week?"

She was startled; she hadn't expected this line of conversation. "It was a long time ago."

"Even so." Jared said. "But actually what I meant was, in the sober light of day are you okay with the fact that you told me about it?"

"Oh." She blushed again and was happy the pub was dark. "It felt good to tell you. I trust you; not just your opinions, you."

"Good." He leaned back. "I was afraid you were avoiding me. I'm glad you know you can trust me. Because you can."

"I know." She paused. "Was I avoiding you?"

Now it was Jared's turn to blush. "Weren't you?"

She fiddled with her napkin. "I'm not sure."

He cocked his head.

She brushed a crumb off the table.

"Megan." He took a deep breath. "Do *you* think I should ask Suzanne out again?"

Megan looked up; her heart was beating fast. "It sounds like you like her." Her foot jiggled under the table. "But it's not up to me."

"It could be. You know, I wouldn't be going out with Suzanne, or anyone else for that matter, if there was a good reason not to."

The noise from the debate in her head was deafening.

"Okay, I'm just going to say this, although I wish I had a few more beers in me for courage," Jared said. "For a long time now, I've been wondering about us. Together, as more than friends. Maybe I'm an idiot and I've just been hoping for too long." He paused. "Oh hell, I'm already out on a limb here, so I'm not even going to preface this with 'I think.'"

He took a deep breath. "I'm in love with you." He exhaled. "Now you can fire me as a friend and as an employee." He sat back.

Megan leaned towards him. "Are you kidding? I think you just got promoted."

————

Later that night, after a two-hour dinner at which the meal was only a condiment, Jared hailed her a cab. As the yellow sedan screeched up to the curb, Jared whispered in her ear. "You know how we were joking earlier about whether this was our first date or our hundredth?"

Megan nodded as chills crawled up and down her spine.

"Let's say it's our first." He leaned over and kissed her very gently on the lips.

After the cab door closed and she was speeding away, she put her fingers to her just-kissed lips. This time, there was no accompanying terror in her heart.

CHAPTER 8

When I was young, I anticipated Christmas with the same ambivalence that I felt as Matthew's first day of kindergarten crawled toward me. I was excited in both instances because it was the time of year to be excited; the pre-game props of colored lights and Christmas carols or new pencils and a lunchbox can't help but jangle up the nerves. But mostly I dreaded the arrival of Christmas like I dreaded the arrival of that big, yellow school bus I was supposed to shepherd Matthew onto. As always, my polished face hid the queasy feeling in my stomach, "Isn't this exciting?!" Then later, after the sleigh, or bus, lumbered on its way, the world was startlingly quiet, a jolting fresh emptiness; my hand, still warm from the small piece of my heart briefly clenched there, waving, reaching.

We did try back in those cold Decembers. We hung ornaments and had Christmas rituals, although they were performed not so much as an exercise in unity, but as a mask for isolation. I relished my Christmas parties in school—the secret Santas, the sweet berry punch, the brightly frosted reindeer cookies. For a scheduled hour or two, I was a member of a sticky, delirious joy.

Dana's boyhood Christmas' on the other hand, were steeped in ceremony and love; holidays to the hilt. I imagine a lush, *Town & Country* celebration with polished silverware, gold-rimmed china, red velvet bows and black velvet dresses, a roaring copper fire, a snowy white neighborhood, a majestic green pine, all beautifully wrapped in warm, silky conversation. There was definitely no dread in his countdown to Santa.

Of course, when we were married, Dana and I opted for his family traditions instead of mine.

This year, Dana and I were determined to have a "normal" Christmas amidst a most unusual year, and we made sure that every detail played out as tradition scripted. Dana arrived early on Christmas Eve to help decorate the tree, and the kids, overjoyed to see him and already high on the holiday, clung to him, literally keeping one hand on him while using the other to hang ornaments. Then Dana organized his scavenger hunt, and in our search for treasure around our neighborhood, our joyous shouts—"I found a mailbox with a wreath!"—and bright-eyed laughter blew harder than the icy wind. After we burst back into the house, stomping our boots and peeling off layers, we lit a fire and sang and danced along with Bing Crosby and Frank Sinatra. We were fully connected as a family, and the happiness that crowded into the room took me by the shoulders and shook me, reminding me what a wonderful father Dana is to my children, and what a toll his absence is having on them.

And on me.

Finally, after our dinner of fondue (cheese for dinner, chocolate for dessert), Matthew and Gillian nestled into us for Dana's animated reading of *The Night Before Christmas*. As the kids went up to bed, the stockings were hung by the chimney with care, and there were high hopes, I think, that in the morning Daddy would still be there.

Oddly, the only moment that felt awkward during the whole day was in the late afternoon when Dana went to pour us a drink, and he hesitated in front of the liquor cabinet as if unsure whether he should ask my permission. He looked at me, a thousand questions scrolling through his eyes, and I looked away. The moment quickly passed, and he poured the cocktails with a little heavier hand.

After Matthew and Gillian were finally tucked away, Dana and I sunk down onto our kid-worn couch, not exhausted by the day as per our usual end-of-the-day sink, but I think, quietly encouraged by how well it had gone. It didn't feel strange to be sitting close to him, and although perhaps our edges were dull due to the seductive combination of wine, Christmas lights, and a fire, when Dana reached out to stroke my hair, I longed to melt into him. He whispered in my ear. "You're beautiful."

And you know what? For the first time in a long time, I almost felt it. I leaned into him, and we kissed, tentatively at first—those ultra-soft kisses that awaken deep cravings—and then hungrily. This wasn't about the kids; this was about us, Dana and I, and it was a gift.

The next morning, when the kids bounced into our bedroom at the crack of dawn to announce Santa's arrival, Dana and I greeted them together.

People have always told me I'm beautiful. I remember when I was young, random ladies would pat my head in a pitied response to my mother's departure and ooze a rendition of "poor little girl. And so pretty too." As if it was all the more tragic because I was pretty. As if my beauty should have held my mother in place.

Because everyone knows if you're beautiful, you've got it made, right? It's easy street all the way—emotionally, financially, socially, and of course, romantically. Beautiful people do not get their hearts broken. For me, being beautiful was also supposed to lure my mother back. In my fantasy, she'd breeze in the door, take in her attractive, charismatic daughter, and realize that she made a monumental mistake. See how glamorous I am, Mother? See how everyone loves me? Watch me Eva! Watch me Mommy! You should have stayed.

You should have stayed.

My mother. I guess she'll always have that title, even though it's been so very long since she's worn that crown. For a long time I've thought of her not as Mother or Mom, but as Evelyn or Eva, declaring to everyone—myself included—that she was a person of no real consequence. No title; no import.

But clearly, she will always have enormous consequence. Her actions, and then her later lack of them, have chiseled who I am today. Never more so than when I had Matthew and Gillian. Every single time one of them reached for me with their chubby little arms and eager face and demanded "up," an ache would pulse down deep in my soul, buckling my knees with its surge. While I snuggled my child in close, I also wanted to scream at the top of my lungs: How could you have walked out on me?! At those moments, my kisses served two purposes: bestowing adoration onto a baby-soft cheek, and choking back the desire to just open up my mouth and wail, letting free all the questions, all the pain, all the demons living inside of my heart.

But what would people think once those demons were let loose, and more importantly, how fast would those people sprint away from me? I couldn't let anyone see inside, I couldn't let anyone know that I was not who I hold myself up to be. I know all too well what happens when I do.

So I never screamed.

We all hide pieces of ourselves; beauty just provides better hiding places.

All of my life I have tried to be someone my mother would approve of. It's all the more astonishing when I remind myself that I don't even know her; I really have no idea what she would endorse, what she would find appealing. My lifelong endeavor has been based purely on an assumption.

Beauty's in the eye of the beholder, isn't that the saying? But it is oh so ironic that most of the time we have no idea what the beholder actually considers beautiful. We assume we know and proceed accordingly. But so often we're only trying to attain some ideal that we ourselves have created; an ideal that has nothing to do with what the "beholder" in reality considers dear.

JANUARY 1995
New York City

The snow was tapering off in Manhattan, and already the white fluff was grimy, gray slush. Megan's white Nikes were soaking wet and filthy, and drops of cold, gritty snow had sprayed up her stockings, leaving textured black polka dots on her calves. Megan knew that Zoe—who could afford a cab anytime, anywhere—would have a heart attack if she saw the sneaker/stocking combo. She sighed. She really needed to get her boots back from Jared's.

At eight o'clock in the morning, she was already having one of those days. Somehow she'd overslept, and when her alarm finally broke through her thick dreams, the time on the clock shot her straight out of cozy and into the rudeness of her shower, which on a good day needed 10 minutes to warm up. She yelped as she stepped into the icy cascade, then held her breath and lathered fast while goosebumps duked it out for space on her skin. She rinsed and reached for the conditioner, only to remember with horror that yesterday she had banged out the last drop. There was no time to mourn however, or to celebrate the warmth of her towel. She ripped through her tangled hair with a brush, ripped through two pairs of panty hose, and then ripped a nail down to the skin as she hurried to lock the apartment door.

She cursed several taxi drivers as they cruised by her, and then, as she caught a glimpse of herself in a deli window, forgave them. *I wouldn't stop either.* She tried to smooth down her halo of frizzy, Ronald McDonald hair.

She began to speed walk, New York style—long gait; arms swinging; focus straight ahead, alert and ready to dodge the prancing poodle on a leash, coffee-guzzling pedestrian, or open manhole. With each long stride she tried not to think about Jared, but she knew that he was as much a part of the chaos of her morning as were all of the logistical malfunctions. She was mad at him, she was confused about him, and most of all she missed him. They had been apart for a few weeks, but the hole he'd left this past weekend at Tess's wedding was different from the one gaping inside of her; this new hole was outside of her body, right next to her, a void that occupied space and volume but couldn't hold her hand.

Of course, the wedding itself had been salt on the wound. But as much as she wished to be a bride, she still wasn't sure whether Jared should be the one waiting at the end of the aisle in a black tux and incandescent expression of wonder. He had no such doubts, and ironically, it was his certitude about their future that had created the rock-solid stage for her vacillation. At least until recently, when it became obvious that Megan's long-standing excuse for their gridlock had been a mirage.

"It's not the job, is it?" Jared challenged her a few weeks ago after he started work at a new agency. The broken glass in his eyes hurt more than the angry, thorny words or their decision to spend some time apart.

Time to myself; time to meet different guys, and see…

But she didn't have much interest in meeting new men, at least not yet. And really, the men she met had been yawns compared to Jared. At Tess's wedding, Megan walked down the aisle with a prematurely graying accountant who was nice enough, but had her plotting her escape after five minutes together at the bar. Derek however, was not to be deterred; he appeared at her shoulder every time she switched groups, following her across several conversations and then clear across the room to Allie. Even her "I'm sorry, I have a boyfriend," said with a polite smile and dash of the Heisman strong-arm hadn't helped. And neither had Allie.

Megan chuckled to herself as she remembered it, and then glanced at her watch and forgot all about it. She urged the elevator to hurry up. She was late to a meeting and needed to pop into the ladies room to clean off her stockings and put on some makeup. She rushed into her office with a flurry of apologies and pulled out her chair.

Her boots.

She spun around.

"Jared stopped by early and left those for you," her assistant said in answer to the question mark on Megan's face.

Red roses. They were the only flower Tess wanted at her wedding reception, and they were everywhere. The bride carried a bouquet of long-stemmed red roses, the bridesmaids carried sprays of red mini-roses, and Gavin and his groomsmen each wore a rose on their lapels. Roses bloomed on all the tables, on the bar, and on top of the towering tiers of cake. Women needn't have bothered with perfume as the sweet, flowery scent overpowered every-thing else in the huge dining room, including the body odor from the band.

Allie wrapped up a conversation with a guest she didn't know, and turned towards Megan, who had just joined her from the bar. Megan rolled her eyes at Allie as a moment later Derek sidled up to them.

"Dance?" Derek said to Megan.

"Not right now, thanks."

"Come on, that's what we're here for."

"I'm sorry, but I have a boyfriend."

"Really?" He looked around. "But he's not here?"

"Don't let her fool you, Derek," Allie said. "She's currently unattached. And she loves to dance." She smiled innocently at Megan.

"Derek, have you met my *best friend*, Allie?"

A confused Derek nodded to Allie. Then he turned back to Megan. "So, do you want to dance?"

"Go," Allie put her hand on Megan's back and gave her a nudge.

Megan threw up her hands. "Thanks a lot," she mouthed over her shoulder at Allie as she followed Derek out onto the dance floor. The band started a poor, and painfully slow, interpretation of "Unforgettable."

Allie dropped down onto a chair next to Zoe.

"You do realize that you just sent my date off into hell," Zoe said, referring to Megan.

"I didn't know the band was going to switch into romantic mode. But you can cut in if you want to."

"I'm not sure this crowd is ready for two women dancing together. But you just keep your merry matchmaking hands off of me." Zoe's chortle was cut short when Gavin and Tess floated onto the dance floor. She said in a low voice, "There's no one here I'm interested in."

"How are you doing?" Allie leaned in.

"I'm okay." She smiled at Allie's furrowed brow. "Really. It's not like I haven't had years to get ready for this day, right?" She sighed. "I'm just thankful for two things right now. That I'm not wearing that bridesmaid dress," she smirked at Allie, "and that there's an open bar."

Allie laughed.

Zoe continued, "Actually the only thing I'm worried about is that Megan's not strong enough to carry me home tonight." She drank from her wine. "What about you? Why aren't you out on the dance floor kicking up your heels?"

"Well, I am glad to be *wearing* heels, but I don't think they've got a lot of kick in them. I'm pretty much running on empty right now."

Zoe peered at Allie.

"Matthew was up all night with croup," Allie said.

Zoe nodded and drained her wine glass.

"He and I camped out in the bathroom. I think I have tile marks on my butt."

"And where was Dana during this little adventure?"

"He offered to take a shift or two, but I let him sleep. He's been working so hard... "

Zoe poured herself another glass of wine.

"I wouldn't have slept anyway," Allie said.

"How is the little man?"

"Better." Allie checked her watch. "I should call the sitter. This is the first time Dana and I have been out for longer than an hour or so."

"In 10 months?" Zoe's mouth fell open.

Allie lifted her chin. "Sometimes we grab a quick dinner, but it's hard to find a good sitter, and I have to pump if we go out for too long." She could feel her breasts grow heavy at the thought of her little boy in his blue sleeper.

"That's a visual I'm going to stay away from." Zoe smiled. "But a sitter's a sitter, right? All she has to do is plunk him in his crib."

Allie felt a surge of anxiety. *What if Matthew was crying for her? What if...* She scoured the room for Dana, and saw him over at the bar, laughing in a group. She felt a pang in her heart.

"Basically. But she has to give him a bottle, read to him, rock him to sleep, and he might get upset... " She watched Zoe's eyes casually scan the crowd. Zoe would never understand. It was like trying to describe childbirth to the girls; they were somewhere else, back in the city, mulling over their inboxes, and Allie's words failed her, deflated on her tongue, the intense experience becoming just a jumble of syllables strung together. She knew that there was no way she could describe her love for Matthew, how it had taken over her life to such a degree that she wasn't even sure it was hers anymore, and that that was okay. How she could feel suffocated by his needs and moods but that the moment she had space to breathe she ached to touch him; how she dreaded his growing up and yet clapped and danced with his every achievement—first smile, first cheerio, first crawl; how in the shadow of her feelings for him she was tiny and vulnerable. Her heart, her soft underbelly was now Matthew, out of her body and so conspicuously exposed. How could Zoe understand that in her head she knew that even if Matthew cried for her, he'd be fine; that in the big picture, it didn't matter. But in her heart it did. It mattered more than she could say.

Allie looked at her watch, and then across the room again at Dana. His back was to her.

Megan arrived back at the table with Derek close on her heels. She rolled her eyes at her two friends and sat down, her back to Derek, who stood for a moment behind her and then meandered off.

Zoe raised her eyebrows at Megan.

"What?" Megan giggled. "I said thank you. And anyway, what was that all about?" She eyeballed Allie.

"Sorry, but I couldn't resist." Allie smiled. "Hey, not 20 minutes ago you said you needed to date other guys so you could figure out your feelings for Jared. Derek can be your first guinea pig. And he's cute."

"He is cute." She sighed. "You're right, this is what I wanted. But now I feel like I'm betraying Jared every time I smile at someone. What's the matter with me?"

"I don't know, but I'm pregnant and nauseous, draped in a tent of red velvet, drinking seltzer with a limp lime. I'm hoping to live vicariously through you guys, so get to work. Have some fun!" Allie said.

"I hate to tell you this, but your yardstick for fun has deteriorated drastically," Megan said.

"Tell me about it," Allie said. "I feel warped. And old. And this dress isn't doing me any favors." She took stock of her long red velvet bridesmaid dress. "Three months pregnant is a fashion nightmare. I've got just enough of a belly so that my clothes don't fit, but I'm not big enough to be obviously pregnant. I just look fat."

"No, not your best look," Zoe said.

Megan kicked Zoe under the table as she said, "But not mine either. And I don't have the pregnant excuse." Megan glanced down at her own red velvet dress.

Allie ran her hand over the velvet. "Gorgeous in theory, heinous in reality."

"I'm not even sure it was gorgeous in theory," Zoe said.

"Didn't I read somewhere that the bridesmaids are sacrificial? We're supposed to be unattractive, better for the bride's glow," Megan said.

"And who best for the job but the bride's closest friends?" Allie said.

"If Jared and I ever get married, please shoot me if I'm excited about a cookie-cutter bridesmaid dress or red velvet anything."

"That's a deal I'm happy to make, as I could be wearing one of those scary dresses," Zoe said.

"Should I point out that you're still contemplating marrying Jared, yet you broke up with him?" Allie said.

"Only to underscore that I have no idea what I'm doing." Megan pretended to pull her hair out. "Here's this great guy, he loves me, I love him, we're comfortable; but because I can't tell if I'm *in love* with him, I've cast him away."

"First of all, you haven't cast him away," Allie said. "You guys are just taking a breath, and like you said, Jared loves you. He'll wait. And second of all, you guys had some issues. Not just theoretical issues, but real ones, like the fact that you worked together. That was real."

"But it never really was about the job." Megan held her hand up like a stop sign. "I know, that's what I said, that was the billboard I hung on it so that I could slow it down until I had the moment of knowing. Isn't that a thing, the moment of knowing? But really, the job was just the most top of mind excuse I could grab onto. It was convenient."

"But authentic," Zoe said.

"And easily surmountable, as Jared has so aptly proven," Megan said.

"He's very resourceful, our Jared. Nothing's going to stand in his way," Zoe said.

"What's wrong with comfortable anyway?" Allie's eyes flicked to Dana. "Last time I checked, comfortable was a good thing. A comfortable couch, a comfortable bed; and in our house growing up, we had fistfights over the comfortable chair."

"Except in relationships, comfortable is the kiss of death," Megan said. "Like nice. He's nice. We're comfortable."

"Some people search their whole lives to find comfortable," Allie said.

"But that's just it. We're like a 50-year-old couple. We've arrived at a place on the spectrum of coupledom without going through the fire and angst to get there."

They all watched Gavin and Tess click glasses. "What's so great about angst?" Zoe said.

"What I mean, I guess, is spark." Megan turned to Allie. "The you-and-Dana spark, the Rhett-and-Scarlet spark. You know, the can't-live-without-him, have-to-get-naked-right-now-or-I-just-might-explode spark."

"I think those are two separate things," Zoe said. "And the last time we talked, getting naked wasn't a problem with you and Jared."

"Our sex life is good, it is. But it's not, I don't know, urgent."

Allie giggled, "Like having to pee urgent?"

Megan laughed. "You know what I mean."

Allie was about to say that urgent wasn't all it was cracked up to be, and that even if there was urgency, it could easily get buried under the landslide of other, more basic emergencies, like groceries and changing diapers. "And the can't-live-without-him?" she asked instead.

"I guess that's what I'm trying to find out."

The band switched back to lively and the girls watched guests jump out of their seats, arms and legs already flapping as they made their way to the wooden dance floor.

"And where, may I ask, is your date?" Megan asked Allie.

"I've released him to the bar with all the non-hormonal, skinny people. He was sweet, chaining himself to me earlier, but honestly, it felt good to let him go." She leaned back. She and Dana had both been looking forward to this wedding as a chance to unwind, a chance to refill their depleted buckets with new energy and some time together without Matthew. She wasn't sure what to think about the fact that they were across the room from each other, laughing at different jokes, sharing this event—and conversations about their lives—with other people. "I think we've passed comfortable and moved on to exhausted."

"Why don't we go find a couch to sink into for a while? I'd love to hide from Derek, who thanks to you, now thinks he's getting lucky tonight."

Allie held out her hand to Megan. "If you can pull me out of this uncomfortable chair."

Zoe asked Allie, "Can I sneak you a glass of wine?"

"Oh, that sounds good. One won't hurt, right?"

"You're asking me?" Zoe asked.

Allie laughed. "I'd love a glass."

Allie found a couch and Zoe brought back three glasses of lukewarm chardonnay. Megan disappeared for a moment and returned with three pieces of white frosted wedding cake.

"Things must be bad if you're eating cake," Zoe said to Megan as she accepted a piece.

"I went to a killer aerobics class this morning, so I'm covered. Oh, guess who I saw there? Jane Powell."

"Was she high-kicking people in the back?" Zoe said.

Allie looked from Megan to Zoe.

Megan laughed. "No, but she tripped me on the way to the locker room." Zoe's eyes widened.

"Just kidding. I steered clear of her, I'm not sure she even saw me."

"Who's Jane Powell?" Allie said, hating that she needed background on the hair-trigger conversation.

"A bimbo who was backstabbing Megan at work," Zoe said. "We stabbed her back, though. We got her believing that her boss is into her. So now she pretty much makes a fool of herself every day."

Megan held both hands up in the air. "It was Zoe's idea."

Zoe rubbed her hands together. "I am slowly initiating Megan into my Machiavellian ways."

Allie forced a chuckle and moved her wrist so she could spy her watch. She had to call the sitter.

"Hi ladies," Dana stepped into the conversation. He put his hand on Allie's shoulder. "How're you doing? Do you guys need anything?"

"Actually yes, but nothing you can help with." Zoe grinned.

"That's where you're wrong." Dana smiled and turned to Megan. "I ran into Jared the other day."

"You did?" Megan sat up straight.

You did? Allie's shoulders sagged. *You never told me.*

"We ended up having a beer together. I didn't realize you'd broken up," Dana glanced at Allie, "but he filled me in."

Allie watched Dana talking and tried to remember the last time they had chatted about anything other than the nuts and bolts of their growing family. They were both working so hard; in the evenings they usually just sagged onto the couch together, clicked on the TV, and self-edited stories or feelings about their days down to the barest of details, down to scraps that would fit into the hole of a 60-second commercial.

"How was he?" Megan said.

Dana sat down. "Sad. I mean, he wasn't weeping or anything, but he said he was sad. He misses you."

"He said he was sad?"

"Unapologetically."

Megan finished the wine in her glass.

"That's a good thing right?" Dana asked as he surveyed the women's faces.

"It hurts to think he's hurting." Megan picked at her cuticle. "But I guess I wouldn't want to hear that he was popping champagne and hooking up with other girls either."

She sighed, her eyes shuffling between Allie and Dana. "You guys don't know how lucky you are. You're through all this jockeying for relationship clarification. Now you're just sailing along."

Allie and Dana caught eyes for a moment; then with a blink, their connection was broken.

Allie was glad that she had cake in her mouth and couldn't reply that they may be sailing along, but it often felt like they were on different ships.

————

Only a few miles away from Megan's grungy commute, the snow in the suburbs dressed the shivering trees in white velvet and sequins. Matthew's first snowfall! Allie jumped out of bed into the chill of the morning and rushed to the window. The last fat flakes were drifting in the breeze, floating down onto a yard that had become white frosting overnight. She pulled on a sweater and thick socks, and flew down the stairs to see what Dana thought of the snow. "Dana!"

The note on the table was her answer; he had left for work early because of it. She laid her hand over the words for a moment, then slid the note into the garbage. She clicked on the TV and flooded the kitchen with the gang from the *Today* show.

At Matthew's cry, she sprinted up the stairs and burst into his room. "Good morning handsome." He grinned and held up his arms. She gathered him up, held him close, breathed in his sleepy smell. "Okay, okay." She smiled as he fumbled with her shirt. She settled onto the chair in his room with his head in the crook of her arm and Matthew drank from her breasts hungrily, his eyes twinkling at her while he sucked. This was one of her favorite times of day, just the two of them connected in a quiet hush. For a few precious minutes, she didn't rush to fill the world with music, TV; she didn't panic in the silence, she reveled in it.

"I have a surprise for you," she said as she bundled him up in his blue snowsuit. "See the snow out there? No, keep your mittens on," she said as he started to pull them off. She laughed as he pulled at his hat. "Your hat too." She smoothed it back down on his head and kissed his nose.

"Ready?" She wedged his Michelin-man bulk into the backpack and they set out into the whispering white grandeur.

It was slow going; even on the semi-plowed street her boots sunk to mid-calf. The crunch, crunch of the snow and her soft monologue with Matthew were the only variance in the snowy hush; the world had bowed to nature and was holding its breath, one long exhale on the weekday chaos. As she chatted with her son, a thick mist swirled in and around her voice—"See the bird? Look at the smoke snaking out of that chimney!" She imagined aloud for Matthew the scene in each of the houses they passed: fires crackling, pancakes flipping, kids burrowing into their down comforters, grateful for the unexpected day off. Occasionally Matthew answered her with a sweet gurgle or a brush of his wool mitten on her cheek.

Back home, she flipped on the music—a little Bach before she switched into top-40 pop—and opened the fridge to a cornucopia of homemade baby food. She warmed pureed pears for Matthew and percolated coffee for herself. Then she let him loose in the playroom to pull himself up and "cruise" the edges of the wooden side tables and oak bookcases lined with child development advice and award-winning children's books. She trailed him closely, alternately warning "careful" and thrusting out her hands, and cheering his attempts to steady himself.

Finally, when both of them were tired, she read him a story and put him down for his first nap of the day. She jumped into the shower, and as she closed her eyes and rubbed shampoo into her hair, remembered that she hadn't had breakfast yet.

————

Zoe reclined in a salon chair at Cashmere, her knee-high black boots still glistening with wet snow. Her head was jammed into a white porcelain sink and the painful crick in her neck shrieked over any relaxation that the shampoo girl was trying to massage into her scalp. She wasn't sure if relaxation was something she could attain anyway, as she was still smarting from the slap of Gavin's wedding a few days ago. The whole miserable event looped endlessly through her thoughts, like a bad song on the morning alarm clock that becomes mental muzak for the rest of the day. She craved a cocktail, but as she was on her lunch hour and due back in the office, she had settled on a haircut and blow-dry instead. The cocktail was going to have to wait a few hours. But just a few.

Once her hair was wrapped in a plush black towel, she paraded back over to the tall woman with the Long Island accent who had been cutting Zoe's hair since high school. Sherette was a talkative, opinionated, and potentially attractive lady who wore too much makeup and snapped her gum while she worked. Zoe was always nervous that one of her enormous pink bubbles was going to end up stuck in her hair, but not nervous enough to change stylists. Sherette was a genius with scissors, although she checked herself out in the mirror just as often as she looked at her client. She was the one who had encouraged Zoe to cut off her long dark hair before college, and after the initial alarm at seeing her shorn locks carpeting the salon floor, Zoe had loved her new look. She'd been wed to Sherette ever since.

"So, what's new with you?" Sherette chomped as she wrapped a smock around Zoe.

"Well, let's see… " Zoe stared at herself in the mirror. "The guy I've been seeing for forever got married on Saturday."

"Ouch. What's the story with that?" Sherette combed Zoe's wet hair. "I assume we're doing the regular here."

"Yeah, although I should ask for a totally new look. This one hasn't done me any favors." Zoe sighed. "But no, just do your thing."

"So, what happened? How'd this girl steal your guy?"

"The million-dollar question." Zoe snickered. "Actually, I guess he wasn't really my guy. I was borrowing him." She bit her lip and stated more to the mirror than to Sherette, "They've been engaged for almost a year now." *Surely enough time to get the message and move on.*

"Leasing with an option to own."

"Although my option was never stipulated in writing. It was all up here." She tapped her damp head. *And it still is.* Even now, there was part of her that refused to let go of Gavin. She loved him. Never more so than when he had stayed by her side during her abortion, nervously fidgeting in the waiting room and ferrying her home afterwards. It was a new side of him: caring and concerned with nary a sexual innuendo in sight. The surprising and sad thing about it all was that they had now developed a strange sort of friendship; the piece that had been so lacking in their earlier relationship was now their only tie. Although they didn't see each other often, when they did it was with a quieter and deeper commitment than before. The sexual zing was gone, or at least the certainty that it would be acted upon, but the beginnings of a comfortable bond was there.

"Now that the lease is up, the good news is you can move on to a newer model," Sherette said.

"In theory."

"Don't tell me you're still hung up on him?"

"I'm still not sure I've figured it all out yet."

"Get a grip girl. They said 'I do' didn't they?"

"That they did. I was a witness."

Sherette's eyebrows shot up. "You were at the wedding?"

"With bells on." Zoe had considered just not showing up, but she knew that whether she was there or not, she would feel the same way. Better to see it for herself. Besides, her absence would say something to Gavin that she would rather not repeat.

"You're a sucker for punishment."

She wondered again if she had made the wrong decision. Even with a year of mental prep—reciting her "It's not a big deal" mantra, staying busy at work, and partying into the night when the other tricks didn't deaden her pain—she hadn't quite grasped how deeply it would cut to see Tess and Gavin celebrating their togetherness (she still couldn't bear to think of them as in love). She shuddered as she remembered Gavin dressed to the nines, attentive to Tess, holding her close on the dance floor, whispering intimately with her; she realized that she had rarely seen them together, and that it was obviously only in her own mind that Gavin was dismissive of Tess. "I'm kind of friends with the bride."

Sherette stopped snipping. "You're kidding, right?"

"No." Zoe studied her hands on the black vinyl smock. It sounded awful to her too.

"The plot thickens." Sherette moved around to Zoe's back and blew a huge pink bubble.

Almost to herself, Zoe said, "I just don't see what he finds attractive about her."

Sherette chuckled. "But she's your friend, right?"

Zoe exhaled slowly. "Let's just say we run in the same group." Sherette didn't comment and so Zoe continued, "She's a nice girl, and maybe under different circumstances… but there's always been Gavin." She shook her head. "She's so demure with him. I mean, I know guys like to have control, but to call all the shots all the time? How can men find that attractive?" Zoe thought of her mother and stepfather, who lived an older version of the Tess-Gavin dynamic, and shook her head. "I just don't get it."

"Honey, if we knew what men found attractive, we'd all look alike."

Zoe laughed.

"She never knew?" Sherette said.

"No. I mean, I really don't think so."

"How about your other friends? That must have caused some switching of teams, some divided loyalties."

"They never knew."

"You kept this all to yourself?"

"Don't you feel honored?" Zoe sighed. "My best friend knew how I felt." She thought about Allie squeezing her hand as Mr. and Mrs. Gavin Keller were ushered to the dance floor for the first time. The wordless squeeze had given her a powerful shot of support, and perhaps, had also held her in place so that she didn't leap onto the floor and rip them apart. "But no, I didn't tell them we were together because it was none of their business."

"And because you knew they wouldn't understand. You were afraid they'd side with the quiet mouse."

Zoe caught eyes with Sherette in the mirror. She had wanted to tell Allie, and even Megan, but she could never bring herself to do it. Although they would've tried to understand, she knew they would have eventually sided with Tess, who on paper was Gavin's rightful partner. But Zoe liked her reason better, it hurt less. "She wasn't always the fiancée. We were actually together first," she said with a lift of her chin. "It was one of those things, I just couldn't help it."

"That's bullshit."

Zoe winced.

Sherette backtracked from her sharp tone. "I mean, I'm just being straight with you here, right? I've known you a long time. Take it from me, I've been where you are. Asshole told me he loved me and that he'd leave his wife." Chomp, chomp. "Took me a long time, and a lot of mascara to figure that game out." She peered at herself in the mirror before her eyes focused back on Zoe, the scissors motionless in her hand. "Don't fool yourself. You can always help it. You're a smart girl."

Zoe stared into the mirror.

Sherette went back to snipping and cracking her gum. "So there's my two cents." Sherette smiled warmly. "Can you believe this weather?"

———

It wasn't snowing in the Caribbean. The blood-orange sun was on fire, melting through the horizon towards the turquoise of the sea, and the whole sky was glowing pink and purple with its effort. The tinny beat of reggae music provided a seductive soundtrack. Gavin stood quietly, absorbing the display, thinking it should be captured on a postcard with "Wish you were here!" scripted across the top. He took a sip of his rum punch and squeezed Tess's hand. "Whoever invented the honeymoon was a genius."

"You mean you're tired of the votive versus tall candle debate?" Tess said.

Gavin smiled. "It was the seating chart that put me over the edge."

"Can you believe after that whole debate that my crazy uncle Jim never even showed up?"

"I think my grandfather's speech filled in for anything crazy uncle Jim might have pulled off. Although your mom seemed to like it."

"She was just happy that the food was garnished appropriately."

Gavin laughed. "I think there are more pictures of the food than of us."

"Sorry we're late," Robert called out as he sauntered over with his new bride, Traci (with an "i" she had informed them upon introduction; Gavin could almost see the heart as the dot).

"I thought the word 'late' was outlawed here. Weren't we supposed to leave our watches in our suitcases?" Gavin said.

"I can't do it," Robert confessed, peeking at his wrist.

"At least I got him to switch off the alarm," Traci said, and the other three laughed with a communal noise more about making connections than about humor.

The two couples had met the day before, bumping into each other first on the tennis court, and then later on the beach. Tess and Traci had instantly bonded over the fact that they had gotten married on the same day (overlooking the fact that most of the honeymooners at the resort had undoubtedly done the same), and they'd agreed to meet for dinner on the terrace.

"Cocktails first or straight to the table?" Gavin said.

"Despite the watch, I'm in no hurry." Robert smiled at his new bride as if to say, "See?"

Gavin waved the white-jacketed waiter over.

They sat down in wooden armchairs facing the hypnotic blue of the water and were momentarily silent, a combination of breathing in their surroundings and not knowing where to start the conversation with relative strangers. Traci, a tall, thin woman with a supernatural blond bob, broke the quiet. "So, tell. How'd he pop the question?"

A smile exploded on Tess's face. "Gavin was acting weird for about a month." She patted his leg. "I figured he was stressed about work, but I didn't really know what was going on, I mean, I was starting to wonder..." She paused, shook her head as if to shake those thoughts out of her head again. "*Now* I know that the ring was burning a hole in his pocket all that time. So anyway, one night he came home with red roses and champagne and got down on one knee." *Said he loved me, hadn't been thinking clearly* (she still wasn't sure what that meant*), said he didn't want to waste any more time.* "And pulled out this ring." She looked at Gavin and smiled. "I cried." She sat back with a contented exhale. "How about you?"

Traci clapped her hands together. "We met at my friend's wedding six months ago; Robert was friends with the groom. One look and that, as they say, is all she wrote." She flashed a toothy smile at her husband.

"So after one day, you knew?" Tess said.

Gavin picked up his drink and drained it.

Traci nodded like her head was on a spring.

"It all happened so quickly that some people came right out and asked if we were pregnant," Robert said.

Gavin shifted in his chair. He scanned the patio for the waiter.

It was pathetic that his life had only become clear to him when it was threatened, but there it was. In the five quaking seconds that he believed he was the father of Zoe's baby, Tess had fallen into place with trembling certainty. He loved her; he did not want to lose her, he couldn't lose her. And he had been so careless with her, with the one person in his life who didn't expect him to be anything other than who he was. The guilt he had never allowed himself to feel had suddenly swamped him. Even more so because he knew that if Zoe told him he was the father, he would've offered to marry her, and that would have ended up slaying all three of them. All because of him. But he didn't love Zoe. And despite her unintentional and breathless "I love you," he didn't think she really did. The words were still out there though, hovering over them, unconfirmed and unaddressed.

"Get out of here." Traci punched her husband's arm with a closed fist. "Who asked?"

"Some of the guys."

"You didn't tell me."

"I figured you'd flip," he said, and then he chuckled at Tess and Gavin, "and I guess I was right."

"Obviously skeptics about love at first sight," Gavin said. He held up his glass. "Anyone need a refill?"

————

Several rum punches later, Tess staggered into the ladies room with Traci right on her heels, giggling and grabbing onto Tess's arm for support.

"Those punches are strong," Traci said. "And Gavin's cute."

"Are those two things linked?"

"Possibly!" Traci howled with laughter and stepped into a stall. "How long did you say you've been together?"

"About six years."

"Whoa."

Let's get off of this subject. It was tarnishing her inner "just married" glow. For all six years she had wished that cupid's arrow had pricked Gavin with the insta-commitment that seemed to pierce everyone else; instead, it had been years of near misses, with one finally just grazing his chest. Sometimes she felt as if she had won the prize she coveted just because she survived the longest. Not that she wasn't ecstatic that he'd finally come around; but to know that her husband had "come around" to the idea of spending the rest of his life with her was not something she cared to brag about.

"Robert's cute too. You guys seem good together." Tess rummaged through her purse.

"You think?" Traci shouted from behind the stall door. "Guess what? He snores! I'm having a really hard time sleeping."

"Didn't you notice that before?" Tess asked in a more moderated tone of voice.

"Apparently not. I must have been in some kind of engagement fog or something."

Or maybe you just haven't known each other long enough. Tess swiped on her berry lip gloss, silently thanking Traci for validating her and Gavin's long courtship. "They say that love is blind, right? Maybe it's deaf too."

CHAPTER 9

JOURNAL ENTRY #9
February 21, 2001

Ghosts wear a white sheet over their nothingness so that they are visible, so that someone knows they're there. We wore clothes. In our last few years of marriage, Dana and I were invisible to each other in all but outward body. We moved around the house not so much unobserved, but overlooked; breezing past, gliding through each other. Our big dreams, our trivial desires, our daily temperature were all at best obscure shadows to each other.

It was not an earth-shattering fissure that pushed our marriage to the very edge of a deep crevice, it was slow and simple erosion; it was presumption. The base presumption of love, of our knowledge of each other, of the foundation of each other was initially an asset of ours, but we took that basement for granted for too long. As we built our life together, the normal fault lines that open up within any relationship were patched over with a sense of invulnerability, not new cement. And so ironically, our sedate presumption of strength left us fundamentally weak, and as the earth continued to shift underneath us, we were ever so gradually split apart.

Within this growing divide, our vulnerabilities slowly became a liability. The human flaws that we had once tentatively shared with each other, held out in front of us on a silver tray like a trembling, intimate offering, were locked away. Our failings were not something we were going to expose when so many other, obvious things went unsaid as well.

I can understand now how so many empty-nesters get divorced. In the living room of their lives, one theme—most likely the children—has bound them, dominated all conversation, all passionate emotion, all tangible exchange. Meanwhile in their kitchens, offices, yards, cars, the individuals are still dreaming, still achieving, still accumulating new friends and new interests, but for any number of reasons these personal pursuits aren't shared over the living room coffee table. The partners open their fingers and let go, just for a moment, of each other's hand as they inch away into these separate corners of their lives. The inch becomes an arm's length, then more, just out of reach; maybe they even look over their shoulder and watch their spouse disappear behind a different door. The living room becomes an empty formality; at first lacking life zest, and then after the children have shifted out of eyesight and daily mindsight, devoid of conversation as well.

And one day, the husband and wife park themselves together in their spotless living room and discover that they're sitting across from a stranger.

Right now Dana and I are trying to rebuild our foundation, to create a shared room we live in. We're dating again, a one-step forward, one-step back getting to know each other, and in so many ways, it's more hesitant than our initial head-first dive into each other. We know every crease and crinkle of the other's smile better than we know our own, and yet we now tiptoe into conversation, not knowing when we're going to tread on a scar, all too aware that we don't always know what prompts that smile anymore. But we both want to find out.

And if our feelings are a little less cloudy, the logistics of this interim relationship are still quite gray. The whole will he/won't he spend the night is actually rather comical—in hindsight—although quite prickly in the moment. This is our house, our bed, but it feels like my call, which is strange. If I say no, the assumption zipped into the tiny word is that there's something we need to discuss, some boulder in our way. If I say yes, *what* am I really saying yes to? The night or our marriage? Perhaps both.

Sarah knows all this by the way, so it's legit. Dana joins me now at my weekly sessions, and the conundrum of the end of the date is something we talk about in therapy together, sometimes even get a good laugh out of. It feels good to laugh again with Dana, like every shared chuckle cancels out one bitter thought, one forgotten goodnight kiss.

But the meetings aren't always amusing; they are often a wrenching dissection of the layers of our marriage, of our feelings for each other, of the way we experience each other. As Sarah has coached, we try to stay away from the word "you" as in "YOU ALWAYS MAKE ME FEEL..." And "always," that's another one. But it isn't easy, especially when we've kicked down the repeatedly re-hinged door of propriety and are violent with tears, clenched jaws, raised voices. But we're smashing through our assumptions about each other, digging deep into ourselves and each other and coming up with our eyes open, able to see not just the outfits that clothe us, but inside each other again. And most of the time, after our hour is up, we take a deep breath and throw out our tissues; and when we walk out it feels as if we've patched up a piece of our basement. With cement.

MAY 1996
Greenwich, CT

Allie and Dana pulled up to the enormous white colonial at 7:30, amazed that they were only 30 minutes late after spending what seemed like hours extricating themselves from Matthew's superhuman grip. After both begging and bribery failed, they finally just pried the two-year-old's arms off of Allie's leg and sprinted out the door, amid shrieks from both Matthew and the baby, who at 10 months was uncannily empathetic to Matthew's distress.

The couple shared a shaky sigh as they were backing down the driveway.

"Wow," Dana said, his eyes on the rearview mirror. "I thought he liked Heather."

"He does. He just likes us better."

Dana digested that for a few minutes—or maybe he thought about work, Allie was never sure these days—and focused on the dark road. The radio sang several songs into the silence.

"You okay?" Dana asked as the DJ came on.

"I'm fine." She was so drained from their harrowing escape that she didn't have the energy to think up a topic of conversation. *Why is it that when I'm quiet, something's wrong, but when he's quiet, it's normal?* They used to have so much to say to each other; anecdotes and opinions used to froth up and over them like the head on a beer that was poured too fast. They could be silent together too, but the silence had been binding, not isolating. She sighed. Then she straightened her shoulders. She'd been excited about tonight. She and Dana hadn't had much time together lately, and now that they were out, she didn't want to waste a moment. She pulled down the visor mirror, reapplied her lipstick, and ran her hands through her long, wavy hair.

Dana peeked at her out of the corner of his eye and smiled. "You look nice," he said as they pulled up to the house.

"Thanks." Allie snapped the mirror closed. He rarely complimented her anymore. She wasn't sure if it was because she was usually in a sweatshirt or because he didn't think she looked good, or maybe didn't think of her at all. Melancholy swelled up inside her. His small compliment felt like gold, but it also tapped into sadness, a deep yearning, a longing to be close, to be connected. He felt so far away. She felt so alone.

The intense feeling took her by surprise and she turned to look out her window. She didn't want Dana to see; it felt so out of place on the way to this party. She tried to swallow the lump in her throat.

After a minute or two, she smoothed down her black crepe pants and turned to him. "Ready?"

———

Dana could feel the mood in the car shift; he sensed her turn away from him, heard her sigh. The sigh seemed to hiss *"you've let me down, again"* and those words slithered through his heart and into his stomach. He assumed she was irritated with him but he certainly wasn't going to ask about it, as that might throw gasoline on whatever it was. He racked his brain for what he had done wrong. He didn't know. He'd been busy most of the day and although he could feel some tension between them earlier, he had tried to stay out of the way so they wouldn't bump heads.

He glanced up at the house they were about to walk into, all his colleagues, his boss, the partners. He needed to be on his game tonight.

He could still feel her sigh in the pit of his stomach.

————

The deep toll of the doorbell echoed off the walls as they were ushered through
the front hall and into the formal living room filled with vases of fragrant, bright
flowers and a dozen or so lawyers and their fragrant, bright wives. Dana and
Allie were sucked into a group near the door, a circle that included their hostess,
a thin, powdered woman with a choker of pale pink pearls around her neck.
Allie assumed Dorothy had been a bubbly blond debutante 30 years ago; now
however, although the bubbles still popped in the exclamation point at the end
of each sentence, they resembled the dime-store suds that are forced through
a wand, not the champagne effervescence of an 18-year-old.

Okay, stop it. Allie chided herself. *You're feeling awkward with Dana
and out of place in this room. It isn't Dorothy's fault.* She looked at Dana.
Did he feel it too? She wasn't sure.

She needed to shake her mood, and she was desperate for a glass of wine,
as much for something to hold as for something to drink. She slid her hands
in her pockets and sized up the crowd. She recognized a few faces—Charlotte
and Frank would be good for a few laughs, she'd avoid Nancy for fear of being
lured into a corner and bored to death. And hooray, there was Hannah.

Her eyes settled back onto Dana, one of the young stars in the room.
She knew it was his hard work that had opened the door to this high-
powered group in the office and subsequently at this gathering. She watched
him, absorbed him for a moment—his earnest smile, the way he spoke without hesitation and without bulldozing, the way he gestured with his hands
when he was energized. A powerful synthesis of pride and love washed over
her, and she reached down and squeezed his hand. He glanced down at her
with a fleeting public smile, and then turned back to the group.

Dorothy tapped her fingers to her pearls and said, "Oh, I haven't offered
you two a drink!" She flapped her hand at a young girl carrying a silver tray
and weaving her way through the knots of people.

"This is my daughter, Courtney," Dorothy said as the girl scurried over. Courtney flashed her silver braces. "May I get you a cocktail?"

Allie examined Courtney for some sign that she was annoyed at being sold into servitude, but saw none. "I'd love a glass of chardonnay, thanks." Dana opted for scotch. Allie snuck a glance at him. *Scotch?*

"Allie darling, you look fabulous!" Dorothy said as Courtney pirouetted away. "I can't believe you have two small kids. Dana, you're a lucky man."

Allie bit back a crack to Dana about his luck and focused on Dorothy. "Little kids are easy. You're dealing with teenagers. Now that's a job." She watched Dorothy's smile spread as she continued, "Courtney's lovely. How old is she?"

"14, the baby if you can believe it. Grace, who's not here, is 16. She's our tricky one. And then Adam," Dorothy turned towards the bar and exhaled as if life drained out of her, "is off to college in August. We're letting him tend bar tonight."

"I can't imagine Matthew tending bar, much less going to college." Allie party-smiled at Dana.

"It'll be here before you know it." Dorothy shook her head. "Excuse me." She breezed away to greet another couple.

Allie sipped the wine that Courtney had delivered with a smile just short of a curtsey, and thought that after this glass of wine, she should call and check in with the sitter. She tuned back into Dana—who was dissecting a case with the other men in the circle—and inserted suitable exclamations to a story she'd heard several times. Finally, as her negligibility became obvious—at least to her—she wandered out into the party. Her final destination was Hannah, but as she was on the far side of the room, Allie braced herself for pit stops along the way; it wouldn't do to make a beeline through the throng. She slid into a group of four.

"How are you, dear?" Susan, a woman with short gray hair, smiled at Allie. She was married to senior partner Henry Drake, and as such, was the assumed matriarch of the firm. Allie knew they had grandchildren and thought briefly that she should ask her how they made their long marriage work. She realized she'd never had anyone to ask before.

"We're great." She flashed a smile she didn't quite feel. "It's good to see you all again. Hi, I'm Allie." She extended her hand to the one woman in the circle she hadn't met: a tall, stunning brunette. Several compliments lined up on Allie's tongue—the wave of this woman's hair, the flawless cut of her turquois dress—but she swallowed them back down. Something told her it wasn't appropriate.

"June."

Allie tried not to stare at June's enormous diamond ring as they shook hands. "It's so nice to finally meet you. Dana talks about Jim all the time; he enjoys working with him." This wasn't exactly true, but she was hoping to pump some warmth into June's cool demeanor.

June blinked, as if reorienting herself to the conversation. "Thanks. Yes, I've heard about Dana too."

There was an awkward silence and Susan waved Courtney over.

"Oh June," a sleek blonde named Katherine tentatively said. "I heard that Jim just got the Clayton case."

"He did." June smiled, although it did not reach her eyes. "He's been working incredibly hard; in fact, we postponed our vacation to Bermuda." She turned to Susan and plugged for her husband. "I think he was happy not to go, he'd rather be working."

"Good for him, he deserves the case." Susan patted June on the arm. "Just make sure you get that Bermuda trip."

Allie got the feeling that all these women were being careful with June. She guessed that along with June's style and obvious money, she had a lot of social power. And maybe not in a good way.

"How are your kids, Allie?" asked Margaret, a woman in a hot pink dress.

"Asleep, I hope."

"I'm so glad I'm done with the toddler years. Honestly, I don't know how you get through the day. Even with a nanny, I barely made it," Margaret said.

"Some days are longer than others." Allie smiled.

June excused herself, and there was a momentary silence in the hole of her absence.

Allie peered around the room. Dana was deep in conversation with one of his colleagues, so she edged as gracefully as she could out of the circle and continued to make her way through the room towards Hannah. Along the way, she merged into small groups of women and chatted briefly. Each conversation was similar—perfunctory questions or comments about the kids, spouses, or someone at the firm, or perhaps a compliment on an outfit or accessory.

Finally, she reached her friend. Hannah was dressed just to the provocative side of tasteful tonight, wearing long, swingy white silk pants and a white halter, under which she was notably braless. Her wildly curly, dark blond hair was loose and hung to the middle of her back. As Allie approached, Hannah wrapped up her conversation with Bob Crabtree, one of the partners, with a kiss on the cheek that was just a twitch away from his lips.

"Aren't we the minimalist couple amid all this color," Hannah said. She hugged Allie; unusual in this room of work relationships.

Allie stepped back to eye their monotone outfits. "Mine was intentional. Black hides the baby weight."

"I wonder what it says about us that we're devoid of color amid this tropical rainforest."

"We're scared colorless?"

"Scared?" Hannah laughed. "Of what?"

"Have you seen the cast of characters in here?"

"Well I know you have; I saw your slow dance across the room. Were you campaigning?"

"Maybe, although I don't think I was getting a lot of votes. I can't tell if they just don't like me or what." She smiled. "I guess I was hoping to crack the ice a little."

"You'll get there. Hey, if they've warmed up to me… Now they actually talk *to* me instead of just behind my back."

Allie didn't know what to say. Hannah laughed again.

"Come on, this group? Even if I didn't know what they were saying, I could guess. Greg's handsome, a partner on his second marriage, a much younger wife, no kids. I'm sure there's imagined scandal in there. Greg and I have given them fodder for years."

Allie nodded.

"I have to admit, I like to egg them on." Hannah leaned in. "My lack of an undergarment must be a great conversation starter out there." She smirked.

Allie laughed. "It definitely saves them from talking about themselves."

"Oh no, that's taboo. It's a cocktail party, and a work one at that. We're all trying to be sparkling and pretty. No tarnish allowed."

Allie nodded. "Even 'how are your kids'—which could be loaded with lots of dirty laundry—it's all wonderful and shiny."

"These parties take practice. It's like skating really, gliding along on Waterford crystal, trying to avoid the thin ice."

"I must be drinking the Kool Aid. A little while ago, someone asked me how I was, and I said, 'we're great.' *We're.* As soon as it came out of my mouth I wanted to shove it back in, but no one blinked."

"That's one slip of the tongue I don't have to worry about." Hannah paused, sipped her drink. "I think the 'do you work' question has the most landmines."

"But no one asks it anymore. Because if the answer is no, then the whole group's embarrassed, as if they've just denigrated Motherhood. And you feel defensive, like they've just asked if you're a Useful Person and you've answered no, and there's a rush to fill the awkwardness with a list of everything that keeps you busy all day."

"You've thought about this." Hannah smiled.

"One of the many things I do all day." Allie's eyes twinkled.

"Deflection is the name of the game. Admire me, applaud me, but don't *really* ask—certainly not at a party like this. But not with your good friends, not with Dana, right?"

Allie was quiet for a moment.

"How is that cute husband of yours?" Hannah said.

"Good, busy. He puts in a lot of hours."

"Sounds familiar." Hannah sighed. "You okay?"

"I'm busy too. The kids keep me on my toes."

"I knew there was a reason I don't have any." Hannah's eyes were fleetingly sad. As if to cover it up she grinned and said, "And what about after hours?"

"You're looking at it." Allie waved her hand in Dana's direction. "Opposite sides of the room." She sipped her wine.

"Hopefully you're getting out with your friends."

It had been quite a while, Allie realized. The garbled noise of a hundred conversations filled the space between them.

"So did you pick up any interesting news while you were making your rounds?"

"Other than your halter?" Allie grinned.

Hannah turned and accepted a merlot from Courtney. "How's June holding up?"

"Jim's wife? With the enormous ring? I just met her." Allie tucked a chunk of hair behind her ear. "She was pretty cold. Her polish was so thick I thought it might crack if she smiled."

Hannah didn't say anything.

"What'd you mean 'holding up?'" Allie said.

"Her son died last year in a drunk-driving accident."

Allie's hand flew to her mouth.

Someone across the room laughed loudly.

"I think the coldness you saw is paralysis," Hannah said. "The polish is protective."

A deep wave of melancholy rolled through Allie. "That poor woman."

They were quiet for a moment.

"She's really funny, razor-sharp funny, and nice. But I can't imagine she finds much funny now." Hannah swirled the red wine in her glass. "I worry about her. I know all about suiting up for events, or suiting down." Hannah smiled and adjusted the strap of her halter. "But I make sure I have a place where I can take the suit off, be real."

Allie avoided Hannah's gaze by scanning the crowd. Dana was across the room, a stranger in a clump of navy blazers. She hadn't seen Megan in weeks. She suddenly felt queasy. *When was the last time I checked my suit at the door?*

She smiled for Hannah. "Thanks for the life lesson; now I'm thoroughly depressed."

"Anytime. Now let's go outside and have a cigarette, and you can regale me with tales of your kids, or Dana, or yourself if you dare." Hannah's eyes twinkled.

Allie zeroed in on Dana once more. He was still deep in conversation and had not, to her knowledge, even looked around for her. Then she stepped outside with Hannah to tell her a funny story about someone else.

———————

Much later that night, on the car ride home, the passing streetlights gently stroked the silence in the front seat. Allie was warm and woozy from the wine, and introspective in the way the right amount of alcohol and circumstance can render. Dana was quiet as well, perhaps all talked out from discussions with colleagues. As they drove down the familiar streets toward their house, the bright lights and chatter from the party slipped under the tires along with the gritty asphalt underneath them, and the dark gulf between the two front seats yawned, enormous and unbridgeable. Allie stared out the window into the black night and thought that there wasn't a car big enough to encase the separateness between them right now.

———————

The next Friday night, Tess had a decision to make. Close her eyes and drift off to sleep or break a sweat struggling to get off the couch. Unfortunately, the nap was a pipe dream. She planted both arms behind her and rocked front to back, building up enough momentum so that she could tip into a standing position. She laughed at herself—a noise that burped out into the quiet house—and walked, or rather waddled up the stairs.

She tried to ignore the mirror as she undressed, but she caught a glimpse of herself anyway. *Hard to avoid; I fill up the whole room.* Her belly had swollen so much that it now served as a shelf for her huge breasts, and her belly button had vanished; in fact, all excess skin had been called upon to stretch tightly over the 50-plus pounds she had gained. Early in her pregnancy, she had tried to stick to vegetables and grilled chicken, but she had been so ravenous that after the second month she just threw up her hands. And of course she craved anything laden with excess fat and packing zero nutritional value: mayonnaise, French fries, potato chips, or absolutely anything chocolate.

She climbed into the shower, hoping to be in and out and dressed before Gavin came home. She hated being naked in front of him now. She hated being pregnant in front of herself for that matter, and perhaps (although she was afraid to think it) she just hated being pregnant. *I love the baby*, she thought in a rush, afraid that someone might read her mind and scorn her; it was already fully entrenched in her heart. Its fully entrenched position in her body was the problem. She was just not one of those women who reveled in being pregnant. When she stumbled on magazine articles like "Sensuous and Sexy, The Untold Pregnancy Bonus!" in which perky celebrities waxed on about their pregnant bodies and revealed that they felt so much more sexy in the family way—and that P.S. their husbands agreed—well, she wondered what planet they could be living on. They certainly couldn't be carrying an active human in their giant bellies.

She had to admit, that although she didn't think Gavin would describe her as sexy, he seemed oblivious to her growing girth. He had doted on her for the past seven months, heroically alleviating her discomfort with back rubs, loving words, and once in a while, surprise weekend getaways. The baby, just the idea of it, had transformed him into Gene Kelly—tap dancing with a delirious smile while putting the laundry away or taking out the garbage. In bed at night he would often whisper to her belly, an intimate act that nearly moved her to tears with its sweetness, and swathed her whole world with promise.

But when she was alone, she slumped into her enormity. She became her stomach, pasting her mother's "fat" label across her own forehead. She had grown up watching strangers' eyes glaze over when they were introduced to Ann; in response, her mother would yank her coat or sweater more tightly around herself. Tess never knew if this was to cover herself up or to remind herself that she was real. Either way, it wasn't the stuff that creates healthy self-esteem, or a healthy marriage; Tess's father's eyes were equally glazed over. Tess was terrified that privately, under the singing-in-the-rain, Gavin was just as disregarding.

She toweled off and waddled over to her closet, selecting a huge tent of a shirt and black maternity pants—shapeless, stretchy things with a spandex panel instead of a zipper. She heard the door slam downstairs and she tugged on her shirt and stepped into the gigantic white maternity underwear.

"Hi honey." Gavin walked into the room and threw his tie down on the bed. "How're you doing?"

"Okay." She grimaced. "For a circus freak."

Gavin laughed, which elicited a laugh from Tess. "Sorry," she said, letting the humor purge some of her negativity. "Being hugely naked in the bathroom brings out the beast in me."

"Sounds interesting." He grinned as he stepped towards her.

"Get out of here!" She giggled and swatted at him. "We've got to get ready to go."

"I know. It was just the image of you naked; I thought maybe we could be late."

"Don't forget the word in front of naked: hugely," Tess said, sitting down on the bed to pull on her pants.

"Naked any way, anytime sounds good to me," he said, and he kissed her on the forehead before disappearing into the bathroom.

"It may sound good to you, but the reality is a little frightening," Tess muttered.

"I heard that!"

"Okay. I'm leaving the attitude here. Hurry up, Allie said 7:30."

———

An hour later, Dana and Allie were seated and quietly perusing their menus as if they were studying *The New York Times*. When Tess and Gavin arrived, Allie leapt up out of the silence and hugged them both. Dana and Gavin shook hands, and then Tess walked over and kissed Dana.

"Meg called," Allie said as she sat back down and happily relinquished her menu. "She and Jared are going to be a little late. And I haven't heard from Zoe, but I always assume she's going to be late." Allie watched Tess's face shift ever-so-slightly at the mention of Zoe's name. "So we might want to order an appetizer if we're all hungry."

"Starving is now my permanent state," Tess said. She fiddled with her gold necklace. "Is Zoe bringing anyone?"

"She wasn't sure."

Gavin opened his mouth as if to say something, and then closed it.

Dana leaned back in his chair. "Well, it always adds entertainment when she does. Conversation for tonight's dinner and the next few to come."

"Remember that last guy? What was his name? Vic?" Gavin smiled. "The guy who couldn't stop petting her?"

Dana laughed. "Like she was an exotic poodle or something."

"I can't believe Zoe made it all the way through dinner without biting his head off," Allie said.

"And remember that guy who scowled all night?" Tess said.

"Except when he had the chance to talk about himself," Gavin said.

"He was bad," Dana said. "At least The Petter was interested in her. I'm not sure what The Scowler brought to the table."

Tess turned to Allie. "Have you met the new man?"

"No, but I've heard a little. You know Zoe, she's never excited enough about anyone to color in the details." Allie shrugged and her eyes shot to Gavin. It was reflex; although Zoe didn't talk about it, Allie knew that she still had feelings for him. She and Gavin caught eyes; Allie looked away, embarrassed, as if she had just stumbled in on something intimate. Their discomfort spread between on the tablecloth between them like the soak of spilled red wine.

"Or they're spun through her revolving door and the details are lost in the blur." Tess snickered.

The other three politely guffawed and picked up their menus.

"Did I spy new shoes?" Allie asked Tess.

Tess stuck her black-sandaled foot out beyond the table. "Shoes are the only thing I can buy right now in my regular size."

"You're lucky," Allie said. "My feet grew during pregnancy and never shrunk back."

As if on cue, the men turned to each other and started talking about sports.

Tess groaned. "I swear if that happens to me I'm throwing in the towel."

"That bad, huh?"

"Like a Mack Truck."

"You don't look like one." Allie reached across and squeezed Tess's hand. "Just a few more weeks."

"I am so ready."

Allie stifled an, "Enjoy the peace while you can," and instead said, "Me too; so's Matthew. When he heard we were going to see you tonight, he wanted to come and see the baby."

"How's my favorite little man?"

"He's awesome," Allie said. "Chatting up a storm."

Movement near the table caused Allie to look up. "Ah, the newlyweds!" she said with a wide grin.

Chairs scraped back in unison as the girls leapt up to hug the couple; Dana and Gavin kissed Megan on the cheek and shook hands with Jared.

"How was the rest of your honeymoon?" Tess asked, as Jared pulled out Megan's chair. "We all wanted to stay with you!"

"Amazing," Megan said as she settled into her chair. "We didn't want to come back either."

The waitress appeared with her pad, and everyone's attention veered to beverages and appetizers. Allie peeked at her best friend and was relieved to see her glowing, a combination of the Caribbean sun and possibly the peace that came with finally committing to Jared. After many months apart, Megan had realized that the answer to the can't-live-without-him question didn't have to involve urgency and anguish, it could just be a simple fact: she didn't want to be without him. She had decided that their love could create its own kind of fire, the kind that kept you warm on a frigid, snowy night. And it obviously did, as soon after they reunited, they were scrambling to organize a small, casual wedding in the British Virgin Islands due to the yet-to-be-showing, but certainly extenuating circumstances.

Allie watched Megan reach out and squeeze Jared's hand, and she swallowed a lump of envy. Her green eyes flicked to Dana, ordering calamari from the waitress. She loved him deeply, but differently now after 11 years and two children. The spark, the giggle was all but extinguished, and whether it was a temporary outage or a permanent loss, they now plodded, as opposed to danced, through life. She didn't know if it was a normal evolution or something that was just happening to the two of them.

As the waitress rushed away with a promise to be back with their drinks, everyone at the table leaned in to hear Megan and Jared's tales of cloudless days, water sports, and gourmet food.

"Stop! Don't tell me any more, I can't stand it," Allie leaned back. "It's been so long since we've been on a vacation."

"You don't consider every day in our new kitchen a vacation?" Dana said.

"I seem to be missing the five-star service piece."

"You are the five-star service piece." Dana smiled.

"More conventionally called the maid." She heard the edge in her tone and bit the inside of her cheek.

Dana glanced at his wife and cocked his head.

Megan jumped in. "I'm expecting homemade chocolates on our pillow the next time we stay in your guest room."

"Absolutely," Dana turned to Megan, "although payment for the turn-down service is a tour with Gillian's night duty. What is it these days Allie, two times a night?"

"Oh, God. Don't tell me," Tess said. "After 10 months you're still getting up twice a night? When does that stop?"

"Ask Gillian," Allie said.

"There's nothing you can do?" Tess's mouth hung open.

Dana patted Gavin's shoulder. "Get ready to give up all control."

Gavin reached for his drink. Tess laughed, but it sounded like a panicked cough.

"Hi everyone," Zoe sang out as she slung her black leather purse over a chair. "My date's behind me, he saw some ass to kiss at the bar. Please tell me we're not going to talk about babies all night."

Once again everyone rose to hug, a veritable do-si-do of quickly switching partners.

"I'll see if I can dredge through my attic files for another topic of conversation," Allie said as she kissed Zoe.

"How was that party the other night?" Megan asked Allie as they all sat back down.

"Let's just say I needed a night out with my friends who knew me back when."

"Should I finish that sentence?" Zoe said. They all laughed, Dana a little less heartily.

A tall man with dark hair and an air of confidence appeared at the table. Zoe smiled. "Everyone, this is Doug." She flicked her hand to indicate the group. "Doug, everyone."

All eyes scanned his left hand as they introduced themselves.

"So, what, is everyone here pregnant?" Zoe raised her eyebrows and fired a scowl at Tess. "Where are the cocktails?"

"Ordered and hopefully arriving any minute. Sorry Tess, but I really need a drink," Allie said, hoping, as always, to soften the tension between Zoe and Tess.

Gavin twisted around for the waitress and waved her over to take Zoe's drink order.

Tess rubbed the pendant on her necklace. "Zoe, you look great." Her words floated across the table like a sigh.

"Tess has cute new shoes," Allie said.

"Oh," Tess stuck her feet farther under the table. "They're nothing special."

"So Doug," Megan said, "do you work with Zoe?"

"Doug is my married boss," Zoe said.

The buzz at the table died as if someone had pushed *stop*, and then Doug guffawed. "Actually, I'm divorced. And in a different division." He looked at Zoe like she was an amusing child.

"For a moment there I thought you'd learned nothing from Megan and Jared's boss/assistant dilemma," Allie said.

"What we learned there was that true love prevailed," Zoe said. Her blue eyes sought Gavin's, and trembled there for a moment.

Allie noticed Tess's eyes move slowly between Gavin and Zoe, and back again. Then she put her hand over her stomach and was very still.

The waitress plunked down drinks and appetizers.

Zoe held up her martini in a toast. "Here's to a new baby," she looked at Tess and Gavin, "a new marriage," she looked at Megan and Jared, "a new kitchen," she looked at Allie and Dana, "and a new drink." She chuckled and took a big gulp.

Doug raised his glass and smirked. "I guess I'm in the *new drink* category."

Megan cleared her throat. "And one more thing." Everyone turned to her. "Add another baby to that toast." Megan beamed and reached for Jared's hand. Jared leaned over and kissed her.

Zoe stared at Megan. "Wow."

Allie smiled; she had known the news. "Congratulations."

"Ten weeks," Megan said. "So unbeknownst to most of you, you attended a shotgun wedding."

"I wish we'd known that. We might not have come," Gavin said with a twinkle in his eye.

Tess rolled her eyes at Gavin.

"Congratulations Meg," Zoe said quietly to Megan. "Wow. Another baby." Then with more of a public flourish, she joked to the table, "I guess it's contagious." She raised her glass again. "Catch the glow."

Allie caught Gavin's quick glance at Zoe.

Zoe turned to Doug. "Don't worry though, I prefer to catch my glow from other sources." She finished the rest of her drink in one smooth swallow.

Dana helped himself to fried calamari, and the movement broke the conversation up into small groups. Allie, who was sitting next to Zoe, leaned in and asked, "Are you okay?"

"Sorry, I had a couple of drinks before I came. Couldn't do it on a sober heart, you know? Don't mind me. How are you?"

"Well, it's hard not to mind you, but I'm fine."

"Are you?" Zoe stared intently into her friend's eyes. "I'm hearing fine, but I'm not so sure I'm seeing fine in your eyes."

"I forget that you have paranormal powers. Things are... I don't know what's wrong with me to tell you the truth. But basically fine."

"You know, you say fine and I say fine, and we just add to the giant myth that everything's great for everyone else and we're the only ones who can't quite cut it. Sometimes the brave face isn't the most useful."

"You're right." Allie did a double-take. "Such insight."

"It's the alcohol talking." She chuckled. "Don't tell anyone."

"We need a date. It's been too long since we've talked."

"I know. In the meantime, have a drink." Zoe pushed Allie's wine closer to her. "I don't want to be the only one making loud and inappropriate comments at the table. And get a job. It gives you something to talk about when what's really on your mind won't do." Zoe flashed a grin.

Allie ran her finger along the stem of her glass. "I can't get a job. Matthew and Gillian are too young."

Zoe sighed. "I don't know how you do it. I'd be bored out of my mind."

"No you wouldn't." Allie touched Zoe's arm. "Not if they were your kids."

"What's this about getting a job?" Tess jumped in. "You're not going to leave me hanging after I've gone ahead and quit now are you?"

Allie shook her head.

"You quit?" Megan said.

"I did," Tess said with an excited twinkle. "I've been flip-flopping for so long, but as D-Day approaches… due date," she said to Jared who looked perplexed, "it just seems like the pros of being home with this little bambino outweighed the cons. You know, going for walks in the park versus managing a client's tantrum over the fact that some magazine didn't mention their product in the 'Got To Have It For Summer' article. It was really a no-brainer." She sighed. "And Lord knows, I could use a vacation."

Allie smiled at the idea that a newborn was a vacation.

"What about you, Meg? Now that you guys are going to be changing diapers every five minutes, do you think you'll quit?" Zoe said, spilling her drink a little.

"Oh God. I… we haven't really thought about it." She paused. "But that being said, I love my job. I can't imagine leaving it."

"Maybe I'll stay home with the baby," Jared said.

Everyone but Jared chuckled.

———

Gavin, who was sitting with Tess on his right and Zoe across from him, was becoming concerned about how much Zoe had obviously had to drink. Ever since her abortion, he felt responsible for her. Maybe it was the "I love you" she had exhaled so long ago; maybe it was their long history; maybe it was the bowling ball of guilt he carried around, guilt and shame around how very close he had come to hurting Tess, and Zoe, and himself. He was trying to make that up to Tess by being a good husband. He tried to make it up to Zoe by being a good friend.

They still saw each other for drinks once in a while, but their relationship stayed planted in the public arena—drinks, conversation, end of story. He was just as attracted to her, and all else being zero he'd jump at the chance to be with her. But all else wasn't zero now. He had made a vow to Tess, and he was happy to know that it truly mattered to him.

The last time they met for drinks, Zoe had had one (or really several) too many; not all that unusual for Zoe, especially lately. What had been unusual was that for the first time since her abortion, she'd climbed out of her emotional straightjacket and become pretty loose. At one point in the conversation, Gavin mentioned that Tess was feeling uncomfortable in the last days of her pregnancy, and Zoe had responded lasciviously, "Which must make you pretty uncomfortable."

A few years ago, Gavin would have assumed the comment was sexual and would have batted back the flirty pitch. But now he was an umpire, and played strictly by the book. "It's just hard to see her feeling so awkward in her own skin. It's hard to know how to cheer her up."

"I actually, believe it or not, wasn't really talking about Tess. I was talking about you, and whether you needed cheering up," Zoe slurred.

"Me? I'm fine."

"Are you sure?" Zoe put her hand over his on the bar.

He moved his hand gently out from under hers. "I'm sure, Zo. Thanks," he said lightly, playing ignorant to what had unmistakably been put on the table. He wanted to say "I'm sorry" but didn't want to highlight the rejection. Better for her if it remained innuendo, not an explicit offer.

There was a brief, awkward silence while Zoe absorbed the sting. She focused on her bare hand, pale and slim against the dark mahogany bar, and then quickly reached for her vodka and drank deeply.

———

With her hand firmly clasped together with Jared's, Megan left the restaurant so exuberant she could have sprinted a marathon. She was alight with luck and good fortune, a feeling she hadn't had in a long time. Her job, her friends, Jared, the baby, all the puzzle pieces, everything that was important to her had finally snapped into place. She adored feeling like she was carrying around an amazing secret, a secret that only she and Jared, and a few select people of their choosing, knew anything about. She now understood why pregnant women glowed; she certainly felt like she was lit up.

Strangely, when she had discovered she was pregnant, certainly a surprise on the scale of premeditation, she hadn't been panicked. The second she saw the positive test, the world had narrowed down to the eye of a needle—this breathless moment, her trembling hand, the extraordinary double pink line, and the certitude in her heart. When the world opened back up again a moment later, she was in Oz, and everything had turned from slightly washed-out ordinary to lemon yellow, fire-engine red.

The four walls of the apartment had quivered with excitement as she waited for Jared to arrive home that night. The minute the door creaked open, she exploded into his arms with the white stick in hand, sending the mail flying and almost knocking him to the floor. Shortly afterwards, barefooted and silhouetted against the Caribbean sunset, their vows and rings were exchanged with quiet conviction, the gently breaking surf and the tearful sniffles of both families and a few friends the only background music.

Now on the heels of their honeymoon and their first dinner out in the city as husband and wife, they returned to their little apartment—they had already planned where the crib would go—and fell onto the couch together. A few times during their walk, Megan had felt a strange twinge in her belly, but she attributed it to walking too quickly and once the feeling passed it had disappeared from her consciousness. But now that they were home, the twinges started again.

She left Jared on the couch and went into their closet-like bathroom, closing the door behind her. She pulled down her underwear and sat down on the toilet seat. It took her a full minute to register that she was bleeding.

CHAPTER 10

JOURNAL ENTRY #10
March 18, 2001

Get ready to give up your heart. Not many people hear these words when they're pregnant with their first child, when they are eagerly stockpiling receiving blankets and colorful rattles. Family and friends help us prepare with lists of gear must-haves (diapers, pacifiers, 10 more arms), with logistical suggestions (an extra changing table downstairs), and with self-care advice (sleep when you can). But no one sits us down and asks: Are you ready to be moved to corners of your heart you've never been before? Are you ready to love so fiercely that you'd kill if you had to? Are you ready to be knocked to your knees by the overflow of adoration, grief, rage; emotions that previously were manageable but are now Herculean in their depth and power?

Our conversations are so often peppered with emotional qualifiers about other people in our lives—I love him, I'm furious with her, I despise that man. And we talk about our children all the time, either casually with acquaintances or in depth with family and friends, but I've never once heard a parent reflect on their feelings for their children. The situations are analyzed to death; the underlying emotions aren't debated. There are whole genres of creative arts dedicated to romantic love (love songs, romantic comedies, romance novels), and comparatively few pieces of art dedicated to the feelings we have about our children. Why is that? Is it because words, despite all the fat dictionaries chock full of interesting choices, can't begin to capture the encyclopedia of feelings we have about our children?

Or is it because the premise of loving your children is so instinctive, so organic that it doesn't need detailed description, and that *that* feeling is the only emotion in the encyclopedia that is internally, and certainly publicly, sanctioned? Everyone cherishes their children; it's as simple as that. But does this simple blanket of impermeable love render any other strong feelings—natural feelings such as anger or frustration—an act of ultimate betrayal? Does allowing ourselves the bad days and negative thoughts constitute treason, signify deviance?

And if just feeling or speaking of moments of ugliness is taboo, how can some people so publicly declare themselves aberrant by walking away from their children? And what does that say about their children?

What does that say about me?

That was meant to be rhetorical.

I wonder if other parents ruminate as much as I do about their own death. My worry isn't narcissistic; it's an Arctic dread for my children. Of course selfishly, I can't bear the idea of not knowing these quirky, beautiful, charismatic little people, can't bear the thought of not watching, supporting, cheering for them as they grow up. But even more unbearable is the thought of them facing the world without me, without the bubble wrap of my unconditional love, without that one person in their lives who can barely stand it she adores them so.

Random times when I'm behind the wheel of mindless errands, a flash of disaster shatters my semiconscious maneuvers on the road, and for a split second I envision slamming into a tree or crashing through a guardrail into the rippled reservoir below. What's most horrifying about these images is that it would be a day like any other. Matthew and Gillian would be at home with a sitter, happily playing outside on the swings, or in their rooms, contentedly imagining stuffed animals ruled the world, confidently anticipating my arrival. The clock would tick... and tick... and tick... and I just wouldn't show up. The house would become hushed with their confusion, and they would wonder why Mommy wasn't sailing through the door, as only a few hours earlier she had sung a cheery "Be back soon! Love you!" as she had hurried out of it. After a while their worry would become cranky frustration. The clock would continue to tick; the big hand would patiently make its way around again.

Matthew and Gillian would be left only with questions, and I wouldn't be there to cuddle them close, to smother them with soft kisses and offer answers. They would be forced to digest death and loss and insurmountable sorrow without me to put sugar on the spoon for them.

When these nightmares wash over me, I try not to look, I try to turn the channel, but like a turnpike rubbernecker, I can't tear myself away. I'm glued to the scene, tears in my eyes and despair in my heart as I think of the grief I've unintentionally wrought. And then another image steps forward from the recesses of my mind: an image of a scared little girl and boy, huddled together on a blue couch, wondering and worrying about their own mother. And I am reminded that unanswered, insurmountable sorrow is exactly what my mother knowingly handed to me.

Apparently I was inconsequential.

I have spent my whole life trying to show Eva that she shouldn't have walked out; I realize now that no matter what I do, and no matter what I did when I was a child, she's not coming back. And that her leaving was not my fault. NOT MY FAULT. (Repeat after me, Sarah coaches gently, "Not my fault.") Sometimes now I believe it. And through Matthew and Gillian I see that kids are what they are: lovable, awe-inspiring, life-redeeming, pure and passionate joy. They are also exhausting, challenging, and button-pushing. There's no getting around that. It didn't matter how hard I tried to be fun, to be exciting, to be an "easy" child, my role as a child and my mother's role as caregiver would have been the same. I was four. I was a responsibility; I put unspoken and unknown demands on her. Sometimes I was a pain in the ass. And there was nothing I could have done to keep her from bolting.

I try to remember that when Matthew's face lights up with pride and his eyes instinctively search for mine among the parents in the audience, or when he falls off his bike and needs a kiss before he needs a Band-Aid; every time Gillian joyfully prances around me in the kitchen, or shakily yells out for me in the middle of the night. I'm not going anywhere.

And I am not inconsequential.

Electric guitar smashed through the sleepy, gray dawn, jolting Allie upright and into consciousness. She reached behind her, over her warm, crumpled pillow, and smacked the alarm; silence flooded back into the room. *The kids must have played with it again.* Her heart was pounding like she'd just run a marathon. *And there's my cardio for today.* She sighed and rolled out of bed.

Through the baby monitor, she heard Gillian's "Mommy-Mommy-Mommy!" and wondered whether it was the classic rock or Gillian's own internal clock (set for daybreak) that had woken her. She stumbled bleary-eyed by Gillian's door—*coffee first*—and down into the kitchen, where she started to fill the coffee pot with water. In the corner of the room, the overflowing laundry basket sneered at her. *Damn, I meant to do that last night.* She'd better throw in a load fast; Matthew's best friend, Jack the Rabbit, was encrusted with mud and lying limply on top of the pile. If Matthew spied it, she wouldn't get Jack into the wash without an epic call to arms.

She blindly spooned coffee into the machine and made a mental note to get more at the store. *I should write that down.* She glanced around for a pen, but as Gillian's cries grew more adamant, she abandoned the idea of a list and rushed back upstairs.

"Juice, Mama," Gillian demanded through her pink pacifier as Allie walked into her room. "Juice." Underneath the mop of dark hair that was sticking up in all directions, her green eyes were very serious.

Allie smiled; it had been the same greeting since the two-year-old could say the word. Clearly she believed if she didn't insist on it each morning, she wouldn't receive it. *Which judging by the fact that I forgot to start the coffee machine, could mean that Gillian belonged in the talented-and-gifted program.*

She wrapped her arms around her daughter and held her close, breathing in the little girl's warm, rumpled scent as she tread down the stairs, cherishing for a moment the little arms wrapped snugly around her neck. Allie one-handedly poured orange juice into a sippy cup, started the coffee, and stepped cautiously over the obstacle course of toys in the playroom that she'd sighed and turned her back on last night. The red couch was mercifully clutter-free, and she and Gillian sank in for a round of stories while they both regained consciousness. She could hear the coffee machine gasping and grunting as it began to percolate, and Allie silently urged it to hurry.

A moment later, Matthew padded in and curled up in her lap as well, but he had no patience for the board book and demanded his morning addiction, hot chocolate.

"Let me just finish this book sweetie, and then I'll make you the most delicious hot chocolate."

"Mooooooooom." Matthew looked at her with big brown eyes.

"Sweetie, please don't whine. I'll get it in a minute."

"Read!" Gillian jabbed her chubby finger into the book.

"Mooooooooom."

Kids must be taught in utero that the more compelling the whine, the faster the action. That and the best way to find something is to dump everything out.

"Matthew, can you help me read this story to Gillian? Tell her which animals the gorilla is saying goodnight to."

Matthew's face lit up and he began to point to the colorful pictures.

"*Mommy* do it!" Gillian said, pushing Matthew's hand off the page.

Matthew drew his eyebrows together in a deep frown and thumped his finger down on the book.

Allie took a deep breath and smoothed a lock of hair behind Gillian's ear. "Gill, Matthew knows this better than Mommy. He can help us."

Gillian opened her mouth to protest, and Allie interrupted with her best cheerleader voice. "Okay guys, let's go get something to eat."

"And hot chocolate too!" Matthew scrambled off of the couch.

And coffee, Allie thought. She toted Gillian into the kitchen with Matthew close on her heels and passed a pile of unopened mail waiting to be sorted; bills most likely. *Balance my checkbook, oh and RSVP to that party.*

Still juggling Gillian, she opened a cupboard. "We have Cheerios. Want Cheerios?"

Both kids nodded.

"Matthew, with milk or without?"

He nodded absently as he climbed into his chair.

"With or without?" Allie said.

"Without," Matthew said. "I mean with!"

Gillian nodded. "Wid." Her wide eyes were solemn with the importance of the decision.

"Yellow bowl!" Matthew yelled. He had to eat and drink everything out of yellow dishes.

"Yellow bowl… " Allie tilted her head and raised her eyebrows at Matthew. "Pleeease."

As Allie was pouring the milk into two identical yellow bowls, Matthew gave a squeal of delight. "Jack!"

Oh no. She turned toward him with a smile. "Jack's been waiting for you to help him with his bath."

Matthew grabbed the filthy toy and clutched it against his chest. "He's not dirty."

"Sweetie, he's very dirty, can you see?" Allie buckled a squirming Gillian into her high chair and squatted down to Matthew. "And he was so excited for his bath, he told me this morning."

"He can take one with me tonight." Matthew was pleased that he'd thought of a solution.

Allie had visions of her son swimming in a tubful of black water. "But Jack needs a special bath, a fur-washing bath. Hey, you know what? Maybe we can give him a bath outside later, fill up the plastic pool with bubbles and have a giant bath for animals." She held her breath.

Matthew grinned and clapped his hands. "Now?" Jack fell to the floor in a cloud of dust.

"How about we wait for the sun to come up?" Allie smiled.

Matthew started jumping up and down and Madaket, their yellow Labrador retriever, pranced and barked around with him, not sure what the commotion was about, but more than happy to join in. Gillian bounced up and down in her high chair and cheered.

The dog snatched up Jack from the floor and froze, looking at Matthew, hoping for a chase.

"Jack!" Matthew shrieked with gleeful indignation and jumped towards the dog, who took off, tail wagging. Matthew bounded after him.

Allie put her hands on her hips and smirked at Gillian. "Ladies and Gentlemen," she said in a deep voice. "The man-eating lion has broken out of the ring, and is loose in another tent. Please stay where you are." She tickled Gillian under the arm.

She heard the shower turn on upstairs, and was relieved to be handed an easy way to slow things down, or at least move the circus to a different adult—um, room. "Daddy's up."

"Daddy!" Matthew veered away from the dog and ran for the stairs.

"Matthew, your Cheerios!"

"I'm all done."

"Me too!" Gillian said.

"Really, Gill? You don't want this?"

"I wanna see Daddy." She pushed her cereal away and Allie reached out to grab the sliding bowl before it dumped soggy Cheerios all over the floor.

"Okay." She sighed, unbuckled Gillian, and watched her scamper after Matthew, noting her giant, soggy diaper and gambling that the levee would hold another half-hour. *Or maybe Dana will change it.* She stood at the bottom of the stairs to supervise Gillian's half-walk, half-crawl up the steps, and once the toddler had reached the top and was weaving her way to the bathroom, Allie went back into the kitchen, poured some coffee, and threw a load in the washing machine.

Above her head the kids charged into the bathroom and Allie heard Dana's hearty "Good morning!"

She sipped her hot coffee (she had long ago graduated from milk and Sweet-N-Low to rocket-fuel black) while she unloaded the dishwasher and mentally began a grocery list, until a clean-shaven Dana tagged her for bathroom time. As she started up the stairs, Allie spied Gillian waddling into the playroom with a dirty diaper the size of a watermelon hanging behind her.

Half an hour later, her long hair hanging wet down her back, Allie walked through the kitchen with a ball of dry cleaning tucked under one arm and a garbage bag of dirty diapers gripped in the other hand. She dumped it all by the back door.

"Can you get the garbage on your way out?" she said to Dana.

"Sure, and can you go to the—" he glanced at the pile of dry cleaning. "You're way ahead of me." He glanced at his watch. "What's on tap for today?"

"We're meeting Tess and Juliette at the pool."

"Sounds like fun." He smiled absently. He kissed them all goodbye—one, two, three. "I'll be home by six."

"The garbage!" she called after him.

Allie took a sip of her now cold coffee and peeked in on the kids, who were frozen, mid-play, in front of *Barney*, as if they had just been slapped in freeze-tag. She was indebted to that big purple dinosaur; the final gurgle of "I Love You, You Love Me," was a very sad moment indeed. She glanced at the clock—6:46 am. Too early to make any of the calls she needed to make. She picked up the newspaper; she had 14 minutes to catch up to the world.

"Mom, I'm hungry." Matthew wandered into the kitchen as the top of the hour commercial kicked on.

Allie put down the paper. "Hi hungry. I'm Mom."

Matthew smiled. "May I have something to eat?"

That face, he was so cute! She bent down and kissed him on his nose, on both cheeks. "Toast?"

"No." He bent down and picked Jack up off the floor.

"English muffin?" Allie took Matthew by the hand and led him to the sink. "No."

She eased the filthy rabbit out of Matthew's grip, soaped up his hands, and rinsed. She handed him a towel. "Oatmeal?" *Oops, don't have any.*

"No." *Thank God.*

"Liver and onions?"

Matthew giggled. "Toast," as if he'd just thought of it.

"You got it." Allie raised her voice. "Gill, do you want some toast?"

"Melon."

Allie sighed. "We don't have any melon." She grabbed a pen and added oatmeal and melon to the list. "How about toast?"

With one eye on the toaster, Allie flipped through the pile of bills and scribbled out two checks.

"Butter?" Matthew said when she brought him his toast.

"There's butter on it."

"I don't see it."

Allie pretended to spread more butter on it. "Okay?

Matthew smiled. "Good."

"Thanks Mommy, you are fabulous and beautiful," Allie said to him with a smile.

"Thank you," he said, his mouth full of toast.

"You are fabuwous and bountiful," Gillian said solemnly.

Allie laughed. "I'll take it."

Leaving Gillian strapped in her high chair, Allie raced upstairs to gather diapers, wipes, pacifiers, toys, bathing suits, towels, hats, and then clomped back downstairs to load up snacks, juice, and suntan lotion. She wrestled the two kids into clothes (literally wrestled, as she had to first catch and then fight a struggling, howling, clothes-averse Gillian), and settled them down in the playroom with some toys—trains for Matthew, plastic animals for Gillian—while she cleaned up the kitchen and jotted down a few last groceries. Then she answered the enthusiastic cries of "Come play with me!" and brought her coffee into the playroom for an interesting game of trains chasing animals, and the animals retaliating by knocking the trains off of the tracks.

———

"Okay, guys, we're going to go in a minute, Mommy just needs to go potty." Allie dashed to the bathroom, gambling that the kids would be fine alone for 60 seconds.

A moment later, while she was sitting on the toilet, both kids came in, sat cross-legged on the bathroom rug, and looked at her expectantly. "Pee or poop, Mom?" Matthew asked. Allie sighed. There was nothing sacred anymore.

———

Madaket sat patiently by the back door, his long, pink tongue hanging out and his soft brown eyes watching the morning finale—a mad hunt for shoes. His patience snapped however, when the three bodies rushed past him and out the door. He let out an indignant bark.

"Oh, Madaket, you haven't been out yet." She opened the screen door wide and the stocky dog bounded down the steps. *Vet appointment.* She swung her purse and the overstuffed beach bag onto one shoulder, hoisted Gillian onto her opposite hip, and reached out for Matthew's hand as they followed Maddy down the back porch steps.

Once the kids were buckled into their car seats, Allie ushered the dog back inside and grabbed the pile of Dana's dirty shirts. She didn't know if they'd make it to the dry cleaners today, but just in case. Today the priority was the grocery store, and although after the pool it would be like dragging them to the dentist after Disney World, the refrigerated stuff would spoil if they went beforehand.

As she pulled away from the house, her stomach growled. She hadn't eaten breakfast. She eyed the sea of spilled goldfish on the seat next to her and grabbed a few.

One Disney song later ("Hakuna Matata" 11 times over) and half an hour late, they arrived at the pool, and after locating Tess and her cherubic one-year-old, Allie released all the gear in her arms onto a lounge chair that she had no hope in hell of reclining in. "Sorry I'm late."

"We just got here too."

Allie leaned over and riffled through her giant bag. "If Mary Poppins could magically fit all that crap in her carpet bag, why the bag in the first place? Why didn't she just carry it all in her pocket?"

"My nanny has a bag of tricks like that." Tess sighed. "She's always whipping out fun things for Juliette to do. It makes me wonder why Juliette wants to be with me when I'm always cleaning up the kitchen for the umpteenth time or dragging her on errands."

"She's working out?"

"Maria? She's a better mom than I am." Tess lowered Juliette down in the pool. "I'm thinking of going back full time."

Allie looked up from the bag.

Tess shook her head. "It's just a fantasy."

Allie took a longer look at her friend. "You look great."

Tess blushed and glanced down at herself. "Well, I'm not Zoe, but I've lost weight, although I still have a ways to go."

"How'd you do it? Because my diet of stale Teddy Grahams and half-picked-apart chicken fingers isn't working."

Tess smiled. "Mostly it's that I'm not eating Hershey's Kisses while I sit on the couch and breastfeed. And I'm not popping M&Ms while I stress about whether to go back to work, and I'm not—"

"Hang on," Allie said. She turned to her kids. "You guys need lotion before you go any further."

"No lotion!" Matthew yelled.

Allie rolled her eyes at Tess.

"How's Gavin with the whole back to work thing?" Allie said as she lathered up a squirming Gillian.

"He encouraged it." Tess chuckled. "I'm sure he wanted me to stop eating chocolate too."

Allie took Gillian's hand and they stepped together into the pool.

"So, I wanted to—Oh!" Tess said, as she reached for Juliette. "That's not yours honey." She eased a green plastic shovel out of her daughter's hand and handed it to the mother standing nearby. "Sorry."

"No problem," the woman said. "Hilary doesn't mind sharing, do you Hilary?" She handed the shovel back to Juliette; Hilary screamed. The mom sighed. "We're just learning to share."

"I'm so sorry," Allie said. They all laughed.

A fourth mother, who was in earshot, joined the conversation and the women became a temporary sorority, sharing pretzels, juice boxes, and bottles of water, and throwing out half-sentences from their strategic positions around the pool deck, never quite getting more than a few thoughts out into the warm summer air before one of them was leaping to a corner or calling out to one of their kids.

As lunchtime approached and the tears started to rival the dimpled smiles, Allie strategized the next hour of her day, weighing toddler crankiness against the sheer necessity of the supermarket.

"This is going to be fun." Allie rolled her eyes at Tess as she started to pick up the Lion King figurines, which were strewn all around, and in, the pool.

"Promise them a lollipop if they're good," Tess said.

"Any more sugar is just going to work against me," Allie said. "And anyway, it's my fault for waiting so long. I deserve whatever they dish out. I'm just going to hold tight to the cart and never let go." She glanced at her watch. "Six more hours."

"Until relief walks in?"

"It's the golden bullseye in my day. It doesn't matter what time he tells me it's going to be, I start looking forward to it around lunchtime."

"It doesn't matter what time?" Tess smiled.

"Okay." Allie smirked back. "But I can at least deal if I can aim for a time. It's when he's really late and doesn't call that I want to throttle him."

Tess nodded. "Hey, I wanted to talk to you about something, but it's too hard to talk here; it's like being at an ADHD convention, I'd get about half the story out, and you'd hear even less."

Allie appraised her friend. "You okay? Is it an emergency?"

"I'm fine and no." They decided on dinner next week.

Allie arrived home and breathed in the cool peacefulness of her house, relishing the relief of home after a meltdown at the store. She savored it for 15 seconds before the sleepy abode shook back into life and she rushed to get the kids into fresh diapers and dry clothes, lunch on the table, and groceries put away, all with Maddy trailing her so closely that she kept tripping over him. Finally, after Gillian was down for a nap (or at least captive in her crib), and Matthew was snuggled up on the couch for quiet time (a half-hour video of a real construction site—pure genius), she took the desperate dog out for a few quick throws of the tennis ball.

All dependents taken care of for the moment, Allie slapped together a peanut butter and jelly sandwich. She was quite definitely a waitress during the kids' lunch—retrieving more milk, another napkin, a dropped spoon, or wiping up some kind of spill; her own lunch waited until the kids were settled into their various prone positions. She didn't mind; in theory, eating lunch alone was a quiet luxury, although in reality she stole bites while doing other things. She found it hard to sit still while so much lay in wait for her during this midday hole: bills, phone calls (*I've got to call Megan*), laundry, various messes. Food had now become simply fuel.

With a full tank and a few things crossed off her list (and a few more added), she settled down on the floor with Matthew to play cars. While she drove her red Matchbox Corvette around the colored curves of the oriental rug, she debated whether he could spare her attention as long as he had her motions, at least for the few minutes it would take her to call Megan. But Megan wasn't at her desk, so after leaving a message, "Just checking in to see how you're feeling," she dialed Zoe.

"I have about one second before I have to get my butt into a meeting," Zoe said. "What's up?"

"Not much, just driving my Corvette."

"Hang on a sec. No, that needs to be copied," Zoe's muffled voice said to someone in her office. "Sorry," she said to Allie.

"No problem. How are you?"

"Actually, a little hungover," Zoe said. "I'm on my fourth cup of coffee and it's… oh my God, it's three o'clock."

"Hungover, that sounds interesting," Allie said as Matthew drove a car up her leg.

"Eric took me to a fundraiser last night. Potentially deadly, but it turned out to be highly entertaining, or at least, our table was. There was the most amazingly gorgeous man, have you ever heard of Colin Parkman? As in Parkman Books? The son and heir apparent; I couldn't keep my eyes off of him. Anyway, we were up until four or so, and I basically crawled into work this morning."

"And how was your date with the fact that you were ogling someone else?"

"Ogling?" Zoe laughed. "Oblivious, I think."

Allie heard papers shuffling.

Zoe continued, "That Parkman guy had a date anyway. I just hope I run into him again. I'm going to have to work on that. A new project."

Allie chuckled. Zoe's lifestyle amused her, and she liked to think that she lived vicariously, if not a little enviously, through her friend's latest dates, fabulous clothes, and special events.

"How's Meg?" Zoe asked. "I keep meaning to call, but I've been swamped."

"She's more confident now that she's at 12 weeks. But I think she's still nervous."

"Can you blame her? How far along was she the last time?

"About 10 weeks. It was just after her honeymoon."

"I remember. That was awful." Zoe paused. "A few more weeks and she'll be out of the woods, right?"

"I think so. You can miscarry at any time, but the chances decrease the further along you are."

"Oh shit—Allie, I've got to run, sorry. I'm going to the Hamptons with Eric this weekend, but maybe next week we could get together? Any interest in coming into the city?"

"Sounds great. I—" Allie could hear someone coming into her office as Zoe hung up the phone.

———

Five thirty. Dinnertime, a.k.a. Hell Hour. Or really more like purgatory, a frenetic holding area where one false move drops you down into fire and angst and absolute chaos. There was a sense of urgency—panic really—quivering inside Allie as she raced around the kitchen. Everyone needed her, right now, this minute; the kids, the dog, the boiling macaroni.

Thank God Dana will be home soon.

The shrill ring of the phone was just another needy hand clawing at her. She ignored it. She had to get this mac and cheese on the table before there was a meltdown of catastrophic proportions. Megan's voice echoed out from the machine—"Allie, you there?"—and Allie leaned over and grabbed the receiver as Matthew roared indignantly from the other room.

"Oh Meg, hold on a minute. Matthew, what's going on?"

"Gillian's messing up my game!"

"Dinner's almost ready, just play with her for a minute."

Both children screamed like they were being stabbed in the heart.

"No! I was playing that first!" Matthew shouted.

Another scream.

Allie wanted to scream too. "Okay you guys, hang on a minute, I'll be right there!"

"Bad time, huh?" Megan said.

"You combine exhausted and starving and it's not pretty," Allie snorted. "And I'm just talking about myself. Can I call you back? So sorry," Allie said over the shrieks from the other room. She hung up as the timer on the stove screeched. She dumped the steaming macaroni into the colander in the sink and sprinted into the playroom.

Gillian and Matthew were red-faced with rage in the middle of an explosion of colored blocks; they looked like soggy-diapered prizefighters, each sizing up their respective opponent with pursed lips and narrowed eyes. Along the edges of the room, empty plastic bins were upside down next to heaps of Legos, cars, dolls, balls, plastic Happy Meal figures. The room looked like the town dump, minus the flies.

"What is going on?" Allie's words were clipped, her jaw clenched.

"Gillian kicked over my tower!" Matthew swiped at Gillian and connected with her plump leg. Gillian fell backwards onto the blocks. She started to wail.

A scream surged up through Allie's throat and out into the room, a scream erupting from some primal place. She clenched her fists. "*Enough,* you guys. Enough!" She was shaking as she scooped up Gillian; grabbed Matthew by the arm, bent down to his face, and growled, "We don't push." Her heart was pounding. She marched into the kitchen, holding Gillian stiffly in one arm, and towing Matthew with the other. She had a flash of her mother's face, twisted with rage, and Allie was in pigtails again, standing underneath her mother's wild-eyed glare, anger and shame and guilt and dread knotting together in the pit of her stomach.

She deposited both kids at the table and slapped macaroni and cheese into two blue bowls. She stomped back over to the counter to pour milk, mumbling about manners, the mess, the missed call with Megan.

She plunked the bowls and the milk down on the table. "Eat your dinner."

Matthew opened his mouth to say something.

She knew he was going to cry. She didn't care. "The yellow bowls are dirty. Eat." Allie's voice was steel.

Both kids looked at her with wide eyes, their faces wet with tears.

Allie turned away and stared into the sink filled with dirty dishes. The emotional vomit in her stomach curdled into a wave of self-loathing. It roiled inside of her, obliterating all five senses. She couldn't see, she couldn't hear. Black self-hatred became everything she was. Her body buckled with it, surrendering, as if succumbing to a familiar demon's clutch. She clutched the edge of the sink to stop from collapsing.

I hate myself.

I hate my kids.

I hate my mother.

I hate myself.

She slid to the floor into a broken pile and put her hands over her face. She was a failure; a wretched daughter, a witch of a mother. The weight of self-hatred was crushing her; soon she would extinguish. She waited for it. She closed her eyes.

Some minutes later, Matthew's warm body nestled into the curve of her body on the floor. The whisper of his breath grazed her face. She put her arms around him and squeezed him close.

———

At 7:30, Dana braced himself as sat in the car in the driveway, the funny story about a colleague that he had wanted to share with Allie now buried under his growing defensiveness about the time. He was an hour and a half late. She was going to be simmering.

He hated feeling this way at the end of the day, as if he was going to get punished for simply doing his job. His success or failure, once something that had felt recreational, now had deep repercussions on the people he loved. He was fully aware that as the breadwinner, their sovereignty as a family rested solely on him. Ironically, the more freedom that his job provided them, the more he felt as if his own personal choices narrowed.

He glanced again at his watch, although he knew exactly what time it was. He should go in. He massaged the back of his neck.

He had had another frenetic day at the office. The morning had started with his boss berating him about an unhappy client, and the day hadn't improved after that. He had worked right through lunch, placating his empty stomach at four o'clock with another cup of coffee and a semi-crusty muffin from an earlier meeting, and he hadn't come up for air until he noticed that it was getting dark. And he was late again.

He should've called right then. But he knew she'd be mad, and the funny thing was, he understood; he just didn't think he could handle hearing it right then. Of course he knew that by not calling he was making it worse, but his head was pounding, his stomach was grumbling, and in that particular moment, procrastinating felt like the best option.

Now, not so much.

The bang of the screen door closing behind him set off an instant reaction inside the house, and he was tackled with the fresh aroma of baby shampoo and the slightly damp and pajama-ed kids that went with it. He laughed; a deep, joyful sound. To be barraged like this at the end of the day was something he looked forward to throughout the long commute home. He let all the petty and monumental pressures from the office ease off of his shoulders for a moment as Matthew and Gillian, like puppies, jumped and climbed all over him, reclaiming him. Dana growled like a bear as the three of them rolled around on the floor in the ecstasy of their reunion.

After a brief wrestling match, he tucked one child under each arm, and tread carefully into the kitchen to greet Allie, who was at the stove, stir-frying vegetables.

"Hey," he said to her, a tentative smile on his lips as he tested the mood in the room. Feeling the air heavy with what he assumed was anger, his kiss hello—never intended to be a passionate embrace in the first place—was decidedly perfunctory.

"Hi." She glanced over her shoulder at him, then back to the vegetables.

"Sorry I'm late." Dana felt impotent, then defensive as he spoke to her back.

The kids scrambled out from under his hold and scampered away.

Allie turned around to face him, the spatula in her hand raised like a weapon. But her tone was more tired than angry. "It's okay."

He wondered where she had tucked her anger, and whether it was going to resurface at another time.

"How was your day?" Dana said.

She turned back to the stove. "Fine." She reached for the salt and sprinkled the vegetables. "Busy."

He opened the refrigerator and took out a beer.

"Gillian discovered that markers work not only on paper, but also on the walls," Allie said.

"Oh no," Dana smiled into the safe discussion. "Was the artwork permanent?"

"No. I scrubbed it off." She glanced over her shoulder at him. "How was your day?"

"Busy too." His stories from work charred and died away under what he thought he heard in her tone: You have it easier; you don't know what it's like all day with these guys. "I didn't even stop for lunch."

"I'm sorry," Allie said without remorse in her voice. She turned off the burner under the sizzling vegetables. "Lunch with these guys was a whine fest. Without the benefit of alcohol."

Here they were again, engaged in a subtle contest as to whose job, whose day was harder. He felt like Allie had no idea how stressful his days were, but the more tension there was between them, the less he wanted to share with her. He worried that anything too lighthearted might come back to handicap him in the future, and that any serious worries would be met and dismissed by something stressful from her day.

Matthew and Gillian tore back into the room and the next hour was spent reading stories, brushing teeth, tucking and re-tucking them into bed, and putting together the rest of their own dinner. When they at last sat down to eat, Allie and Dana filled in the bites of silence with edited pieces from the day, and finally, exhausted, they collapsed in front of the television to let someone else's drama take the forefront for a while.

Allie sat in the bustling restaurant waiting for Tess, happily people watching, reveling in fact that she was in the middle of commotion and that none of it required her. She wondered what Tess needed to talk to her about, and assumed that it had something to do with Juliette, as Tess often called Allie with baby questions. *I'm now the resident child-rearing expert. Incredible.*

She watched Tess glide through the restaurant towards her, smiling at people as she passed, turning heads of others, and was struck by her friend's meet-the-world posture, her walk just shy of a swagger.

Tess slid into the chair opposite Allie with a huge grin on her freckled face.

"Wow, I know said this the other day at the pool, but you look amazing. A manicure, even. Whatever you're doing, you need to share the secret," Allie said.

If possible, Tess's grin grew even wider. "Okay." And, as if it was gushing up out of her chest independently, she leaned across the table and lowered her voice. "I'm having an affair."

Stunned, Allie twitched back a fraction, away from this news, this piece of information she had not been expecting. Her eyes dropped to her wine-glass as she tried to regain her bearings, to reconcile the shot of conflicting emotions she was feeling—alarm and a surprising thrill, thrill not only for Tess, but a vicarious one. Then, knowing she needed to respond to her dear friend's news flash, she looked back up and took her cue from Tess's beaming face. She smiled. "Nothing like coming straight to the point."

"Sorry, I couldn't contain it. I mean, I literally can't contain myself. I feel like an idiot because I'm walking around all day with this ridiculous shit-eating grin on my face."

A waiter hovered nearby and Tess said, "Chardonnay," to his as-yet-unasked question.

Allie noted the uncharacteristic snip; Tess was always over-the-top congenial to everyone. She usually waxed on and on to every random waiter, salesgirl, and taxi driver she shared a moment with. Not tonight, apparently. Allie nodded towards her own full glass, "I'm okay, thanks." The waiter moved off.

"Yeah, you look ecstatic," Allie said. "But it's not ridiculous; it looks good on you." She paused, examining her friend. "Not that it seems like you need a lot of prompting, but tell me, who is he?"

"A guy from work, Rob. And okay, we're not actually having an *affair* —at least no one's gotten naked yet. I just like the taste of the word in my mouth. It's more an affair of the heart right now."

Allie's initial pangs of concern receded a little, and the voice-lowered attitude of collusion emerged in their wake. "Flowery memos and sweet serenades by the copy machine?"

"Nothing that poetic, or that out of the ordinary even. God, Allie, he makes me feel so good. He can do that with just a glance, a look from clear across the room. He has this way of looking at me—it's hypnotic really—as if he is truly seeing *me*, thinking about *me*. It makes me feel so substantial. Not substantial here," she grabbed the sides of her stomach, "which is how I usually feel, but substantial as a person. Like I'm a complex mystery that needs puzzling; like in a crowded room, I'm the one that matters."

Allie sipped her wine; she could imagine the flush of someone redis-covering her. And maybe in the process, the flush of rediscovering herself.

"We started working together after I went back and," she shrugged, "we just connected."

The waiter placed a glass of wine in front of Tess. "Thanks," Allie said, looking up at the waiter.

"He compliments me all the time, not only my work, but me." Tess reached for her wine. "It feels like harmless flirting with a chance card."

"And is that what it is? Harmless?"

Tess paused, her glass in the air. Then she put it down like a gavel. "Yes. Nothing's happened." After a moment, she smiled. "Although the idea of it, the promise of it is so seductive."

Allie nodded.

Tess continued, "The... 'thrill' is the word I keep coming back to... the thrill I now feel, all day long, even when he's not around, is incredibly energizing. I'm ultra-aware of my body, of the way I move, of my hips swaying when I walk in a room. I feel sexy. Honestly, I feel like a teenager picking out my outfits in the morning."

"And the chance card?"

"The chance card." Tess blushed; her cadence became slower. "We've been out to dinner a few times. And I think both of us know that the potential for more is right there on the table, like the salt. One of us just needs to reach for it."

"So what's stopping you?"

Tess held Allie's eyes. "You mean besides Gavin?" Tess's mouth was a straight line, the sparkle from a moment ago substantially tarnished.

Allie nodded. She hadn't heard a lot of Gavin in the conversation's undertow. Of course there was Gavin, but she could tell there was something else. Although Allie was hoping that it *was* simply the import and weight of Gavin that was holding Tess back. She could easily imagine being mesmerized by that kind of attention and electricity, and she prayed that if she found herself in a similar position, she wouldn't need anything other than Dana to give her pause.

Tess hesitated, and Allie filled in the momentary silence with a solemn, "He's married too."

Tess nodded. "Three kids."

"And what's the deal with his marriage?" Allie avoided asking Tess about her own marriage; they would get there when Tess was ready.

"He says they've just grown apart; nothing more dramatic, nothing less significant. There are no plans for divorce, which is fine. I don't want that."

"What *do* you want?"

Tess sighed, her giddy glow now extinguished as they stepped deeper into the conversation. "I don't know. Right now this just feels so good. And nothing's happened," she said again with her chin lifted. Then her chin dropped. "But I know it's wrong. Believe me, I know it's wrong. Right now we're consciously speeding, but keeping it steady at 10 miles an hour over the limit so that no one will pull us over."

Allie nodded. There was a part of her that wished she were speeding too. She so often found herself driving down a one-lane road, silently cursing the car in front of her for driving so damn slow, only to glance at the speedometer and realize she was going the speed limit.

"But Allie, I don't want to stop. I feel good about myself in a way I haven't felt in a long time. He makes me feel," Tess blushed again, "like a siren that invades his thoughts and cramps his focus. I've never been that woman before, the kind of woman that drives men wild. It's empowering."

"And Gavin? You don't think Gavin thinks of you like that?"

Allie watched Tess's face slowly fall, all of the features pulled down by her frown like a Venetian Blind. "Gavin?" Her brow creased; she shook her head. "I don't think so. With Gavin I'm a frazzled, frantic mother, and not a much better wife." She took a big gulp of wine and looked at Allie. "I love Gavin, you know that. But no, I'm not that woman for him. At least not now. And maybe not ever."

"What do you mean, not ever? You guys met and that was it. Classic love at first sight."

"Gavin thinks of me in sweats with unshaven legs." She smiled weakly, "He doesn't see the brilliant, attractive, successful woman I am at work."

Allie reached across the table and gave Tess's hand a squeeze.

"I know what you're thinking. Why not ditch the sweats, shave the legs?" Tess said.

"Actually I was thinking: wasn't that what we dreamed of when we were younger, someone who loved us even at our worst?"

Tess took another big gulp, finishing her wine. "I'm just going to get drunk here, do you mind?" She waved the waiter over.

"We'll have some calamari too. Thanks," Allie said to him. She looked at Tess. "We should eat something."

"I do shave my legs," Tess said. She absently fingered her gold necklace and sighed. "I imagine presenting myself to Gavin in a sexy teddy and it feels so contrived. I would feel ridiculous."

Allie looked at Tess and said gently, "It's not like I'm prancing around in sexy lingerie right now either. But there's a lot in between Frederick's of Hollywood and Hanes."

"I know, but I can only imagine it with Rob, not with Gavin. Why is that? I fantasize about telling Rob to touch me a certain way and it feels sexy. I think about telling Gavin the same thing, and I'm embarrassed, I can't do it. I might hurt his feelings; maybe he'd think I haven't liked the way he's been touching me all along."

"I know what you mean," Allie said. "Our sex life is good—great sometimes—but it's definitely choreographed. Which makes it easy, I guess. Time efficient. And we definitely never brainstorm. But that's my fault too."

They were quiet for a minute, each looking down at the table.

"Let's face it, Gavin's had a lot of women in his life," Tess said. "And sometimes I think he married me because I represent something different, something safe, warm, comforting. Not Madonna, but *the* Madonna." She looked at Allie. "I'm not the wild passion in his life."

"How come you're just telling me all this now? I thought all was great with you guys."

"Maybe I didn't want to admit it to myself. Maybe the affair is giving me confidence." Tess glanced around the restaurant, then looked back at Allie and leaned in. "Look, it's common knowledge that Gavin was a cheater before he met me. We could come up with lots of names, and those would only be the ones we know about." The waiter arrived with their wine and started to pour. "What's stopping him from cheating on me now?"

Allie glanced at the waiter, who was pretending not to hear that last comment. He finished pouring their wine and scuttled away.

"Tess, really? You really think that?"

Tess shifted uncomfortably in her chair. "See? I gain a pound just thinking about it." She exhaled loudly. "I'm just going to say this, and please don't get mad, just hear me out." She took another big swallow of wine. "I think he's cheating on me," She held Allie's eyes, "with Zoe."

"No." Allie leaned forward to emphasize her point but Tess cut her off.

"I know it sounds outrageous, paranoid even. But there's something going on with them. What's with the fact that they're friends now, that they meet after work for a drink?" She shook her head. "I just don't get that."

"I don't know," Allie said slowly. "But maybe they *are* just friends now; water under the bridge and all that. There's a lot of history there. But they're not having an affair, they can't be. Gavin wouldn't do that to you. Neither would Zoe, for that matter."

Tess raised her eyebrows.

"Zoe's not cruel," Allie said. "I know there's been this weird thing between you guys, I guess ever since college. But she wouldn't do that. And

I'd know it if she was." Allie was certain. She knew Zoe was still in love with Gavin, but she couldn't believe that she would act on it.

"Like you say, there's so much history there. And from what little Gavin's told me, that history was pretty wild. Does that just go away?" Tess ran her fingers up and down the gold chain around her neck. Up and down.

"What does Gavin say about it?" Allie asked.

Tess guffawed. "He'll come home and tell me he's had a drink with her, like there's nothing wrong with it, and I just want to shriek at him. Doesn't he know how that makes me feel?"

"So what do you say?"

"Nothing," Tess shook her head and looked at the table. "I don't want to be a bitch. And Zoe's a friend, which would make me sound even more bitchy. So I probably smile and ask him how it was, how she was. But inside my blood is boiling and all kinds of alarms are going off." She exhaled. "And then my imagination takes over and I envision Gavin in Zoe's Chanel life. It makes mine feel so Walmart."

"Have you talked to Gavin about any of this?"

"What's he going to do, admit it? I'd just sound like a crazy, paranoid wife. Which maybe I am." She paused. "Plus, how can I accuse him now?"

Allie didn't answer. There were now so many issues on the table she didn't know which one to tackle.

Tess jumped in for her. "So we're full circle, and even to me it sounds like I'm having this little... flirt, for lack of a better word... with Rob because I want to get back at Gavin. And maybe it's true, at least maybe a little. Or maybe Gavin's cheating just gave me license to do what I wanted to do." She twisted her necklace. "But it feels more about timing. I wasn't *looking* for something to happen, it just did. Rob came along and made me feel good at the precise time when I couldn't remember what that felt like, either within my marriage or within myself. I was buried under all this weight, both figuratively and literally, and I think I just felt... heavy."

Allie held Tess's eyes. "So what are you going to do?" she asked softly.

"I don't know."

"You still love Gavin?"

"I still love Gavin. God I still love him. And I wish with all my heart that it was Gavin who made me feel this way. And I'm so mad at him that it's not."

"Then you have to talk to him. This whole Gavin-cheating scenario isn't fact. You're making yourself crazy about a rumor, although you're the only one who's heard it. But maybe you've been whispering it to yourself for so long that it's turned into truth."

Tess rubbed her forehead. She whispered, "I'm so afraid to ask him." She closed her eyes. "What if it's true?"

Allie leaned towards her friend. "I've never for a minute thought Gavin was cheating on you. He loves you. And he loves Juliette. It's going to be okay." She desperately wanted to offer her friend reassurance, wisdom, but her words fell flat on the table—extra silverware, lame and useless. The silence however, was making her feel even more helpless. "And this thing with Rob? Don't beat yourself up; if you're like me you do too much of that already. Hell, I go to bed every night and berate myself for every ugly moment of the day."

Tess nodded.

Allie ran her hand through her hair. "We're all looking for someone to make us feel special, to reassure us that our ugliness is okay." She smiled. "That's the glass slipper."

"Are you saying you don't have it? I think of you and Dana as having it all."

Allie sighed. "Dana and I? We're basically living two different lives right now. Sometimes I feel like I don't even know him anymore." Allie fingered her wine glass. "I think we've gone back to hiding the ugly."

A cocoon of silence wrapped around them.

Allie realized with horror that she just added to an already overwhelmed Tess. "But we'll get through it. I honestly don't know how you do all of it and work too."

"I've learned it's better if I work. I feel like I'm accomplishing something." Allie sank back in her chair.

Tess leaned in towards her. "You're the only one I've told about this. I can't tell Megan, not yet at least. She's been through so much this past year. And... I love Megan, but she can be judgmental. I knew you'd listen without getting all moralistic on me."

Allie wondered if Tess suspected that on some level at least, Allie would be sympathetic, maybe even excited about the idea of an affair. "Don't worry. Your secret's safe with me." Allie paused, and then tentatively said, "Before we order, can I say one more thing?"

"Please."

"If you do end up taking this further with Rob, make sure it has nothing to do with getting back at Gavin."

Tess was quiet for a moment. "I'm not so sure I can just separate that out."

Allie nodded.

CHAPTER 11

As I perch here at my desk, I am stunned into sobriety, an observer at the window, and the world is reeling around me, inebriated. The bright, pungent colors of spring and the tiny screen squares through which I see them are blurring in and out of focus, and I half-expect towering giraffes to walk by and graze at the oak tree in the yard. I close my eyes, hoping that when I look again everything will be as it should—the grass here, the daffodils there. But no; when I look again, everything is unfamiliar, backwards, and still in motion. The only thing that seems solid and unwavering is the journal page in front of me, and my pen bleeding blue onto the crisp white page.

Right now this journal, this brown leather book that has grown into a patient friend, is the only thing that will keep me sane and stop the spinning. My pen is poised above it, itching to capture the chaos that is ricocheting around my world, begging me to release it onto paper, to remember and relate the whole of the story; not only our words, but our essence. In its precise markings, the ink assures me that if I can deliberately attend to and reconstruct the narrative on these pages, then maybe I'll be able to assimilate the enormity of this truth in a way that my imagination alone now cannot.

Sarah has always urged me to write. And so I do.

Over the course of many, many years, and more intentionally over the past few months, I've been building up the courage to confront, or rather to just plain ask my father for more details about Eva (I always view any contact with my father as confrontational). For almost three decades now—30 *years*—her shadow has loomed over all of us, clouding not only our past, but as I have learned, my present as well. And now I know that I can't fully patch together my marriage—or myself—until the fog around my mother has dissipated, and the holes in my past have been filled in.

So with my heart in my throat, one afternoon while the raw drizzle outside turned the shy spring buds fluorescent green and shiny, I picked up the phone and dialed my father's number, and with each push of a button, began my ascent up Mt. Everest. He seemed surprised, and then happy to hear from me, then slightly wary, or maybe more resigned, when I blurted out that I wanted to talk about Eva.

He changed the event from lunch at a restaurant to cocktails at his house with a nervous guffaw, and the conversation was over.

After I put the phone down, I realized my shirt was damp and sticking to me. Not your normal response to making a short phone call to your father.

As Dana and I have sworn, in Sarah's presence of course, to make a heroic effort to *communicate* with each other, I immediately called Dana. He too, sounded happy, but wary (I must make people cagey). He asked if I wanted him to go with me. YES! I wanted to shout, but old habits die hard, and I said something about doing it myself.

"Why?" he asked me.

Fair enough. Why indeed? Because I'm scared. Because I'm finally going to ask the question that has been lodged in my throat my whole life. Because I might completely, utterly break into a thousand pieces when I hear the answer. Because I'm afraid of you seeing me like that.

I'm afraid of you seeing me.

"I don't know." I laughed nervously. I took a deep breath and with it, a giant step. "Actually, it would be great if you came."

"Okay," he said, and I could hear him smiling over the phone.

I smiled back through the plastic.

After a moment I said, "That was really good of us. Sarah would be so proud."

Dana laughed. "Yes, she would."

About a week later, after reminding myself that this wasn't a festive occasion and casting aside a black dress and my initial urge to accessorize, I settled on worn jeans (to keep me grounded) and a white silk blouse (a warning to myself, don't spill, don't sweat). I did both in the car on the drive over.

When we arrived, Joseph and Dana formally shook hands; then my father and I shared an awkward, adolescent moment in which our eyes connected briefly and then mine dropped to the floor, ostensibly to study the intricacies of the carpet. After a minute I said hello and bolted by him, not wanting to be deterred from my mission by the confusing emotions that were washing over me. He immediately poured us a drink, and I could see from his wet glass that he had started well before we arrived. *Whatever gets you through*, I remember thinking. He refreshed his scotch, the glistening liquid glowing in his eyes like a craved elixir. I noticed a platter of cheese and crackers on the coffee table—an unexpected touch—and I wondered if there was a lady in his life who had advised him, or had maybe just bought the cheese party for him.

Dana and I sat next to each other on the living room couch, and I stole a quick look around. The house was not at all what I'd envisioned—which was an austere, spartan shrine to my mother, kind of like a cellblock with photographs. This house was comfortable, definitely masculine in variations of blues and browns, but soft and lived-in. And as far as I could tell, there was not one picture of my mother on the walls or shelves. There were however, several very outdated pictures of us kids: traditional, posed snapshots of birthday parties and graduations. There were no pictures of us all together.

Once my dad sat down, the painful small talk commenced with chatter so porous it was translucent—Dana's job, my dad's job, the kids. The cheese waited patiently, untouched, smirking at our discomfort. We all sat back a bit in our chairs, trying to seem casual, but we held ourselves straight up, as in, one wrong move and we're out of here.

Finally, my dad, designating himself as the adult in the room in a way I never remembered him doing even when he *was* the only adult in the room, opened the Q&A. "So you had some questions about Eva."

This was quite obviously my prompt, and I took a swig of my chardonnay and nodded, unable to locate my voice.

He waited. I remember hearing distinct sounds—birds chirping, kids on the street laughing and screeching, a lawnmower. The everyday noises somehow calmed me, gave me my voice. "When she left I was only four. I can barely remember her. Can you tell me about her?"

His shoulders softened, possibly with the relief of a lob. He looked up as if he was retrieving the memories from the air. "She looked like you, that's for sure. Same long dark hair, same green eyes. Even when you were a baby, when all three of you were small, people would joke that it was clear who wore the pants in the family, because you all looked so much like her." He paused. "Even my genes were submissive to Eva."

It was a typical comment—a husband or wife amusedly reflecting on the dynamic in the family—and the appropriate response would have been a polite chuckle. Except in that instance, laughter would have been grotesque as there was no amusement in his demeanor, none of the requisite twinkle in his eyes, delight on his lips. Even 30 years later, his reminiscence was tinged in acrid remorse.

He continued, "She had so much energy. She was like fireworks exploding into a room with crackle and flashing red lips. She always had a slightly uncouth idea for something to do, and whether or not you knew the details of her plan, you were up for it because you knew that with Eva in charge, it was going to be fun." He rattled the ice in his glass.

"I met her when I was 20. I was just one of her many admirers; at 19 she had lots of them. Lots of admirers and lots of aspirations. She was convinced she was going to have a big life—those are actually the words she used, 'big life.' It was this sunny, buoyant thing she would toss out: 'let's have a big life.'" He offered a feeble smile. "She didn't often say 'let's,' but when she did it felt pretty great. I'd get swept up." He paused. "And I always assumed she meant 'full.' A full life. I could provide that, right?" He looked into his glass.

I remember cringing during this part of his monologue, thinking *here it comes, I'm going to hear that my mother couldn't stand being bottled up with the three of us,* that we were not part of her 'big life' plan. I waited, but my father had stopped. He seemed stuck.

"So how did you two get together?"

He was jolted back from far away. He sighed. "Eva had some dark times too, days and days in which she would just sit in the dark. Shades pulled, lights off, dark. It seemed almost fitting, as if that was her way of recharging after expending so much energy. And during one of those times, I decided I was going to save her; I was going to be the one to step up and offer myself to her. While everyone else just marched by her raised drawbridge, I was going to be her knight in shining armor.

"And it worked." He still looked astonished. "We were married six months and several rescues later. We bought a house, had Paul, had you, had Kevin; boom, boom, boom. Everything was going as planned." He exhaled deeply. "Except that about a year and a half after Kevin, she went into one of her dark periods and never really came out of it."

I was trying to get my mind around what he was saying, what he was inferring. "What do you mean, dark periods?" I looked at him intently. "Are you talking about depression?"

"Oh God. We certainly never called it that. Depression wasn't as common a phenomenon, or maybe it was just as common, just not commonly understood like it is today. Like I said, in college we all assumed it was just her way of recharging her batteries. And even after we were married, that's the way I understood it.

"Let me backtrack." He shook his head as if to rewind his thoughts. "You never knew your grandparents, your mom's parents. We told you that they'd died, but really, your mom had broken off all contact with them."

I looked at Dana; he squeezed my hand.

My dad shook his head again as if to ward off questions, although none had formed yet on my lips. "I'm not sure exactly what happened, she never went into it with me. All I know is that they were terrible to her." He added softly, "Maybe I never really asked her." He reached for his drink and got lost for a moment somewhere in the amber of his scotch. After a gulp, he said with certainty, "I just know she had a bad time of it. So you see, for her to sink into herself for short periods seemed... appropriate."

I hadn't known any of this. "Did you ever get help?"

"No. She didn't want to, and I didn't force it because I didn't want her to think I was accusing her of something. Besides, every time it happened, I just assumed she would emerge from the darkness as her old self again, like she always did."

"But she didn't?"

"Not that time. She was depressed," he looked at me, "to use your word, for months; the longest she'd ever been that way."

In answer to my wide eyes, he said, "She was functioning. It wasn't like we had to hire a babysitter for you guys or anything. But she was low. Really low."

It seemed impossible to me that this had all gone unaddressed. It was pretty clear that something had been going on with my mother, whatever the diagnosis. How had this not been investigated? For the millionth time in my life I thought, *I do not understand this man.*

The noises from the street dripped into the room intravenously, trying to hold us in the present.

"And then," he sounded like he was choking, "I came home one night from work and Eva's eyes were wild and the house was mayhem." He looked at me, cleared his throat. "Do you remember any of this?"

I shook my head slowly. He looked at the floor.

Dana took my hand again.

"She was crying. She was hysterical actually, all four of you were, and it took me a few moments to grasp what was going on." He took a deep breath. "Eva had just broken Paul's arm—I mean literally minutes before I walked in the door—by accident. She was frantic, both because of Paul's pain and because of the enormity of what she had done. God, I think of it now," he rolled his eyes towards the ceiling with a little shake of his head, "and know that she must have been out of her mind with shame, guilt, fear, panic, and obviously extreme alarm for Paul, but of course I couldn't begin to see all that. My focus was Paul; Paul who was in pain, Paul who needed to get to the emergency room. And I think you and Kevin were terrified and upset empathically from all the commotion and chaos.

"So I scooped up Paul and took him to the hospital. I was so furious and upset that I don't think I said two words to Eva after we got home later that evening. This was hours later, and I still didn't trust myself to hold it

together, and I certainly didn't want to yell and reignite all of you. She tried
to explain, she was desperate to explain it to me: everyone had been cranky
and irritable all day—I think the house itself was tantruming—and Paul had
thrown something across the room. She had reached out to stop him as he
tried to run away from her and she grabbed him too hard, his arm twisted... "

I grimaced. My father affirmed the horror with a nod. He continued,
"Eva couldn't bear the guilt and I think, although I certainly didn't consider
this at the time, she thought that what happened had been preordained
somehow. I think she believed this proved that she was fated to live out
the legacy that had been slapped on her when she was a little girl; that this
accident with Paul was the beginning of the recycling of the abuse she had
suffered. I think that at her core she was suddenly afraid of herself, afraid
of the hurt that she had the power, and now she believed the disposition,
to inflict on you and your brothers.

"Of course I couldn't see this, couldn't begin to understand what her
nightmares were that night. I was furious. All I could think was, she should
have been able to control herself, control her feelings. And underneath that,
I was furious with myself. I felt guilty that I hadn't had the power to pull
her out of her darkness, as I'd always been able to do in the past."

He paused and said softly, "Then further underneath all that anger and
guilt, I was also confused. What was I supposed to do? I had lied to the
doctor—in front of Paul—and told him Paul had fallen. I was panicked,
scared you all would get taken away from us." He paused, rattled the ice
in his glass, watched the cubes settle back to stillness. "And I think I was
also questioning Eva. Had it really been an accident?"

"Oh my God, so she left because of Paul? Because of you?" I was desperately ransacking old memories, dumping out broken pieces to see how
they fit back together.

He lifted his glass in slow motion and took a long sip, almost an inhale,
the scotch a yellow oxygen mask that had dropped from the ceiling. The
ice cubes clinked in the glass as he lowered it from his lips. "So it's still your
understanding that she walked out?" He was looking at me so intently that
his eyes looked crossed.

I froze.

Dana answered for me with a puzzled, "Yes." He squeezed my hand tightly, a powerful clamp.

My father took a deep breath. "I wasn't sure. I wasn't sure what you had found out, what you knew."

I had the sensation that I was sliding backwards. The sounds outside the window disappeared as if someone had pressed mute, and all I could hear was the blood pounding in my brain. I wanted to put my hands on the sides of my head to contain it, to stop my head from imminent explosion. I'm not sure if I actually put my hands there or not.

My father moved forward in his chair, possibly to reach out for me, to stop me from sliding even farther away from him, but if that was his intent, he changed his mind at the last minute and rested his elbows on his knees. He sat there for a moment, looking down at his hands.

"Allie, the next day... " He looked up at me. "Your mother killed herself."

I don't know who reached for whom first, but in milliseconds, Dana was pulling me in close with both arms. Which was lucky, because if he hadn't been anchoring me, I might have slipped away.

"What?" was the only word to creak out of my dry mouth.

Although I had heard him clearly.

OCTOBER 1998
New York City

Zoe forced herself to get up off of her cushy couch. Darkness was descending over the city, a curtain of indigo bumping up against the preternatural, rebellious glow of the street. She had to get in the shower or she'd never be primped and ready for Colin. She didn't feel like dealing with the icy attitude she'd receive if she kept him waiting. *Such a prima donna. So gorgeous he can afford to be a pain in the ass.*

She walked into the kitchen, poured herself a glass of merlot and popped two Advils. She paused, then shook a third out and swallowed it with another wash of wine. She was still nursing a killer hangover from last night and needed to squelch it fast. It wouldn't do to be a drag.

A long, hot shower later, she emerged feeling better as the Advil and the wine worked its magic. She brushed out her now shoulder-length hair and walked over to her closet naked, unfazed that all the curtains were tied back and the huge apartment windows gave any interested neighbor a clear view. The expensive window dressings were strictly decorative, and the thought of giving her neighbors, whoever they were, a little thrill amused her. She slid into a short black cocktail dress that crossed her bare back, impassively noting that it didn't fit as snugly as it once had. She took time applying her makeup, masterfully covering up the shadows under her eyes, and finished her face with two strokes of deep red lipstick. Lighting up a cigarette, Zoe stood back to admire herself. Once she put on her mile-high heels, heels that even with her height only brought her to Colin's nose, she knew she would wow him. She smiled.

She padded back into the living room, cigarette and refilled merlot in hand, and sat down to wait for Colin. She dialed Allie's number.

"Hi!" Allie said happily.

Zoe heard commotion in the background—the unmoderated voices of young children, the murmur of the television. She pictured the kids and the dog surrounded by a sea of tiny toys. "Is this a good time?"

"Dana's here, he can handle it."

Zoe imagined Allie gesturing for Dana to take charge.

"How are you?" Allie asked.

"Now? Great. If you had asked me a few hours ago, however, I might have moaned."

"Oh God, don't tell me," Allie said. Zoe heard her loading dishes into the dishwasher. "I'm not sure I can tolerate hearing about a night out on the town. I myself had a date last night, with poor Gillian who was throwing up into the wee hours of the morning."

Sounds a lot like my own night, Zoe thought, although she couldn't really remember all of it. "Sounds like hell."

"It was actually. Poor little kid, throwing up is the worst."

Tell me about it. Zoe's cigarette fired red with an inhale.

"And now we're all on standby, wondering who's going to be bent over the toilet next."

"Now that's a visual I hope doesn't haunt me all night."

"Sorry, enough about vomit. Are you ready to go?"

"Ready and waiting."

"I'm so bummed we can't go. Although I guess with Gillian sick we wouldn't have been able to come even if we had found a sitter. You need to remember everything and call me tomorrow."

"Better tell that to Meg and Tess. I plan on getting very drunk. As the girlfriend of the birthday boy, I'm the de facto hostess to 100 of Colin's most intimate friends. I don't plan on doing that sober."

"So it's 'girlfriend' now."

"I need a title, at least for tonight. We'll see if he behaves himself though. That's another reason for boatloads of booze—if he starts getting moody on me, I won't notice."

"Don't get so drunk that you can't give him a good kick in the butt if he deserves it."

Zoe laughed. "You got it."

"I actually wasn't kidding."

Zoe heard a knock on her apartment door. "Gotta go, Colin's here. Unbelievable; he even charmed my doorman, he didn't buzz me."

Her cigarette smoke trailed her as she walked to the door and opened it to a tall and tuxedoed Colin. Zoe thought once again that he was the most handsome man she had ever seen.

"Wow," Colin said to her with a dazzling white smile.

———

Allie put the phone down slowly. She was worried about Zoe. She had been drinking so much—more than usual, more consistently, and with more intent—and Allie was sure that she wasn't privy to half of it. But by combining concerning stories with Megan and adding up the number of Sunday afternoon get-togethers that Zoe had skipped because she couldn't get out of bed, Allie got the general picture.

To add to it she was dating Colin Parkman, a charming sociopath who skated from oozing charisma to raging jealousy to cold, calculating disregard with frequency and ease. He strutted around the city with Zoe on his arm as if she was a beautiful new purse or coat; a designer accessory that served a role en route, but was just slung onto the back of a chair once they stepped into the chosen festivity. At that point, Zoe became immaterial to his good time, which seemed directly proportional to the number of pretty young things who velcroed themselves onto him for the night. His bottomless wallet and chiseled features had given him celebrity status—not just in his own mind, but apparently in the eyes of many single women as well—and like a self-absorbed, B-list musician, the starry eyes of his roadies were his lifeblood. Allie knew from hearing the recap of several of their arguments that Colin expected Zoe to be president of his fan club, and that he had accepted her sarcastic reply with a smile on his lips and bitter steel in his eyes. After that, his random indifference had become intentional, cruel. Where he got the balls to behave like that, Allie didn't know, as Zoe was certainly no wallflower. But for some reason, Zoe continued to date the sadistic bastard. Allie just didn't get it.

Although maybe a little romance is better than none, she thought as she heard Dana throwing up in the bathroom upstairs.

———

Several hours later, the birthday party was in full swing with over 100 New Yorkers dressed to the nines and celebrating Colin's birthday as if it were their own. Electronic dance music boomed through the room, its pounding beat reverberating in the oversized cocktails, the artistic hors d'oeuvres, and the glittering guests' veins. It gave the room a dramatic, otherworldly pulse and further revved up the night's engine.

Zoe, with a constantly-replenished martini in hand, leaned against the bar with her new best friend Chip, a guy who hadn't known what hit him when Zoe sauntered up to him and turned on her cool, silky charm. She had abandoned Colin after he fired his first grin at some simpering blonde, and she had started to walk across the party towards Megan. But she saw Gavin and Tess glom onto Megan first, and Zoe had decided mid-step that tonight, she couldn't quite muster up a life-is-great face in front of the

Kellers—at least not without a little more lubrication—so she spun on her heel towards the bar and into the unsuspecting Chip. Since then Chip—who thought he'd just won the lottery—was gleefully oblivious to his role as pawn in the various chess games that were being played out.

While batting her eyelashes and making fluid conversation with Chip, Zoe had one eye on Gavin and one eye on Colin, who was smoothly holding court with several young waifs at the end of the bar. She suddenly had an eerie feeling that she was watching her life, and that she wasn't in it. She looked around the room—people were laughing, kissing, singing, dancing—and she was hanging off to the side, biding her time. *For what?* Through her haze of gin and detachment, she realized that hanging on the sidelines was something she had perfected over the years; she ran in circles, other people moved forward.

She had lost her heart to Gavin nine years ago—*nine years ago,* she thought as she chugged her martini and held her empty glass up to the bartender—and had never fought for it back. Instead she had run from it, choosing men who chased her but who she could outpace without breaking a sweat, or her heart; keeping them and any feelings at all at a manageable distance. Colin was the first in the long procession however, who didn't chase, who didn't want more. He'd made it clear that all he wanted was adornment and a convenient companion. And impersonal, fiery sex. She had met her emotional match. And the abyss created between them was dark and unforgiving.

So now I'm stranded in no man's land, cowering between all I want and all I don't want. The circles she was running weren't complete circles, because she never came back around to Gavin; they were spirals, and she was going down. Above her was Gavin, a fantasy. She bit her lip, hard. He had never loved her the way she loved him. The relationship she'd wanted back had never really existed.

And below her was Colin, offering her a glimpse of the cold and murky bottom.

I'm not going to go there. She shivered. *I deserve better. And P.S.,* she tossed her hair over her bare shoulders, *better is not Gavin.*

Chip was prattling on (and on) as Zoe accepted her drink from the bartender and then, without re-checking Colin's status, she turned her back on Chip and marched as purposefully as she could while balancing on her heels and on her many martinis over to the little circle of Gavin, Tess, Megan, and Jared. *Just going over to hang with my friends*, she thought as she spilled a little of her drink on her Manolo Blahniks.

The birthday bash roared on, reaching a feverish pitch as groups of revelers—like the cocktails fueling them—mixed up and refilled, merrily consuming the unique potion of glitz and disinhibition. Then, like a pin-prick in a fat balloon, the energy gradually dissipated as two by two, guests leaked out to catch the tail end of other parties or to wave down cabbies for a ride home. Somehow, during the last-minute bathroom runs, coat quests, and goodbyes, Gavin and Zoe found themselves standing alone together.

"You okay?" Gavin leaned in and peered at Zoe.

Why didn't you ask that question in front of Tess? "Yeah," Zoe said with a sneer. "Are you?"

"Because if there's anything wrong... I mean, what's with this Colin guy?"

How dare he comment on who she was seeing! She wanted to slap him across the face; instead, she would slap him with words. She opened her mouth to spit venom.

"You're right," he said, holding up his hand like a stop sign. "None of my business. It's just that I'm worried about you." He paused. "You know you can count on me if you ever need anything, right?"

Zoe narrowed her eyes. "Thank you, but I'm fine. I don't need a baby-sitter. And I don't need you."

Gavin took a step back, put his hands in his pockets. "Because you seem really wasted."

Zoe's red lipstick smiled, but there was no smile in her eyes. "You're very perceptive. I am really wasted." She took a slug of her martini for emphasis. "What a good choice of words, Gavin. Wasted. I was thinking that very thing, that I've wasted so much time on people, on men who've led me farther and farther down the stairs." She waved her drink in a circle and some splashed over the side of her glass. "And you know what? They're happy, or happy enough where they are on that staircase; their lives are all chugging along just fine, it's not like it changes when I come in or out of it. And *I'm* always the one who ends up a little lower on the spiral, and wasted, or maybe just null. Ha! Null and void." She was swinging her drink around, swaying a little on her heels, and mentally poking her finger in his chest. In her drunken haze, she was making complete sense; she was Confucius.

Gavin scratched his head, looked around the room, then looked back at her with a frown. "Zoe?"

She continued her rant. "That's it! Null and void, like a canceled check that gets thrown in the garbage. Originally signed with a flourish—such high hopes for that check—and ultimately not worth the paper."

Gavin reached out to touch her arm. She batted it away.

"And you know what, Gavin? You're not on top anymore. I mean, you've been a good friend, and I appreciate your concern. But you're not on top. You've been displaced by," she swayed and almost fell, but caught herself on the back of a chair, "well, I don't know who yet."

Tess appeared suddenly, looking flustered. "What's this I hear about someone being on top?" She chuckled, a strangled cough.

Gavin guffawed and stepped toward Tess. There was a brief silence, and then he said, "To tell you the truth, I'm not really sure. Zoe, I think your martinis are catching up with you. Actually, I think they've won the race. Can we get you a cab?"

"No, thank you, I'm fine," Zoe said, directing the most plastic smile she could muster at Gavin. Just then, Colin, who hadn't said boo to Zoe in hours, slithered up in back of her and wrapped his arms around her from behind.

Gavin and Tess looked at each other.

"I'm fine," Zoe said again.

Zoe watched Gavin put his arm around Tess, then watched them cross the room and go out the door. She caught him look over his shoulder at her before the door closed behind them.

She noticed that Tess saw him look too.

———

Zoe and Colin pushed the scraped-clean mirror away and leaned back onto Zoe's couch with a collective sigh. They both licked their lips and ran their tongues around their gums to test the cocaine's freeze. Then after a moment and without a word, Colin leaned towards her to begin the next activity on their regularly scheduled itinerary. Zoe pushed him back as his face joined the rest of the room in a wild spin.

"Too drunk," she slurred. "I feel sick. You should go."

She clearly didn't have to convince him; Colin grabbed his jacket and practically sprinted for the door. Zoe guessed the waifs were still at the bar.

After his exit, Zoe's living room began to spin so violently that even though she was still seated on the couch, she thought she was going to fall over. She opened her eyes, shut her eyes, tried to lie down, and then shakily sat back up. There was no position that slowed the manic merry-go-round. She knew she was going to get sick, so she slid off the couch onto her hands and knees and crawled towards the bathroom. Halfway there, she vomited all over the polished hardwood floor of her living room, and continued retching for forever, her stomach contracting and twisting, her dark hair swinging in and out of the liquid bile with each heave.

When she was finally depleted, she rolled away from the mess and curled up in a fetal position, whimpering, her soggy and splattered black silk dress hiked up around her waist. In a small crevice of her mind that was not pleading with the apartment to slow down, she began to panic. *I'm going to die.* Her sweat-soaked body convulsed with shivers.

She spied the cordless phone wavering on the living room coffee table, right where she had left it after her earlier chat with Allie, and dragged herself over to it. Her hands shook and the numbers in front of her swerved in and out of focus as she tried to punch in Allie's number, forgetting that she could have just hit redial. A three-note tone shrieked in her ear and a robotic voice announced "The number you have reached is not in service."

Zoe's whimpers turned into tears. *I'm going to die right here, right next to this pool of brown vomit.* She begged the buttons to stand still as she stabbed at Megan's number. Megan's cheery, pre-recorded voice kicked on. Sobbing now, her hands quaking uncontrollably, she tried Tess. *Please pick up, Tess. Help me.*

"Hello?" Gavin's voice croaked, a combination of sleepiness and call-in-the-middle-of-the-night alarm.

His face floated through Zoe's mind, and along with his image, a flood of sorrow and remorse rushed through her. *What did I do tonight?*

She couldn't remember. All she felt was searing shame and a deep sense of loss in the pit of her stomach. Still sobbing, in a rush of words she cried, "Gavin, I'm going to die. I'm so wasted. You were right, wasted. And I'm so sick and the room is spinning and I can't... Help me Gavin. I'm going to die."

"Hang on. I'll be right there," he said in a steady, deep voice. "I'm calling 911. Don't worry, I won't let anything happen to you. I'll be there as fast as I can. Do you hear me? Hang on."

———————

Tess sat up in bed, her sleep-puffed face dimly lit by the bedside lamp to her left. "Who was that?"

Gavin faced her with the receiver still in his hand. His face was white. "It was Zoe."

"Zoe?" Tess looked pointedly at her watch, although they both knew exactly what time it was from the red, glowing numbers on the clock next to the phone. "It's 3:30 in the morning." Her voice was shrill.

"She's in trouble. She's beyond drunk and she thinks she's going to die. I'm calling 911." He spoke urgently into the phone.

Tess stood up, then sat down again as she listened to the call, her emotions careening between genuine concern for her friend and years of unleashed resentment that she suddenly could not quell.

"What are you doing?" she said as Gavin started pulling on his clothes.

"I'm going over there. I told her I would go over there."

"911 will get there before you."

"I hope so." He zipped up his jeans.

"Oh my God. I should come, but Juliette... " She stood up again.

"Do you want to go instead?"

"No," Tess said, sitting back down. "She called you." A flood of emotions coursed through her head, her heart. "Why did she call you, Gavin?"

"I don't know, Tess. We're friends," he said as he pulled on his shirt.

"Friends? She's got lots of friends." A sharp edge of hysteria sliced into her voice. "Why'd she call you, Gavin?"

"I don't know."

"Oh, yes you do." She despised herself for starting this argument now, for scratching at her biggest fear in the middle of this crisis, but bitterness had taken over and was rising unedited out through her mouth.

Gavin stopped moving and looked at her in astonishment. "Can we talk about this when I get back?" He paused for a moment longer, and then turned and hurried out the door.

His words, his tone kicked her, full on. All the more so because she knew he was right; someone was in trouble and all she could do was argue about a phone call, argue about the fact that Zoe chose to reach out to them. But her shame only added to the fury that was now running riot through her body. *It wasn't "them" Zoe had called, it was Gavin.* And her heart was hammering with that implication. It took every ounce of her self-control not to shriek at him as he walked out of the apartment, "You're screwing Zoe!" *Goddamn him.*

————

An hour and a half later, Gavin slumped back into their York Avenue apartment, exhausted and discouraged. With no cab in sight, he had run most of the way to Zoe's Park Avenue apartment, and by the time he had arrived, panting and sweating in the crisp October night, the paramedics were already wheeling an unconscious Zoe out. Helplessly, he stood and watched them race by him. One of the paramedics had taken pity on him—"There's no point in following us; go home and check on her later." She was probably going to be fine, he had added, but she had to have her stomach pumped. The ambulance raced away, sirens screaming, lights flashing, and the revolving colors pulsed across his damp face: red, white, red, white. Then, silence.

He stood motionless in his grey Erikson sweatshirt, shivering while the sweat dried on him. Then, before he started home, he went into Zoe's building to call Tess and let her know that Zoe was on her way to the hospital.

———————

Tess, still in her blue men's pajamas, sat stiffly at the round kitchen table with a cup of untouched coffee in front of her. As she listened to Gavin's voice boom out from the machine, her finger absently ran around the inside of the mug handle, tracing half-circles over and over again on the warm ceramic. When the message ended, she stood up and walked around the apartment, methodically flicking switches, flooding the dark rooms in light. Once every light but Juliette's was bright, she sat back down at the table to wait. Her finger resumed running mindless laps.

Gavin took one step into the kitchen and froze. He blinked in the bright light.

"I packed you a bag," Tess said evenly, her eyes on her coffee, her finger still in motion on her mug.

Gavin glanced at the small, bloated duffel bag lying on the floor and then looked back at Tess.

Tess looked up. "Why would she call you, Gavin? She's got lots of other friends."

"Tess." He rubbed his eyes. "I honestly don't know. Maybe... I told her at the party that if she ever needed help, she could count on me."

"Why would you do that?"

"She seemed like she was in trouble. Come on, Tess. You saw her, she was a mess. I wanted to let her know we were there for her."

"We or you? Just how often have you been *there* for her Gavin?"

Gavin began to move towards her. "Tess," he said gently. "I'm not cheating on you with Zoe." He paused. "Look, I know we've been having a hard time lately, but it's just a hiccup, everyone has them. We're good, we're fine. I love you; I care about Zoe. Big difference."

Tess was softening. She wanted to believe him, but she was afraid. Was she just being stupid?

Gavin began to kneel down next to Tess's chair. He said quietly, "It's just ridiculous."

Ridiculous? Ridiculous? The bile peaked in Tess' throat again and she wanted to drown him with it, to choke him with her own vitriolic doubts.

"I know all about that big difference, Gavin. It's like the big difference I feel when I'm with Rob."

Gavin stopped mid-kneel and straightened up again. "What?"

Tess put her head in her hands, suddenly deflated. "Oh, Gavin, this isn't working. You're cheating, I'm cheating."

"Tess?" Gavin paled.

"Us. Our marriage. It's not working," Tess said, depleted now after vomiting her own admission.

"You're sleeping with Rob? Rob Landry?"

Yes, she wanted to say defiantly, the whole purpose of the admission having been defiance, revenge. But she was too dejected to be defiant; too disheartened about where this conversation and their marriage was going, had gone. "Once. I slept with him once."

Gavin's face crumpled. "Oh my God." He took a deep breath and leaned on the back of the chair. He was so slumped over Tess thought he was going to lie down on the floor.

Tess looked up at him. "And you?"

"I'm not sleeping with Zoe." He took another deep breath. "I admit, I cheated on you a long time ago with her, but it was years ago, before we were married. I've wanted to tell you, but then I thought maybe the past is best left in the past." He looked her in the eyes, his spine straightened again. "It was wrong, both the cheating and the not telling you. But since we've been married, since we've been engaged for that matter, I've been faithful to you, I swear. I love you. I have no reason to cheat." He waited. "What's your excuse?"

"My excuse?" Her head was stuffed with thick white cotton, all her staunch, lined-up reasons suddenly unwieldy fluff. Why had she done it? Had it really been as simple as the fact that Rob made her feel special? And if so, then that highlighted a malignancy in herself, not in Gavin. "Oh Gavin, look at me. My excuse is that you have a fat, tired, nagging wife. The farthest thing from a Victoria's Secret model. And there's Zoe—beautiful, funny, *beautiful*—the contrast is too striking. And there *is* something between you two, I can't be that paranoid."

"Wow, Tess. I'd like to be sympathetic here. Maybe another man would come over and hug you, make you feel better, tell you how much I love you, and that oh my God, the way you just described yourself is the farthest thing from how I see you. But you've just knocked the wind out of me. To put it mildly." He backed up. "I think I'll take this," he picked up the bag, "and go to a hotel for a while. I need to think."

She watched him walk down the hall and peek in on Juliette, sleeping peacefully in her stuffed-animal-filled pink room, oblivious to the damage and destruction right outside her door. He stepped into her room and Tess imagined him leaning way over the crib side, giving Juliette a soft kiss on her cheek, maybe tucking a strand of blond hair behind her ear, the way he always did before he went to bed. Then he re-emerged from her room and gently closed her door.

He walked back through the kitchen—Tess hadn't moved from her seat at the table—and clutched his duffel bag to his chest like he was holding a flotation device. He paused at the front door, his hand on the gold knob. Tess watched the muscles in his shoulders tense, and then, without a word, he opened the door and walked out. The apartment door clicked shut behind him.

————

Out in the suburbs a few hours later, the day had burst into a New England postcard—a rare October Sunday where the cool air and the hot sun duke it out with equal muscle, and the deep violet blue of the sky is only outdone by the vivid fire of the fall foliage. Allie and Megan were stretched out on top of a red fleece blanket, toasting their faces in the sun and trying to stay as still as possible so as not to catch the wind's cool sting. Crumpled white sandwich wrappers stained with mustard and pickle juice were pushed to the side, and two huge bags of just-picked red apples—the product of their morning's efforts—were parked in the shade of a nearby tree. Dana and Jared (who had 10-month old Maggie in a carrier on his back) were chasing Matthew and Gillian across the worn grass, and once caught, the kids were scooped up for a quick, squealing squeeze-kiss, then released again for a new round of "Can't catch me!" (*catch me Daddy, catch me!*). The chase was just far enough away from Allie and Megan that specific words were lost in the breeze, but the melody of ecstasy was loud and clear.

"So what time does Maggie nap?" Allie said, her eyes closed.

"She totally missed her morning one, so I'm surprised she's not asleep in that backpack right now. She'll probably conk out in the car on the way to my mother-in-law's."

"You're going to Rose's?"

Megan nodded, picking a blade of grass.

"I thought you guys weren't making that weekly pilgrimage anymore." Without turning her face, Allie glanced sideways at Megan.

"We've cut way back to every other week." Megan laughed, her long copper hair ablaze in the sun. "It's not so bad. She's great with Maggie, and we'll get an amazing meal."

"I still salivate when I think of her lasagna."

"I just have to steel myself to all the heavy sighing and oh-so-subtle cracks about my job and Jared's staying home with Maggie." Megan reflected back on their last visit to Rose's. Maggie had been cranky and tired, and when Megan rushed over to soothe her, she'd screamed herself scarlet, arching away from Megan and stretching out her milky white arms towards Jared. Even though Megan understood that she was reaching for the person who most of the time held her when she cried, it hurt enough without her mother-in-law's, "It's normal dear. You work such long hours." The *tsk-tsk* in her voice had been deafening.

"She totally disapproves, and doesn't do a very good job of hiding it," Megan continued. "Come to think of it, I'm not sure she *is* trying to hide it. Every time Jared tells a story about something cute that Maggie did, Rose makes a point of looking at me as if to say, see what you're missing? And most of the time, I'd been there to see Maggie do it! I could've been the one telling the story."

"You would think she'd be happy that her son is an amazing dad." Allie paused. "It's a great reflection on her actually, that she raised such a warm and loving son."

"Oh, no. She sees it as a blemish on her, that her kid has a screw loose." Megan sighed. "The whole thing's just too unconventional for her. She thinks I'm cold because I'm working, that Jared's making this huge sacrifice because I refuse to. So she blames me and pities him."

"But Jared wanted to stay at home with Maggie."

"I know. She can't see that this, right now, is what works best for all three of us. Here's my theory: in her mind, what Jared's chosen to do is unmanly for two reasons—he's doing woman's work, and he isn't providing for his family. That's unacceptable to her, so she rewrites the script. Rather than thinking of her son as stripped of his manhood, he's heroic, a martyr that is holding his family together by the skin of his teeth. And I, of course, am the wicked witch."

"That's so unfair. She knows how much Maggie means to you."

"It's not her fault really. She's traditional; thinking outside the box isn't her forte. It's not a big deal." She shrugged her shoulders. "Sometimes I think her real issue with me is that we didn't name Maggie after her."

They both gazed at their husbands romping in the sun with the kids. A minute or so later, Megan continued.

"She's not the only one who looks at us cross-eyed once they hear that Jared stays home with Maggie. I can see the questions popping into people's eyes like little thought bubbles. 'Was Jared fired? Was he unsuccessful? And what about that mother? Is she so selfish that she couldn't take a few years off?' I know other working moms get that too, but people can write that off as all about the second income. With us, one of us *is* staying home, it's just not MOM."

Allie nodded.

"Sometimes I question myself too," Megan said softly. "Especially after I'm riding home and it's later than I thought, and I ache to hold Maggie, to see her smile at me, but she's sound asleep when I get there." Megan felt a hot flash of anguish. She looked at her friend. "Don't judge me."

Allie shook her head. "Never."

Megan sighed. "Well, I judge myself."

"You're doing what we're all doing. Your best."

Megan smiled at her friend. "I know there are times when Jared wishes he was at work, but he loves staying home with Maggie. And I know myself, I would get antsy staying home all day. I need to be busy, I need to work or I might just go crazy. Plus I really love my job. Is that terrible?" She rolled her eyes. "Don't answer that."

"You're an awesome mom. Maggie's lucky to have you." Allie watched Matthew running across the grass, his arms swinging determinedly. Allie smiled. "You're like the woman who can bring home the bacon, fry it up in a pan and never, ever let you forget you're a man."

Megan laughed. "I think there's a reason there are no kids in that jingle." She looked at Allie. "Now that song is going to haunt me for the rest of the day. What was that ad for anyway?"

"Some perfume, I think," Allie said.

Then they dissolved into laughter as the finale of the old commercial rang through their minds and they both sang out the name of the perfume in unison, "Enjolie!"

"Is there a reason that song has survived in the archives of our minds for decades?" Megan said.

"It has to be the brilliant lyrics; the copy is always the key," Allie said, smirking at her friend.

———

Gavin did not notice the gorgeous autumn weather outside his hotel room window. He didn't notice much of anything. He had been sitting on the edge of a gold-and-brown polyester bedspread for hours, paralyzed with disbelief, unable to lie down, and too exhausted to even click on the TV. *Tess slept with Rob Landry. How could I have missed that? Why?* Questions knocked back and forth in his head like a racquetball that he couldn't hit. He wasn't angry; he assumed the anger would come later. Right now he was in deep shock and he was bleeding.

The wail of a siren jolted him out of himself and into the morning, and stiffly, like an old man whose joints are shot through with arthritis, he showered and dressed for work. He was halfway down the street before he realized it was Sunday. He slowed—a braking train pulling into a station—and then stood still on the sidewalk in his gray suit, despondence rooting him to the pavement, snuffing out his smallest decision. He lost 15 minutes—a well-dressed statue forcing blue-jeaned strollers to detour around him. Finally, a pretty woman who gave him a wide berth and a wary look impelled him forward, and he trudged back to his hotel, blind to the fat stacks of *The Sunday Times* on the sidewalk, unaffected by the smell of coffee steaming out from corner delis. He spent the rest of the day in blue jeans, slumped in the armchair of his small, stuffy room, reexamining the old files of every conversation, argument, and romantic exchange he and Tess had recently engaged in. Every so often he stumbled onto a statement or remembered an odd moment that in hindsight raised a red flag, but that in the landscape of their life had seemed completely benign.

Every so often, he glanced at the phone. He was dying to talk to Juliette—Sunday mornings were his special time with her and they often went out for breakfast before embarking on a toddler-sized adventure together—but he didn't want to call and have to speak to Tess; he was afraid he might say something that he could never take back. The thought of being cut off from his daughter spurred a fresh wave of sadness, and with it, the first surge of anger.

By late afternoon he was too agitated to stay in his room, and as he needed more than a bartender to talk to, he found himself back out on the street, his feet marching the well-worn path to Zoe, who he assumed was now home in her apartment. He felt a brief pang of guilt, a single bell toll, once his destination became a clear goal in his mind, but his anger snuffed it out and loudly drummed out a faster pace.

"A Gavin Keller here to see you, miss."

Gavin stood with his hands in his pockets and looked around the lobby, even though he'd seen it hundreds of times.

The doorman looked at Gavin. "She's not up for visitors right now."

"Tell her "please." Tell her for just a minute."

The doorman hesitated, then relayed the message. He looked at Gavin. "Go on up."

"Hey," Gavin said as the door opened into Zoe's apartment. He was instantly hit with a flash of Zoe on a stretcher, only a few hours before.

Zoe smiled faintly, her scratchy voice a decibel above a whisper. "I hope you don't mind," she indicated her fluffy white robe, "my comfortable look."

"How are you feeling?"

"Okay, I guess. Considering my insides are somewhere back on the hospital floor." She lay back down on the couch.

Gavin slouched into the chair across from her.

"But how are you?" She looked more closely at him. "You actually look worse than I do, if that's possible." She adjusted the pillows under her head. "Can I offer you a robe? Notice I didn't say drink. I think the smell of it might send me leaping out the window."

"I'm not going to stay long," Gavin said. "I just wanted to check on you, see if you were okay."

"And?"

"You seem to be okay… "

"No, I meant *and* what else? You look as if there's a something else." She chewed on her lip. "Do you want to tell me what happened last night? I'm braced to hear if rock bottom is just one step lower." She paused. "Or do I not want to know?"

Gavin gently sketched out what he knew of her ordeal, and then described his own train wreck with Tess. Zoe listened with wide eyes.

"Tess had an affair? I'll be damned," she said softly.

"What's that supposed to mean?"

"I don't know. I just never expected it from her."

"You sound like you respect her now," Gavin said.

"Sorry. It's not that. Some people just surprise you, that's all."

"Tell me about it." Gavin slowly exhaled all his oxygen.

Zoe swallowed hard. "Gavin, why are you here?"

"What do you mean?"

"You know if Tess knows you were here, it's going to make all this worse, right?"

He shrugged. "I'm visiting a friend."

Zoe frowned.

"And anyway, how can it get worse?" He sank a little lower in his chair.

Zoe grimaced as she tried to sit up, and ended up just propping herself a little higher up on her pillows. "Gavin." She waited until he looked her in the eyes. "You know even if I could sit up, I can't be The Shoulder here."

Gavin closed his eyes and nodded.

Zoe stared at Gavin's face until he opened his eyes again. They held each other's eyes for a moment, then Gavin looked down.

Zoe sighed. "Oh Gavin, for so many years we've been stuck in this purgatory between being friends and being lovers, at times wanting one thing, at times maybe wanting neither. But if I was Tess, our relationship—whatever the definition de jour—would have been a needle in my side too."

Gavin leaned forward, listening attentively.

"For a long time I didn't care what Tess thought—hell, I *wanted* to needle her," Zoe said. "I blamed her for coming between us." She shook her head as he started to say something. "Don't comment; I know it's not true. I know you and I were never ideal. The point is, I don't really know how to fix this," she waved her hand between them, "but I think we should try."

She inched up on her pillow and grimaced again. "You need to go back to Tess and Juliette. We both know if you don't do that, you're going to regret it for a long time. It's where you belong."

Gavin rubbed the stubble on his chin.

"I'm going to go away for a little while. A little family spa called rehab." She smiled feebly. "And maybe when I come back," she bit her lip, "we won't make it a point to get together and talk about old times."

Gavin nodded. He was mute with fatigue. And surprisingly relieved at what Zoe was saying to him.

"Obviously we'll see each other when we all get together, that's unavoidable. But we can handle that, right?"

"Absolutely." He watched her close her eyes, lay back on her mound of pillows. It looked like the couch was swallowing her up; she looked tiny.

Zoe's eyes stayed closed as she said in a steady voice, "Gavin, go back home and make it right with Tess. Don't lose her."

He was still for a moment, then he pushed himself out of his chair and walked towards the door.

"Gavin."

He turned around.

Zoe looked straight at him. She bit her lip; then set her mouth in a straight line. "It really was Bob's baby."

Gavin couldn't breathe in. His knees wobbled as he forced himself to walk to the door, step out into the long hallway, close the door behind him. Click.

He leaned against the elevator bank and started to cry.

CHAPTER 12

Some of the best, and certainly most provocative dramas are the ones in which the denouement lifts up the sheet on our assumptions and in one shocking revelation, forces us to reconsider the whole story. In a world where theaters empty as though someone has yelled "Fire!", there is no mass exodus after a movie or a play in which a secret is laid bare in the finale. The lights may brighten, but the unsettled audience lingers, mouths agape, struggling to squeeze the puzzle piece of extraordinary information into their foregone conclusions.

And so I am just sitting in the theater after almost 30 years of a reality that I now know is wrong. I can fully appreciate people's disbelief and fear when they discovered the world was round, after they had always, always walked on flat earth. Or the disorientation of hearing you're adopted, when all your life you had assumed, without consideration, that you were the biological offspring of your beloved mom and dad. Or the utter devastation of learning a spouse is cheating, has had a lover for a number of years, and you'd never had cause to doubt that your favorite-sweatshirt marriage was anything other than faithful and preferred.

Most of our basic assumptions about the people in our life and the history we've lived through become indelible and self-evident over time.

Like the permanent features of our face, they just are; they are our truth. We then build our lives on these assumptions, on this truth, on this face of ours. The many marks of wisdom and maturity pile on—the warm freckles of life-lived, the deep wrinkles of heartfelt expression, the soft gray of worry and courage and risk. But what if one day, you wake up, slog into the bathroom to brush your teeth, and when you glance into the mirror, a different face, a fun-house distortion of yourself gapes back—your eyes are a different color, your skin a different tone, your nose a foreign shape. Shock and terror rocket through your body as you try to grasp that the familiar "you," the truth you have always trusted, is gone.

When this happens, when a fundamental truth of your life is shattered, do the unique characteristics that make up who you are—the freckles, the wrinkles, the gray of your life—lose their meaning as well?

And how do you assimilate this new face, this new piece of information into your carefully constructed life? Does it radically alter who you are, who you've been? After a month or so to digest all this, I think not. It may alter where you're going. But who you are? Who you've been? I don't think so.

What happened with my mother will continue to be powerful and haunting; but it's just one of countless experiences that have been accumulating over time, building up a fatty cushion around that piece of my life, diluting its influence with the sheer volume of alternatives. So the crush of this news, this truth, is well buffered. It has changed my perceptions, shifted my outlook and my insight in ways I can touch, and I'm sure in ways I can't guess at. But I do know this: it hasn't negated everything I am. My reflection has been changed forever, but the splintered one will come into focus again; this strange image will become lived-in as I weave this piece of history into my story.

And it is *my* story. The poetry of life is that I'm the author. Of course, life dumps out a bagful of incredible and sometimes horrible characters and subplots that must be included. But I have the luxury of interpreting each new scene, establishing my own cadence, and arranging all of my life chapters into my own unique epic. And if one life episode is particularly heinous, I have the prerogative to assign its symbolism, and perhaps, to surround it with beautiful prose. And of course, I have the power to determine its significance—is it a paragraph or the whole story? Yes, it is a piece of my experience, but I am the one who decides how it fits.

The truth is subjective. You see and understand what you want to see or what you're capable of understanding. I think about all the dinners I've had with Dana's or Megan's family, times when their parents will recycle favorite family stories, the ones they think are especially adorable and representative of their children. "For Dana, even lemonade stands weren't impulsive; he had a whole marketing scheme mapped out weeks in advance… " or "While I cooked dinner, Megan would sit on the counter next to me to make sure I followed the recipe exactly… " Both Megan and Dana listen to the hundredth retelling of these loving anecdotes and laugh along, humoring their parents because they know that to argue their truth would be fruitless, they would only receive a puzzled look and a "Where were you when this happened?" ("Well Mom… actually, I was there.") Afterward, when their parents are out of earshot, they will roll their eyes and quickly set me straight on how it *really* was. But all of them believe their own stories, and they are sticking by them.

And sticking by them adamantly, as my family did with each of our versions of what happened to my mother and why. My mother obviously had her own edition. My father's guess as to what that was… well, he finally told me that night at his house that he now believes Eva killed herself because she loved us, and because she was so afraid of hurting us, so terrified that she might lose control again. And again. She believed she was damaged and refused to pass that on.

My father said to me, "I've spent so much of my energy analyzing, guessing, and re-guessing. Of course the other explanation that haunts me is that I failed her. Maybe she thought that if I couldn't rescue her that night, or worse, if I didn't *want* to rescue her, then she might never climb out of the darkness. And then that begs the question, for me at least: if I couldn't pull her out of the abyss, what was *I* good for? That was why she chose me, that was our dynamic. She fell; I picked her up. That last time she fell, I failed her."

I can still hear his intake of breath, deeply weary, age-old. "The first scenario is obviously easier to live with, although I was stuck in the more grisly, self-lambasting explanation for years and years. Isn't that just the thing? The explanation that pollutes our life the most is sometimes the easiest to believe."

I don't know what Kevin or Paul believed, although I'm guessing from the theme here, that they blamed themselves, viewed themselves as failing in some way too. My father said that Paul knew the truth. No wonder he pulled away from Kevin and me. What a toxic secret to hold.

My own understanding of my mother's absence—that she walked out on us for something better—had a hefty "hence" attached to it: hence I wasn't worth her staying put. This belief, along with my desperation to bring her back, to prove to her that she was wrong (and maybe to prove it to myself too), drove me a certain way in my life. When she didn't come back, or when life just weighed me down, it confirmed she was right. I was not worth it.

A heart can only be broken so many times. At some point, you learn to self-protect. I realize now that the ways I tried to protect myself, to keep Dana from finding out the truth as I knew it—that I wasn't worth it—just pushed him away. And as he stepped back, my truth was confirmed.

The sad irony is that yes, a deep moat around your heart keeps you safe, but it also keeps you alone.

But maybe I can change that. After all, I can decide to cower behind my moat all by myself, or dare to put my drawbridge down.

MAY 2000
New York City

"Sorry guys." Tess eased into a chair at the table for four and smiled, "Although it looks like I still beat Megan."

Allie chuckled. "You're not going to win any awards for that."

"No, I guess not. What are we drinking?"

"Vodka tonics," Zoe said.

Tess's eyes darted to Zoe's tall glass.

"Just kidding, everyone relax. It's San Pellegrino." Zoe smiled. "See, I don't have to be drunk to have fun."

The waiter came over and hovered by the table.

Tess hesitated.

"It's okay. Have at it," Zoe said.

Tess ordered a San Pellegrino.

Zoe's eyes softened, and all three women were quiet. Then Zoe smirked. "Don't tell me you're pregnant."

"I better not be," Tess said. "The new house is a handful enough. Although I guess 'new' is not the operative word." She turned to Allie. "You didn't tell me renovating would be so much work. I keep telling myself I'm going to love the finished product, but I'm not sure there'll ever be one."

"It's like childbirth, if people told the truth, no one ever would do it." Allie smiled. "What are you working on now?"

"We just finished our bedroom, so that's where we're all camping out for a while." Out of habit, her ears pricked towards Zoe, expecting a snort or a sarcastic comment. She was so surprised she didn't hear anything that she almost forgot what she was saying. She continued, "We're saving the kitchen for last. Maybe we'll throw a party when we finally rip out all that avocado green laminate. Although I'm worried that Gavin's becoming attached to it. He's started cooking."

"Gavin's cooking?" Zoe's mouth hung open.

"So far just paella and blueberry pie, but both are pretty damn good."

"Paella?" Allie said.

Tess shook her head. "You got me."

They all laughed.

"What's Megan working on these days that's keeping her tied to her desk?"

"I haven't talked to her in, wow, about two weeks, which is a little weird." Allie looked at Zoe.

"Don't look at me, I haven't talked to her either." Zoe shrugged.

"Here she—" the last word of Tess's statement died away, and all three women looked towards the door. Their banter and cheer crashed to the floor like a tray full of glasses. It was obvious that something was very wrong.

Megan—once the unofficial "borrower" in college—now had the salary and the fashion sense to never leave home without some gorgeous and trendy outfit, usually culled right from the pages of the most recent *Vogue*. Tonight however, she was approaching the table in jeans and a long-sleeved tee; her belt loops were empty and no funky accessories hung off of her. Her long red hair, usually neatly pulled back somehow for work, was loose and looked as if a brush had been raked through it out of habit, not out of a desire to actually detangle it. She looked so pale and bedraggled that Zoe's eyes darted to the window to see if the weather had turned stormy. No one uttered, "it looks like it's been a bad day," as it had too obviously been that. They waited, concerned, for Megan to offer an explanation.

She deep-sighed her way onto her chair and sagged back against it. "Maggie's sick," she said to her captive audience. "She has leukemia." Tears trickled down her bare cheeks. She made no move to wipe them away.

There was a collective sharp intake of breath around the table. "Oh my God," Allie exhaled, and reached for Megan's hand.

Zoe, who was sitting on her other side, gave Megan's shoulder a squeeze. "I'll get you a drink," she said, and moved to signal the waiter.

"No, no. I'm only staying for a minute." She reached for Allie's glass with a shaking hand and drank deeply.

"It's just water," Zoe said with a furrowed brow. "Let me get you a—"

"I just came because I wanted to tell you all in person, and honestly, I wasn't sure I could do this on the phone three separate times."

"How is she?" Tess asked, her brown eyes intense. "How are you?"

Megan chewed her thumbnail. "Me? I'm a wreck." She pressed her lips together, perhaps in an attempt at a smile, and then she choked back a sob. "And Maggie, God, she's such a trooper. She's so sick, and she's two, and she has no idea what's happening to her, why she's in the hospital, why all these worried faces are peering down at her. I try my best to be cheerful but," she tried to chuckle but it came out as a snort, "you guys know how good I am at putting on a face." She grabbed a white napkin and wiped her eyes. "She senses my tears just under the surface, I know she does."

Three bodies inched closer to Megan, closing a tight circle around her, their faces a wall of solemnity.

"She's just lying in this big white hospital bed feeling awful, I mean *awful*, being poked and prodded, with tubes coming out of her and poison going into her... " She took a deep, ragged breath as she slumped lower in her seat. "I feel so helpless."

"Oh, Meg," Zoe said as she squeezed her shoulder again.

Megan twisted the cloth napkin in her hands. "I'm numb, and when feelings do break through, it's terror or... agony." She swiped at her eyes again with her napkin. "You know how in the movies someone always says 'I wish it was me instead of her?' I can honestly say that I get that now."

"What do the doctors say?" Allie said quietly.

"The good news—isn't that an oxymoron—is that it's a kind of leukemia that has a really high cure rate, something like 70 percent. All we have to do is blast it all right out of her body with liquid Drano." Bitterness spiked her tone. Then she breathed deeply, and feeling Allie's grip on her hand, Zoe's hand on her shoulder, and Tess's soft brown eyes hugging her from across the table, she sat up a tiny bit straighter. "And she's in what they've told us is a low risk group, so," she looked at her friends, "we're going to beat this thing."

"Absolutely," Zoe said. Allie and Tess repeated the word as if they were saying *amen*.

"How's Jared?" Tess said.

"Hanging in there. Like me I guess; some days strong, some days not so strong. He hides it better than me though. We've both been basically living at the hospital. Work has been great about giving me time. But they're going to want me back at some point, and to tell you the truth, I really just want to quit. But we need the money, and now we definitely need the benefits." She smiled wanly. "My penance as the breadwinner."

"What can we do?" Allie said.

"Pray." Her voice was grave.

Everyone was quiet for a moment.

"Can I come back to the hospital with you? Keep you company?" Allie said.

Megan's big brown eyes, raw and rimmed in red, looked into Allie's and held on for a few moments. Then the slight movement of Zoe and Tess leaning in broke the mental hug and Megan shook her head slowly. "No," and she continued as Allie started to protest, "no, really, thank you. I just want to get back to Jared and Maggie. I can't explain it, and it's not that I don't appreciate it, but I just need to be alone with Jared right now."

"How about tomorrow?" Allie said. Even just for a little while to hold your hand?" Zoe and Tess nodded.

"That would be great." Megan glanced at her watch. "I should go. Sorry." She looked around the table as her eyes welled up with tears again. "You guys are the best; it felt really good to sit here, even for a few minutes." She stayed in her chair for a deep inhale and then pushed herself up. "I'll see you tomorrow."

Allie, Zoe, and Tess leapt to their feet and rushed to each give her a long embrace and whisper words of hope through their own tears. They didn't want to let her go and their hands lingered on her arm, on her shoulder, one last hug. Finally, Megan pulled away from them with an anguished whimper that she tried to chuckle over—it sounded like a hiccup—and started slogging across the floor as if it was thick mud. Then her shoulders straightened and her pace picked up as she strode out of the door and into the night.

Allie jumped up from the table, her white napkin fell to the floor. She mumbled something about being right back and sprinted after Megan.

It was cold out on the sidewalk, and Megan—trying to hail a cab—was shivering and small against the honking headlights of the city. Allie put her hand on Megan's shoulder, and Megan turned and collapsed into Allie's arms, her shivers becoming great, shaking sobs.

"Oh Allie," Megan said, her words choppy and hoarse.

"I'm right here, Meg. I'm right here."

———

Later, after Megan had cried herself into a trembling and exhausted quiet, Allie tucked her into a taxi. As she sped away from her friends, she realized that she'd forgotten to tell them that she was pregnant.

———

Back inside the restaurant, the three women stared at each other, shell-shocked. Around them music danced; wine flowed; diners chewed, chatted, laughed. The waiter sauntered over and asked if they were ready to order.

Zoe waved him away. "I'm not sure I can eat right now."

"I'm not sure I can even speak right now," Allie said.

Tess fiddled with her necklace.

Sorrow and concern circled the table like vultures.

"I need to get out of here," Tess said. Her chair screeched backwards. "I'm about to jump out of my skin. I just need to be home right now," she glanced at her watch, "and there's a train leaving in 15 minutes that I just might catch."

Allie leaned over and gave Tess a quick hug. "Go," she said, and then she looked wearily at Zoe. "I think Zoe and I are right behind you."

Tess stood up. "I have a morning meeting tomorrow. Does anyone want to go to the hospital early?" Tess glanced at Zoe, let her gaze rest on Allie.

"I can't go until around 10," Allie said.

"I'll go with you," Zoe said. "Eight o'clock?"

Tess hesitated, then nodded. "Great."

Tess sprinted for the train in her black heels, bumping into briefcases and shoulders as she ducked and weaved through the crowd of commuters heading for Grand Central. The fact that there was another train in 25 minutes did nothing to assuage her panic; if she didn't make this train, the world was going to end. She leapt on just as the doors started to slide closed, and sank onto one of the few remaining red vinyl seats. Beads of sweat trickled down her temples. She almost cried with relief.

Gavin, Juliette. Like a mantra chanted over and over, the two names chugged in time with the rhythm of the speeding locomotive. They were a powerful magnet pulling her away from the devastation and pain of Megan's news, home to the safety of Gavin's arms and Juliette's sweet chatter. They were the only salve that could nurse the creeping mold of nausea and worry taking over her heart. Maggie. Megan. This was surreal. *How can that little girl be so sick? How are Megan and Jared dealing with this?* She stared out the window at the dark buildings racing by and knew that if anyone on the train looked at her crosswise, she would dissolve into tears.

Juliette would be sleeping with them tonight.

She checked her watch again; 30 more minutes. Gavin wouldn't be expecting her home this early. She imagined his smile as she walked in the door. She closed her eyes and let her thoughts drift with the white noise of the train.

New house, fresh start; it had been Gavin's idea and Tess had been overjoyed at the forgiveness inherent in it. When he walked out a year and a half ago, Gavin had closed the door behind him calmly and deliberately, which Tess found more frightening than a raging slam; anger was temporary, resignation much more permanent. Another interminable minute later, she had heard the more final swoosh of the elevator door in the hall.

What have I done?

She sat frozen at the kitchen table for hours, dazed by the quiet after the explosion, her cold, cloudy coffee in front of her and the dawning of a new day filling in around her. The ticking clock, like the lonely beat of a heart monitor in ICU, was the only sign of life in the apartment, until she heard Juliette shout out, demanding that she move, that she focus.

She didn't call anyone. She didn't go to work; she canceled the nanny. She only left the apartment for groceries. She couldn't even face the teen-age cashier with the green smock and bored affect; instead she pretended to fumble in her purse for her credit card—"Where did I put that?"—while the girl tapped out a tune on her silver braces.

Shame rotted deep and heavy in her core; the sour taste of bile fermented in her mouth.

Gavin called every day to speak to Juliette, and every day Tess rushed to the phone and blurted out an apology instead of hello. His tone of voice terrified her—it was ashy, dead; not hot fire.

She never asked him to come home. She couldn't think of anything appealing enough to offer him.

A week later, Gavin called and told Tess, "Get a sitter to take Juliette. I'll be there in an hour."

———

Tess showered, made coffee, stashed Juliette's toys and the dirty laundry and her towers of magazines in a closet and threw her weight against the door.

The elevator in the hall groaned and then stopped.

The apartment door banged open.

"Now I'm mad." Gavin stomped past her and into the kitchen, marching with a sound. His every step matched the thumping in Tess's heart.

"Gavin, I'm—"

"I don't want to hear that anymore." He clenched his fists. "I want to hear why."

"Why." Tess stood in front of him, feeling tiny in the face of his anger. The makeup she had brushed on suddenly made her feel plastic. She had the urge to wipe it off with her hand. "The easy answer is I thought you were with Zoe."

He crossed his arms over his chest. "And the hard one?"

She sighed, sunk into a chair. "The hard one is that I gave up on us. Everyone else's 'What's Gavin doing with her?' made me feel smaller and smaller. And it got to the point where I couldn't remember the answer."

Gavin sat down in a chair across the table and looked directly at her. "You never talked to me."

Tess hung her head.

"That's the worst part," Gavin said.

They sat in silence.

"But I didn't talk to you either." Gavin looked away. The kitchen clock ticked into a long pause. He sighed heavily and looked back at her. "Tess, before we were engaged," he dropped his eyes to the table and then it seemed like he consciously dragged them back up to meet hers. "I cheated on you with Zoe. I know I told you that a week ago—years too late—but I slipped it into our fight, and didn't tell you the way I should have, the way I wish I had. What I wish I had said, what I want to say now is: it was wrong. I was wrong. I loved you and I slipped into a thing with Zoe like I've slipped into so many things in my life, without the courage to say 'I want something different.' And I am just so sorry, Tess."

They let the silence fill the space between them. Tess reached out her hand to laid it over Gavin's.

"Wait, there's more," he said. He eased his hand out from under hers and put it over his mouth. He breathed in and then exhaled slowly through his fingers before dropping his hand onto the table. "Back then—and again, this was before we were engaged,—Zoe got pregnant." Tess looked up at him, wide-eyed. Gavin continued, "She told me it was Bob's, remember Bob? But I wondered, just a little bit, if it was mine. I wondered if she was just trying to let me off the hook, and to help you too. All these years, I had this tiny, shard-of-glass worry that the horror on my face when she told me she was pregnant had chased her into a lie. A life and death lie. Afterwards, every once in a while, when I moved a certain way, that shard of glass would cut me with the thought: I let her go through with the abortion, I let her believe that I believed the baby was Bob's." His voice wobbled, cracked. "Because I couldn't bear to lose you, our life. Tess, I love you so much." He cleared his throat, shook his head. "The baby really was Bob's. But that doesn't change the fact that I was afraid to really ask."

Tess and Gavin sat across from each other, still and silent.

"So you weren't crazy to think there was something going on with Zoe," Gavin said. "And part of me feels like I deserve what just happened with you and Rob."

Tess reached across the table and touched her fingertips to his. "Gavin, come home."

―――――

During the next several months, both Gavin and Tess rode an emotional rollercoaster, and various pillows and blankets moved from the bedroom to the couch and back again as they relaxed into the warmth of forgiveness and exploded in bitterness and blame. But they buckled in, they fought through it, until finally, all the pillows and blankets stayed resting on their bed, and the couch became once again, just a place to sit.

―――――

Allie and Zoe lingered at the restaurant in the wake of Tess's hasty exit. Zoe itched for a martini; she licked her lips and then pressed them against each other, her fingers twitched on the tablecloth. She lit up another cigarette and ferociously sipped her Pellegrino.

The two friends leaned over the unused silverware, grief and worry soaking their every syllable. They brainstormed ways they could help, but while their ideas attempted strength, their gestures—hands running through hair, nails mindlessly scraping cuticles, cigarettes rapidly moving up and down—highlighted helplessness. After a while, they needed to move, needed the night to just end so that they could at least do something, even if it was only showing up at the hospital in the morning.

"Are you going to be okay?" Zoe said as they walked out.

"I guess so. Are you?"

Zoe nodded. She noticed Allie's eyes held hers for two beats too long. "What?"

"You're not going to drink tonight, right?"

"No, Mom." She held up a pack of cigarettes. "I'm armed and ready. And, seriously, if Megan can face this, I can stare down a bottle of vodka, seductive as it may be. I'm going straight home; my apartment's clean. I'm okay." And she smiled because she knew she meant it.

———

Allie unlocked the back door, stepped into the bright kitchen, and lobbed her keys onto the corner table. As an answer to the crash of metal against the smooth wood, she heard Madaket's toenails click-clacking towards her across the tile floor.

Allie stooped down to scratch her dog's blond head, and then aimed towards the den where she expected Dana would be eating pizza and watching TV. All was quiet in the big house except for the low drone of the television, and Allie was longing to sink onto the couch next to Dana and weep with Megan's story. Before she rounded the corner however, long, bell-bottom denim legs slunk towards her. "Hey, Ms. Sexton. How was your night?"

Allie stopped. "Hi Carrie." She glanced at her watch with a furrowed brow. Why was the 16-year-old babysitter, who had come to cover the hour between Allie's six o'clock departure and Dana's seven o'clock arrival from work, still here? "Is everything okay?"

"The kids were great." Carrie smiled. "I had to read Gillian like 10 stories—*Madeline* over and over again. I think I can recite it now. But they're both asleep."

"Good. Actually I meant, where's Mr. Sexton?" Allie felt foolish asking, as if with that one question, she was exhuming the state of their marriage for this teenager.

"He called around seven from work. I guess something came up, and he asked if I could stay and put the kids to bed."

Allie frowned.

"It was okay; not a problem. I just did my homework here."

"What time did he say he'd be home?"

"Around 10. He said you wouldn't be home until after that."

"Thanks Carrie. I really appreciate it." They walked back into the kitchen and Allie dug around in her purse for some money. "Are you okay walking?"

"It's only three houses, Ms. Sexton." She smiled at Allie as if she had gray hair and a cane. "I'll be fine."

After Carrie left, Allie stood alone in the clean kitchen among the organized Calphalon and gleaming appliances and felt a black, moonless loneliness engulf her. She leaned onto the granite counter and put her head in her hands; she was surprised that no tears let loose. Fatigue stood on her shoulders and kept her wilted over the counter, her eyes wide open but shuttered to sight. She was so numb, so immobilized, that for the first time, the absence of energy around her was not frightening. She couldn't feel anything; she wasn't sure she was even breathing.

Her grumbling stomach broke into her tomb, reminding her that she hadn't eaten anything except for a piece of bread at the restaurant, and she opened the refrigerator and then closed it, already intimate with the contents without having to look, and knowing that the leftover Scooby-Doo macaroni and cheese was not what she was looking for. The murmur of the television beckoned from the other room and she was drawn to it as if it was flannel pajamas and a cup of warm milk. She collapsed onto the couch and flipped through the hundreds of channels. No sarcastic banter or dramatic affect grabbed her attention, but she stared at the changing channels, hypnotized by the rhythmic color shift. She finally clicked the

TV off after a kitschy used-car commercial broke the spell. With a heavy step, she climbed the stairs.

She wished she could crawl into bed with Matthew or Gillian, to hold them close in the hope that their smattering of freckles and sweet soapy smell would begin to close the cavern that had opened up inside her chest. But she was afraid that once she curled them into her arms, the dark, stormy sobs that had been threatening since she left the restaurant would thunder and wake their peaceful slumber. So she placed a tiny, tender kiss on each of their baby-soft cheeks, and hesitated in their toy-filled kingdoms a little longer than usual, allowing the rise and fall of their breath to become her own.

She exhaled into her king-sized bed and curled up into the fetal position, listening in the dark for the swoosh of a car in the driveway. The earlier longing for Dana was being slowly supplanted by the caustic wounds of old times—wounds that always lay patiently waiting for a hapless new hurt to infect; wounds that ensured that new arguments weren't as much about the here and now as they were about the unraveling of their togetherness in general.

You're never here. Even when you're home you aren't here.

The bullet points of tonight's offense ricocheted through her mind. *The kids had been looking forward to some time with you, what the hell was so important at work? I hardly ever go out, couldn't you have tried to get here on time tonight?* It felt sneaky somehow that Dana had called Carrie after she had already left, as if he had only changed the plan once Allie could no longer have any input.

Underneath her gathering rage she could hear his defense: *I couldn't help it, it was a last-minute thing. The kids were fine with Carrie. I assumed this was a good night to stay late because you weren't home either.* Still further beneath that, Megan's news festered, scorching a hole in her heart, fueling her anger with hot kindling.

How long had it been since she'd cried in Dana's arms? How long had it been since they had shared something more than logistics, more than the Sexton household breaking news of the day? She wasn't sure what happened first, had they stopped talking, or were they never in the same place long enough—physically or emotionally—to hear each other?

Allie tossed and turned for an hour, her fury spreading from a small pill on her tongue to venom boiling in every muscle, every joint. Her body was rigid under the covers.

She clenched her fists as the floorboards on the stairs slowly creaked, one by one, like Dana was an old man making sure of his footing, leaning all his weight on one leg before taking the next step. He paused in the bathroom, turned on the light. She heard the water, the swish-swish-swish of a toothbrush, the clatter of a few Advil shaken out. Then the click of the light.

"You're home early," he said as he pulled back the sheets and sank onto the bed. "How was your night?" He fluffed his pillows and crashed down on them, turning on his side towards her.

Part of her wanted to move into him and bury her head in his familiar chest and wail that her night had been horrible, that she was sick with worry about her friend and about Maggie; dump out the poison she was feeling into the space between them that had once been so intimate and sacred, and most of all, healing. But that crawlspace had over the years become a widening gulf, a gulf that could only be crossed with a running leap and a good deal of faith, and she just couldn't find the strength, or the faith, necessary to initiate the hurdle.

What's changed that makes reaching out for each other so daunting? I need you. Please. If I jump in here, will you catch me?

But in the end, or rather in the five seconds it took her to dismiss the tiny butterfly of chance—one of many that often fluttered in between them—the chasm felt too deep, the leap too huge, and the other part of her ambivalence stepped forward. Without turning over, she said in an even tone, "It was okay." She paused. "You were at work?"

He sighed. "I realized I was way behind in some reports. It seemed like a good night to tackle them, you were out anyway. It was either stay late or get there at the crack of dawn."

His reply was reasonable, but she wasn't feeling particularly reasonable. Anger kept her rooted in place, her back still to him. "And you just realized this tonight? Why didn't you tell me this morning?"

"I thought that I could get more done during the day." He injected levity into his tone. "So, why are you home early? Did you guys have a fight?" He forced a chuckle.

"Would you have told me Carrie stayed late if I came home after you?"

"I'm not hiding anything, for Chrissake. Of course I would have told you." He paused. "What's going on with you?"

She turned over to face him and spat her words at him. "What's going on with me is that Maggie has cancer. Megan's a wreck and I'm terrified for them. They're facing the most unimaginable nightmare." She shot up in bed.

"Oh my God," Dana said.

"I came home early to see you; to just see you. But once again, you weren't here." She crossed her arms over her chest. "You weren't here."

Dana shot up too. "I'm not a mind reader, Allie, how the hell was I supposed to know that? I was at work. Earning the dollars that keep this family running? It's not like I was out slamming down beers and cheating on you; I was at *work*."

"You may as well be cheating, it's the same thing. You're not here, Dana. You're at your desk, talking to clients, eating with colleagues, captivated by other things. And we're back here, waiting for you to waltz in the door. We're always second. Always."

"I'm somewhere else because I have to be." He rubbed both hands across his face. Then he smashed his pillow again. "I can't be two places at one time, although God knows, I try. When I'm at work I feel guilty because I know I should be home, and I *want* to be home. Then when I'm home, I feel guilty about everything I've left undone or patched together at work. You think I don't make sacrifices at work to get home, but I do. I just don't play the martyr about it."

He grabbed his pillow and lurched out of bed. "God, Allie, I'm not sure how many times we can keep having this fight. I'm tired in my bones." He pivoted roughly and stomped out.

Now the tears came, burning hot and heavy. Allie fell face down on her pillow and sobbed like she'd never be able to stop.

The next morning, Allie and Dana spoke only when they had to during the usual sprint to get all four of them up, dressed, breakfasted, and loaded with the various briefcases, backpacks, lunches, jackets, lists, library returns, and all the other props they would need for their respective days. The kids didn't notice the difference.

Both Allie and Dana had spent sleepless nights, wrenching back and forth and side to side, oblivion only briefly granted as the inky night ebbed into the soft pencil-gray of dawn. Their emotions had thrashed around as well, from anger to grief to anger to loneliness to optimism to despair. Both of them had landed briefly on the necessity of taking time for just the two of them to get away and reconnect, re-romance. And both had summarily dismissed the possibility as the immediate demands of a busy life elbowed in. In the guest room down the hall, deadlines and deals, phone calls and reports filled Dana with anxiety as the mini-vacation with Allie packed up and fled his imagination. And under the twisted blankets in their king-sized bed, Matthew and Gillian's end-of-school pageantry and accompanying emotional regression paraded across Allie's thoughts of holding hands with Dana on the beach. She also knew that there was no way she could go away and leave Megan right now.

As they climbed into their separate cars, both Allie and Dana resigned themselves to the fact that this fight, along with all their other ones, would get stuffed into the attic trunk of unresolved angst, to be brought down and aired anew another time. They knew that stowing it away just increased the dangerous undertow between them, dragging them in different directions, but neither of them knew if they were capable of the enormous strength it would take to swim back against the unforgiving current.

And they tried not to watch as they drifted further and further apart.

A month later, Dana moved out.

CHAPTER 13

JOURNAL ENTRY #13
July 11, 2001

My mother never left a note. Was it because she had nothing to say? Did she feel that her motives were so obvious she need not explain? Maybe the act was so impulsive that she never had time. Or perhaps she was simply in too much pain. I'll never know. Nor will I ever know her frame of mind at the time; what made her consider it, what the final, determining factor was that spurred her to take her own life. I can guess, and as my father has for 30 years and as I may for 30 more, re-guess. But I'll never know.

I think that even if she had left words on a piece of paper, they wouldn't have been sufficient. They would have been two-dimensional, monotone in both the black ink and the state of mind. We would have had just as many gnashing, piranha-like questions: Is this how she felt the day before? The previous year? All her life?

And how could a few scribbled sentences portray all that dumped her at that option, that decision? How could a note give us all we crave to understand? No matter how lengthy the explanation, we would have been left with empty pages, gaping holes into which we would have read our own conclusions, assigned our own interpretations and beliefs. Her true intentions would have been lost in the limitations of black and white, in the struggle to articulate the depth of her feelings, and in our struggle to grasp the intricacies of meaning—layers of delicate lace beneath the words.

It's a rare thing to truly understand another person's experience. Even if we are familiar with the story, it's rare that we are privy to all of the ingredients, can grasp the richness, savor the taste, feel the texture that each fragment of the story had for the teller. We're shown pieces of someone's narrative, specific editions that are polished and palatable enough to present. Then once shared, once the chosen words are set free into a conversation, they become pureed with the listener's own momentary mood and long standing history—as much as he may try to remain unbiased—ensuring that with the retelling, the tale has been filtered into two slightly disparate versions of the original. Both the narrator and the audience then operate on these adaptations as if they're real; and they *are* real to each person.

We all have a story. And much of the time, we don't even know another person's table of contents. But there I am, standing in a cocktail conversation, chatting with casual friends and acquaintances and sharing a bit of my own tale with the group. I describe an abbreviated experience, using a dictionary of adjectives and verbs that sketch a decent overview, and perhaps drench it all in a humorous tone for effect. There's obviously a much longer story behind the one I tell, an elaborate framework as to why I felt that way, how the scene unfolded as it did. And I assume people get that, they understand where I'm coming from, we're on the same page. I'm socially gliding, at the top of my game, entertaining this group of people who are smiling and laughing along with me, getting it, getting *me*; only to reconsider the story later through a different lens and realize, "Oh my God, they must think I'm crazy or stupid or a cold bitch." Or even worse, to later learn something about one of the people in that group that makes what I said and how I said it totally inappropriate and even hurtful.

Obviously with strangers, there is no way we can know their story, although we almost always think we do. A woman pushes her creaky cart through the grocery store and based on the few things we observe—the items she's grabbing, the way she's dressed, the way she's snapping at her kids—and bang, we know this person. We've got it all figured out. She's a bad mother, she's rude, she's trash, she's no one we would spend time with. We have no idea whether she's just lost her father, whether she's at the end of her normally saint-like rope with her children, or whether she's reached a dead end.

We're only human. And while it's human nature to assume, to stereotype, it is also human nature to defy categorization. We tend to forget that side of humanity, we forget to allow for ourselves and for others to be what we are—imperfect, defying stereotype. In the recesses of our minds we understand that everyone has flaws and pain. But all too often in the reality of the moment, we want to catalog, to *know*, and so we thrust people up on shimmering pedestals of awe, or we snicker at those who we think are more human than the rest of us—people whose stories, we think, are a little easier to read.

As I move through the supermarket now, I try to remember that we're all just doing our best; our best at juggling all the observable and invisible balls that life has thrown up in the air for us with such high expectations. And maybe at times there are just too many in the air and our best is stymied; some balls fall—our work slips, our patience is thin, we *are* rude in the grocery store. But as we desperately try to keep the most challenging spheres of our life off the ground, maybe that's the best we can scrape up at the moment. Tomorrow may be easier, or harder, and our best will look different.

Most importantly, when I get home from the store now, I'm working on sharing my dropped balls. It's terrifying to peel back the layers and stand before Dana, cold and naked, exposing a vulnerability, offering a shameful secret, baring a scar. I tremble—will he leave? And there is no script, no snappy music in the background to assure me it will all be okay. But Dana is there, listening, holding my heart.

And giving me his.

There are many reasons why my mother could have taken her own life. I'll never know those reasons, and in my eternal quest for understanding, it would be so easy for me to believe the worst about myself. But this time, I'm not going to walk the easy path.

I think she did it because for her, it was the ultimate gift to my brothers and me. In her mind, she took her life to spare us ours; ours which she treasured so much that the possibility that she might hurt us, and the knowledge that she had already hurt Paul, was literally unbearable. Of course, I'm not saying that the choice she made was a good one, far from it. But I guess in that moment, it was the only one she could see.

This theory may not be the truth; but it means I was loved. So that's the story I'm going to go with.

JULY 11, 2001

Nantucket, MA

Allie closed her journal and inhaled the thick, salty air. It was early morning and along with the screech of seagulls and the background deep breathing of the ocean, she could hear Dana, Matthew, and Gillian downstairs trying to stifle a bout of laughter and not being entirely successful at it. So often over the years, at five in the morning and stumbling around in the dark, she and Dana had cursed the fact that their kids were perky and raring to go as soon as the sun peeked over the horizon. But this week, in this house packed with four families, she and Dana relished rising early and getting the worm; the worm being a bit of time on their own before all cheery hell broke loose.

After years of wondering aloud about the four families vacationing together, Allie, Megan, Tess, and Zoe had taken the plunge and rented a six-bedroom house on Nantucket. And so far, five days into the adventure, everyone had given themselves over to the potent cocktail of hot-sun relaxation and saltwater buoyancy. The weather had been beautiful, the house just a few barefoot steps from the beach, and everyone, from baby Rose (Megan and Jared's eight-month-old, who loved the beach so much that she ingested fistfuls of sand at every opportunity) to Matthew (who at seven had become a champion body-surfer) to the four significant others (who had all thought a week with the group seemed, well, daunting) was having fun, to which the spontaneous and constantly erupting laughter was testament.

———

Dana and Gavin shared a chuckle as they jumped into Dana's minivan. Zoe had asked if someone would run to the store to pick up a few things, or rather she had yelled, "Can someone go to the store?" over the riot of five tired children all clambering for snacks, juice, dry clothes, hugs, and stories at the same time. Both of the men had literally raced each other to the door.

"Was that obvious?" Dana grinned.

"Oh man, I don't know. But I needed to get out of there." Gavin smiled back and took an exaggerated breath.

"You know we're getting old when a trip to the store in a goldfish-infested minivan sounds exciting," Dana said.

"Pretty sad, huh?" Gavin said. "You'd think we'd have a higher tolerance for the kid-craziness because we're at the office all day; we should be able to handle them for a few hours, or even a week. And I only have one!" Gavin often felt guilty asking Tess for a break. Hadn't he just been away from Juliette all day, all week? He believed he should be "on" once he was home, reacquainting himself with his daughter, making up for the lost hours at his desk. To go for a run or to read the paper in solitude felt like a luxury he had no right to request. "Sometimes I don't know how Tess stays so calm. I feel like a short-tempered ogre next to her."

"Maybe you only get thick-skinned if you're around it all the time. My mom had four kids, and she was really patient. Bossy, but patient."

"I'm one of four too," Gavin said, "and my brother has Down's. Somehow my mom always held it together. Or maybe that's just what I remember in hindsight."

Dana took his eyes off the road and glanced at Gavin. "I didn't know about your brother." He paused. "So, your new job at Special Olympics… "

Gavin smiled.

Dana looked back at the road and nodded.

"My whole life I felt all this pressure to be… I don't know, stellar… for my brother, for my parents. But in the end, they were happy when I was on Wall Street and they were happy when I quit. Turns out, they just want me to be me. I thought they wanted me to be someone else."

They watched the road in a comfortable silence.

"How is it that the generations before us had such huge posses of kids?" Dana said. "Were they more intelligent or completely insane?"

"I think it was lack of contraception."

Dana chuckled. "You ready for number two?"

"Are you ever ready?"

Dana shook his head. "For Allie, the second was a piece of cake—she was already knee-deep in diapers and sleepless nights. It was adjusting to the first that was challenging for her. For me though, Gillian's arrival was harder. With number two there's no sitting on the bench; you're a full-time player."

"I love being a player, it's definitely the best game in the world. But the bench time is key."

They parked and walked into the store, their flip-flops clicking.

"You've got the list?" Gavin asked.

Dana pulled a piece of paper out of his pocket. "Fish, bread, cheese, salad stuff, hot dogs, wine." He chuckled. "The wine is in all caps."

Gavin grabbed a bag of Doritos and held it up with a twinkle in his eye. "And Doritos." Dana laughed.

"You guys thinking about moving from man-to-man to zone?" Gavin asked as he pushed the cart down the aisle.

"We're thinking about it, but right now we're just taking things one step at a time."

Gavin nodded as he threw a bag of potato chips into the cart. "After this vacation, I'm cutting all this stuff out. I've got to lose a few pounds." Then he grinned as he threw in a pound bag of M&Ms. "After vacation."

———

Ever since Tess had floated the idea of this vacation—ever so casually over steaks one night—Gavin had avoided the conversation if possible, and had been vague when pressed.

"We've got to give them an answer," Tess finally said one day as they were painting the nursery light green. "We've dragged our feet for as long as we can."

"You're nice to say 'we.'" Gavin smiled.

"Well, now I've got you trapped in here, notice my strategic position near the door? And you're not getting by this stomach without a decision." Tess stuck out her pregnant belly so that it blocked the door.

Gavin sighed and continued painting long, even strokes of Spring Fern. "There's just so much going on, I'm not sure it's a great time to take off. My new job, your job, the house, our new addition… " He leaned over and kissed the top of Tess's stomach.

"Don't think that's your ticket by me."

He looked up at her. "Are you sure you want to go?"

Tess was quiet for a moment. "The elephant in the room here is Zoe, right? And P.S., how great is it that I'm not making a fat joke?" She smiled. "But seriously, I know you're worried about Zoe and me, in a sweet, pro-tecting-me way."

Gavin stared at her.

She smiled again. "I on the other hand, am looking at it differently, as a chance to start, maybe not fresh, but just again." She sat down on a chair and put her hand over her stomach. "It's funny, Zoe and I have been in the same group for what, 10 years? But we've never really been friends." She snorted. "In fact, we've often resented each other, all while being connected in this tight little circle. But we know a ton about each other, maybe now more than ever."

Learning about Zoe's unwanted pregnancy and witnessing her obvi-ous alcoholism had humanized her for Tess. There was after all, a chink in Zoe's expensive suit of armor, a scratch in her brilliant 24-carat life and persona. No glee accompanied this realization, no vengeful satisfaction; just acknowledgement that even Zoe could, at times, feel powerless.

Gavin had also told Tess about his visit to Zoe the day he walked out. She listened with wide eyes to how Zoe, after hearing the whole story of Tess's affair, had told Gavin to go home, to forgive Tess. *Support from Zoe?* Tess was shocked. She wondered if she had just misread this woman through her own veil of bitterness.

Tess looked at Gavin. "I feel like we might be able to move on. Honestly I'm ready, and I think Zoe is too."

"But we're not just talking about a dinner here."

"I know it's weird for you when we all get together now. I know you feel like I'm watching, she's watching." Tess shrugged. "Old habits die hard. But it's not with the same vinegar in my mouth. And if you and I can talk about it at the end of the day…"

"You really want to do this?"

"So much has changed, for the better, right? Hey I'm pregnant and some days, I actually feel sexy." She smiled.

He smiled and then kissed her on the mouth. "You want to prove it to me?"

———————

"This is truly decadent. I could get used to this," Tess said as she eased onto a lounge chair in the sun next to Zoe.

Zoe put her magazine down on the wooden deck and squinted at Tess. "I know, I think I've become one with this chair. I'm not sure I could move even if I wanted to. Although I have to say that every so often I have a powerful urge to go and check my email. How's your work withdrawal going?"

Tess shrugged. "Not bad. Working from home has been good training. Once I'm done with what I need to do, I've gotten to the point where I can just walk away."

"I think I'd be the opposite. Knowing it was all just steps away from me, halfway finished and fermenting, I'm not sure I could ever just walk away." Zoe smiled. "Either that, or once away, I'd never get myself to go back."

"It took a while to get used to it. At first I was constantly jumping up to do the laundry, whip up a snack, or run a quick errand. And I'm still way more distracted at home than I'd be in the office. But it's a good distracted." Tess looked at Zoe's cell phone on the deck next to her. "It would definitely be the walking away that'd kill you."

Zoe nodded.

"And anyways, I can't quite see you jumping up to do a load of laundry." *Oh no, that sounded bitchy.* Tess's fingers reached for her necklace, but she had taken it off.

Zoe laughed easily. "If I wasn't working in an office, I guess I'd have less dry cleaning and more laundry, right?"

"Somehow I doubt that." Tess smiled and glanced at Zoe, who never failed to look amazing, even stretched out on a lounge chair in her pink bikini. She felt a pinch of jealousy, but nothing like the bitter surge that used to course through her whenever Zoe would waltz into a room. *This I can handle.*

Tess shifted in her chair and moaned as she ran her hand over her huge belly. "I think my bikini days are gone for good."

"They'll be back. When are you due again?"

"October."

"And you don't know if it's a boy or a girl?"

"No. I want to find out, but Gavin doesn't. He likes surprises."

Zoe opened her mouth like she was going to say something, and then cleared her throat instead.

They were quiet for a moment, listening to the surf in the distance. Then Tess took a leap, opening a layer of conversation between them that had always been bolted. "Anyway, I think I've kept enough secrets from him."

Zoe peeked at Tess, then out over the deck towards the rolling dunes. After a moment she said, "But you guys are good now?"

"I think so. Although sometimes I can still see something in his eyes, some kind of question, some shadow…"

"But that will get better, right?"

"I don't know. I guess he and I both have scars, faded now, but still there. Maybe they'll never go away. Maybe those secrets, that betrayal is something we will always be fighting against."

Zoe didn't reply, and Tess closed her eyes and mentally kicked herself. *Too much information.*

"But maybe that's okay," Zoe said after a moment. "Maybe on some level it will remind you what you're fighting for, keep top-of-mind what's important." She sighed. "You know, there's not a day that goes by that I don't itch for a drink. Even now, the thought of a thick, spicy bloody Mary is wiggling just underneath this conversation. I've even imagined the walk into the kitchen, the gathering of the ingredients… except when I start to imagine the sweet burn of the vodka I need to quickly focus on something else. Luckily you sat down." She smiled and then bit her lip. "But it's a daily struggle. And I'm not sure that will ever go away. But even though it's relentless, it reminds me to focus on what's really important. Without the itch, it's easy for the important stuff to get lost." She looked at Tess. "At least that's what I tell myself when it gets hard. That if the 'fighting against' wasn't intense, it would be too easy to pick up a glass and wind up right back where I was." She shuddered. "I'm not sure I'm making sense."

"You are." The sound of the pounding surf filled an amiable silence. Tess was about to comment on their current teetotaling solidarity, but then thought better of making a joke. "Is it harder for you when everyone's cocktailing?"

"Sometimes very."

"Would it be easier if we didn't drink?"

"Probably not. It would just make me feel guilty, like my choices, my mistakes, now impacted everyone else's un-fucked up lives." She paused. "One Shirley Temple in a room is enough." She looked at Tess's belly. "Although it looks like I've got an ally for a while."

Tess smiled.

————

Now sober, Zoe could finally see that what was wrong in her life was not Tess's fault. On the other hand, Tess's pain, some of it at least, had definitely been her fault. So when the discussion of this vacation started to solidify, she had at first balked—after all, letting the tension between her and Tess just fade away sounded so much better than tackling it head on. But then she had straightened her shoulders and decided that this could be the perfect time to show everyone who had stood by her through the haze, and everyone who had suffered because of it, that she was in a better place. Maybe that would be the best thank you. And the best apology.

Zoe's boyfriend had become tangled in her enthusiasm and had agreed to the vacation as well. Drew was a teacher (in fact, he had been Matthew's teacher and Allie set them up), and with the whole summer off, a week away was no big deal. They had been dating for four months—*a miracle in itself*, Zoe thought, as their first date had almost ended before she had even said hello to this guy that Allie had convinced her she couldn't pass up.

"Not quite your type," Allie had said. "But I think he's great. And the other day when he made a comment about being single, I immediately thought of you."

"Is that because I'm your only single friend?" Zoe said.

Allie laughed. "It was either you or my anorexic aerobics instructor. No really, I think you might like this guy. He's adorable." She watched Zoe's dark eyebrows rise.

"I'm not too sure 'adorable' is my thing."

"But maybe working against type isn't such a bad idea?"

Zoe smiled and held up her hands. "You're right. And how bad can it be? It's only one night."

But as Zoe saw a goofy-looking guy with strawberry blond hair and a wide grin lumber over to her in the bar, she wanted to sprint out the side exit. *Oh my God, Allie, you set me up with Howdy Doody?*

Before she could strategize an escape however, he had loped up to her barstool. Without an introduction, and flashing a huge, dimpled grin, he leaned in and said, "I wore my running shoes so I could hightail it out of here if you said you were a cat lover."

Zoe turned a poker face towards him. "I have two of them."

Drew's smile dimmed a few watts. "Oh well, I had a 50-50 shot at an immediate bond." He grinned again and looked around. "I'm assuming they're not with you?"

"No, they're at home, waiting in my bed. They sleep with me." Her blue eyes remained stone-serious.

"Really?" His smile disappeared. "What are their names?"

"Romeo and Juliette," Zoe said after a brief hesitation. The hint of a giggle flickered across her face.

He paused, then chuckled. "You're kidding right?"

Zoe full-out laughed. "You can take your sneakers off. I hate cats."

Dating had always been a competitive sport for Zoe. The instant any initial attraction glinted off of an approaching lance, she assessed for weakness and assumed her opponent was doing the same. Then she led a guarded, one step forward, one step back dance—always keeping an eye on the other player—with full understanding of the dual nature of the goal: to stay in the game and to avoid the cut of getting too close.

But as her night with Drew wore on, it was clear that the only thing he was armed with were funny, endearing stories about himself and his life as a first grade teacher. He wore his shirt and his heart untucked, his feelings and opinions hanging out without edge, without challenge. He had a habit of running his right hand through his short, confused hair, which gave him permanent bedhead. But his deep blue eyes belied his absent-minded professor look; they glittered like the early evening sky, daring her to come out, gently mocking any pretense with an I-can-see-through-your-crap twinkle.

Under his tousled delight, Zoe laughed at herself, at her own cynicism; a deep, resounding laugh that wasn't carefully measured out in teaspoons and gauged for effect. Overall, the evening was like a ride in a convertible—a rush of pure inner freedom, of shared glee without deep insight or intensely personal revelations. At the end of the night, after a mediocre meal and without the augmentation of alcohol, Zoe surprised herself by saying yes to a second date. Which turned into a third, and months later, a vacation together.

Zoe was looking forward to having everyone meet; and nervous too, which felt strange. She had never really cared what her friends thought of her men before, possibly because she herself had never cared much about the men. Or possibly because the whole point of dating hadn't been about interviewing an emotional partner, it had been about numbing pain.

Once they were all ensconced in the beach house however, the reviews were good; Drew was an immediate hit. It wasn't long before they all discovered he was an excellent cook, and after he had whipped up a chunky bruschetta that infused the whole house with the aroma of garlic and basil, there were immediate cries of an encore.

"No wonder you go out with this guy," Megan said as she swallowed a bite of his grilled swordfish with homemade pesto. "He's got a secret weapon."

"Why do you think I keep him around?" Zoe smiled at Drew.

"Are you saying that you don't like my cooking?" Jared said to Megan; he stuck his bottom lip out.

"Honey, I love you dearly. But what you do isn't cooking; it's called heating." They all laughed. "But you heat like a pro."

———

Megan gazed at Jared across the candlelit table and thought for the millionth time how lucky she was to have married him. Somehow through all of Maggie's sickness and treatment, and through all the other craziness of life that didn't stop just because they prayed it would, they had tunneled through together, sometimes side-by-side, sometimes one of them cradling the other and scraping up the power to provide what the moment called for, whether it was a strong arm, a sympathetic shoulder, a silly joke, or just spaghetti. And sometimes, they found themselves clinging to each other while the waves of despair threatened to drown them both. But instead of being pulled under, they emerged from their sobbing hopelessness with a strong sense of solidarity; and whether or not each particular cry was cleansing, afterwards they were at least able to find their feet again and put one in front of the other, simply because they had each other, because they felt understood.

When they were home with the kids, Megan and Jared put all their strength into creating happiness—as if it was a delicate cake that needed just the right ingredients to rise—and they hated themselves when their exhaustion or crankiness was visible through their threadbare exterior. Oftentimes at night, after Maggie and Rose were in bed and asleep, they would make love, sometimes in an attempt to erase their worry, and other times in an attempt to connect with something profound, something hopeful. Either way, the sheer power of their converging emotions would often reduce one or both of them to tears.

The pregnancy had been a blessing, an amazing sign of life amidst the bleakness. It gave them all something to focus on. And as Megan's stomach began to pop, Maggie finished the worst of her treatment, and the doctor declared her prognosis excellent. Hours after Rosie was born, Jared and an awestruck Maggie had cuddled up into the small white hospital bed with a battered but glowing Megan and the tiny, wrinkled baby girl. It had been one of the happiest moments of Megan's life.

———————

"This is so gorgeous," Megan said softly as she and Allie ambled along the deserted beach. The morning was fresh, holy in its beauty; a deep breath. They sipped hot coffee from metallic travel mugs as they walked, and the shiny canisters reflected the cloud-splattered sunrise, allowing each of them to briefly hold a small piece of its multicolored magic. The dark green waves—rowdy teenagers trying to steal the scene—crashed at their feet and rhythmically caressed their ankles in white bubbles and clear, cool water. "Thanks for dragging me out of bed."

Allie smiled. "Anytime."

"Is Dana going to mind when he realizes he's on duty with the kids?"

"He likes to do the mornings now actually. I think in a way, he's trying to make up for lost time. And the kids are pretty self-sufficient now. At least in terms of getting breakfast and stuff."

"God, I can't even imagine that right now."

"You'll get there. Faster than you might like." Allie paused. "Maggie looks really good."

Megan smiled at her friend. "The doctors are really optimistic. She's gained some weight back and some color, even before we got into the sun. And she doesn't seem to care that she lost her hair." She paused. "At first the hair loss was hard for Jared and me. It was scary. And it felt symbolic." She looked at her hands as if she was holding her daughter's hair. "A concrete loss. But then Jared suggested we focus on 'it will grow back.' Like *of course*, no doubts, it will grow back, which was like saying, of course she will get better. No doubts. And that became our mantra, it will grow back. That helped, a little."

They were introspective as they crunched slowly on, their brightly painted toes—courtesy of their daughters—making soft, wet imprints in the sand.

"Will Jared care that he's waking up on duty?" Allie said.

"Nah, he'll be fine. He rolls with everything, and he's used to the mornings. I've been going to work at the crack of dawn so that I can leave early to get home."

"Your boss is okay with that?"

"She's been nice, but I think my safety-pinned schedule isn't going to fly much longer. She said as much when she gave me this vacation time. It was a gift with a warning label; take it and then enough."

"I don't know how you did it, with Maggie in and out of the hospital, a baby at home."

"I didn't do it alone. All of you guys, and our parents really stepped up. Hell, Rose pretty much moved in with us for a while there." Megan smiled. "Payback for rolling my eyes at her."

"You made it up to her when you named Rosie."

Megan nodded. "And Jared's amazing, he's a rock. Oh Allie, thank God I—" She swallowed hard. "Thank God."

Allie reached out and squeezed her arm. They crunched along in silence and sipped their coffee.

"You and Dana seem good," Megan said.

Allie smiled. Dana had moved back in a month ago, and Allie was thrilled with how well it was going. They had been working hard on staying connected both physically and emotionally, infusing the everyday logistical machinery with unadorned feelings, purposeful attention, and spontaneous, tender gestures. "We may be still in our honeymoon phase—our second one—because things are sailing along. We're trying not to fight." She looked out across the water. "Actually, at least from my perspective, there doesn't seem to be anything to fight about."

"That's good."

"I'm not so sure. It seems a little unrealistic. I keep wondering when the shit's going to hit the fan and real life will bully its way back in."

"Or maybe it already has, and you haven't noticed. You guys were made for each other. And if you can weather a year apart, then maybe real life doesn't stand a chance."

"That's where we screwed up before, thinking we were somehow above falling apart because Fate had brought us together." A wave crashed over their feet, washing in tiny shells and a brief silence. "Now we are working on... trying. On talking, asking, on not assuming. That was a big one; I just assumed I knew what he was thinking so after a while didn't bother to ask. And of course as we got more disconnected, I wasn't assuming golden thoughts and sweet intentions." Allie smiled. "So now I'm trying to check in and check things out, give him a chance. Who knows, maybe he'll surprise me."

Megan paused for a minute. "And Dana?"

Allie looked appreciatively at her friend. "Well, he certainly wasn't asking either. He assumed if he asked, he'd open up some can of worms, so better not to ask. And in his mind, Voilá! No ask, no conflict." She sighed. "Of course the irony is, when he didn't ask, it felt like he didn't care."

Megan nodded.

Allie continued, "You know, he'd come home to a clean house, pajama-ed kids, and he'd feel like family fringe. Certainly we jumped all over him when he got home—sometimes even in a good way." She chuckled. "But I think he felt like some fabulous uncle who'd pop in with presents. I set the rules on the fly, and he'd have a hard enough time catching up on all the adventures, never mind the other stuff. He started to feel like he'd worked himself right out of the picture. Which just increased the pressure of suc-ceeding at the office; after all, that's where he thought he was most useful. Which made him that much more unavailable."

"I get that," Megan said. "That 'MOMMY'S HOME!' shout is an amazing rush, but it's loaded. The minute I'm walking in the door," she snapped her fingers, "I'm switching gears from frazzled and stressed into peppy superwoman—both to the kids and to Jared, who's happy to see me, but probably even more relieved about the extra set of hands. I have about an hour to prove my worth, and of course it's witching hour."

Seagulls shrieked above them, swooping in and out of the wind.

"I thought it was all going to be a piece of cake." Allie sighed. "Mar-riage? I envisioned love and romance and a quick pat on the butt as you pass each other in the kitchen. And parenting? How hard could it be to adore, have fun with, and even discipline your kids? I envisioned happily-ever-after with lots of crafts and witty banter." She smirked. "Who knew about all the sticky glue and silence?"

Megan nodded.

"And you know me, silence was never my friend. That's when I used to panic. Literally." She glanced at Megan, who had lived through a few of Allie's panic attacks. "Now I try not to let that stuff throw me. I know that the 'conquering' in 'love conquers all' implies effort." Allie smiled. "Isn't therapy great?"

A huge wave crashed and sent them scrambling to higher ground, their legs dripping with ocean water.

"Did I ever tell you what my mother told me about an hour before I walked down the aisle?" Megan said.

Allie turned towards her and shook her head.

"Not the best timing really, and not the kind of revelation you want to hear on your wedding day—things she and my dad have had to work on, times when they were really unhappy with each other."

Allie's eyebrows shot up. Megan's parents always seemed so happy and in love.

"I know; I had no idea. They always seemed so perfect, they made it look so easy. And at the time I was thinking: too much information, Mom." Megan smiled. "But she told me something I've remembered when Jared and I are arguing or just zooming in different directions. She told me, love is an incredible feeling, but it's one of many, and marriage is the container for them all. Feelings morph, shift, get big, get small, and sometimes with all that feeling you just want to run away. Then you bump into the container wall and you have to turn around and figure it out together."

"I like that," Allie said. Then she did a double take. "You never told me that."

"I always think you know everything I know."

They walked a bit farther in comfortable silence.

"Should we turn around?" Megan asked.

"Yeah. Let's go back."

Dana had moved back into their house in the beginning of June, after a full year of living in an apartment on the other side of town. The move back in wasn't a trial run, and they weren't doubtful. He and Allie had been working up to this beginning for some time now, getting together casually as a family on the weekends, and just the two of them during the week for what they playfully, and by default, called dates. And of course, they got together more formally in Sarah's office where they cried and clawed their way through the overgrown, tangled hurt and frustration.

Settling back underneath the roof of marriage was something they had considered very carefully, and they held off a little longer than they both would have liked, not wanting to jump back in too soon. But finally, when their "I wish you didn't have to go" at the end of a date or weekend was no longer accompanied by a tiny "but it's okay that you do" and instead was hitched to an ache in their hearts and palpable hole in their lives, they knew that the time had come. And they couldn't rent the moving van fast enough.

They had prepared the kids as best they could, and it was fair to say that both Matthew and Gillian were over the moon about their reconciliation. But there really hadn't been a way to prepare themselves for the strange combination of nervousness and excitement that both Dana and Allie felt once Dana's bags were unpacked.

Allie found him sitting on the bed beside his empty duffle bags, gazing around at their bedroom and at his bureau, which was now back in the place it had occupied a year ago. She came in and sat on his lap, something she hadn't done in years. "Are you okay?"

"Just soaking it all in."

"Do you want to be alone?"

"Not a chance." He kissed her.

Allie looked around at the room. "Maybe we should move the furniture around or something. Or paint the room."

"Sounds good." Dana smiled. "Just not orange."

She grinned. There was a moment of silence between them. "So… " she said.

Dana laughed. "You want to redecorate now?"

She hit him with a pillow. "No. I mean, so now what?"

The kids answered that for them as they both bounded in and leapt onto the bed.

"Now, this. Just this." Allie answered her own question as the four of them rolled around in a giant group wrestle.

Matthew and Gillian were in bed. It was nine o'clock—a little late for dinner—but Allie and Dana had decided that once or twice a week, they would wait until the kids were in bed to eat. Whether it was pizza or a meal they made together, they were going to unplug and sit across the table from each other. Allie lit the candles.

"So you're really okay with Nantucket?"

Dana smiled. In the candlelight his face looked ten years younger. "You kidding? It sounds like the perfect way to kick off a new beginning." He uncorked the wine. "Nantucket is ours."

"I know." Allie smiled back. "But I meant, are you okay with the whole gang on Nantucket with us?

Dana poured wine into a glass. "I'm okay with anything right now. Life is good."

"Thank you."

"For what?" He poured wine into the second glass.

"For your enthusiasm about spending a week with the bride's side."

He walked around the table and wrapped his arms around her. "They're my friends too."

She melted into his arms. "That may be one of the nicest things you've ever said to me."

He looked down at her in his arms. "Oh yeah? Well sit down and drink your wine. I'm just getting started."

The last day on the island. The house was stripped of personality; bags were packed, beds were bare, the refrigerator was empty. The morning routine of loading on the SunSense and toting coolers, chairs, and sand toys down to the beach—once completed in lightning speed and with prancing energy—was heavy and tinged with melancholy. The weather remained impervious to the mood on the beach however; the turquoise blue sky fluttered like a kite above them as they dove into their last rendezvous with the ocean. For this year at least.

Five-year-old Juliette and three-year-old Maggie—her peach fuzz covered with a blue baseball cap—were on a mission. In order to distract them from their last-day pout, Gavin had challenged them to create the best sandcastle of the week, and so with their mouths pursed in determination, they were hard at work on their project, while baby Rosie, who was sitting on a blanket near them, tried her best to eat each new turret. Megan and Gavin were elbow deep in wet sand helping to fill buckets and shore up the sides of the ill-fated structure.

Matthew, bobbing out in the water, was gleefully high-fiving the approaching waves on a bright yellow boogie board, with Dana bodysurfing and coaching enthusiastically along next to him.

Tess and Allie were lounging on red and white striped beach chairs, chatting and watching Gillian intently hunt for shells. Jared had just collapsed on the big blanket next to them after lugging bags of chips and a huge cooler of cold drinks down from the house.

Tess nodded in the direction of Zoe and Drew, who were holding hands and leisurely strolling back up the beach after a long walk. "They've been such good sports about all the kids."

"I think that Zoe puts on a good show of indifference, but secretly she likes kids," Allie said.

"They seem good for each other, don't they?" Tess said.

"He's a great guy," Jared said.

"Do you think they'll end up together?" Tess said.

"I don't know," Allie said, turning the idea around in her head.

"He seems perfect," Tess said.

"I wonder what his story is?" Allie said almost to herself as she closed her eyes and lay back in her chair. The sun and the quiet seeped into her and she melted into herself. She didn't feel the need to get busy, to make some noise or make something happen, and when she opened her eyes again, it was with peace, not with panic. She looked around at all her friends and family on the beach and felt a rush of warmth, of gratitude, of love. Shading her eyes with her hand, she focused on Dana in the water with Matthew, and watched them surf the green waves. She couldn't hear what they were saying but she could hear their joy float up and into the roar of the waves and the screech of the seagulls.

She took a deep breath of the salty sea air and looked at Tess. "I'm going in." She pushed herself out of her comfortable chair, walked down to the water's edge, and dove into the cold waves. When she surfaced, she aimed for Dana and swam out to join him.

THE END

ACKNOWLEDGMENTS

This book is a years-long love and endeavor. I would like to thank everyone who helped me write and publish *The Truth is a Theory*.

First and foremost, I would like to thank my husband Steve. Thank you for your quiet support and your unfailing patience in all things but especially for the many (many) times that I was absorbed in my writing and basically, lost to the world. Most importantly, thank you for giving me your heart and cradling mine.

I want to thank my kids, Sam, Katie, and Jack. To say I adore you does not even begin to capture it. Your laughter lights up my world; your hugs stop time for a sweet moment. Thank you for being uniquely you.

Thank you to my parents, for their unabashed, unedited love and support. Thank you for teaching me what determination looks like, and for the invisible yet palpable scaffolding of safety and love.

I am forever grateful to my friends, whose unconditional love and laughter has buoyed me more times than I can count. Thanks for making me a better person, a better listener, and a better "sharer". Special thanks to Kirsten Bushick and Kirsten Krinsky for reading this book in its infancy, and offering genuine encouragement and honest, red-ink edits.

Thank you to my editor Fran Lebowitz for her thoughtful insight and honest critique. Thanks to Kevin Barrett Kane at The Frontispiece for his beautiful book design and general guidance. Thank you Harry Groome for offering invaluable wisdom and experience.

Thank you to Dr. Sue Johnson, who created a life-changing model of couples therapy, Emotionally Focused Therapy. Even though I wrote this book before I ever had heard of EFT, my intense training in this model helped me to see what I was writing about and better describe the negative cycle in Allie's marriage. Thanks also to Sue Johnson for the idea that sometimes we can protect ourselves so well from hurt that we end up all alone.

Thank you to everyone who pre-ordered the book during the month-long Publishizer campaign in 2018. Your genuine enthusiasm gave me the confidence and support to fulfill my dream of publishing *The Truth is a Theory*. Special thanks to all those who pre-ordered 5 or more books:

Brian Abraham, Maria Arakil, Nahla Azmy, Tracy Bennett and Bob Bristol, The Breen Family, Brian and Susannah Bristol, Steve Bristol, Ted and Nellie Bristol, Christine Brown, Eugenie Brunner and Paul Egan, Kirsten Bushick, Robert Carder, Caryl Capeci, Lisa DeMarino, Mimi Drummond, The Elfland Family, The Eyl Family, Elizabeth Gift, Wanda Gilhool, Harry and Molly Groome, Karen Halls, Erica Hanson, Matt Hartnett, Ben and Lizzie Lewis, Tyler Lewis, Maria Lorditch, Donna and Mark McDonnell, Cheri Mitchell, The Moriarty Family, Fritz Plickert, Hans and Sandy Plickert, Lindsay Schwartz, MaryBeth Shay, Scott Sodokoff, Meg Soriano, Laura Spiller, Donna Usiskin, and Linda Weber.

Made in the USA
Middletown, DE
19 June 2019